Pressure Points

"[AN] ADDICTIVE THRILLER. . . .
Performance seminars have long been the bane of the corporate world, yet few authors have explored them in fiction to the candid degree that Brooks does here. [He] crafts his characters with care, lending them opaque dimensions that make them appear both sympathetic and loathsome."

—*Publishers Weekly*

"LARRY BROOKS HAS DONE IT AGAIN!
Pressure Points is a clever, twisted, bone-chilling tale that grabs hold and doesn't let go. Everyone's a suspect and the twists and turns keep coming until the final moment." —Danielle Girard

"LARRY BROOKS HAS WRITTEN AN
EXCITING THRILLER
as the reader, like the group, never knows what is deadly and what is an exercise. In *Pressure Points*, ignoring reality could mean death. . . . Mr. Brooks keeps it fresh because reality is so blurred."

—*Midwest Book Review*

continued . . .

Darkness Bound

"Grabs you by the throat and doesn't let go . . . it's as scary as hell."
—*New York Times* bestselling author Lisa Jackson

"Teasingly erotic, [*Darkness Bound*] is that rarest of sexual thrillers, in which sex isn't gratuitous but a convincing means to an end . . . a high-stakes game of strategy and deceit, in which the prize is life. The novel's final scenes burst with the intensity of a first-rate horror film, and it's difficult to detect a loophole in the intricate plot."
—*Publishers Weekly*

"Dangerous, diabolical . . . and absolutely delicious in the creepiest way! The twists and turns gave me whiplash. A wild, thrilling ride!"
—Thom Racina, author of *Never Forget* and *The Madman's Diary*

"Full of surprises, *Darkness Bound* is one sneaky read." —Leslie Glass, *New York Times* bestselling author of *The Silent Bride*

"Erotic obsession, sexual betrayal and murder . . . fast-paced." —*The Oregonian*

"So believable and very frightening."
—*Midwest Book Review*

"I found myself enjoying *Darkness Bound* in the same way I'd enjoyed . . . Hitchcock thrillers two generations ago."
—Norm Harris, author of *Fruit of a Poisonous Tree*

SERPENT'S
>> DANCE <<

Larry Brooks

A SIGNET BOOK

SIGNET
Published by New American Library, a division of
Penguin Putnam Inc., 375 Hudson Street,
New York, New York 10014, U.S.A.
Penguin Books Ltd, 80 Strand,
London WC2R 0RL, England
Penguin Books Australia Ltd, 250 Camberwell Road,
Camberwell, Victoria 3124, Australia
Penguin Books Canada Ltd, 10 Alcorn Avenue,
Toronto, Ontario, Canada M4V 3B2
Penguin Books (N.Z.) Ltd, Cnr Rosedale and Airborne Roads,
Albany, Auckland 1310, New Zealand

Penguin Books Ltd, Registered Offices:
Harmondsworth, Middlesex, England

First published by Signet, an imprint of New American Library,
a division of Penguin Putnam Inc.

First Printing, February 2003
10 9 8 7 6 5 4 3 2 1

 REGISTERED TRADEMARK—MARCA REGISTRADA

Printed in the United States of America

PUBLISHER'S NOTE
This is a work of fiction. Names, characters, places, and incidents either are
the product of the author's imagination or are used fictitiously, and any resemblance to actual persons, living or dead, business establishments, events, or
locales is entirely coincidental.

For Laura and Nelson

Acknowledgments

Whatever insights to the human experience an author imparts to the work are most valid when borne of personal experience, particularly where love and romance are concerned. The rest is research and imitation, shaped by conjecture and too much television. In the past I have written about the consequences of flawed parental love and the tribulations of romantic treachery, and while it may seem strange, I must thank those who have contributed to the context of that understanding. Truth really is stranger than fiction. But when it comes to love and romance, the kind that transcends daily experience and connects us to something bigger than ourselves, I have been blessed with a soul mate and a tutor in the fifth decade of my life, in the form of my beautiful wife, Laura, who is also the smartest person I know. As it has been and will always be as long as I draw breath, this book is dedicated to her—friend, coach, critic, editor, mentor, partner, dreamer, lover, angel. Thank you, sweetness, for saving my life. I love you forever.

Thanks to my son, Nelson, for the abundant love and companionship. We made it work, didn't we? You make me proud, and your goodness humbles me. Always remember, buddy—the sky's the limit.

Thanks to my A-team: Mary Alice and Anna of Cine-Lit, my extraordinary agents; to Dan Slater, my editor; to the Oregon Writers Colony for all your support; to PSI for the crash course in life; to Dick and Bev Barber, my sister, who proves that angels do indeed walk the earth; to the clan—Sybil and Lester, Tracy and Eric, Kelly and Paul—and to Scott, who goes back into the will if he actually reads this, and to their collective seven children. You are all tremendous blessings in my life, and in Nelson's.

To Bernadette and Lee Koehn, Mike Wustrack, Rick and Robyn Dillon, Denny and Robin Damore, Sybil Melin and Tom Manning, Michael Land, George Souza, Cal Vaughn, Roger Davis, Jason and Patti Hillman, Lynn Mattern and others who steadfastly spread the word, thank you. Thanks to Blaine Borgia for the tech tips. Special thanks to Frank Consalvo for your friendship and for modeling excellence; and to Louise Burke, a very special lady who saw it first and made it happen for me, as she has for so many.

To the booksellers who went the extra mile—especially Page, Maria, Victor, Chris and Pat—and the readers who took the time, you have my sincerest gratitude. You are, after all, the entire point.

The prologue is respectfully dedicated to Elmore Leonard.

Above all, thanks to the good Lord, from whom all blessings flow.

> Prologue <

Fort Worth, Texas

They were proud and they were pissed off, not necessarily in that order. And they were all of twelve years old.

Theirs was a small congregation, one whose body language gave off a decidedly sinister energy and, if you came too close and were under a hundred pounds, a certain potential for violence. Jimmy Dub—little Jimmy Weirbosky had become Jimmy W. and then, in the name of further efficiency, Jimmy Dub—was the tallest and clearly in charge, his buzzed hair anchored by patchy, prepubescent sideburns. The others mimicked the don't-give-a-shit way he pocketed his free hand and cupped his Marlboro with the other. They had nervous eyes and a tendency to spit frequently. Most students remained clear of this particular patch of turf, tucked under a breezeway between two buildings, and the boys assured each other this was their reputation at work. But the truth was they didn't have much of one, and those few who were aware of them weren't remotely interested in either challenging or investigating. To the rest they were as invisible as the moss in the cracks of the sidewalk upon which they stood.

They held court here every day during seventh-grade lunch, safe from harassing eighth-graders and wandering teachers, who preferred an hour's respite in their air-conditioned lounge. Smokes came courtesy of Jimmy's mother, who, understanding this little social significance because she had started at the age of eleven herself, didn't want to stoop to the parental hypocrisy of her childhood. She figured Jimmy would score some anyhow, either stealing them from her purse or the 7-Eleven, so what the hell.

Today the boys were gloating about the kick-ass thing they'd done yesterday, which had broken new ground. Suddenly one of them tapped Jimmy Dub on the shoulder and, with the flick of an eye, indicated that he should turn and look.

Two people were heading their way, crossing the grass from the parking lot—a local chick from the high school and a guy with WWF shoulders. They walked with purpose, displaying the focused expressions of hunters who'd just spotted dinner.

The boys ceased their chatter as they turned. Eye contact and the maintenance of cool was essential. The big dude stopped ten feet shy, folding his arms as he leaned against one of the breezeway roof supports. But the girl kept coming, a strange and perky little grin on her face. She wore a leather car coat over snug jeans that were easy on the eyes, and expensive boots. Snotty little rich girl, you could tell, though not so little anymore. Her long dark hair was pulled severely back and tied with what the girls called a scrunchie, and the exchange of glances among the boys acknowledged that she was, by their prepubescent estimation, hot as hell.

She honed in on the tallest boy as if the others didn't exist.

"You must be Jimmy Dub," she said. She extended her hand, very businesslike. "I'm Bernadette."

The young man took a drag on his Marlboro and flicked the butt over her shoulder before accepting the handshake with limp enthusiasm. He blew the smoke in her face.

"So?"

When the young woman said, "Peggy Kane's sister,"

Jimmy's grin began to fade. He tried to pull his hand away, but Bernadette's grip tightened.

"You remember Peggy, right? Sixth-grader? Long straight hair, like mine? Plays basketball? She knows you, Jimmy. Told me all about you."

The color in Jimmy Dub's cheeks bled away as quickly as his smile.

"Cat got your tongue, Jimmy Dub?"

Jimmy didn't move. His friends inched away, exchanging glances.

"Peggy said you'd be here. She told me that right after she told me what you did. That *was* you, wasn't it, Jimmy? I don't want to make a mistake about this."

He started to speak, but hesitated. When Bernadette offered a friendly *go on* with her eyes, he said, "It was no big thing . . . Peggy's cool."

Bernadette nodded as her companion shifted his position slightly, the leather sleeves of his letterman jacket creaking loud enough so all the boys noticed. There was trouble under those sleeves. Jimmy Dub kept his gaze fixed on Bernadette.

"Peggy's cool?" she said, her own smile giving way to something darker now.

"Yeah. We were just, I dunno, having a little fun. No harm, no foul."

"She bled, Jimmy. Did you know that? When you put your fingers inside her, you broke her hymen. But you don't know about hymens, do you, Jimmy, because you're just a dumb little fuck with less brains than balls. You were just playing around, right?"

As Jimmy Dub tried to pull his hand away, Bernadette switched her grip to his wrist with a lightning-quick move.

"What is this, man?" Jimmy twisted in an effort to free his arm, but Bernadette was stronger than he was. The other boys looked at each other, checking their options, which were dwindling. "What, you gonna have Tonto over there kick my ass or something?"

Bernadette smiled. "No, Jimmy, but that's close. Here's what we *are* gonna do. You get to choose. I give you two options, you pick one. That's the deal, okay?"

Jimmy Dub's face contorted into an expression of complete bewilderment.

"Option one, I report you to the police, the school, your parents and a few guys like Tonto here. Very bad for you . . . something like that might keep you out of med school someday. Option two—you deal with me. Right here, right now."

He didn't flinch. She wasn't sure—nor did she care— if he was processing the choices or if he was too stupid to comprehend them.

"Ever fight a girl, Jimmy Dub?"

Then she slapped him across the face, keeping a firm grip on his wrist as he tried to spin away. Reflexively he raised his free hand to his cheek, and for a moment it appeared he was seriously considering option two. She had him by two or three inches, but their weight was about equal.

"They call that a bitch slap. Wanna see it again?"

She whacked him once more, this time curling her hand into a fist and popping him squarely on the ear.

"Choose, Jimmy. Right now."

Bernadette's escort, whose name was Eric, had moved closer to one of the other boys, and was now standing with his arm clamped around the boy's shoulders. Any temptation to help Jimmy Dub out of this mess was immediately overwhelmed by sheer common sense. Besides, hassling Peggy had been Jimmy's idea, all they'd done was hold her down. All they'd done was what Jimmy Dub said.

Jimmy started to speak, but only a stuttering little whine came out.

"What's that?" asked Bernadette, just before she popped him on the ear again.

"I . . . I said I'm sorry. . . ."

"Say what? You're *what*?"

She hit him again, harder, this time squarely on the

nose. He started to sink to his knees, but Bernadette's grip on his wrist kept him from going all the way down.

"Look at me!" she demanded. When he didn't, she kicked him between the legs, striking the inside of a thigh inches from never-never land. "*Look* at me!"

He did. Penitence rained down his face, mixing with the blood streaming from his nose.

Bernadette flicked her head toward her companion with the bridge-abutment neck. "Tonto's the starting middle linebacker at Central—you may have heard of him. You go near my sister or any of her friends, you'll see him again. You don't want that."

Eric grinned, tightening his grasp on the other boy's shoulders. The boy he was holding began to cry.

Bernadette said, "We cool, Jimmy? You and me?"

Jimmy Dub lowered his eyes as he nodded. Bernadette again kicked out, this time nailing the field goal dead center as she let go of his wrist. The boy sunk to his knees, coughed, then threw up the peanut butter sandwich his mother had made him, delivered in a brown paper bag with a fresh pack of Marlboros.

A bell rang. The boys backed away, then turned and ran into the school building.

Bernadette and Eric walked across the grass toward the parking lot in silence. From the set of her jaw and the fixed nature of her stare, Eric was pretty sure she wasn't quite ready to move on with the rest of her day.

When they arrived at his car, she touched his arm and said, "Thanks for coming."

"Any time," he said, holding her door open. "Remind me never to piss you off."

The faintest trace of a smile played across her lips as she got in. But it was gone by the time he joined her inside the car, replaced by that same icy stare.

PART ONE

>><<

Fourteen Years Later

Dearly beloved, avenge not yourselves, but rather give place unto wrath: for it is written, Vengeance is mine; I will repay, saith the Lord.

—ROMANS 12:19

> 1 <

Sometimes I am possessed by the thought of killing him. I visualize every delicious moment of it, his expression of surprise as he recognizes my intention, the way his eyes evolve toward fear and then, as doubt becomes expectation, into utter terror, the salty flavor of his tears, and then the slow bleeding of his awareness, the last moment of which is consumed with me, and by me. I smile as I kiss him good-bye. The kiss is cold, as dead as the smile, tasting of bitter memories built on sweet but unfulfilled possibility.

And then he dies. And I am free.

This thought and the vision it paints consume me. I wonder when it is that thought becomes temptation, at what point sin is rendered mortal. After all that has happened, I should know by now.

As I drive to meet him I am reminded of these things, past and future suddenly inseparable, and I wonder which is the more damning to my soul. Then again, I haven't given my soul a second thought since he and I began. What a strange and funny time to yearn for grace.

My lover has summoned me, and I must go to him.

I go not to forgive or even to kill, but to listen. Closure does not discriminate between the betrayer and the betrayed. This I know because I am both, and the thirst for closure torments me from both sides of that judgment. I can't imagine why he wants to see me now, after the time that has passed. After what he did. A part of me continues

*to hope that his desire has smothered his pride, that he
has discovered he cannot live without me after all. Ah,
the eternal deceit of the fallen ego. Of course, there is
always the chance that he simply wants one final taste of
the fruit he has forever rendered forbidden, on that final
night when the music died, to borrow a phrase.*

*I am sick as I drive to the place. Our place, it was.
How fitting for this final dance. I have been sick now for
months—has it really been months?—perhaps tonight the
book will at last be closed.*

A fucking apology would be nice, too.

*The more I think about it, the more I am sure that, for
this thing to really end, to bring peace to all those who
have suffered by our hands, one of us must die.*

*I am unarmed, unprepared. Then again, a girl can al-
ways improvise if she has to.*

Plano, Texas

They were wrong about the chocolates. Her girlfriends
claimed they'd done it, more than one book on the subject recommended it, she'd even heard Dr. Phil talk it
up on *Oprah,* and God help us if you can't count on
that. But bless their well-intended souls, they were all
full of shit. When her boyfriend of two years decided he
just wanted to be friends—an epiphany, he'd called it—
Bernadette Kane had, in good faith, wolfed down two
boxes of Godiva while watching back-to-back reruns of
Friends. And now here she was, enthusiastically throwing up, her perspective on love no brighter than before.

Then, just when things couldn't get any worse, the
telephone rang. As anyone with a broken heart knows,
the sudden ringing of a telephone can send bolts of
white-hot adrenaline straight to an already traumatized
stomach, as hope for an olive branch collides with the
cold probability that he's calling to ask for his CDs back.
This was Bernadette's prevailing line of thought as she
stared at the ringing telephone, saying the word *hello*

out loud several times until she was satisfied with her tone of indifference.

She didn't answer it.

As it rang, it occurred to Bernie that this was a singularly feminine moment. Most men in this position—that of the dumpee—would be diving across the bathroom tile to answer. Women, on the other hand, courageously put the desire for a poised façade above their own desperation. This was why God invented voice mail, so women could hear the pleadings of their capitulating lovers without compromising their pride.

Funny what betrayal does to the thought process. In the midst of her wallowing, it also occurred to her that it was time to buy a house. Condo living—right here in Stucco Land, as she called it—with its communal parking lot and pool, was designed for singles on an alimony budget. It was as cliché as her life suddenly felt, and she wasn't even divorced. She didn't belong here. Too many people at this close proximity made loneliness all the more poignant. She and her loneliness would be happier in a house.

With her head in the toilet, listening to her ringing telephone, Bernadette also considered the relationship between her boyfriend's so-called epiphany and the sudden frequency of the dreaded L and M words in their conversations. She had uttered them first, of course, making this whole thing her fault. It was hormonal, something that historically clicked in at the twenty-four-month mark in her romantic relationships. In the last three, the mere mention of marriage had been like plopping a biopsy specimen into the petri dish of love—they all tested positive for that most dreaded of male maladies: Fear of Commitment. Once uttered there is no turning back, and the relationship is rendered terminal.

Besides, this last guy kept a horsehair car duster in the trunk of his Audi and actually used it. Daily. Swear to God, he even had a leather case for the thing. Maybe she was better off just being friends after all. Maybe she was better off reevaluating her tastes in men with big chins, big jobs, dust-free cars and colossal intimacy issues.

It suddenly occurred to her that the acronym for the dreaded Fear of Commitment—FOC—rhymed with the word "fuck." She found this both ironic and interesting.

Bernadette loved men. She really did. She just didn't *like* the ones who rang her bell all that much, particularly of late. She and her sister shared a common weakness— they were doomed to sleep with hunky jerkoffs. These three guys with their FOC and their horsehair car brushes had cost six years of her life. Throw in a year between each relationship for the recovery of her self-esteem and the renewed realization that the single life sucked, and that about summed up her adult life thus far.

The telephone rang again. More insistently this time, it seemed. Bernadette rallied and made it to her nightstand. She put her hand on it, then remembered to check the Caller ID readout, at once thankful and devastated that it wasn't *him*. But the number was familiar. Maybe he was having one of his beer buddies call to plead his case from the sports bar, high school style. He would do that. But in that case the number would be completely foreign. No, this caller was from somewhere on her side of the fence.

She cleared her throat, tested a final cheery "hello," then picked it up.

"Hello?" Perfect. As if she were between orgasms.

"Bernadette."

Like the number, she recognized but could not place the voice. Male, older, not a particularly happy camper. Her pause tipped the caller to her confusion.

"Walt Hopkins," said the voice. Walt was her sister's father-in-law, a flirtatious guy who still had his Clairol blow dryer from the seventies. She'd met him over a handful of family holiday functions, forming no particular opinion one way or the other, which was how she felt about most men of the previous generation regardless of their hair. What made this call interesting was the fact

that Peggy and her husband, Brian, had recently commenced divorce proceedings after the nasty affair that
had split them like a pair of Vegas aces. Also interesting
was the fact that Walt's voice, usually self-affected,
wasn't nearly as peppy as hers.

"Walter . . . how are you?" Using the more formal
iteration of his name was her way of telling him to
back off.

An ominous pause, then he said, "I have bad news
for you, Bernie."

Something deep in her stomach quietly disintegrated.
She didn't respond.

"Peggy's dead. I'm so sorry."

Silence dominated the line for several seconds. Then
Walter Hopkins added, "Your sister killed herself last
night."

Bernie wasn't at all sure she'd be able to attend the funeral. The pain came in waves, disguised initially as anger before yielding to a helpless grief, and finally to complete confusion. Memories overwhelmed her waking hours and dreams haunted what little sleep she could manage. The most painful images were from the early years, when Bernie had introduced Peggy to the sports that would define their shared youth—soccer and basketball and softball and later, their favorite event, boys. After high school came golf and a failed attempt to introduce Peggy to the martial arts, which Bernie had taken up in high school. The boys became men, and the need for sisterly counsel was greater than ever. Bernie's advice wasn't always heeded, Peggy's marriage being the best example of her unhealthy independence. But Bernie never sank to I-told-you-so hindsight. Her love for her sister had been unconditional, the purest of her life.

There had been no secrets between them, ever. Even during the affair.

The images came with a narrator. During the day it whispered that there was no way her sister committed suicide. At night it screamed that Bernie had somehow failed to protect her, as she always had . . . protected her from neighborhood bullies, from predatory boyfriends, even from the truth about their parents' alcohol-fueled divorce. Bernie had been there through Peggy's affair and the ensuing separation, listening, resurrecting hope. The affair and therefore the scorn of blame had been Peggy's—again, she had thanked Bernie for her warning, then ignored it—but the domestic soap opera that motivated it had been understandable, if not justifiable. Everyone who knew Peggy's husband would agree that he was an emotionally retarded, misogynist bore, the kind of guy whose life goal was to buy a Fat Boy Harley and whose idea of a romantic vacation was a week in a tent next to a trout stream. Bernie certainly never condoned Peggy's relationship with the mysterious and exciting business executive from Phoenix, but when it all went to hell, Bernie's was the only hug available. With Bernie's support, Peggy had managed to accept and release her guilt, and she was finally looking forward to rebuilding her life. She was no more a candidate for suicide than she was for Junior League Wife of the Year.

Not quite lost in the swoon of her self-persecution was Bernie's realization that her own romantic meltdown was but a trivial speck of spilled blood on the canvas of her life. If that relationship had been viable then she would have yearned for the man's shoulder in this time of suffering. But such was not the case. She had left a message on his cell phone about Peggy's death, just a courtesy, really. No, let's be honest, she was baiting the bastard. But big surprise, he didn't call back. The L word had been tolerated but the M word had never been in the cards.

Someday she'd send the guy an e-mail and tell him how easy it had been to bury his memory, with a well-timed F word or two tossed in for emphasis.

The day before the funeral she put her Stucco Land condo up for sale.

The funeral itself was a predictably wrenching affair, conducted to the relentless percussion of rain pounding the sanctuary roof. Bernie had insisted on cremation over the protestations of her very-old-school Iowa parents, who after fifteen post-divorce years were now clinging to each other in the front row. What remained of her sister had been poured into a bronze urn and displayed on a marble pedestal in front of the congregation of wet-headed mourners. In a month Bernie would scatter the ashes from the stern of a sailboat off the coast of Mazatlan, where five years earlier she and Peggy had vacationed together in celebration of Peggy's graduation from college.

Peggy's husband, Brian, spent the entire ceremony with his gaze fixed on his shoes, knowing that everyone seated behind him was staring a hole through the back of his head. Suicide, however inexplicable, always demands a defendant. He never spoke a single word to Bernie or anyone else, and when it was over he departed through a side door alone, the first person out of the room. To go fishing, Bernie was certain.

As Bernie left the church, avoiding a handful of well-intended conversations waiting in ambush along the way, she saw Eric Killen and his wife huddling under an umbrella as they descended the stairs. Eric had grown close to Peggy when he and Bernie took a swing at romance during their senior year in high school. As it turned out it was a swing and a miss, so they settled for a friendship forged on mutual respect and the love of laughter. A by-product was his continued relationship with Peggy, which had a touching big-brother quality to it. Bernie remembered Eric showing Peggy how to ride a motorcycle, how it pissed her father off to the point that Eric was ordered from their property until the return of Christ. In the years that followed Eric had taken a different road, one that for him was fraught with detours and disappointments, and while it had separated them for years, they were forever linked. Childhood friends are the best friends, and even inept adolescent sex and a decade of other priorities couldn't screw that up. Years later, after the second of three busted relationships, Bernie began to regret the decision to let him go. It was then that she also realized that marrying one's best friend was the Holy Grail of love.

Bernie tapped his shoulder, and Eric immediately

turned and opened his arms to her. They hadn't spoken in a year or two—Eric never said it, but she knew she subconsciously threatened his wife, Shannon, making their friendship hard on him—but the birthday and Christmas cards had a perfect attendance record over the previous decade, always written by hand. He was still a drop-dead poster boy for testosterone, his thick black Latin-in-the-blood hair combed back, a strand casually falling down toward irrepressibly electric eyes, his body filling out his suit in a manner that stirred the imagination of women and men alike. Shannon was petite and fashionable in her funeral attire. She waited her turn before hugging Bernie, her eyes moist. Any unspoken friction between them was put on the back burner.

"You okay, little darlin'?" Eric asked as the two women parted. He'd called her that in high school, and it had always sort of bothered her. But not today.

She didn't answer, but rather than just stand there in tears she embraced him again. After a moment Shannon joined in, and the three of them held each other under the umbrella there on the sidewalk as other mourners passed at a respectful distance.

Bernie pulled back and dabbed at her eyes, which she fixed on him with a steely expression. "I need to talk to you," she said.

Eric nodded. He was aware of what had happened to Peggy, the affair that precipitated the suicide, and because of this he instinctively knew what Bernie wanted from him now. An alarm went off somewhere in his mind, and he wondered what would come of it all. Before answering he exchanged a quick glance with Shannon, who nodded subtle permission.

"Whenever you're ready," he said.

"I'll call you. This week." She hugged them both once again. She looked at Shannon as she said, "Thank you both for coming." Shannon's smile was at once empathetic and relieved. It vanished as soon as Bernie turned away.

Bernie rushed off, her pace quicker than all the other folks hurrying to their cars in the rain. Eric and Shannon watched her go, her hand cupped around his substantial arm a little tighter than before.

When she was gone, Shannon said, "Am I crazy, or has she put on a few?"

Eric shot her a look. Not funny. Not funny at all.

> **3** <

There wasn't a day that passed in the next month that Eric Killen didn't think of Bernie and her promise to call. It didn't happen the week after the funeral, as she'd said it would, but that didn't for a moment suggest to him that she'd changed her mind. Bernie would never back down from injustice, especially where family was concerned. Not then, not now. No, she was probably just waiting for something to let its guard down before she took its legs out. Eric was neither dreading nor looking forward to her eventual appearance, and neither feeling had anything to do with residual emotions unresolved from their youth. He was, he had no reason to remind himself, a happy enough husband and the proud father of a three-year-old boy who needed his father to teach him to keep his eye on the ball. Of all the things in his past with which he needed to come to terms, Bernie was not one of them. Eric had gently placed her in a proper place in his heart, one that was acceptable to all parties concerned.

She would come when she was ready, and Eric would be ready when she came.

As it turned out, she didn't call at all. She simply appeared at work on a Friday, toward the end of the day so they would have time to talk after his shift.

Eric worked at a privately funded juvenile detention facility known on the mean streets of Dallas as Da Slamma, a sort of white-collar repository for disciplinary cases with deep pockets. Lots of drug offenders, the occasional rookie rapist, and more serious cases of vandalism and street violence. If the family lawyer was good enough and the parents were so inclined—or, as was often the case, had country-club connections to the judge—a teenaged first offender in that gray area between hopeless and hopeful could avoid the county and state institutions and work off their penance here. Eric Killen was the camp drill instructor disguised as a big brother, the muscle in charge of physical education and intramural diversions. He was also the school's primary deterrent to any guest who thought he was Mike Tyson. Five years earlier Eric had started there as a guard, but it was quickly apparent to the administrators that he was more than just another lock jockey, that he was someone the kids would both relate to and respect, and who would step up when someone went ballistic in the hall.

Eric was playing three-on-three basketball with the residents when word arrived that he had a visitor waiting in the office. When he was told who it was, he asked that she be told to wait for him at the Starbucks in the strip mall just down the highway. His guys were up six-two, and he didn't believe in quitting when he was ahead.

He arrived a half hour later, his hair still wet. Bernie sat alone at a tiny table by the window, nursing a cappuccino, looking as if she was about ready to leave. Across the table waited another paper container, its contents now cold.

"I hate this place," he said as he bent to kiss her cheek before he sat across from her. "They act like they're saving the world. But I do love cold coffee."

He took a sip, tried not to wince.

"Did you win?" she asked, grinning at his expression.

"He told you? Damn, I told him to tell you I was polishing the shotguns."

"He said you're a hero to those kids. And that you never let them win."

"Some things never change."

"The hero part? Or the competitive asshole part?"

"Both." He winked, tried another sip. "This isn't too bad."

Her smile turned to a smirk, then faded to that warm, approving glow reserved for old friends.

"You look good," she said. "Happy."

"So do you. You look . . . employed."

"Freelance. Opposite of employed."

"It's working out?"

"It was. Then I sold my condo and went to Mexico. I'm in debt, and I can't sleep."

"Which is why you're here."

"I can't have cold coffee with my oldest best friend?"

Eric smiled. Both took sips from their respective cups, as if it was choreographed.

"How are things?" she asked. Her tone was softer now, the staccato repartee set aside for the moment. He knew what *things* meant—his son, who'd had heart surgery before his first birthday and had since suffered through a series of life-threatening maladies that would have disenfranchised Norman Vincent Peale. The other *thing* was his career, about which she never failed to ask.

She knew the story all too well, and her asking was her way of acknowledging that things shouldn't have turned out that way. That life was unfair. What had happened was Eric's cross to bear, the chuckhole in his chosen path. He'd always wanted to be in law enforcement, alternating his dreams between the FBI and military intelligence. But one day in college, where he'd gone on a football scholarship, the car in which he and some teammates were riding was pulled over. The boys had been drinking, and one of them, a black pulling guard named Montgomery who could bench press a paddy wagon, started to mouth off. The two white policemen took one look at his tattooed arms the size of utility poles and began spraying mace. In the ensuing scuffle Eric landed a solid left hook that landed him in the county lockup. He was charged with assaulting an officer, complicated by being under the influence, which he wasn't. His scholarship and his law enforcement career were both history. His scholastic transcript suddenly had a smudge on it that no police department in the country would forgive.

"Max is good," he said, his eyes wandering as he pictured his little boy's infectious grin and Tupperware-bowl haircut. "He's got a few blood problems now, anemic and all that, but the doctors say that as hiccups go this one is a cakewalk."

Bernie nodded as she smiled approvingly. "That's good. At least I think it's good. Shannon?"

The energy between the two women required no tone in her inquiry.

"Shannon is Shannon. And the job is fine, thanks. You?"

Bernie's stare drifted toward the parking lot. Eric sipped his cold cappuccino, in no hurry to get to the point of all of this.

But the small talk was done. Like well-practiced music, it all had a rhythm. Following this awkward moment of quiet would come the real reason for her visit.

She looked him in the eye and said, "I can't let it go."

"Never thought you could." His voice was soft, resigned yet gentle.

"Peggy didn't jump."

The conventional wisdom—the story the police and the coroner and anyone else who wanted to shelve the file on Peggy's death would have you believe—was that she went to the Embassy Suites hotel, smoked a few sticks of hashish and jumped from the sixth floor, landing in the atrium rock garden next to the restaurant, completely ruining the night of a rookie front-desk clerk who quit the very next day. This was the same hotel in which her affair with the mysterious Arizona big shot had ended ugly—on the sixth floor, in fact—the details of which were known only to Bernie and Peggy's shrink, whose testimony convinced the police that this was all there was to it. A broken heart gone mad.

But Peggy wouldn't have jumped. The shrink tended

to agree, conceding that it seemed unlikely. But only Bernie believed, and the police didn't care.

Bernie swallowed hard before she said, "I thought it might pass. The rage, the need to fix it. Spend some time alone, go to Mexico, get drunk, say good-bye, then get back to work."

She seemed to choke on whatever was next.

"But it didn't pass," offered Eric.

Bernie shook her head. "She didn't jump, Eric."

They both sipped from their cups again, this time with less symmetry.

"Let's say you're right. Now what?" Eric shifted in his chair, trying not to sound impatient.

"I want you to find the guy."

"The Phoenix dude."

She nodded, as if this was all she intended to say on the matter.

"You think this guy had something to do with Peggy's death."

She nodded again.

He raised his eyebrows and said, "Based on . . . ?"

"Based on this." She thumped her chest. "My heart knows. *I* know."

"And the police won't help you."

"The police have a suicide note and a psychologist who will verify that my sister was traumatized by an affair that terminated in that hotel. That's all they want to know."

"You asked them to check this guy out?"

"They need more than a first name, which is all I have. No last name, no company name. Peggy's boss won't provide any of the vendor names unless she's subpoenaed, and that's not happening. I asked a couple of her friends, but they didn't even know about the relationship. Boss lady doesn't want to piss off any vendors, coworkers don't want to piss off boss lady. Bitch threw me out of her office."

"Sensitive."

"I need your help, Eric."

"You have a first name and a city, and you want me to find this guy."

"He has a jet."

"Pardon me?" Eric's eyes were round as quarters.

"Turns a girl's head. I know his first name and the fact that he has a jet. Should narrow it down, don't you think?"

"Not in Arizona. Ever been to Scottsdale?"

Bernie leaned forward. "Peggy worked for a software firm. Cutting-edge stuff. We can narrow it from there, categorize potential vendors."

"Sure. Narrow it down to, say, ten or twenty thousand companies that might do business with a major software developer in Dallas, Texas. I'm a freaking coach in an alternative high school for privileged brats, Bernie."

"You're a pit bull, is what you are. And you're good at this stuff. You once told me you have contacts, friends with big computers who can go where you can't. And I know you dig this kind of undercover thing."

Now it was Eric's turn to survey the parking lot. He chewed on his lip, tried not to shake his head.

"I'll pay you," she said.

"No, you won't," he shot back.

Her chin quivered, and she had to look away.

"Why?" he asked. "I find this guy, what then?"

Bernie blinked, her eyes betraying any sense of calm she'd maintained until now.

"I don't know," she whispered.

A tear fell, hitting the plastic top of her drink.

Eric reached across the table and took her hand. They locked eyes and Bernie smiled, knowing her friend would help her.

"This is bad, Bern."

"I intend for it to be bad. For him."

"Bad for *you*," he said. "Let it go."

She looked away, setting her jaw.

"I can't."

Eric nodded, shaking his head slightly. "What's his name?"

Her eyes snapped back. "Wesley," she said.

"That and the jet . . . that's all she told you."

"I was trying to talk her out of the affair, not celebrate it. Based on how it ended, I'd say this Wesley guy is one flaming asshole jet jockey with world-class credentials."

"Then I'll just follow the smell," he said. He was already going over his ledger of favors owed and owing, vacation time accrued, what he'd say to his wife.

Bernie got up, came to Eric and hugged him. He was sitting, she was standing, so his face was somewhere between her breasts. For a moment the past flooded in, then was gone. As usual, they would leave this little unspoken volume unopened.

"It may take some time. There'll be expenses, too. . . ."

"Just shut up and let me love you for a minute here," she said, still hugging him.

Eric harbored a familiar thought from their past: *Remind me never to piss you off. . . .*

4

Denver, Colorado

The young man couldn't take his eyes off of the woman in front of him. She was on her hands and knees, naked, the small of her back curving upward in an almost unnatural way, presenting her exquisite ass to him. His gaze alternated between her back and her buttocks, both of which were like nothing he had ever seen. It was enough that her skin was perfect and eerily smooth to the touch, that her muscle tone was that of a gymnast half her age. It was enough that she'd come on to him in the hotel bar, fawning over his clothes and what she assured him were his movie-star looks, buying the drinks, eventually inviting him up here to her room, no strings, just two mature people on business trips, living on the edge, taking advantage of a singular moment in time and space. She was beautiful, but more than that she was stunning in a dangerous sort of way—ink-black hair only slightly longer than his own, perfectly styled with just the right spike effect, bright blue eyes framed by makeup that leaned toward the theatric, deep burgundy lips perpetually moist, all of it accented with expensive jewelry and the quintessential little black cocktail dress, which, in a bit of creative couture license, had a high collar and tight long sleeves that bloused over her wrists. She was a hybrid vision of femininity, part uptown glamour, part neo-goth chic, with wall-to-wall attitude that said she liked to party. This woman knew

what she wanted, and tonight, for some reason, she
wanted him.

He knew nothing else about her, except that she was
the most sexually provocative woman he had ever met,
and here he was, doing her in her hotel suite. If into
every life a little rain must fall, then tonight he'd caught
a serious break in the clouds. When he told her he'd
never done anything like this before, she replied that
she had, many times, in fact. He suspected that this diversity in their moral compasses was what made it exciting for the both of them—tonight she ordered vanilla,
and he was eating Cherry Garcia.

He couldn't argue, so upstairs they went. Other than
her handing him a prophylactic in the elevator, anyone
looking on would conclude that they'd never met.

Now, gazing down at her naked flesh, he realized that
no self-respecting gymnast on the planet would do to
her skin what this woman had done. On the left cheek
of her ass was a bright red tattoo of a tongue protruding
from puffy lips, which he recognized as the logo of The
Rolling Stones. It was to scale, too, not some subtle little
girlie thing, as if Jagger himself had loaned his fabled
tongue to the tattoo artist. But this tongue on her tush
was nothing compared to the masterpiece that had been
etched across the entire landscape of her back, a mael-
strom of sweeping, wispy strokes framing a darkened
netherworld background, like the cover of a sinister
comic book. The centerpiece was the image of a coiled
serpent rising up, morphing into a woman's wrist and
hand, also done to scale. The hand itself, with long serpentine fingers and daggerlike nails the color of dried
blood, held an apple. The entire image was laced with
what appeared to be leafy vines, as if the serpentine
arm and its apple were being thrust upward through the
branches of a vaporous tree. It was frightening, actually,
because there was no mistaking its metaphoric intention,
and from there it was an easy leap to the character of
the owner. Who in this case had shamelessly seduced
him and was now crouched on her knees accepting his

most enthusiastic thrusts, greedily touching herself with
one hand as she watched their bestial dance in the mirrored closet doors with fascinated, half-hooded eyes.

She had insisted on this position, carefully positioning
the angle of attack that would permit her to watch in
the mirror. Hanging from her neck was a pendant, a
cylinder of deep red, which swung back and forth as he
entered and withdrew. Her eyes remained open the entire time, and he thought he saw her smiling at the mirror. Even that was provocative because the smile was
unmistakably wicked, as if she knew a delicious secret.
The smile of a woman with a portrait of sin forever
carved on her spine.

Her movements became more urgent and her eyes
took on a familiar glaze.

"Come with me," she said, her line of sight in the
mirror never meeting his.

When they came she reached between her legs and
grasped his testicles, squeezing firmly as the spasms overwhelmed him, the pressure of her grip unrelenting until
he had emptied into her completely. He would never
forget her face, the way she stared at the mirror at the
moment of release, all abandonment and freedom. As if
she were cruelly laughing.

He slumped onto her, relishing the moisture on her
back. Her knees had collapsed, and she was now flush
with the mattress as he lay flat on top of her, still inside.

Her chest still heaved and her eyes had finally closed.
He noticed the other tattoos now, a bursting sun on the
back of her neck, a pair of snake's fangs on the top of
one shoulder, a biceps encircled with what appeared to
be barbed wire, Asian lettering on one of her ankles.
There were others, smaller ones, too many to count, including an intricate band of braided ink around the third
finger of her left hand. Funny, he hadn't noticed that
downstairs. There was also a thin brass ring through
each nipple, which because of the abbreviated foreplay—
they had assumed the canine position within seconds of
entering the room—he also hadn't noticed until now.

She said, "I want you to leave."

He rose to one elbow, as if to better see her face. "Excuse me?"

"Go. I want to remember you like this."

"What . . . confused?"

A little smile played at the corners of her mouth. "Precisely."

He pulled away, his penis withdrawing. He could feel the deliberate constriction of her vaginal walls, as if to keep him in place.

"I'd like to stay," he said, ". . . make love to you again." He was tracing the outline of the snake on her back with his finger. He was lying, and both of them knew it.

"No."

She was staring at him now, her expression leaving no doubt. He shook his head and began to dress. She lowered her face back to the mattress and again closed her eyes, her face expressionless. As if she was already bored.

When he was dressed he bent to kiss her forehead, but she didn't move.

"Good night," he said as he opened the door. "Thank you." He waited for a response, but there was none. "I'll never forget this."

Without opening her eyes, he heard her whisper, "I know."

As the door swung shut behind him, the woman quickly got up and went to it. She connected the security chain and the dead bolt before turning back toward the closet.

She stood before the mirror and smiled.

"Hello, lover," she said aloud.

She pulled the doors open.

Inside the closet was a man. He was naked, kneeling upright with his hands aloft, bound to the clothing rod with a necktie. A belt had been wrapped around his face, holding in place the pair of her black panties stuffed into his mouth. He had been carefully positioned to see through the crack between the doors, out into the room, with a clear line of sight to the bed.

Like her, his body was covered with elaborate tattoos. An eagle on one shoulder, a cross on the other. What appeared to be Asian lettering around one perfectly sculpted biceps. And like her, he looked more like a model than an ink enthusiast. He had dark hair that appeared greasy because it was soaked with sweat. A matching pendant necklace, cylindrical and bloodred, hung from his neck. And at the moment, he was perfectly, gloriously erect. The black tattooed image of a snake entwined itself around his penis.

She sank to her knees in front of him so they were eye to eye. Maintaining eye contact, she smoothed his hair back as she tenderly kissed his forehead. Using her other hand, she began stroking his tumescence.

She smiled warmly, closing her eyes as she pressed her face on his shoulder. She kept stroking until he came, screaming from behind the gag.

The lovers were motionless on the bed. The room was dark, the only light coming through the window emanating from nearby Coors Field. Muted traffic sounds could be heard, and muffled television audio wafted through the wall, a sound unique to hotels. They lay on their sides under a sheet, the bedspread and blanket thrown back as they cooled. The man lay behind her, his body seamlessly cupped around his lover's fetal form, her head on his biceps while his fingers stroked her forehead. For many minutes they listened to nothing before he broke the silence.

"What are we?" he said softly.

"Lovers," she said. They'd done this before, the form consistent, the content always a fresh take on a familiar theme. They repeated nothing in their lives.

"Lovers of lust," he countered.

"Lovers of passion."

"Fuck buddies from hell."

A pause, then she said, "Seekers."

"Seekers of pleasure."

"Seekers of suffering." She used her voice playfully here, and he moaned.

"Yes. Adventurers."

"Carnivores," she said. "Ravished predators."

"How about ravish*ing* predators."

"Obviously."

"We are explorers."

"Of boundaries and limits."

"Who have no limits."

"Who know no boundaries."

"Perversions of nature."

"Keepers of a secret flame."

"I like that."

"Thank you."

"Devils."

"Demons," she said. "Demons are sexier."

"Diana and Damien, demons at large."

"Which is the more dangerous, I wonder?"

"Definitely Diana, the Huntress," said Damien.

"I think Damien, the Serpent," said Diana.

A moment of quiet passed between them. The television from another room was definitely tuned to Leno.

"One wonders what's next," he said.

"One wonders."

"Something . . . dangerous."

"Something sick and wrong."

"Deadly, perhaps."

She reached behind, feeling the return of his erection. She moved her hips and lifted her leg, guiding him into her.

"Ooh, Damien likes *deadly*."

"Damien likes Diana deadly."

"My little alliterative boy toy."

They didn't speak further as they moved, the game suspended. It was a slow, unhurried dance, tender in pace, soft in conclusion. His fingers playfully tugged and twisted the brass rings in her nipples as he made love to her.

When it was over, as his breathing returned to normal, he kissed the back of her head and whispered, "What are we, really?"

A moment passed before Diana answered. He could not see her face, did not know that her eyes were open and staring.

"Nothing," she said, her voice barely audible. "We are nothing at all."

5

Peoria, Arizona

He had feared this moment for as long as he could remember. He knew it would come, but knowing didn't keep him away. Not now, not in his previous life, not in his next. We die a million little deaths along the way—this would simply be another. It had happened before, and he'd survived. He was what he was, and this was his thing, his secret passion. The suits might own his days, but these were his nights, his sweet, delicious nights, and the risks be damned. He entered the establishment with an eye on the lot for familiar cars, scanning the aisles for the wrong face. He'd even rehearsed his response to the moment of exposure, a shrug that made light of it, a piss-off grimace if it turned ugly. What could they do, anyhow? This wasn't the twentieth century anymore, and Jerry Falwell was little more than a trivia question. Besides, whoever saw him here would be burdened with the same dirty little secret.

A tap on the shoulder, and his world would never be the same.

Tap tap tap.

Tonight was the night. Busted.

There were two levels of risk, actually, and luckily this was the lower of the two. Not a suit or a coworker, which would have spelled the end of his gig at work. No, this was just a face, someone he knew in passing, someone who knew where he worked. And while you could never tell from the outward signs, this was a face he was surprised to see here, in this adult superstore on the other side of town. After midnight in the middle of the week. Here in the gay section, a copy of *Tunnel Man* in his hand.

The face was smiling sheepishly, a good start.

"I'll be damned," said the man, nodding gleefully, as if this was the goof of the year. Jason thought the man sold office supplies, a guy who dropped in once a week or so, a nameless face you ran into in the elevators or the parking lot.

Adrenaline coursed through Jason Hillman's system, and he fought off the sudden urge to simply turn away. All he could do was smile back, easier said than done with so much adrenaline urging him to bolt. It was a critical moment, requiring just the right humility and a dash of indignance, without too much shame and absolutely no guilt. How he played it would dictate how much face he could show tomorrow.

"Lemme guess," said the man, "just browsing, right?"

Jason said, "Getting crowded here in the closet, I think."

The guy kept nodding, his contrived little smile fixed in place. Something was going on behind those eyes, serious processing at work, options being weighed. It looked like fear, but it was a mask for something else.

Jason was doing some processing of his own. He was standing across from his polar opposite, someone who hadn't given him the time of day the few times he'd seen him at the office. Jason was a byte-head, a programming prodigy. This other guy was a stiff with golf clubs in his trunk, the kind of guy who liked to wear Polo shirts with his company logo on the chest and had a burger every day for lunch. Jason was a vegan skinhead and a *Star Trek* buff; this guy had Richard Gere hair and a letterman jacket from forty pounds ago in storage somewhere.

"No one knows I'm here," said the man. "How about you?"

"You know," said Jason.

"Too true. Listen, I won't tell if you won't."

Then he winked. The sonofabitch actually winked. Here it was, the covenant, the leverage, the devil's deal.

Jason nodded. "Okay. This never happened."

The man smiled, took a deep breath. "Never happened. So . . . come here often?"

They both laughed at this little icebreaker, suddenly pals.

The man looked at his watch. "Listen," he said, "you wanna have, like, a drink or something?" He shrugged. Just the right humility. Not a trace of shame.

"I don't think so."

"Look, I'm not coming on to you. I just . . . need to talk. Please."

Jason felt a new jolt of adrenaline, a different vintage. It wasn't lust, though this guy wasn't too bad if you were into ex-lineman. And, to be honest, there was something hot about nibbling the forbidden fruit, if just for a lost evening. Suddenly there was desperation in the air . . . the guy was scared. And Jason Hillman found that exciting.

"I've got an important meeting in the morning," said Jason.

"Me too, actually. I just want to explain about, you know . . . this." He indicated their surroundings with a dramatic sweep of his hand.

"Nothing to explain," said Jason.

"Let me try. Please."

Jason wasn't sure what to make of this. The guy just needed some reassurance and maybe a quick parking-lot hummer. With each other's balls in a sling, anything was possible.

"All right," said Jason. "Something nearby."

In the parking lot, the man said, "Let's take your car. I came on the bus. You know how it is."

The first of several silent alarms went off in Jason's head, but not loud enough to change the course of fate. Later, he would realize this excuse had made no sense, that this was the moment when he should have run, but for now he was too excited to assign meaning.

Jason drove to a bar called Zeke's on Bell Road, one of the few establishments still open at this hour on a weeknight. As he started to turn into the lot, the co-worker instructed him to keep going straight.

"What?"

Jason turned, and a second alarm went off, this one loud enough to silence his raging hormones. The course of fate was already written.

The man had a gun in his hand.

"Keep driving," said the man. The seductive little smile was gone now, replaced by a nervous tic.

"What is this?" demanded Jason, wheeling his '94 Nissan back into the lane.

"Capitalism," said the man.

Scottsdale, Arizona

Jerry Grasvik checked his watch and swore aloud. He was alone in the lab that he shared with his partner on this project, so he could sling profanities all he wanted, play his favorite rap-metal bands full out, pass gas, sip a beer, whatever. There were no rules at this level, only the expectation that you deliver, on time and on budget. In return you got your food brought in for you, free of charge, and once in a while there were Coyotes tickets or, if you were really on fire, an extra check waiting in an envelope in your In box.

It was only ten after nine, but he was notoriously impatient, and Jason Hillman was anal retentive, notorious for being on time.

He picked up the phone and dialed the receptionist's desk.

"Hey. You seen Jason this morning?"

"What am I, your bitch?" Nadine was always busting his balls. It was how she flirted. She was attractive because she worked at it, all makeup and fashion and attitude. She was pushing forty with only a few extra

pounds, but nonetheless the woman had a way with the
guys. Jerry had noticed she had different shticks for different men in the company, a consummate political animal who knew everything about the various comings and
goings here at Oar Research. Right now, he was interested in the coming of Jason Hillman, his assigned partner on the company's most important programming
project, one that would put them over the hump in the
highly competitive security software arena.

"No, but we both know you're my love slave," he said.

"You know how bad I could sue your ass for that?"

"Takes two to tongue-dance, babe."

"No Jason," she said without missing a beat.

"Thanks. Nice fuck-me pumps today, by the way."

He hung up and brought up the address book on his
desktop computer. He found Jason's number, picked up
the phone and punched it in.

After two rings he heard a voice speaking in mono-
tone: "This is Jason, you know what to do." Then the
beep.

Jason. A laugh riot, that guy. Grasvik hung up without
leaving a message.

He waited until nine thirty to call the boss, who answered on the first ring.

"Yeah."

Wesley Edwards. A real piece of work, that guy.

"Jason's a no-show," said Jerry.

"What's that mean?"

"It means I can't run the test."

"Can't, shouldn't, or won't?"

"It's his code, man."

"It's his ass if he doesn't show, too. Can you run it
without him?"

"It's his code, but it's my application. Of course I can
run it."

"Then run it."

"You'll back me on this?"

There was a pause, uncharacteristic for Wesley Edwards, who ran the place with the frenetic energy of a

football coach on Ritalin. Jerry wondered why all the guys in suits in this business, all these Larry Ellison protégés, were such insufferable pricks.

"You free for lunch?" asked Wesley.

The new pause was Jerry's. This had never happened, and he'd been here three years, since before the dotcom apocalypse that brought Wesley Edwards to the company, ego in tow, gilded résumé in hand. The thought of breaking bread with this guy was about as appealing as a high colonic.

"Uh, yeah. Okay."

"Twelve thirty, then."

The line went dead.

As Jerry prepared to implement the critical simulation of the remote-access security system he and Jason Hillman had developed together, he had two thoughts. He wondered if Jason was okay, and if he'd finally get to ride in Wesley's slick new Cadillac SUV on the way to lunch.

6

Portland, Oregon

The IT Center took up the entire two floors of the bank's regional headquarters complex, which stood adjacent to a thirty-two-story downtown tower that bore the bank's name. It was Portland's second tallest building, which was like saying you were the second tallest player on an intramural basketball team. The place looked more like a county library than the digital nerve center for a trillion-dollar financial institution.

The shit hit the fan on what was supposed to be a typically quiet Sunday. In the entire seventy thousand square feet of the building there were only three people working, one a janitor, another at lunch when it all started to fly. Kim Greenwood was in charge of the whole shooting match while senior IT staffers were at home having a life. Most of the bank's data for the week had been processed in real time, and any batch work and periodic reporting had long since been finished, filed, archived and electronically distributed. That left little more than cash machine transactions active on the system, and though the division encompassed six states and some thirty-three hundred ATM machines, it all amounted to a blinking light on Kim's PC screen about every six minutes, for which she was paid $12.65 an hour to watch. She had court time reserved at six, so today she was wearing her tennis sweats, sitting with her feet on the control console as she checked out the latest Doc

Marten's catalog. She ran her fingers through thick curly hair as she considered a little mid-shift catnap and a fourth can of Coke for the day.

A woefully understated beep signaled the first anomaly. Looking up at the screen, Kim saw that seventeen hundred ATMs were being accessed simultaneously.

On any business day this wouldn't be all that unusual, but on a Sunday in March this was statistically impossible, something the artificial intelligence component of the program instinctively understood, prompting it to offer a feeble little toot to anyone who happened to be paying attention. Even more unusual, however, and far off to the left on the bell curve of probability, was the fact that all seventeen hundred machines were dispensing precisely the same amount of cash: $200.

Kim bolted upright and grabbed her reading glasses. This couldn't be right. Even in training modules, where instructors with warped senses of humor amused themselves by playing stump the rookie, nothing like this was within the realm of possibility. She quickly typed in instructions that triggered a real-time diagnostic program, then sat back with held breath to see what happened next.

In twenty seconds a readout confirmed that, indeed, $200 had just been withdrawn from a whole shit-load of ATMs. Only now, it was up to twenty-five hundred machines.

Kim tore into a Rolodex on the console—high tech had its practical limitations—to find the home number of her supervisor, who was a football fanatic and would be pissed as hell at the interruption of his religious observance of the game. The guy wasn't home, but she caught him on his cell phone on the way home from a halftime beer run.

Either this happened all the time or he was surprisingly calm. He told Kim to hit the Panic Button, a master control switch—like everything else in the room, it was a keystroked system command—that was supposed to immediately disable the bank's entire ATM network.

She entered the Panic Button code, immediately freezing the system. She hung up with the assurance that she'd stopped the bleeding and that the boss was on his way in. Meanwhile, the bank's clients were about three million dollars poorer.

The freeze lasted all of two minutes. Despite the overriding failsafe, the withdrawals began again.

Her supervisor arrived twenty-five minutes later. It seemed like twenty-five hours to Kim Greenwood, however, because she could only watch in horror as the master control screen told her that continued withdrawals were taking place from all corners of the region every two minutes at twenty-five hundred of the bank's ATMs. She had the presence of mind to access the underlying account numbers of the withdrawals, and this proved to be the most puzzling aspect of the whole incident. The withdrawals were all coming from the same account. The account belonged to a local billionaire, by far the richest man in Oregon, who had founded a little shoe company favored by people like Michael Jordan. Apparently this guy liked to keep ten or twenty million easily accessible bucks handy, in case he wanted to Just Do It. One never knows when one might want to buy a new jet or something.

Kim watched as the account balance dwindled by a half million dollars every two minutes. While this certainly sent Kim's blood pressure into the panic zone, part of her rationalized that the guy would never miss the chump change.

And then it all stopped. As suddenly as it began, the withdrawal frequency dropped off the chart to zero. At first she thought the Panic Button program had kicked in again, but there were still a few random accesses happening across the system. She ran diagnostics of her diagnostics, checked and rechecked the system on redundant processors, grabbed the cross on a chain around her neck and said a few Hail Marys. By now her coworker had come back from lunch and was poring through a manual in search of a clue. Both were certain Mr. Big

Shoes and his friends on the bank's board would have them fired first thing in the morning.

The last thing she did before the boss arrived was take another look at the shoe czar's account balance. To her great surprise and even greater relief, it was back where it started, as if none of this had happened.

Right about then an e-mail reached the control room.

When the supervisor arrived several minutes later, Kim was sitting with her feet up on the console. She was shaking her head ironically, a slight smile evident as she held out a printout of the e-mail.

"Know anybody pissed off enough to pull something like this?" she said.

"The Indonesians," offered her coworker, referring to the shoe company's political cross, borne with the arrogance of the obscenely wealthy.

The supervisor didn't get it. His knowledge of the shoe company's geopolitics extended to the cross-trainers on his feet.

He squinted at his subordinates in turn, then read the note.

It said: *Thanks for playing, and do come again.*

7

Plano, Texas

Bernie realized she was uncomfortable when she returned home from work to hear Eric's voice mail, asking if she could meet him the next day at a nearby Starbucks. It was not the reaction she expected, given her initial fervor on bringing justice to the man who she believed had caused her sister's death. A month had passed since she'd sent Eric off to locate him, and she'd actually taken Eric's counsel and tried to put Peggy's death and all that it implied behind her. Negative energy, he'd called it, a cancer of the spirit. She was well on her way to remission, too, aided by a freelance assignment producing an online tutorial for a local training company. The gig paid fifteen grand for about six weeks' work—she was looking forward to some hands-on work after her life as an upper manager, which consisted of little more than wall-to-wall meetings—and her condo didn't close for another few weeks, so life was good for a while. A few casual dates, a girlfriend's birthday party—complete with a stripper who looked like George Clooney—and a dinner with her parents that didn't erupt into an argument over religion, and she was back on top of the world.

Eric's call was like going back on medication. You ordered it, you knew you still needed it, but you didn't really want it anymore.

"I thought you hated this place?" she said as she arrived at the Starbucks, leaning in to kiss his cheek in greeting. For some reason she had never understood, there were about fifteen people waiting in line.

"Passionately. But I figured you liked it here. Eric giver."

"Not me, Mr. Giver."

He slid a paper cup across the table. "Room-temp cappuccino, your favorite."

She nestled in and sipped as she nodded a thank-you.

"So here we are, wishing we were someplace else. What else is new?" He paused, blushing as he quickly changed his countenance. "You look good, as usual."

"Thanks. So do you, as usual."

Both of them were being honest, in a way that only old friends can be. Bernie had never copped to the Gen-X fashion sense common to her profession, opting for a more California-hip style, as evidenced by today's crisp black slacks and square-toed boots, and a fluffy black turtleneck under a buttery black leather blazer. With her tied-back raven hair and understated earrings, she looked like a rich lawyer heading for the mall on her afternoon off. Eric wore spanking new Texas-friendly boots, fresh designer jeans and a caramel leather bomber jacket that looked soft enough to swaddle a baby. He'd cut his hair since she'd seen him last, giving him a militaryesque sharpness accentuated by his square jaw and muscular neck. He looked like a rich professional athlete.

The awkward moment of quiet following their exchange of compliments was full of meaning. Their legacy was as precious as it was beyond reach. But there were new rules now: don't call too often, don't talk for too long, be there if you're needed. Shannon's unresolved sensitivities about her husband's relationship with Bernie remained an unspoken governor, which was why they met for coffee instead of lunch. Lunch would simply not be okay.

"You found him," she said, trying to come off nonchalant as she sipped her drink.

"Think I did."

"Okay." She exhaled loudly and smiled, as if this announcement was the opening bell, which it was.

"I want to talk about it first," he said.

"I figured you might."

"You still want to do this?"

"I don't know what I want. Let's start with who he is."

"You going to kill him or something?"

She made an incredulous face. "Right."

"I'm serious."

"No, I'm not going to kill him. Jesus, Eric, what kind of question is that?"

"One from a friend who cares about you."

"What about the friend who *knows* me?"

"That too."

Her gaze wandered. There was no bullshitting Eric Killen.

"I just need to know," she said.

Eric shifted impatiently. "Know what? That this guy dumped your sister? That your sister's marriage was history? What else is there to know, Bernie?"

"For starters, what kind of man does that to another human being."

"Does what?"

"Wrecks a life. Then goes away, like nothing happened. And gets away with it."

Eric's cheeks billowed as he blew out an exasperated chest full of air. He rubbed his forehead for a moment before continuing.

"You think this guy somehow killed Peggy, and you want his balls in your fist."

"Something like that."

Eric shook his head. He was losing his patience, caught between loyalty and empathy. Being a friend, the real deal, was tough sometimes.

"You do this, he'll wreck your life, too."

They locked eyes. Bernie had no response, which invited him to elaborate.

"There was no evidence of foul play," Eric continued.

"I talked to the coroner's investigator, and they went over everything. There's nothing to implicate your guy or anyone else, no matter what you think. I'm sorry, but that's a fact. Which means you're on your own with this thing, whatever this *thing* is. Why don't we start there . . . just what the hell do you intend to do?"

Bernie tried to lighten the moment with a grin. She put her hand out, palm up, and balled it into a fist.

"Squeeze."

"I'm serious. You don't give me a good story here, I'm not giving you the guy. I care too much about you to see you run off and fuck up your life."

Bernie drew another deep breath, the grin long gone. "You still don't believe in revenge, do you? The little altar boy in you keeps hanging on to that one."

"Revenge for *what*, damnit?" He slammed his palm flush onto the table. Several other patrons shot them quick looks, and they both sipped their coffee reflexively in an attempt to downplay the moment.

Bernie leaned closer. Eric could see that her eyes had glazed over, that she was near her breaking point.

"I just want to see this guy. Get close to him. See what Peggy saw, try to understand. If I can turn something up, some evidence, I'll call in the authorities, okay? If there isn't any, but if I think he was connected to it, maybe I can do something to stop it from happening again."

"That's the part I'm worried about."

She grabbed his hand, held it with both of hers. As intently as he was listening, he quietly prayed to God that his wife or one of her friends didn't crave a Frappaccino right about now. He fought off the urge to check his flanks and held her gaze.

"Give me the name, Eric. You've got to trust me. I'm not going to break the law and I'm not going to wreck my life."

"Tell me you're not going to go all Lorena Bobbitt on him, either."

She let a moment pass, then said, "Please."

Eric closed his eyes, his chin sinking to his chest. He

froze that way for a moment, then reached into the inside pocket of his jacket and withdrew a folded piece of paper, which he set on the table in front of them.

"Wesley Edwards. CEO of Oar Research in Scottsdale, Arizona. Software for high-end system security systems. Started in 'eighty-eight in virus protection, tried for a branded product, but it bombed. Did some custom applications, found a niche, grew too fast, ran out of cash, flirted with Chapter Eleven when dot-com went dot-bomb. Board fired the founder, hired a consultant to find a new wonderboy—enter Wesley Edwards. Single, dedicated, megalomaniacal, drives an Escalade, the whole enchilada."

"And he has a jet?"

"Not exactly. Oar Research has a jet. Same difference."

Bernie stared at the paper. Eric stared at Bernie. Both remained motionless for nearly a minute.

"Wow," said Bernie.

"Wow? I bust my ass for this, nearly get fired, not to mention divorced, and that's all I get? Wow?"

She looked up at him, relieved to see that he was grinning. And as usual, part of her mind registered just how magnificent a grin it was.

"Okay," she said, "how? Rhymes with wow."

"I was hoping you'd ask." He drained his cup, shifted in his seat. "Frankly, I didn't know where to start with this thing. Arizona's a big state, lots of Wesleys out there. Lots of money, which means lots of jets, too. So I'm thinking, let's start there, try to find a Wesley who owns an airplane. So I call my friend the American Airlines pilot, Michael from L.A. Michael tells me what I need to do is hack into the FAA ownership database, wishes me luck. I say thanks, hang up, call a fraternity brother who, God being with us thus far, is an air traffic controller. Which means he works for the FAA. He says he'll make a call or two, I don't hear back for a week. Guy finally calls, says there are no Wesleys with their name on a jet, not in Arizona or any other state. Says that nine out of ten civilian jet aircraft are registered to corporations anyway, and wishes me luck.

"So, God still being with us, I call a former teammate, a tight end who used to knock defensive backs into the next county for kicks. Guy's a lawyer because he still likes knocking people around, which means you owe him a blow job for this. Just kidding about that. He does a search on Arizona articles of incorporations for the name of Wesley, first or last, which wasn't a high probability for us because a lot are registered in other states, like Delaware for some weird reason. Nobody's ever *been* to Delaware, so go figure.

"He calls me back, says he got eighteen hits, fourteen first names, four last names. E-mails me the list, I call the air traffic guy back, ask him if I send him eighteen corporate names, can he see if any of them happen to own a jet aircraft. He says sure—he'll take a blow job, too, by the way. Two of those companies have a jet registered in their names. One of those is an insurance outfit in Flagstaff with a chatty receptionist. Your sister's company buys insurance, so I'm thinking this might be good. That Wesley is a fifty-nine-year-old actuary of the Mormon persuasion, and they don't usually give the keys to the jet to their actuaries, if you get my drift. The other firm, Oar Research, is in Scottsdale doing security software, which Peggy's company probably uses, and their Wesley is thirty-eight years old and drives an Escalade. Am I good, or what?"

"Modest, too," said Bernie, grinning slightly.

"I'm not done. I ask my FAA guy if there's any way to monitor the activity of the airplane. He says yes, they file flight plans, says he'll call me back. Calls me back in two days, says the Oar Research aircraft, a Cessna Citation, filed nine flight plans in and out of Dallas in the six months prior to Peggy's death."

He paused, then added with a wink, "Blow job, anyone?"

"Wesley Edwards," said Bernie, more to herself than Eric. Then her eyes snapped back to him, the grin gone.

"Do you know what he did? How it ended between them?"

Eric shook his head. He didn't want to know now, either.

Bernie's eyes took on a distant glaze.

"He called her, asked her to come to the Embassy Suites, where they'd met several times before. Gave her the room number, said he'd leave the key at the desk for her, that he had a dinner meeting and he wanted her to be there when he came in. So she goes to the hotel, picks up the key, goes up to the sixth floor, opens the door. The room is dark, lit with candles. There's a woman on the bed, her legs pointing straight at the ceiling. Wesley's on top of her, and when the door opens he just turns and smiles and says hello, invites Peggy to come on in, he'll be done in a moment. Doesn't miss a beat, just keeps on pile-driving. The woman also says hello, calls Peggy by name, then says to Wesley that she isn't nearly as pretty as he'd said she was. And they're laughing as Peggy backs out of the room."

She allowed a few moments for it to sink in.

"So you see, it doesn't really matter if Peggy killed herself or not. Because if she did, then it's because of this Wesley pig, and he has to pay for it. And if she didn't, then somehow he's connected to her death. And if that's the case, I'll find something that proves it. Either way, I have to do something."

She studied his eyes, then added, "I hope you understand now."

Eric was shaking his head. "How can I help?"

"You've already hit a home run. I can't thank you enough."

"Rain check on the blow job?" He winked again.

"The day your divorce is final, I'm there. I'm not holding my breath."

"You can breathe through your nose."

"Does Shannon think you're funny, too? I bet not."

"You'll call me if you need anything. If you get in trouble. I'm there."

"You always have been."

"I will again. I promise."

Bernie put the piece of paper in her purse and got up. Eric took the cue and rose as well. They embraced, and while their heads were close, he whispered in her ear.

"Revenge is unhealthy, little darlin'. Stay healthy, okay?"

"Count on it," she said. She squeezed his hands a final time and walked quickly out of the Starbucks, back into the real world. Eric watched her go, a familiar emptiness washing over him. And at the same time, he couldn't wait to get home to hug his wife. Who did, in fact, find him to be a laugh riot, and who did, in fact, breathe through her nose when it counted.

He didn't notice that a woman sitting at a table by the far window had been watching them the entire time. He wouldn't have recognized her, but she certainly knew who he was, what he did, and who he was married to.

By the time Bernie got to her car, she had decided on what to do next. As soon as her freelance assignment was in the bag and the fifteen grand was in her checking account, Bernie would move to Scottsdale for a while.

In her mind this wasn't about revenge. This was about justice.

Both were best served cold.

Dinner that night at the Killen residence was a chilly affair, both in terms of the food and the vibe between Eric and Shannon. She'd made him a sandwich out of three-day-old pot roast, served with potato chips. She wasn't eating, complaining of an upset stomach.

There would be hell to pay later. Of course he asked if anything was wrong within minutes of coming in the door, but he never knew the truth until later, and had to stifle a laugh at how bad her acting was in these moments, telling him she was just fine, he was imagining things, then asking pointedly if he had something to feel guilty about.

In retrospect, this was understandable, given the nature and sheer bulk of his transgression. Some cold shoulders just can't wait. He was in the study—the spare bedroom where the computer was, actually—going over a case file when she came in, closing the door behind her. Always a bad sign.

"Nice day?" she began.

He put the file down. He'd learned that paying rapt attention to anything other than her in these moments could have dire consequences. He'd once tried to catch the end of a Mavericks game on television while listening to her complain about one of Max's doctors, and the result was an imploded television thanks to a thrown vase. Actually, she was throwing it at *him*, but she missed.

"Fine. Yours?"

She ignored the question. "I heard from Barbara Bellogus today," she said.

"Who?"

"Barbara . . . from the bunko group?"

Shannon hadn't played bunko in four years, and somehow he was supposed to keep a roster of the women in the group in his head. He'd met them all twice, both times when they'd played at their house and he was slow in vacating the premises.

He shook his head and shrugged.

"Interesting," she said, her tone indicating that the eye of the storm was near. "She remembers you."

"Really?"

"Actually, she saw you today. At a Starbucks in Plano. I have to assume that was Bernie you were with."

Eric stared for a moment, choosing between outrage and amused sympathy.

"Barbara Bellogus saw me today in Plano with Bernie," he repeated.

"Well . . ." said Shannon, her face turning its ritual

red. It should have turned green, given that this was nothing more than a recurring bout of jealousy. "You tell me."

Eric couldn't hide an impatient scowl. "She asked me to check out some information. I *told* you about it, and you said you were fine with it then. I called her, asked her to meet me so I could tell her what I found out."

"That crap about her sister again?"

Eric squinted, forcing back the wrong response.

"What is it with you and her? Bernie's my friend, Shannon. You're my *wife*. And I love you. Okay? I love *you*."

Shannon tried to be tough, hold his gaze, but her chin began to quiver. A moment later she covered her mouth with a closed hand and lowered her head.

Eric got up and went around the desk, kneeling on the floor to put his arms around her. He put his mouth close to her ear and said, "I would never do anything that would compromise you, or us, okay? I keep telling you that, and you keep testing me."

"I'm sorry," she sobbed. "I can't help it."

"You can help it. You can *believe* me. You can get healthy about this. Bernie's not the problem here."

"But I am."

"That's not what I said, and it's certainly not what I meant."

She took a deep, brave breath and sat straight in her chair. She forced a smile and said, "You're right. I'm sorry."

She kissed him, a peck of apology.

"You're a good friend to her," she said.

"I'm a good husband to you," he replied.

Then she hugged him. It was over for now, but he knew this would come up again. Because he knew the thing with Bernie was just getting started, and the emotional extortion of his wife would not prevent him from doing the right thing by her.

Sometimes you had to choose. And sometimes the choice had a price.

> **8** <

Scottsdale, Arizona

Bernadette Kane lurked at the sunny periphery of Wesley Edwards's life for two weeks before she made her move. Eric had provided her with what he'd called a "profile brief," and brief it was: it consisted of an overview of Oar Research copied from a regional business magazine, the company's address and phone number, and a copy of Wesley's Arizona driver's license, complete with its requisite picture. Like most DMV photos, the mug shot held little promise, the features nondescript and the expression impatient, as if the jet was waiting on the tarmac and he had to get going. He appeared younger than thirty-eight, but that was because of the haircut that made him look like Sting on a bad day. Studying the picture, staring at it for extended periods as she plotted her approach, Bernie realized that her emotional agenda was stronger than her acting chops, and that if she didn't go neutral on this guy pretty soon she'd never stand a chance of seducing him.

And so she waited, tending to other business, putting down roots while she sharpened her claws and tried to put her emotions on ice.

The logistics were challenging because it all had to appear as if she'd moved here in search of a new life. After two nights at a Hampton Inn in Tempe she'd scored a sublet furnished condo from the *Arizona Republic* classifieds, and the owner was willing to accept a month-to-month with a ridiculous deposit. It was located several miles east in Scottsdale Ranch—Stucco Land again, but with a better pool—close enough to stay in the game, which would include a lot of surveillance activity. As soon as she recovered from sticker shock she wrote the deposit check and moved in. She'd driven here from Dallas in her Volvo, so that base was covered—a Volvo was very hip, and Scottsdale was a very hip town. All she needed was a convincing sob story and a plausible dream complete with stock options and she'd fit right in.

Though she'd driven past the building where Oar Research was housed several times—a four-story, green-tinted glass cube in a maze of new office buildings that belonged in a time-travel flick, located just a three iron from the Scottsdale airport—she'd waited until day three to break the perimeter. Résumé and portfolio in hand, she put on her best black pants suit and arrived unannounced, just another ace programmer stumping for work.

The receptionist held up a finger as Bernie approached, signaling that she would be a moment. She wore a headset with a stubby mouthpiece that made her look like a Secret Service agent, and her hands were busy attending to the PBX keys as she routed incoming calls.

"Oar Research, can you hold, please?" Click. "Oar Research, can you hold, please?" Click. "Mr. Edwards is in conference, would you like his voice mail? One moment." Click. "Oar Research, can you hold, please?" Click. "Thanks for holding, how can I direct your call? Ms. Damore is in conference, would you like her voice mail?" Click click click.

It went on this way for ninety seconds—Bernie counted seventeen incoming calls—in the middle of which the receptionist rolled her eyes and smiled at Bernie, as if she knew how insane it must all seem. Her tone remained robotically friendly for each new caller.

When a pause in the action arrived, Bernie said, "You're good."

The receptionist grinned. She was old enough to remember disco, but her clothing and hair suggested that a younger spirit lived here, one with a subscription to *Marie Claire*. The hip outfit and the unruffled handling of the calls told Bernie that this woman was a pro and therefore someone who might be useful down the road. Bernie glanced at the nameplate on the countertop: Nadine Worobey. She'd never seen a receptionist with her own shingle.

"Thanks," said Nadine. "Sink or swim in this seat, sweetheart." She paused to check Bernie out, head to toe. "You're here for Wesley?"

Something kicked under Bernie's rib cage, but she maintained a straight face. "Wesley?"

"Guess not. He's got a ten o'clock, I assumed it was you." She grinned. "You *look* like you're here for Wesley."

"Is that good?"

The grin warped into something more complicated, accented with a slight blush.

"Depends. Definitely a compliment, though. How can I help you?"

From there Bernie gave her pitch as a freelance producer/programmer new to the area, asking if there was someone with whom she could talk or at least leave a résumé. As she talked she chanced a few sideways glances around the office, hoping that the gods of deceit would be with her today and Wesley Edwards might stroll through the lobby, coffee mug in hand. Maybe it was paranoia, certainly warranted, but she thought she sensed Nadine watching her closely, as if noting her casual reconnaissance.

"He's in conference," said Nadine. That little knowing grin was back.

"Who is?"

Nadine chuckled softly as she took the résumé folder Bernie had set on the counter. "I'll see that someone gets this," she said.

Bernie felt her cheeks warming and knew that her

complexion was betraying her. Nadine knew it, too, because she said, "You really don't know him, do you? Mr. Edwards, I mean."

"No."

"I'm sorry. It's just . . ." She leaned closer, softening her voice. "He meets a lot of people, shall we say, who show up here looking for work. A lot of women, actually . . . like you. And that's a good thing, appearance-wise. I just thought . . ."

"I'm just looking for work," said Bernie, trying to balance the appearance of indignance and confusion. "Freelance, nothing permanent."

"We use a lot of contractors," said Nadine. She held up her finger again as several more calls arrived within seconds of each other.

Bernie smiled, pointed at the résumé as she mouthed a thank-you, and left.

Back in the car, she realized her stomach was on fire. She hadn't expected much to come of this; in fact, this visit was a plant, so that when she finally met Wesley Edwards there would be what appeared to be an amazing coincidence to talk about.

What she hadn't expected was Nadine and her forthcoming assumption that Bernie had already met Wesley Edwards. The guy was obviously a player; that much fit in with everything she already knew. And Nadine was obviously a world-class gossip with a certain lack of respect for corporate protocol, and perhaps the boss himself. Either that, or she had opinions about Wesley Edwards that transcended common sense, an occupational hazard for anyone on the front line.

Driving away, Bernie decided that a chatty girlfriend, one who happened to work at Oar Research, might make a good and timely addition to her strategic team.

Bernie got her first good look at Wesley Edwards the next morning. Armed with a coffee and a protein bar, she'd parked the Volvo discreetly across the street from the building at seven fifteen and waited for Edwards to arrive, hoping that this wasn't the day he'd decide to hop down to Tucson in the jet for eighteen holes. Cars began arriving around seven thirty, with Nadine Worobey among the first to report in. At ten of eight a spanking new Cadillac Escalade arrived, pearlized white, taking a spot near the walkway that was marked by a sign she couldn't read from where she was parked. She could, however, read the license plate: Big Ed. Bernie smiled and shook her head. The guy who got out of it was not so big—medium height at best—though his build was recognizable beneath an expensive Italian suit as that of someone who spent abundant time at the gym. The man walked with a swagger easily misinterpreted by the naïve as purposeful. The walk of a man who would put "Big Ed" on his license and spent a lot of time on a private jet.

She hadn't expected the reaction that overwhelmed her as she watched Wesley Edwards disappear into his glass building. Suddenly her sister's absence crashed into her consciousness like a morning alarm clock snatching her back from a dream. It wasn't so much that she was looking at the man who had come into her sister's life and wrenched it inside out. It wasn't the impending challenge of what lay ahead or the ambiguous intent of it all. It was something else, something chemical and guttural that defied her very conscious attempt at denial. Hate and hormones were, she realized, mutually exclusive motivators.

The problem was that Wesley Edwards was gorgeous. The big-shot job and the suit and the car and the jet would be enough to turn a girl's head, but to top it off this guy looked like a matinee idol. Better than a movie star, actually—most of them were midgets, yet this guy was a pro-athlete-turned-model-turned-executive kind of movie star. He projected the energy of a man who took his genetic superiority for granted and had moved on to bigger and more important things, like conquering the world. The energy of a man who didn't have time to be a nice guy, because nice guys finished back in the pack and he was light-years ahead of any pack that had ever roamed the corporate wilderness.

Poor Peggy never stood a chance. She and Bernie had always shared the same tastes in dance partners, the same bad-boy, dark-knight-in-shining-armor paperback fantasies. For years they'd laughed about it before Peggy had irrationally put her marriage in hock and, despite Bernie's admonishment, acted upon it. And now Bernie was looking straight at the same book cover, recognizing the buzz of her own percolating, clinging-to-adolescence attraction.

She wasn't sure if this would make the hunt more interesting or more difficult. Perhaps both. Wesley Edwards's looks had nothing to do with what had to be done, and everything to do with the fatal sequence of tumbling dominoes that brought her here in the first place.

At midmorning, still sitting in the Volvo because there was nothing else to do, Bernie used her cell phone to call Nadine. After putting Bernie on hold for almost a minute, she quickly remembered their encounter from the day before.

"I was wondering if you gave my résumé to someone, and who I should call to follow up."

"Of course I gave it to someone," said Nadine. "Our lead programmer is Jerry Grasvik. I put it in his box with a note that you looked very professional. I would have said *hot*, but Jerry's definitely into bytes, not butts."

"I appreciate that. Is he in this morning?"

"He is, but I wouldn't call for a few days. He's a very busy little fellow, and if I had to guess he's not fond of pushy women. Not that you're pushy or anything . . . you know what I mean. Jerry's not exactly Mr. Charming, if you get my drift."

Bernie said, "I work with programmers, so I do get your drift."

"You don't look like a computer geek, if you don't mind my saying."

Something about Nadine's tone confirmed a hunch Bernie had already been nursing in the back of her mind. Like many front-desk types Bernie had known, this woman relished her role as a cultural fulcrum at Oar Research, the woman who knew everyone and everything. Almost as much as she liked the sound of her own voice. And that made her easy.

"You're very sweet, Nadine, and helpful, too. I'm more of a project manager kind of geek. Listen, I think I told you, I'm new in town and . . . can I, like, buy you a cup of coffee sometime? You know, get the lay of the land around here—?"

Nadine interrupted with, "Buy me lunch and you're on. How about Friday?"

"Friday works for me." Maybe the woman was gay. Probably not—she certainly hadn't given off that vibe— but if that was what worked, let it rip. This was covert sexual warfare.

"I'll make sure Jerry takes a look at your stuff. He owes me. The Zinc Bistro at one. It's in the Kierland Commons, you can see it from our parking lot. Just look for The Cheesecake Factory and you're there."

"I love The Cheesecake Factory."

"You and ten thousand other hungry people every freaking day. I don't want to wait an hour and I have no willpower. Besides, you'll love the Zinc, too, even if it does sound like a herbarium or something."

"Okay, I'm there. I can't thank you enough."

"You'll owe me, too, sweetheart. Everybody does. See you Friday."

As the line went dead, it occurred to Bernie that this had gone too well, that Nadine was a bit too accommodating. Nonetheless, she'd use the next few days to prepare herself, both for her lunch with Nadine and for her chance meeting with Wesley Edwards, however and whenever it happened. One would, after all, lead to the other.

9

Everything Bernie did for the next two days was learned from watching television. She followed Wesley Edwards from his office to the bars, where he met people who looked more like contacts than friends, to the gym, where he worked out with obsessive ferocity, to the house in which he lived alone. The place was very middle America, three bedrooms on a cul-de-sac in McCormick Ranch. Not at all the crib of a high-tech CEO, not to mention a major player in the Scottsdale singles scene, which was as legendary as any in the land. On the first afternoon she brazenly inspected the mail in his box at the end of his driveway, and on the second day she took advantage of the garbage can left on the curb for pickup and dumped the whole thing into the trunk of her car. Later that day she followed him from the office across the street to the Scottsdale airport, where he parked the Escalade in the civil aviation lot and climbed aboard a small jet, which she recognized from pictures she'd printed off the Internet as a Cessna Citation. He traveled alone, other than the two pilots. By the next morning the airplane was back in its hangar and the Caddy in its reserved space in the Oar Research parking lot, so Bernie's surveillance would continue without interruption.

Her first observation was that he was always on the phone. To and from his car, while he drove, even when he took a midmorning walk around the parking lot, which he did daily. He used a hands-free mobile, one of those guys in airports talking a little too loudly into thin air, even though their hands were free and therefore quite capable of holding a telephone. Sitting in too many airport gate areas to count, she'd concluded that most of those guys were assholes—like smoking, it was one of those cause-and-effect paradoxes—and it was easy to visualize the rest of their lives and the corrosive state of their relationships. Thus far Wesley Edwards was falling right into that paradoxical profile, complete with headset and, she would bet big money, a thick gold chain around his muscular neck.

Other than that, the results of it all were as inconclusive as they were contradictory to her expectations. Wesley's mail consisted of junk solicitations and a predictable roster of bills; nothing exotic, nothing that tipped his hand to some private hobby or dark fascination. She'd not chanced following him into the two bars he'd visited on successive evenings, but both times he'd emerged within two hours with other men in suits, and from the formal way they shook hands as they parted she knew this was all business. His gym, frequented during long lunch hours, was an upscale club full of upwardly mobile high-tech marketing types—she could surmise this from the cars in the lot—and while she endured a sales pitch from an eager young man with ridiculously massive arms, she saw Wesley working out on an elliptical trainer. True to form, he wore his hands-free phone gear as his eyes alternated between a heart-rate readout and a television monitor. Sensing this might end up being her best shot, she accepted the two-week complimentary membership with a smile and a promise to bring a guest.

Wesley's garbage was only slightly more illuminating—she now knew he drank large quantities of 1% milk, had a weakness for Oreos, subscribed to *Cigar Aficionado* magazine—that fit, she thought—and had recently replenished his stock of hair gel. He drank Canadian beer and not much of it, used creatine and other nutritional bodybuilding supplements still untested or approved by the FDA, and the telephone statement that he didn't see fit to keep bore no long-distance charges. Probably used his cell phone for that, no doubt billed to the company. A guy's guy who didn't seem to hang with other guys. There were no prophylactic wrappers, no discarded greeting cards, nothing that indicated he was in a relationship of any kind or that a woman had recently set foot in his home. Other than a dash of vanity and the interest in cigars, the closest thing to admissible evidence of slime in this man's life seemed to be the fact that he didn't recycle.

He may be gorgeous, she concluded, but besides the hot car he was a blank page. She was looking for a hook, a chink in the masculine breastplate upon which she could prey. A way *in*—it was either buried so deep as to defy the hubris of daily life, or the guy was a clone with no soul. Based on what she knew, it had to be the former. Bernie had learned from experience, as well as her mother's early wisdom, that every man had something to hide, a dark agenda or a camouflaged button just screaming to be pushed, an old scar that still ached in the night. Wise was the woman who sensed these little Achilles' blemishes, because this was both her power and, when the need arose, her weapon. Wiser still was the woman who actually led her man to believe that he liked having his buttons caressed and his secrets embraced.

By Friday she had nothing to use on Wesley Edwards, other than his presence in a health club. But it was one o'clock in the afternoon, and the day was young. She still had Nadine.

The Zinc Bistro was Scottsdale's premier purveyor of California cuisine, whatever the hell that meant. To a Texas girl it meant ten-dollar hamburgers and butter patties shaped like little clams, served by a wait staff wearing aprons and crisp white shirts with skinny black suede neckties tucked in between the third and fourth buttons. It was the only chic little eatery in Scottsdale's newest and most prestigious shopping and office complex, and with competition like The Cheesecake Factory and P.F. Chang's, they had a lock on that particular demographic that looked down their often surgically enhanced noses at national chain concept restaurants. It was a great place to do business and dish news, and this lunch would prove to be a little of one and a lot of the other.

Nadine managed to finish her meal before Bernie despite a nonstop narrative that preempted what she assumed to be Bernie's welcome-wagon questions. Bernie had been content to listen, because Nadine was indeed covering all the right bases. She already knew that Oar Research was one of several high-tech firms owned by an investment group made up of anonymous fat cats who managed to hang on to their money from the early days.

"Be honest. You've really never met Wesley Edwards?" asked Nadine as she drank from her second glass of Chablis.

"Swear to God, I haven't," said Bernie, still working on that ten-spot burger. "I asked some people in Dallas where the action was out here, and Oar Research came up on the short list. I don't know why you assume that I have."

"You wouldn't be the first good-looking job applicant who's shown up after running into Wesley at a club," said Nadine, dabbing at the corners of her mouth with a linen napkin in a faux attempt to hide her smile. She was more attractive than Bernie had noticed earlier in the week, not someone you'd peg as a receptionist or a gossip. At a glance she seemed more like boardroom material, and most receptionists who went for that look rarely pulled it off with this degree of success. The first thing you'd say about Nadine after watching her work was that she was overqualified and underemployed in more than a few ways. Which, upon further reflection, might just explain her seeming obsession with Wesley Edwards.

Bernie returned the grin. "Well, you've brought it up twice now, so I have to assume there's something you're not supposed to tell, but you're dying to."

"Maybe there is. Maybe I am."

Bernie spoke into her iced tea, saying, "So . . . are you going to tell me?"

"That would be office gossip, I suspect."

"I don't work there yet."

"Ah, a loophole. If I tell you, maybe you won't want to."

"Is that the idea? To scare me off?" Bernie sensed that somehow this all had to do with Nadine being threatened.

"Just tryin' to help a sister out, sweetheart. That's all."

"I can take care of myself. And besides, now you've got me curious."

Nadine pursed her lips, and in that moment Bernie figured out what was going on here. Nadine was trying to impress Bernie with her proximity to the boss. Or perhaps with her position as the oracle of the company. Both, more likely, with a boost from her second glass of wine. Whatever came out of her mouth next would make her seem important, and when one beautiful woman was threatened by another, importance was the tiebreaker.

"Okay," said Nadine, grinning like this was slumber-party chatter. "Wesley Edwards, boy-wonder CEO. Face like a Calvin Klein billboard, body like a *Playgirl* centerfold, mind like a steel trap, bank account somewhere north of seven figures, and lest we forget, hung like a fucking thoroughbred."

Her smile was smug as she killed what remained of the wine.

"Would that be gossip or journalism?" asked Bernie, trying for her own nasty little twinkle now. Her instincts had been right on the money.

"We had a night, right after I was hired. Just one. Too many drinks with the gang after a birthday party, all the married people went home early, finally there was just the two of us. He's different one-on-one . . .

the façade goes away, the little rich boy insecurity pops out. Sort of sweet, actually. Very endearing. Like he's afraid someone will tap him on the shoulder and it will all be over."

"Maybe he just likes older women."

"Ouch."

"Just kidding. You're gorgeous and you know it."

"Thank you . . . and I do."

"So you went home with him."

"Not exactly."

"Come on, girlfriend . . . tell me!" Bernie said this with a little squeal, as if the answer would be the highlight of her year.

"Backseat of his Caddy."

"No!"

"Swear to God."

"Good?"

"Hands like a pianist, and that tongue . . . Jesus. First thing he did afterwards was apologize up and down."

"Man knows a lawsuit when he sees one."

"He was really very sweet."

"Sure, most sweet guys do their receptionist in the back of their SUV."

For a moment Bernie thought she'd said the wrong thing, but Nadine's delight only disappeared for a moment.

"Next day I told him I'd leave the firm if he wanted. I had no illusions of a relationship. It was just a lark. Maybe a big mistake. But instead he asked me to stay on, said nothing would come of it. We made a pact, and now we have an arrangement."

"And you've had him by the balls ever since."

"One could say that was part of the pact, yes."

Bernie wondered how often Wesley bent Nadine over his desk to renew his option on their little arrangement.

"A pact which you've just broken."

Nadine's eyes wandered before she said, "You seem like a nice girl. And he's not the sweet guy I once thought he was."

"I'd like to hear about that, too."

Nadine nodded as she took a sip of water. Her eyes were distant.

"Not today. I just wanted you to know . . . he's a player, and a woman like you, that's his game. That's a compliment, by the way. I know what he likes, and you've got a bull's-eye on your ass."

"I just want to work. I can handle Wesley Edwards."

"He's not a bad catch, you know."

"If you like backseat boys who make chauvinistic pacts."

Nadine smiled, though it had a sad, wistful quality to it. "Don't we all, to some degree?"

Their eyes locked. Bernie was the first to smile—Nadine had her number. It was spooky how right she was.

A few minutes later they were walking in silence from the restaurant to the parking lot. Nadine's self-aggrandizing agenda had gone over the top, rendering further idle chit-chat uncomfortable. Bernie had picked up the tab, and at the point at which they were to separate to their respective cars, Nadine extended her hand in gratitude.

"I hope you get what you want," she said.

Bernie grinned—once again this woman had no idea how spot-on she was. "I plan on it. This was very helpful."

They each turned and took a few steps before Bernie stopped in her tracks and spun around. She watched Nadine's retreat, her skirt hugging her buttocks and thighs, and then she called her name.

Nadine stopped and turned.

"What was this all about?" asked Bernie. When Nadine cocked her head to express obligatory confusion, she added, "All this Wesley stuff. Was that girl talk or shop talk?"

Nadine said, "I said too much. I'm sorry."

"I think you're in love with the guy."

Nadine nodded slightly, not in agreement, but in contemplation of Bernie's balls.

"I had my shot," she said. "Wasn't in the cards."

"Now you have your arrangement, and that's enough.

Some of him is better than nothing . . . as long as he isn't taken by someone else. You get to stay in the game."

Nadine's expression evolved into a sad smile. "He's gonna love you," she said.

"And why is that?"

"Because you've got it. You're as smart as he is, maybe smarter, and that'll be new for him. I can't play at that level, but you can. Question is, are you as tough as he is."

"You're a beautiful woman, Nadine, don't sell yourself short."

"So are half the women in the valley. The guy has beautiful women coming out his ears. It's a challenge he wants, someone who's as serious about success as he is. And trust me, he's damn serious. He craves a ball-busting, ruthless business bitch who'll make him work for it and look like Cindy Crawford in the process. Who-ever figures out how to do that lands the prize."

"Sounds like an asshole to me," said Bernie.

Nadine just smiled. Their eyes connected, as if each of them understood the other. But in fact, it was all in riddles now.

"See you soon," said Nadine before she turned and continued toward her car.

"The answer is yes, by the way."

Nadine turned and cocked her head.

"About being as tough as he is," said Bernie.

Nadine snorted a little laugh and nodded. "I have no doubt."

Bernie watched her walk away. She was filled with a fresh but nervous energy, because Nadine had helped her even more than she'd dared to hope. If it was a ruthless business bitch that rang Wesley Edwards's bell, then that's what she would become. As for the Cindy Crawford part, she could hold her own there, too. If she had to get a mole tattooed on her cheek to make this work, then so be it.

10

Wesley Edwards took in the taupe and marble splendor of the Gainey Village Health Club from the last elliptical trainer next to the window. He had a comforting view of his car, which was being washed by the club's lot lackies. If he looked the other way he could see into the gym, where Charles Barkley was loafing through a game of horse with a couple of wide-eyed gym rats. He and Charles were nodding acquaintances, having on several occasions occupied the same departure lounge at the Scottsdale airport, where Charles caught his weekly private jet to Atlanta for his Fox television gig. This particular exercise machine was his favorite for more reasons than those, and if it was occupied when he arrived it tended to put a damper on his workout. Wesley Edwards was used to getting what he wanted. There were two rows of this Life Fitness model with the hand pumps, sixteen machines in all, and as he exercised one of his private little games was to guess the occupation and net worth of each occupant between glances at the CNN market report. That, and imagining them naked as they churned out their aerobic minutes. The lunch crowd was all repeat business, the same faces, lots of suits, too many cheerleader types who chatted up too many fraternity types, including a few obvious ex–pro athletes. How the hell all these people knew each other, he had no idea.

His routine was to push for four hundred calories

burned in twenty minutes on the machine, followed by an enthusiastic punishment of the muscle group of the day on the weight equipment upstairs. Today was chest-shoulder-triceps day, his favorite because he liked the way it made him feel later in the afternoon—validation of life through pain and fatigue. He was working toward a goal of benching six reps at 225—not bad at five eleven, one ninety-five—with the ultimate objective of squeezing off one rep at 300 by his fortieth birthday, still two years and sixty pounds away. The football types warmed up at 225 when they finally got around to it, but he could buy their miserable lives ten times over, so fuck those guys.

Wesley always wore his telephone headset during the aerobic portion of his workout. They were a common accessory here, though most were connected to CD players instead of mobiles. The people he was dealing with didn't like to be kept waiting, and they could be as unpredictable as they were impatient.

He heard the ring and pressed the appropriate button without missing a calorie.

"Edwards."

A female voice said, "You're not sweating yet, Wes."

"Just got started. Who is this?"

"Those look like new Nikes. Jordans or cross-trainers?"

Wesley scanned the packed club. He counted at least five people talking on mobile phones, three of whom were women, none of them looking his way. One guy was actually doing crunches with a phone wedged between his shoulder and his ear. He'd seen people running laps with a phone held to their head, so none of this was out of school, especially in Scottsdale.

"Jordans. What is this? Do I know you?"

"Not yet."

"How did you get this number?"

"Very cleverly, thank you." Bernie had called Nadine that morning and, after making sure they were okay after their little parking lot sparring match, successfully begged for Wesley's mobile number. Jerry Grasvik hadn't called, and Bernie was going around him. Nadine liked her moxie, so she gave up the number on the guarantee of plausible deniability.

"What do you want?" asked Wesley, unconsciously picking up the pace.

"You're out of breath. You should do intervals."

"I'm hanging up. You want to talk to me, talk to my face."

"Testy. I'll be at the bench in ten minutes. I need a spotter. And so do you from what I've seen."

The line went dead. Wesley saw that the three women were still on their phones, all with their backs to him. Could be a ruse, but probably not. This caller was lost somewhere in the crowd, watching him in a mirror, of which there were dozens, probably giggling with her office pals. What a hoot, spin up the boss. God help her if she worked at Oar, which might explain her having his number. He didn't know whether to be pissed off or intrigued.

He had twelve minutes left on his workout. The bitch, whoever she was, would have to wait.

For the next twelve minutes he forgot to watch CNN or indulge in his little net-worth game. Instead he replayed the conversation over and over in his head, realizing that he liked the sound of the woman's voice almost as much as he liked her attitude, and in a world full of major-league women—his world—attitude was everything. This was another of his games, visualizing the face and body of a woman he was scheduled to meet, a business meeting with someone he'd only spoken with on the phone, the rare blind date set up by friends. He was invariably disappointed by the well-dressed reality that greeted him. His entire life was that way, each new fork in the road somehow falling short of his standards. Because he knew he was destined for greatness, he knew there was a woman out there who would one day blow him away at first sight, then live up to the admittedly unreasonable expectation later on. It was a given, and like his impending good fortune, only a matter of time until her met her.

Maybe today. Probably not, but hey, even a CEO can still dream.

There were three benches, all occupied. One had two middle-aged guys working at 185, which meant a spotter was not only unnecessary, it was humiliating. The middle station had a guy in a loose ASU sweatshirt doing quick reps at 225, the prick, without a spotter or signs of effort. The sweatshirt was a sort of reverse ego thing in the gym; tank tops were for the wannabes these days. A woman was sitting upright on the third bench, as if contemplating the impending lift. Some guys—poseurs— sat that way for ten minutes between sets; the heavier the weight the longer the pause.

As Wesley approached she leaned back and began to position her hands on the bar. If she saw him coming, she didn't let on.

Wesley stopped a few yards away. The woman wore nylon warm-up pants, black with a white stripe up the outseam. Her midsection was bare, revealing a six-pack and carved obliques that were the product of more than a Torso Track and a Suzanne Somers videotape—this woman was the real deal. Her top was a tight black sports halter, showing off what appeared to be real yet full breasts, and sculpted shoulders. She had dark hair, pulled back for the workout into a peppy little ponytail that extended through a baseball cap with a 2001 World Series championship seal on the front. Bernie had noted that the license plates on his Escalade were encased in a frame that commemorated the same thing, so today the hat was more strategy than fashion. Modest gold earrings and fingerless black leather lifting gloves com- pleted the ensemble, all of it classic gym couture straight out of a Chuck Norris infomercial. You dressed this way, you better be able to move the metal.

Most impressive of all, at least at first glance, was the weight she was now hoisting into position over her head

with the confidence of a seasoned lifter. She had two 25-
pound plates on the bar, 95 pounds in all. A very impressive warm-up, especially for what appeared to be about
120 pounds of woman, athletically built or not. Hell,
there were guys at the office who couldn't lift that
much iron.

As she began her set, Wesley moved in behind the
bar and extended his hands beneath it, palms up in the
classic spotter position. He noticed that the woman's
eyes never left the bar, no acknowledgment of his presence at all, which meant she had seen him coming. She
worked through ten reps with perfect form, two quick
counts on the press, four on the negative, then placed
the bar back on its brackets with quiet gentleness. Most
people slammed the bar back into place, including Wesley—the rattle of metal on metal was like a mating call
in clubs like these.

Beneath the bench on the rubber mat was a water
bottle, a sweat towel and a mobile phone.

"Nice set," offered Wesley.

Something chemical surged into Wesley's circulatory
system as the woman sat up and smiled at him. In a
world full of ass men and tit men, in locker rooms where
anything below the neck was fair anecdotal game, Wesley was a face man. He had a fascination with women's
eyes, the more mysterious the better, and a keen appreciation for the combined effect of hair, makeup, jewelry and fashion. His thing, no male friend would ever
know, was femininity—give him a six who tried hard
over a nine who didn't give a shit any day. Leave the
earth mothers at home with the rug rats; he liked a
woman you could still smell in the elevator fifteen minutes after they were there. Effort was sexy, vanity was
erotic, and the supreme confidence of a woman who
knew she stopped traffic was, to a man like Wesley, pure
heroin. He was looking at it now, and he was suddenly
conscious that he was wearing his reaction on his face.
Thank God for the state-of-the-art athletic supporter.

"I hope you're referring to my lifting," she said. The

smile told him this was offered as an icebreaker rather
than a challenge, and inherent in it was the mutual recognition that her *set,* apropos of her breasts, was certainly nice indeed. She extended her hand after wiping
it on her sweat towel. "Bernadette Kane," she said. "My
friends call me Bernie, but you may call me Bernadette
until further notice."

He accepted the handshake, actually looking down at
it. It was the kind of handshake reserved for thick-
necked, ex–Navy Seal curmudgeon executives in hotel
bars after a day of listening to boring seminar speeches,
the kind of you-don't-want-to-fuck-with-me handshake
that was either defining or contrived, with no middle
ground.

He said nothing at first, realizing that he was still taking her in. Her hair shimmered like a showroom car,
black as the sea on a starless night, and her eyes popped
with a shade of deep blue that recalled the same sea
under a blazing sun. Her ample lips glistened, a subdued
shade of pink, with a little dip in the middle of the top
one and a subtle pout on the bottom, flanked by tiny
dimples when she smiled, which she was doing now.

It was a face he'd seen before, many times, in fact.
But only in his mind, late at night when he was alone,
dreaming of a time when that would not be the case.

"Breathe, Wesley," she said, not letting the moment
pass. The kind of woman who made it easy to tip your
hand, and nailed you faster than gravity when you did.

Heat rushed to his face, making it tough to keep the
smile cool rather than embarrassed.

"You're up," she said as she grabbed for her sweat
towel and got to her feet.

She sure as hell had *that* right.

Wesley shook his head slightly, signaling that he was
more than willing to play along, that for a while he
would remain amused. He pulled her 25s off the bar and
replaced them with 45-pound plates, the largest available. Bernie took a position behind the bar, but didn't
assume the pose of a spotter—which frankly resembled

a sumo wrestler in the midst of a bowel movement—because she knew these 135 pounds were a warm-up. Instead she drank from her water bottle, all business, as he settled in and positioned his hands.

"So, Bernadette," said Wesley as he lifted the bar off and began a slow rhythm of repetitions, "what's this all about?"

"My career," she said. She waited for a response, but Wesley finished his fifteen reps in silence. He bounced to his feet and began withdrawing the 45-pound plates. Bernie came around from behind the bar, seeing that Wesley was putting the 25s back on.

"Thirty-fives," she said.

"You're shitting me," said Wesley with a smile that would make Gloria Steinem gag.

She stared at him hard, narrowing her eyes. "Do I look like I'm shitting you?" She waited until the smile vanished before she reclined onto the bench.

"How many?" he asked, already in position for the spot.

"Two," she said.

"Lift off?"

"No."

She lifted the bar, slowly lowered it until it touched her breasts, then very slowly pressed it back to the top position, emitting a surge of effort from her lungs as she did. After a moment she lowered it again.

"Come on!" he barked. "Bring it, baby. . . ."

She pressed, only this time the move to the top took several seconds. Wesley kept his hands an inch below the bar, raising them in unison with it, offering his encouragement with more volume than was necessary.

Again, she eased the bar back into its place without a sound.

"Nice," he said. As they exchanged positions he offered a high five, which she reciprocated without enthusiasm. Anyone watching would assume they were married, mostly from the lack of warmth between them.

Bernie pulled one plate off while Wesley attended to

the other. Each of them mounted a 45 on the bar, then
Bernie paused to see what Wesley would do next. He
grabbed another 45, and as he slid it on he nodded for
her to do the same.

"Two twenty-five," he said as he lay down on the
bench.

He didn't see her shaking her head in disbelief. As if
she couldn't add.

"How many?" she asked.

"Let's see."

He lifted the bar and began to lower the weight. Bernie put her hands under the bar as he had done, squatting with the bar as it descended.

"So," he said, pressing up the first rep, "when are you
going to tell me what it is you want?"

Bernie said, "An interview. I dropped my résumé at
your office a few days ago. Some clown named Jerry
Grasvik was supposed to call me back, but he didn't."

"You a programmer?" He was on the second rep, and
his voice was mostly air. His let's-chat-while-I-lift machismo had lasted all of one repetition. "You don't . . .
look like a programmer."

"Project manager. Freelance."

Wesley paused at the top of the third rep. He grunted,
"You any good?"

"Of course I'm good. Would I be doing this if I
couldn't walk the walk? What, I look stupid to you?"

"At the moment you look upside down."

Wesley lowered the weight carefully for the fourth
time. Bernie noticed that the muscles in his shoulders
were quivering. Perfect. When the weight touched his
chest, she put her hand on top of the bar, pressing *down,*
preventing him from pushing it back up.

"Funny girl," he said through clenched teeth.

"Here's the deal," said Bernie. "I don't know who
this Jerry Grasvik guy is. I want *you* to look at my résumé and call my references, and I want you to do it
this afternoon. If you like women who go after what
they want, and something tells me that you do, you'll do

it. If you prefer women who always play by the rules, then I'm toast."

"Cut the crap, lady. . . ."

She kept her hand on the bar. "You like what you see and hear, you call me for an interview. If not, you've got a story for the boys on the putting green. Agreed?"

"Get your hand off the fucking bar—"

"Is it a deal, Wes?" she said with more volume. "Do you mind if I call you Wes?"

He was wheezing through clenched teeth as he said, "Deal."

She removed her hand, but the bar remained on Wesley's rib cage. When she realized he couldn't lift the bar off his chest, she grabbed on with both hands and pulled.

"Bring it, baby," she said softly.

She kept her hold on the bar as he slammed it onto the brackets with a clang significant enough to cause several people to look over.

He sat up slowly, instinctively rotating his problematic right shoulder to illustrate to all what her little drama had inflicted on him. When he turned to confront her, he saw only her back as she walked briskly through the rows of machines toward the running track that bordered the weight room, towel, bottle and phone in hand. He watched in stunned silence as she made her way to the stairwell and disappeared, noticing that Charles and his pals on the court below had stopped to look as well. Charles looked up at Wesley, raising his eyebrows in approval.

The first thing Wesley Edwards did when he arrived back at the office was check his e-mail out of habit. More like an addiction, actually. The second thing he did was order Nadine to retrieve Bernadette Kane's résumé from Grasvik, and quickly. If Grasvik wasn't back from lunch, he suggested she go through his files and find the damn thing, and if Grasvik has a problem with that, which he won't, tell him to talk to me.

He didn't ask Nadine why she was smiling as she listened to these instructions.

11

Wesley Edwards knew full well that Jerry Grasvik wasn't at his desk when he told Nadine to go fetch Bernie's résumé. He also knew precisely where Grasvik was—at home, sitting in front of his souped-up desktop computer, no doubt sipping some putrid-tasting Chinese herb tea, the flaming weirdo, running simulations against every conceivable variable as he waited for a telephone call. From *him*.

Wesley waited until Nadine had retreated to the programming department on the second floor in search of the résumé. The bitch was nosy enough as it was, and the less aware she was of his movements, the better. Sometimes he felt she was watching him, and though he knew what he and Grasvik were doing was completely cloaked in rhetoric and secrecy, it still made him wary. He'd deal with her later, because dealing with her was a certain invitation to litigation, and lawyers were the last thing he wanted on his dance card, especially now. One day soon he'd lay her off and pay her off on the same day, and a convenient and quiet win-win will have been achieved. If there was one thing Wesley understood, it was the need to pay for one's sins.

He told the young woman covering for Nadine at the front desk that he'd be right back. He then went out to his fifty-grand SUV and drove off.

Today's target was a safe but convenient distance away. Not that it mattered—what was about to happen would be as untraceable as it would be brief. Jerry Grasvik may have been a perfect candidate for the nerdy techno-genius on one of those cheesy prime-time spy shows, the epitome of boredom whose personal hygiene was as infrequent as his sex life, but he was one devious and opportunistic little propeller-head. The guy could hack into anything, from the IRS to the Department of Defense to Bill Gates's personal e-mail—he'd done all that, actually—and get out before anyone realized their firewall had been breached, leaving behind whatever mischievous conglomeration of ones and zeroes he desired.

Which was precisely what they were up to today.

As he drove down Frank Lloyd Wright Boulevard heading for the 101, Wesley brought the image of the woman from the gym to his mind. It certainly wasn't the first time he'd been approached by a female in search of a job, some of whom had interesting terms to offer. And there had been no lack of come-ons in recent years—women could smell the money like hungry hyenas smell blood, and in that regard he was an open wound. But he'd never been hit up quite like that, by a woman who'd stepped right out of a Zalman King script, a body by Michelangelo, a femme fatale face and balls of polished brass, the kind of woman Billy Joel wrote about in his song, "She's Just Like a Woman to Me," the one who'll carelessly cut you and laugh while you're bleeding and bring out the best and the worst you can be, yada yada yada. It was enough to sway his thoughts from the task at hand, and that was saying something. Because the task at hand was the culmination of a year's worth of preparation and millions of dollars of potential upside.

He exited the 101 at Shea, turned left into one of the area's most frightening thrill rides—that being the double-lane left-hand turn signal without a center line separating the oncoming cars; traffic management by Disney—then a right into one of the city's many strip malls that were longer than the runways at Sky Harbor

Airport. He went into a Fry's supermarket, picked up a quart of chocolate milk and a PowerBar, then stood in the ten-items-or-less line behind a woman with enough groceries to feed the Supreme Court. Normally he'd say something caustic—it was killing him not to—but today definitely wasn't the day to call attention to himself. When his turn arrived he paid with a debit card, sliding it through the reader and then punching in the code Jerry Grasvik had given him that morning. He was careful to shield the credit card from view, because there were no markings on it whatsoever. It was a simple white rectangle of plastic with a black magnetic stripe from hell.

He walked to the entrance, where he sat down on a bench and opened his mobile phone. He punched in a number and waited for Grasvik to answer.

"Yeah," said Grasvik after one ring.

"We're in," said Wesley.

Wesley could hear Grasvik's keyboard clicking. He waited, knowing what was coming next. Or, what was *supposed* to come next.

"Done," said Grasvik without a trace of ego. "Here we go."

Wesley tore open the PowerBar and took a bite. His gaze was fixed on the check stands, waiting for the body language of confusion to announce their success. He could feel excitement in the pit of his stomach, not unlike the sensation of pulling a woman's underwear down over her hips for the first time, inhaling the scent of victory, knowing that the keys to heaven were right in front of you. No matter how many times you stepped into the ring, the thrill of a new confrontation always brought that little kick in the gut along with it.

A few seconds later Grasvik said, "What's happening?"

Wesley was about to answer, noticing that those keys to heaven in his stomach were quickly melting into something sour with each passing second that nothing happened. Then one of the cashiers turned and urgently

said something to the guy operating the register behind
him. The first cashier's customer had a strange expression on her face, slightly indignant, certainly confused.

A few check stands down, another cashier turned and
raised his hands, as if to communicate his complete and
utter lack of a clue as to what was happening to the
machines.

"What's going on?" asked Grasvik again.

"Hold on," said Wesley, whispering the words.

By now all the registers were at a standstill. Several
of the operators had come out from their posts to look
at the CRT screens on the other cash registers. Some
were manually entering price data from the bar code
labels on the products, as if they suddenly didn't trust
their scanning equipment.

As well they shouldn't.

"We're in business," whispered Wesley into his cell
phone. He was comfortable doing this, because nobody
in the store had any reason to look his way. There was
plenty of sudden energy on checkout row, and none of
it was happy.

Wesley got up and moved casually toward the action,
still munching his PowerBar, just another curious patron
whose interest had been piqued by the sudden chaos.
When he was close enough he could hear the chatter,
simultaneous explanations and justifications and com-
plaints from customers and cashiers alike, none of whom
had the slightest idea what was going on, though several
had opinions as to what to do about it.

As Wesley moved through the store, he passed a man
he assumed to be the store manager—funny, he thought,
how so many grocery store managers looked alike—who
was shoving people aside at the first register, grabbing
products at random and scanning them through, then
staring at the CRT readout as if it had suddenly been
rendered in Russian. Wesley tried not to smile—Grasvik
could have done just that if it had occurred to them.
What *had* occurred to them, however, was to tell the

computer terminals at each of the dozens of Fry's superstores in the greater Phoenix area to move the decimal point two digits to the right on each scanned product entry, effectively turning a twenty-five-cent piece of candy into a twenty-five-dollar investment. Within seconds, the collective transactions across the entire chain of stores had completely sabotaged the inventory and cash ledgers of the company, and perhaps more effectively, brought their business to a complete and utter standstill.

Over the mobile phone Wesley heard Grasvik say, "Talk to me, man!"

"The eagle has crashed and burned," said Wesley, his voice very soft.

He was now standing quietly in front of the in-store branch of Wells Fargo bank and its ATM machine, as aware of the irony behind him as he was the escalating panic in front. They, too, had ceased operations to watch, and they, too, just might experience it firsthand at some point in the near future. Their free-checking program would suddenly become more expensive than it already was.

Wesley felt that delicious rumbling deep in his stomach, more certain than ever of success.

"Fuckin'-A," Wesley heard Grasvik say, imagining the little geek's smile as he sat in the complete anonymity of his apartment, his computer connected via shielded cable modem to the servers at Oar Research, the IP addresses and data flow masked and diverted and cloaked and encrypted and re-encrypted in ways that Wesley couldn't understand to places that made no sense, the details of which Grasvik could recite, always with glassy-eyed awe.

By now the store manager had whipped out his own mobile phone and was trying to explain the situation to some disbelieving IT manager at the Fry's corporate office. Wesley wished he had a zoom camera so Grasvik could see the expression on the guy's face.

"We're good," said Wesley into the phone.

Again he heard Grasvik's fingers making love to his keyboard.

This time Wesley couldn't quite conceal his smile. Once again Grasvik had accomplished precisely what he'd said he would.

Wesley clicked his mobile phone shut and walked calmly out of the store into the Arizona swelter. He didn't need to see what they were looking at now on the CRT screens, because he already knew what each and every one of them was displaying to whomever might be looking on. The punch line had, in fact, been Wesley's idea.

The words on the checkout screens at all the Fry's stores in the Phoenix area read: *Thanks for playing, and do come again.*

By the time Wesley was back on the 101 he'd already punched an out-of-state number into his mobile phone. Listening to it ring, he took comfort in knowing that Grasvik would easily hack into the system at his carrier and erase any record of the call. Of all the marks on the planet, the telephone carriers were the easiest for Grasvik, since in another life he used to design the very systems he now delighted in hacking into. That was before he wrote what became the de facto industry-standard firewall code, which, in turn, came just before he worked for the world's largest credit card company troubleshooting system access problems worldwide.

Jerry Grasvik had been the perfect hire.

"Beta is complete. We're ready to launch. We need to meet, sign off on the timetable. I expect to hear from you by the end of the week that you're ready on your end."

Grinning, he snapped the phone closed and tossed it onto the seat next to him.

12

Bernie waited two days for the call to come. There
was really nothing she could do now, since her plan de-
pended entirely on getting hooked up at Oar Research
so she could get *her* hooks deep into Wesley Edwards.
It wasn't impatience that made the waiting difficult—
indeed, patience would be her greatest weapon in seducing and then destroying the man. Slow roasting versus
flash frying. He would come to her, probably later rather
than sooner, and like every upper manager Bernie had
ever worked for, it would all be his idea. No, the hard
part now was not knowing if her gambit had worked. If
her magic had been potent enough. If she was, in fact,
in Wesley Edwards's league. She tried to fill the days by
making a temporary life seem like a permanent one, so
much so that the line between them was beginning to
blur. The condo complex where she rented was across
the street from a strip mall with a trendy sports bar
called Goldies, an even trendier AJ's grocery store with
designer fruit and meat displays, and a day spa with a
tanning salon. A few workouts and a tan wouldn't hurt
her cause or her psyche, so after an hour of morning
sparring she rationalized a few more hours near the
condo pool's deep end getting to know the locals, which
included a scratch golfer sun goddess, a chatty snowbird-
ing retailer from Yellowstone National Park, and the
gorgeous wife of a writer of paperback novels. Bernie

felt like she'd landed in one of the guy's books, which she'd never read.

And of course, in the midst of all her anxiety about Wesley, there was always Plan B: after a week or so she would call Edwards and play to his well-developed sense of irresistibility. Tell him she couldn't get him out of her head, job or no job. Ask him to meet her for another workout and a lunch down the street at Pei Wei, the hot new Chinese fast-food spot at twenty bucks a pop. If her résumé didn't do the trick, she had a snug pair of leather pants that would.

While Bernie preferred to focus on Plan A, there was something inherently appealing about going straight at this guy, beating him at his own game in his own predatory arena. And, she had to admit, she was looking forward to *playing* that game. Bernie was, if nothing else, a staunch competitor.

It was Nadine who made the call.

Her opening line was, "Never doubted you, sweetheart."

"Pardon me?"

"The power of a woman on a mission. I do hope I get a little credit."

Bernie paused before responding to make sure this voice out of the blue was, in fact, Nadine's. It had been several days since they'd spoken, but after a moment she was sure. The rhythm of the sarcasm was unmistakable.

"I take it you have good news," Bernie finally said.

"You owe me, big time. And payback can be a bitch."

"You have no idea how much I agree. On both points."

It was now Nadine who paused, providing Bernie with a little jolt at what could have been an ill-advised remark. She wasn't yet good enough at this to be remotely cavalier with her agenda. Especially if Nadine's "woman on a mission" crack had been equally loaded with innuendo, if it was dangled bait.

"What are you doing tomorrow?" asked Nadine.

"Are we having lunch again?"

"Only if you're stupid, which we've already established isn't the case. What *are* you doing tomorrow?"

"Okay . . . interviewing with Oar Research?"

"I mean, *all* day tomorrow."

Nadine was playing this out, which was in keeping with her front-desk mentality. The moment she delivered her message she was out of the driver's seat.

"I'll cancel my nails, okay? C'mon, what's up?"

"You're gonna like this. Wesley—excuse me, Mr. Edwards—would like to schedule you for an extended interview with him and our lead programmer to discuss a project. They're flying to Sacramento tomorrow and they'd like you to go with them. I'm talking the company jet here, sweetheart. You fly up, talk nice about yourself for two hours, they have a car for you while they do their customer thing . . . you have lunch, shop until they're done . . . then fly back by dinner, which I'm sure Wesley will try to include in the interview process."

"You're shitting me."

"Welcome to Wesley Edwards's world, dear. Catch him while you can."

Bernie was tempted to ask if there was a backhand in the comment, but changed her mind. She was getting paranoid before paranoia was warranted.

"Is this, like, normal?" she asked instead. "Interviewing on the company plane?"

Nadine's voice was slightly different as she said, "Nothing about this place is normal. Take it from me—the quicker you get that into your head, the better off you'll be."

Bernie was told to be at the Scottsdale airport departure lounge at seven o'clock. Dress was "business casual," which in the high-tech world could mean just about anything, and as a rule, meant absolutely nothing if you were a programmer. After a night of fitful sleep, Bernie found herself spending an inordinate amount of time getting herself together in the predawn darkness. What made the sleep restless, and what made her clothing and makeup

extraordinarily crucial, was not just this interview, the results of which would set the tone for everything to come.
No, it was the recognition of something far more simple
and basic, something both habitual and hormonal. It was,
perhaps, a combination of danger and pheromones.

The man with whom she was meeting was not only
treacherous and beneath all reasonable standards of integrity, he was also astoundingly sexy. It was an age-old
sexual paradox—was this contradiction cause or effect?
Why did one beget the other, when they should have
been mutually exclusive? She instinctively knew that
what made this man a cliché was, in fact, what made
him attractive—the ego, the vanity, the gold chain, the
money and power, the utterly self-centered, scheming
testosterone of his very being. Try as they might to explain it otherwise, no matter how refined the guy on
their arm, testosterone was the drug of choice for most
women with a pulse. While Bernie wanted to put this
truth in a box that had Peggy's name on it, her sister
wasn't the first intelligent, self-respecting woman to fall
head over heels with a nattily dressed, football-pool-
obsessed Neanderthal cad with cigars and hunting rifles
and ice chests full of Budweiser. Hell, she'd done it herself—three times, in fact. Chemistry was too often beyond explanation, and like most addictions, it was almost
always in conflict with reason. Men, after all, had their
whores and their strippers and their dominatrixes;
woman had their exquisite bad boys, their leather-
jacketed James Dean protégés in need of a little moth-
ering. But even after you saved them and made them
presentable, you didn't really want all that darkness and
machismo to wash away completely, you wanted to stash
a little away for those occasional nights of abandon.

Bernie already recognized that what very well might
be an uninvited attraction would ultimately be her biggest obstacle to bringing Wesley Edwards down. But the
recognition didn't stop the churning that denied her
sleep, so in the morning she agonized over every detail,
her thick-heeled shoes from Donna Karan, her black

linen pants by Norma Kamali, her svelte leather jacket by Vacco, her perfectly styled hair and borderline-dramatic, business-bitch eyes.

If it was pheromones this guy wanted, she'd give him a headache he'd never forget.

13

"Good morning. Are you Ms. Kane?"

The *Ms.* was spoken with a respectful and unassuming "z" sound.

Bernie looked up from her newspaper into the eyes of what she immediately realized was the most stunning man she had ever met. Or seen, for that matter, celebrities and professional athletes included. It was that Pitt-Cruise-Lowe kind of pretty boy, not remotely rugged in a Wesley Edwards–Bruce Willis sort of way. It was all centered on the eyes instead of the biceps. She was certain she gasped aloud, though because she was suddenly numb she neither heard nor felt it. She was alone in the Scottsdale airport departure lounge, which was strangely quiet at this time of morning, precisely seven o'clock. Outside the plate-glass windows waited a sleek jet aircraft, an older model Cessna Citation, bathed in surreal illumination, side door open, taxi lights on. Judging from the crisp white shirt this man was wearing, with its shoulder and cuff epaulets and the metal wings pinned on the breast pocket, the man was, God willing, her pilot for the day.

Somehow she managed a nod. In the midst of her hormone rush she had the presence of mind to wonder if he was used to this sort of reaction from women. If so it didn't show, because his smile was almost as shy as his baritone voice was soft.

"I'm Paul Lampkin," he said, extending his hand. "I'll be flying you up to Sacramento this morning."

She said a quiet prayer of thanks as she accepted the handshake. It was warm, as if his hand had just emerged from spending an hour in his pocket, and it was thick with strength. She'd heard other women claim that such a handshake could make them wet, but she'd never believed it before now. A palpable current passed between them as they touched, enough to cause her to look down at his hand in wonder.

There were, she thought, any number of starting points in describing the man's presence—eyes that blazed a brilliant royal blue under dark brows and long lashes; thick dark hair worn long, brushed back neatly and businesslike in Pat Riley fashion, forgivable because he was easily in his late thirties and would have looked silly in a buzz cut and sideburns; velvety tanned skin conforming to neck and jaw muscles that spoke of a body honed by a lifetime of exercise, a lean athletic physique quite unlike Wesley's cultivated bulk; the subtle scent of fine soap or understated cologne; a high-wattage smile, naturally and humbly offered. Some guys in this league—if Wesley was the fullback, this guy was the svelte placekicker—smiled as if they were flexing, but Paul Lampkin's smile was warm and genuine and even sort of coy. He made it easy to convince yourself that he was flirting.

As if all this weren't enough, he had a deep cleft in his chin, something that always grabbed Bernie's attention. An image flashed in her mind—she was on top of him, making love, digging the tip of her tongue deeply into that delicious little valley as she moved.

She snapped herself back to the room. This was a man you noticed, a man who looked equally comfortable escorting a supermodel to the Oscars or casting for trout on his day off. Or, as was the case here, at the controls of a multimillion-dollar corporate jet.

"Can I get you some coffee? There's more on the airplane . . . lattes, cappuccino, soft drinks. . . ."

"What, no flight attendants today?"

That smile flashed again as he glanced out at the jet. "Absolutely. It's just that our flight attendants are all ex–fighter jockeys pulling double duty. It's Starbucks, if that makes any difference."

"Word is they're taking over the world."

"I flew Howard Shultz once," he said, referring to Starbucks' founder. He correctly assumed Bernie knew who he was talking about. "Nice guy. Not all of my customers take the time."

Now here was a rarity—a man unthreatened by the success of other men, yet he took notes on who did and who didn't treat him like the help. She wondered if his comment was in direct reference to Wesley. If so it was risky, and if it wasn't, it was a curious thing to say.

The double glass doors from the parking lot burst open. Two men entered carrying briefcases and, as if the god of coincidence was warming up for the day, paper cups from Starbucks. Both Paul and Bernie looked at them and then at each other. She had trouble keeping her eyes off his chin, consciously pulling her vision back to take in the entire delicious landscape of his face.

"I'll catch you on board," he said with a grin that indicated she might just be busted. Then he turned his attention to the new arrivals as they approached.

Wesley Edwards barely looked at his pilot, seemed irritated that he had to set down his briefcase to shake the man's hand. He wore a dark tan suit, double breasted, and already his strong cologne was smothering the room. After meeting Paul, she saw Wesley in a new light, just a notch down the ladder. It was clear that the other man, obviously Jerry Grasvik, had not met Paul before, and his handshake was not much more enthusiastic. As was typical with many programmers Bernie had known, Jerry avoided eye contact as the two men were introduced. He wore jeans and a tight black sweater with a low neckline that exposed a braided necklace of some sort. He was skinny, especially next to Wesley, who right now reminded Bernie of Sylvester Stallone playing a banker.

Bernie caught Paul's see-what-I-mean? smirk as he disappeared into an office, leaving his clients to themselves for the moment.

Handshakes all around, apologies for the early hour, another offer of coffee that established Wesley as the host for the day. She had been right—Grasvik's handshake had all the charisma of a raw fillet of halibut. He said nothing, clearly more interested in the jet waiting outside.

"You bring your workout clothes?" asked Wesley. A contrived grin was pasted on his face. When Bernie hesitated, he added, "I'm kidding. You look beautiful this morning."

Bernie was about to respond to this inappropriate compliment, but Paul mercifully returned to the lobby with his own briefcase, diverting her attention.

"If you folks would like to board, we're ready to taxi."

Paul held the door for them, his smile neutered now as she went through first. Once outside he hurried ahead of them and was waiting at the steps to the airplane when Bernie arrived. It was already seventy-five degrees, with a cool morning breeze that suggested this was why people lived here. Paul offered his hand as she stepped into the aircraft, and it was still eerily warm to the touch. She felt him place his palm gently on the small of her back.

Wesley and Grasvik didn't so much as glance at the pilot as they boarded behind her, nor were they touched by him as she had been.

Another pilot was already in the cockpit, occupying the right seat as he flipped switches in the ceiling panel. He looked about eighteen, and Bernie suddenly felt old. It occurred to her that it should have been this guy's place to offer the coffee and hold the doors, right before it occurred to her that perhaps Paul had noticed her in the waiting room and taken it upon himself to attend to the niceties.

The flip side of paranoia was ego, and she was immune to neither.

Paul boarded and hit a button, causing the hatch to rise into place with a quiet humming noise. The cabin was surprisingly roomy—she could nearly stand upright as she moved. Plush tan leather seats lined both sides, as wide as commercial first class, with an abundance of buttons and controls on the armrest consoles. Bernie settled into one, soft and buttery as glove leather, sneaking a glance forward toward Paul, noticing how he moved with a confident grace as he secured the door. In contrast, Wesley slammed himself into the seat in front of her—it faced backward, so she was destined to look at him all the way to Sacramento. To balance out the wealth of tasty visuals, there was Jerry Grasvik sitting across the aisle, looking like a roadie for a defunct Seattle grunge band. She was clearly on the grill here, like that halibut fillet, for the entire two hours of this flight. Despite several minutes of occupying the same space for the same purpose, Grasvik had yet to look her in the eye.

"This'll be fun," said Wesley as he took off his suit coat before attending to his seatbelt. "Thing climbs like an F-18."

"I wouldn't know," replied Bernie.

He smiled, as if glad to hear that her acid tongue hadn't become tied since their meeting at the gym. "Ever flown private before?"

"Oh sure, many times," she lied.

He grinned, getting it. "I liked your résumé. Very robust."

"Thank you. Never heard a résumé called *robust* before."

"Jerry here wasn't so thrilled." He glanced over at Grasvik, who was busy gazing out the opposite window, pretending not to hear. "I think you threaten him."

"I doubt it," said Bernie.

"I doubt it, too," said Grasvik without shifting his sight line.

Wesley chuckled, delighted to be stirring it up so soon.

Paul suddenly appeared in the aisle between Wesley and Grasvik. "If I may interrupt . . . there are some preflight issues I'd like to go over with you."

Bernie barely heard, more lost in the pilot's eyes than his words. She noticed that neither Wesley nor Grasvik paid the slightest attention to Paul as he delivered his canned preflight spiel, which she assumed they had heard many times. Wesley opened his briefcase and was removing his telephone headset as Paul demonstrated the seatbelt and the operation of the drop-down flat-panel screen, in case the interview waned and someone wanted to pop in a DVD. At first he divided his eye contact between all three passengers, but soon he was honing in on Bernie, who couldn't help but smile back as she listened. The other pilot was starting the engines, causing Paul to raise his voice slightly.

Nobody took Paul up on his final offer of coffee, so he went back to the cockpit and the airplane began to move.

Wesley made three quick calls as they taxied, all of them to voice mails, none of them particularly urgent. He began each with an announcement that he was on the company plane, and she wasn't sure if he was trying to impress the recipient of the call or her. With her best unimpressed expression she gazed out the window at the morning sky, already a warm Arizona pink. When she looked back she saw Grasvik rolling his eyes at her with a smirk that she knew referred to Wesley's telephone manner. It was a small crack in the ice, but at least it put them on the same page.

They took off to the southwest. Bernie could see the Oar Research building tucked behind the Kierland Commons development off Scottsdale Road, which was lined with headlights in both directions. She suddenly felt disoriented—none of this was real, not this interview, not Scottsdale, not the dreamboat pilot, not even her slightly over-the-top makeup applied for Wesley's benefit. She pictured Eric's face and remembered what he'd said, that nothing good could come of this. She wished he was here now, and as she did Shannon's face appeared with his on the screen of her mind, and the disorientation evolved into a sudden and profound loneliness.

"Earth to programmer girl," said Wesley, jarring her back to the moment.

"It's beautiful," she said, keeping her gaze on the ground falling away from them. They were surrounded by mountains, all aglow in the emerging morning.

"Tell us why you're here," said Wesley. He left it at that, and as she struggled to bring herself back into the cabin, she noticed that Grasvik was looking at her intensely, too. She was on. Time to make them desire her, for whatever reasons they chose.

"Funny, that was going to be my opening line," she said. When neither man changed his expression, she cleared her throat and plowed ahead.

"Combination of push and pull," she said, trying for masculine words that would add some heft to her narrative. "The well was getting a little dry in Dallas, too many little projects and too few big ones. And I've always been fascinated with Phoenix, so here I am."

Wesley smiled as he shifted in his seat. Bernie had the feeling he couldn't sit quietly for more than a minute or so without taking over the conversation of the moment. "Sort of like the most beautiful girl in class," he said. "Nobody asks her out because they assume she's busy every Friday and Saturday night." He paused before adding, "Bet you've been there."

"Excuse me?"

"Those little projects . . . my guess is they don't call you because they assume you wouldn't be interested, wouldn't be worth your time. Close?"

Bernie pursed her lips as if she was thinking about what he'd said. In fact, she was thinking that this was perhaps the most egocentric man she'd ever spoken to. She tried to imagine him with her sister, but the image wasn't clicking yet.

"I suppose. Never thought of it that way."

"Life's a bitch at the top of the food chain," said Wesley.

Bernie noticed that Grasvik was rolling his eyes again, but quickly and just for her benefit.

"You spend much time in Dallas?" she asked, looking Edwards in the eye, hoping to see something flinch ever so slightly. She felt her cheeks flush and immediately regretted the question.

"Too much," he said. He held her stare, though she couldn't discern any meaning to it. Other than her slight resemblance to Peggy, which he certainly may have noticed by now, there was no way he could be on to her this quickly.

Wesley said, "So here you are. A woman who goes after what she wants, in a city in which she knows no one, protocol be damned. Very impressive. At least I think so."

"I needed a spotter." She smiled, hoping to lighten the tone.

"And I need a kick-ass manager for an important new project. How fortunate for both of us." He turned to Grasvik and said, "Tell her."

As Bernie listened to Grasvik's unenthusiastic explanation of the project, she was conscious of Wesley's unflinching gaze. In a normal interview, with normal men, both she and Wesley would be looking at Grasvik as he spoke. She did everything she could to avoid squirming because it would acknowledge something playing out between them, that she was aware of him. Which she was, to the detriment of the moment.

The game was definitely on.

The project was predictable and very much within the realm of her capabilities. Oar Research wanted a new Web site that responded to the latest computer security threats for their customers, allowing them to access online resources for immediate prevention and remedy. Bernie could tell that Wesley's initial comment about Grasvik being threatened had some truth to it, because the overview was peppered with as much keep-up-with-me-if-you-can techno-babble as possible. Whether he was trying to impress her or throw her was unclear, but in either case she just nodded as she listened, tossing out clarifying questions with an equal degree of unnecessarily technical jargon of her own. And she *was* impressed—Jerry Grasvik, bland ego and all, really knew his stuff.

This was good. As a project manager she was all too familiar with the psychology of programmers, how to play to their unique needs to get what she wanted from them. Not all that different from men in general, actually. Jerry Grasvik, the embodiment of the former stereotype, if not the latter, would be no exception.

She caught Wesley grinning as their little verbal duel unfolded. She was already sure these two guys didn't like each other much, stemming, perhaps, from the fact that they had nothing in common except the logo on their business cards. But more certainly than this, she understood that they needed each other. It was a high-tech dynamic as old as the industry itself—Hewlett needed Packard, Moore needed Noyce, Jobs desperately needed Wozniak. The techie and the suit; the builder and the mouthpiece. She made a mental note that there might be something here she could exploit down the road.

"So what's your rate?" interrupted Wesley. He'd heard enough about source code, HTML specifications and graphic interfaces. It was time to cut a deal.

"I usually contract a fixed fee based on the scope of the project," she said. "And I don't know enough about this yet to do that."

"Fair enough. But your fee is based on an underlying day rate, right? Which is . . ."

He waited with raised eyebrows.

"If I said *none of your business* would I be out of line?"

"Absolutely."

"Seven-fifty, ten hours per, full expenses. I use my own subs if I don't like yours, there's no delivery clause,

I bill in thirds based on percentage of completion with a final reconciliation for overages. Today, of course, is outside of the billing."

Wesley was rubbing his chin, which by the way was completely without cleft, nodding as Bernie went through her rate speech. There was no question the man had an agenda of the hormonal variety in play here, but it was all under the table at this point. She wondered when he'd whip it out, metaphorically speaking, and put it on the table for her to gaze at in wide-eyed wonder. He didn't get this confident without hitting a few home runs; he was obviously used to winning at business and pleasure with equal frequency. She couldn't wait to see his expression when he realized she had, metaphorically speaking again, sliced it off at the base with a dull spoon.

Wesley said, "Let's call it twenty-five grand and move forward. Budget is two seventy-five. We know what we're doing, so you can count on that number. Agreed?"

"Twenty-five gets you thirty-four days of my life. On day thirty-five you get another bill. Then we go day rate. Agreed?"

"You'll give me a refund if we wrap on day thirty-three?"

She regarded him a moment. There was an ever-so-slight telling curvature at the corner of his mouth. All of this was a contrived shuck-and-jive designed to test her comfort level in the trenches. And he was enjoying it, seeing how she'd do.

"You say you know what you're doing, so you know that's not how it works."

Wesley nodded again, but not in agreement. More like amusement. He glanced over at Grasvik, who had checked out of the conversation and was looking out the window.

"What do you think? Can you work with her?"

Without turning his head Grasvik said, "I can work with you, I can work with anyone."

Wesley's laugh was forced. He extended his hand. "Welcome to the team, Bernadette."

"Call me Bernie," she said, accepting the handshake, which lingered a moment too long.

The remainder of the flight was consumed with a quickly shifting series of questions from Wesley designed to get to know Bernie better. It occurred to her that he was a posterboy for Attention Deficit Disorder, since he seemed more interested in the unexpected topical shift of his questions than in her answers. One minute he was asking if she had brothers or sisters—she decided to let that one pass without testing him—the next he wanted to know if she'd seen this movie or that, followed by an inquiry about her opinion of foreign policy and then his unsolicited opinion of a particular restaurant in New Jersey. She'd certainly seen men like this before, the fog in their eyes as they failed at the illusion of listening, already formulating their next question, or perhaps picturing her tied to his bed wearing a cheerleader outfit. Grasvik was still checked out, actually falling asleep with his head against the window. At one point Wesley reached over and flicked his finger against his lips to see if he could wake him, greatly amused. The guy was Dennis the Menace in Armani.

At no time during the flight had they talked about their business for the day. At one point Bernie had asked if they were seeing clients, to which Wesley simply nodded with no elaboration. Clearly, it was none of her business.

Upon landing there were two cars waiting on the tarmac right next to the airplane. Just like in the movies, as Wesley delighted in pointing out. Upon deplaning, Grasvik headed for one of them without saying a word. The other was hers, intended to keep her happy while they were going about their mysterious business.

As he deplaned Wesley said nothing to Paul, who stood at the bottom of the stairs, nor did he look at him. Paul held his hand out to help Bernie down, which she accepted with a nice little moment of eye contact.

Wesley had his telephone headset operational by the

time his feet hit the tarmac. He was already connected to someone when Bernie heard him tell the person on the other end of the call to hold a moment.

He withdrew a mobile phone from his briefcase and handed it to Bernie.

"This is yours for the duration of the project. If you need to reach me, call Nadine and she'll forward you. I'll call you when we're done, we'll meet up back here. There's a map and some brochures in the car. Have a nice day, be safe. You see Chris Weber, tell him I said he's a punk. Keep your lunch receipt—you're officially on the clock now, okay? See you, say, midafternoon or so."

"I see Chris Weber, I'm asking for his autograph."

"Careful what you ask for, kiddo."

His grin was smug as he turned toward his car, already back into his telephone call. Grasvik was in the passenger seat waiting—of course, Wesley would drive today. He fired up the engine—they'd rented two identical black Lincoln Continentals—and drove off toward an opening in the fence in a hurry, as if they'd been here before.

Bernie turned her attention toward the airplane, but Paul was gone. The hatch was still open, and for a moment she considered going back to see what he did with his downtime on these trips. Maybe arrange to meet for lunch. But something stopped her; maybe it was Eric's haunting admonition, maybe it was some residual schoolgirl shyness that hadn't made an appearance in a while. Or maybe it was a shift in the sexual dynamic that she wasn't used to, a man who didn't need to pursue his quarry, who could just sit back and wait for women to seek him out. She wasn't sure how she felt about playing the game that way, or if she was even interested in playing at all.

It was an impulse, that's all. And her resistance to it had been nothing more than common sense.

She got into the Lincoln and started it up. Someone had been playing the radio too loud—country music, which was fine with her. Tim McGraw wasn't too bad to look at, either. As she put the car in gear she chanced a final glance at the airplane. She could see Paul sitting in the cockpit, looking out at her, waving his hand. Even at this distance, through the airplane's windshield and the glare of the sun, his smile was radiant.

She waved back as she drove off, wishing now she had followed that impulse, common sense and intimidation be damned. But it was too late for that. To stop and go back wouldn't be good form, and in this little cat-and-mouse game called flirting, Bernie had nothing if not good form.

14

Scottsdale, Arizona

They were in advertising, which meant they were cynics. And with good reason: they knew it was all bullshit. No detergent was really better than another, for the most part domestic beers all tasted the same—like piss-water, actually—and despite continuing claims, no automotive dealer in the history of modern media had actually discounted a single car on their lot, ever. They were man and wife, and they came here to these condominiums every March to soak their weary Minnesota bones in sunshine and take in a few spring-training games, and remember why they had been together for twenty-seven happy years. Her account was the biggest vodka importer in the nation, he threw parties for NFL sponsors, and both rationalized that at least you could get a good buzz while slinging your bullshit at the naïve and willing masses.

They also played games with the locals. Private games, harmless really, but nothing they could or would ever disclose. At night, in the privacy of their bedroom, he would become the tall writer guy with the stunning wife who lived across the pond, pretending he was cheating as he sneaked across the parking lot to ravish the vodka lady from Minneapolis. Or the golf pro who lived two doors down, the one with the massive driver and the sweet stroke. She liked both scripts, and often added her own play-by-play, which tended to lean toward the darker side. On alternate evenings she would pretend to be one of the pool bitches, as they referred to them, whom they sincerely liked in the daylight but nonetheless cast in these little nocturnal productions. The previous evening she had worn a cheap wig from Walgreens and pretended to be the hot new brunette who had recently moved in just across the pond from the pool. They'd met her one recent afternoon and traded sob stories—she was new in town, looking for freelance work as some sort of Web designer. The woman had noticed her husband's rapt attention, and that night she'd narrated a sizzling little lesbian scene for him that lasted sixty minutes, finally making him climax on her shoes because, as a lesbian, she had absolutely no interest whatsoever in his precious bodily fluids. It had been easy for her, too, because the new neighbor—Bernadette was her name—was absolutely stunning. For two days they'd batted around the issue of whether she looked more like Julia Roberts or a brunette Meg Ryan, but they both knew it was just an excuse to bring her into their private world in some twisted little way, and that it worked for both of them.

They were talking about her, in fact, when the man looked over at the condo into which Bernie had moved. Someone was inside.

"She lives alone, right?"

"With a new lover every night," answered his wife.

"I'm serious. There's someone in her condo."

"Maybe it's just her you're seeing."

"Not unless she's doing a John Goodman impression."

The woman squinted, trying to see what her husband was talking about. The late-morning sun was hitting Bernie's patio squarely, illuminating the interior. There was a large man inside, moving about with quick movements. He looked up, seemed to sense that he was being observed, then faded quickly into the shadows.

She said, "None of our business, sweetheart."

"What if it's a burglar? I mean, look at that guy . . . doesn't he look a little suspicious to you?"

"Cable installer, phone man, carpet cleaner, chimney sweep . . . they all look alike. Except for their penises. I hear those cable guys are freaking *hung*."

The woman went back to her paperback—it was written by the resident writer dude, actually, and there were some ideas about ropes in there that had her attention.

Her husband kept looking over at the condo.

Finally she said, "Go check it out."

"I will." He got up, grabbed the gate key and headed off.

He walked around the lake that surrounded the pool area, then went between two of the buildings to the parking lot at the rear. A white van was just disappearing around the corner; he thought he saw a metal ladder affixed to its roof. If there was writing on the side, he couldn't see it from where he stood.

He went up to Bernie's condo and knocked, but there was no answer.

Walking back to the pool, he resolved to return that evening and tell the lovely lady that he'd seen someone inside her place. She'd appreciate that, maybe ask him inside for a drink, get to know each other better. Or not.

That lovely thought, in turn, led him to some ideas about the evening ahead. It was the last night of their stay, and after packing they had planned on consummating their trip with an orgy scene involving all of the regulars at the pool.

By the time he got back to his towel, the notion of talking to Bernie about her condo had faded into the background. Bernie would be with them tonight, though, in spirit if not flesh, in fiction if not fact. And oh, what a fiction it would be.

Bernie arrived home at seven that night, just as it was getting dark. She was exhausted—a full day of shopping in Sacramento and she'd purchased nothing, something she had always taken as a sign of failure. Failure of what, she wasn't sure, but it was certainly a waste of time. Peggy had loved to shop for the simple joy of *being there,* but for some reason Bernie needed to haul away bags. There was probably a red flag hidden in that reasoning, but tonight wasn't the night to psychoanalyze herself.

The flight back to Arizona had been quiet. Grasvik was engaged in a handheld computer game, while Wesley spent the entire trip on the airplane's telephone. He'd manipulated the seating to give himself what little privacy there could be, explaining that he had work and actually apologizing for being a rude host. He gave her a CD containing most of the company's prior marketing media, which she watched on the small LCD screen that descended from the ceiling at the touch of a button on the armrest. *Mediocre* was the word that came to mind, an easy bar to reach with her new project. She'd created better multimedia back when she was breaking in.

She could get used to this, she thought.

At the conclusion of the flight Paul was again at the door with his helping hand and The Smile, but other than that there was no escalation of the game between them, if there had, in fact, even been one.

As all parties adjourned to their respective vehicles, Wesley said to give him a few days, that he'd call to schedule a kickoff meeting for the project. She had a feeling she'd hear from him before that, but it was just another hunch on a day full of hunches.

The condo seemed extraordinarily quiet tonight, though she knew it was just her frame of mind. Like most rentals it was furnished generically, though her landlord had done some interesting things with dried branches pilfered from the grounds. Her mission was progressing nicely, yet there was still something gnawing at her. She looked at the telephone, and for a fleeting instant the thought occurred to her that she'd call Peggy and talk it out. She'd heard other people describe this same fissure in reality, the sudden urge to bring the dead back to life, the conscious forgetting what the subconscious could not. Or perhaps it was the other way around, who knows. But the realization made her melan-

choly; it was the second time that day that she'd been
overwhelmed by a sense of intense solitude.

She considered calling Eric, but that would be selfish,
as well as strategically imprudent. Eric's wife was a
bloodhound on estrogen, and no matter how on the up-
and-up she and Eric were, Bernie knew she was and
always would be a bone of contention between them.
She'd sooner not give Shannon that bone to chew on,
especially after Eric had been so helpful, help that she
would no doubt require going forward.

She decided to send an e-mail instead. His e-mail went
to his office at Da Slamma, and while perhaps not the
best place to vent her feelings, it was better than being
alone.

*E—I decided it best if I not call or email you at home.
Things are going well here, have made contact with W.,
and have been hired on a project, which puts me in the
game. I want you to know how much I appreciate your
help in getting me here, as well as your counsel not to
do this. While I know you are right, we both know how
stubborn I am, and if you don't know it already, how
badly I require closure on this issue. I don't really know
what will come of this, but after meeting W I'm more
convinced than ever that he needs to be taken down. I
promise to be careful. And to call if I need help. Which
I'm sure I will at some point, if nothing more than
tracking down a name.*

*Wish you were here—you could just kick his ass for
me and this would be over.*

Actually, I just wish that you were here, period. B.

She went to bed early, regretting that last line as she
curled up with a book left behind by the landlord. She
found herself reading the first page over and over, her
mind drifting back to her day, to Wesley's aren't-I-cool
manner and Grasvik's complete and total lack of a functioning personality. And to Paul's electric smile.

She lay there until well after midnight before finally

drifting off. Her last coherent thought was that she regretted the final line of her e-mail.

In the morning, there was a response from Eric waiting on her machine.

> *B—good to hear from you. Right on about the call, very dangerous, please don't call the house or office for reasons you can guess. As for email, that's better but also dangerous, getting heat from bosses, please be discreet. Long story. Write if and when you need something, or call if you get into trouble. Will answer as best I can, when I can. Be patient with me. I continue to pursue the issue from this end. Take care—E.*
>
> *PS—happy to kick W.'s ass, anytime, anyplace.*

She read the e-mail several times, not because she was unclear, but because it made her smile. Her sign-off had indeed scared him. In return his message was clear—she was to stay away, avoid putting him in an awkward position. The last thing she wanted was to be a thorn in the side of her friend, a friend who just might be needed down the road.

For now she was, as Eric had warned, very much alone.

15

Santa Clara, California

The bar and grill called Birk's was once a Silicon Valley legend, enough so that it continued to survive on the nostalgia of its reputation, and perhaps the ribs, long after the lights went out on the high-tech industry. In the old days the average net worth of the typical lounge lizard cruising here was something north of ten million dollars, though admittedly there were more than a few hundred-million-dollar boys bellied up to the bar who jacked up that calculation. Even the parking lot drew a crowd of lookie-loos who couldn't get past the doorman on their best day. Located just down the street from Intel's fabled world headquarters, Birk's was the site of some of the most significant venture capital handshakes in history. Rumor had it Arthur Rock knew the bartender on a first-name basis. And of course, like blood washing over the Great Barrier Reef, it was also the feeding ground for leather-clad sharks in high heels with collagened lips and a taste for the brie on the appetizer menu. They hunted in packs of two, and unless you flashed a business plan and a beefy 1040 it was impossible to score a conversation, much less a phone number.

Those days were a fading memory, a time before the dot-com cowboys got the living shit kicked out of them as their hot air balloons sank into a sea of red ink. Now there was gray on the temples of the players from that era, and those that survived had long since traded their stock options and their trophy wives in for eighty-foot sailing skiffs and were last seen somewhere in the vicinity of Aruba. These days Birk's was full of lunching moms whose husbands avidly monitored the family 401(k) on their laptops, and in the evenings came the frat boys and the occasional traveling businessman who, as if returning to Mecca, wanted to get a whiff of the old days when they couldn't get in the door.

The woman sitting at the end of the bar was sipping a lemon drop from a martini glass as she surveyed the room. The bar displayed ten impressive rows of liquor bottles, and Arthur Rock's pal still slung the tumblers with a sense of self-importance. She had shoulder-length blond hair, dark eyes and big earrings. Her top was long-sleeved and tight, made of a stretchy material with black and white horizontal stripes that made her breasts seem bigger than they actually were. She wore black leather pants and stylish thick-heeled boots, the uniform of the night, which happened to be a Thursday. A matching leather jacket hung over the back of her bar stool. She knew she was the topic of conversation being conducted by two young bucks sitting at a high table next to the door, presumably so they could see and comment upon everyone who entered the establishment. One wore a black T-shirt and jeans, the other a Harley-Davidson shirt with words on the back that read: *If you can read this, the bitch fell off.* If their necks were any clue they had once been football players, a hunch corroborated by the volume of their partying and the basic biological slant of their commentary.

They were leaning close now, looking at her, no doubt discussing strategy. She smiled and looked away. The look belonged to that dance along the thin line that divided invitation and shyness, and tonight she was Ginger Rogers.

A minute later one of them came over, commandeering the seat next to her. The place was fairly crowded, and she could see in the bar mirror that other men were watching and disapproving of his move. For one thing this was a mismatch—she was older than this muscle-head, and dressed for cocktails in the dungeon rather than a game of touch football in the parking lot. And, of course, they were miffed because he'd beaten them to the punch. They'd watch, see how he did.

"Hi," he said.

She examined him with a dry expression, then looked back down at her drink.

He added, "I don't have an opening line."

"Obviously."

"But I do have an observation. Several, in fact."

"I'm sure you do." She didn't turn or look up.

"You here alone?"

"You are a true master of the obvious, aren't you."

"I mean, are you waiting for someone? Looks like you are."

"Is that one of your observations?"

"Yeah. And that you're freaking gorgeous."

She turned now, pursing her lips as she looked him over. She focused on the Harley logo on his shirt.

"You ride?" she asked.

"A little. Actually, I just dug the shirt."

"Kmart?"

"Target. Am I bothering you?"

"Fits you nicely. You lift?"

"Yeah. Thanks for noticing. You?"

"No. I fuck."

He tried to be cool with that one, nodding as if this was perfectly okay. A moment later he said, "You a pro?"

"No. I'm just messing with you." Her smile softened. "You're what, twenty-two, twenty-three? I'm thirty-four and wondering what you want. And no, you're not bothering me. I'll be sure and let you know when we reach that point."

He returned the smile. "This is going well, don't you think? My name's Scratch."

"You're shitting me. Scratch?"

"Yeah. Nickname. You?"

He was extending his hand. In the mirror she could see two guys in business suits watching with great amusement. She grinned at them as she took Scratch's hand.

"Who's that?" she said, indicating his friend at the table by the door, who raised his glass to acknowledge her attention. "Sniff?"

"That's funny. Scratch and Sniff."

"Thank you."

He kept hold of her hand. "Your name?"

"Ginger," she said.

"Sounds like a dancer's name. You a dancer?"

"Not anymore."

"You want to join my friend and me?"

"You mean Sniff?"

"Whatever. Sure you're not a pro? I mean that in a good way."

"I bet you do. And no, I'm not."

She picked up her drink and napkin. Scratch took the hint and got to his feet. He was huge, easily six four, smiling like an idiot.

Perfect.

Scratch led the woman down the length of the bar and introduced her to Sniff, actually calling him that. Sniff didn't quite get the name thing at first, and she wasn't sure if he was drunk or had been in the middle of one too many first-and-goal situations. Like his more outspoken friend, Sniff filled out his shirt with what most men admired and the majority of women barely noticed. Three tables of men watched as if they had ticket stubs in their pockets, and judging from the shaking of their heads, they wanted a refund.

"Those guys don't like you," she said as she slid onto the high seat.

"Who?" said Scratch. "Tell me. Let's see how they like me when they meet Mister Fister here." He showed off a huge balled fist. More than one scar was visible on the knuckles.

Also perfect.

"Settle down, boys. Save some of that testosterone, okay?"

"Save it for what?" asked Sniff.

"Who knows," she said. "Night is young."

She took a sip of her drink, watching the two young men exchange a hopeful, holy-shit glance. She flashed on the old Wayne and Garth skits from *Saturday Night Live* and had to contain the sudden impulse to laugh. Scratch and Sniff were too into themselves and too buzzed to notice. And too young to remember "Wayne's World."

Soon everybody was laughing at everything and everyone. It was typical bar talk, which meant it was silly and mean-spirited, and soon it turned the corner from double entendre to the blunt exchange of sexual exploits, including her tying a cherry stem into a knot with her tongue. This transpired over the course of several cocktails, lemon drops for her, Bud Light for the Neanderthal twins.

About an hour in, however, Ginger's mood suddenly shifted. She checked her watch often and seemed inordinately interested in the door.

"You look like you're waiting for the other shoe to drop," said Scratch, who had become the leading contender for the first dance later on.

She bit her lip pensively. "Can I be honest with you guys?" Her eyes were suddenly clouded over. And since they were all so very close by now, the boys were sincerely interested in hearing what she had to say.

"I'm married," she said, her eyes drifting to the floor. Both young men shot a look at her ring finger, where she wore a thick gold band that wasn't obviously of the wedding variety.

"Forgive me, father, for I have sinned," said Sniff just as he threw back the remainder of his beer. Scratch, ever the alpha male, whapped a backhand to his shoulder to demonstrate his sincere and noble compassion for the lady.

Ginger's lower lip began to quiver. Scratch put his big paw on her back to offer comfort.

"Hey, what's up?" he said softly.

She covered her mouth with her hand. "I'm afraid," she whispered.

"Of him?" he asked.

She nodded. Without looking up she could sense the two of them exchanging looks. Like Batman and Robin hearing the bat phone from another room.

"Will you walk me to my car? He knows where I am . . . like I said, I'm afraid. He's . . . unpredictable. It's a long story."

"Well, I'm unpredictable, too," said Scratch, a new boldness in his voice.

"One more drink, though," she said, bravely smiling again.

The two of them simultaneously waved for the waitress with all the seriousness and urgency of surgeons calling for another pint of blood.

Perfect.

Birk's was sandwiched between two pretentious brick office towers, both of which had sprung up hastily in the heyday of the bar's glory. The parking lot was therefore a convoluted maze, with many blind corners and alleys that invited all manner of nocturnal mischief, including a murder back in the mid-nineties. The woman they knew as Ginger led them around one building and behind another, walking in the middle of their three-abreast formation, holding their arms as she professed her immense gratitude for their protection. They were suddenly quiet, as if on the lookout for trouble.

"I just don't know what he might do," she said.

"Not much," quipped Scratch.

"Not tonight," said Sniff.

She was parked at the farthest corner of the lot. There were several other cars nearby, but they were alone and the lighting was minimal. She stopped, suddenly turning to Scratch. Without speaking she put her arms around his neck and pulled him down to her lips. She kissed him gently at first, but after a moment her tongue parted his lips and the kiss became serious.

She held Sniff's hand as she kissed Scratch.

After a moment she withdrew, holding eye contact for a moment. Then she turned to Sniff and kissed him with the same probing urgency. As she did, she pulled Scratch's hand to her ass and held it there.

"Holy shit," mumbled Scratch as he observed the kiss his friend Sniff was getting right before his eyes.

Just then a car door opened two stalls away. A man got out, wearing a black leather bomber jacket and jeans. His thick hair was dark, very Pacino. He began walking toward them, hands pocketed. It was a cocky walk, and he was taking his time.

Ginger sucked in air with a gasp and jumped back.

"That him?" asked Scratch, flicking his eyes from the man to Ginger and back again. She nodded just once, very quickly.

Sniff stood at Scratch's side. Both of them instinctively folded their arms as if posing for a Smackdown ad.

The man stopped right in front of them, his hands at his sides. He was looking at Ginger as if the two massive nose guards weren't there at all.

"What is this?" he asked.

"Go home," she said.

"Not without you."

He took a step forward, which was the cue the boys had been waiting for. Scratch grabbed the guy around the biceps, his fingers wrapping nearly all the way around.

"She doesn't want to go," he said. "But I promise, you do."

The smaller newcomer looked up. He was six foot or so, with a wiry build, though with the jacket one couldn't say for sure. His hair may have been Pacino, but his chin had that little Travolta thing happening, like someone had carved a souvenir out of him.

His eyes were slits as they locked on to the larger man's stare.

"Who the fuck are you?" asked the stranger.

"Your worst nightmare."

"Is that right?"

Sniff now chimed in with an articulate rendering of the words, "Yeah, that's right, asshole."

The man looked at each of them in turn, a small grin spreading on his face. Then he looked at the woman and said, "You did good."

"Thank you," she said, smiling back at him.

"Shall we begin then?"

"By all means."

What happened next was something the two young men would never discuss, not only because it was humiliating beyond words, but because it went down so fast they couldn't agree on the specifics. With a move that neither saw coming, the man drove the palm of his hand squarely up under Sniff's nose, breaking it. Simultaneously he brought a knee up into Scratch's groin. That bought some time, a half second at most, during which a solid elbow slammed into Scratch's temple, knocking him to the ground. The man then went to work on Sniff, bombing his head with blows before finishing him off with a roundhouse spin-kick to the head. Sniff crashed back into a parked car, unconscious before he hit the pavement. By now Scratch had found his way back to his knees, but a kick to the jaw sent him sprawling to his back again. Still game, he tried to rise, grabbing for the smaller man's legs, but let go when the stranger applied some sort of pressure hold to his neck that caused unbearable pain to shoot through his entire body. He kept the hold in place as he slowly pushed Scratch back to the pavement, keeping eye contact with him all the while. Through his pain, Scratch could see that the guy was smiling at him.

Once on the ground, the smaller man leaned over his opponent and said, "Are we having fun yet?"

"Fuck you," burbled Scratch, still unable to move.

The man looked up at Ginger, whom the ex-lineman

couldn't see from this position. "Harley boy here doesn't get it," he said.

But he did hear her say, "Then perhaps you should give it to him."

The pressure hold was released just as a fist came crashing into the big man's face. It was followed by another, then another, a series of blows that took him to the very precipice of unconsciousness. He tried to strike back, but his arms felt useless, connected to nothing.

The smaller man seemed to hesitate, as if giving his opponent the opportunity to give it up. The guy wasn't even breathing hard.

But surrender wasn't what the attacker had in mind. Scratch didn't feel or comprehend that he was being dragged between two parked cars.

Then the dream began. Later he would remember it in terms of a dream because that was the only way he could get his mind around it. His friend, whose real name was Brian, had remained unconscious through the whole thing and was never sure he believed the story about what happened next. He only knew they had both been beaten senseless, and his nightmare began and ended with that.

The woman they knew as Ginger was suddenly on top of Scratch, straddling him so her face was inches from his. He remembered shadows moving behind her, and later realized that his attacker, the skinny dude with the leather bomber and the Navy Seal moves, had come up behind her and was kneeling. Scratch could see his face clearly in the reflected light, all business now. Scratch moved his hands and encountered the woman's legs straddling him, but they were no longer sheathed in leather. Her legs were now bare.

Her fingers gripped his throat tightly, nearly constricting his ability to breathe. With her other hand she pulled off the blond wig, revealing very short dark hair.

"Lie still," she whispered, and in that moment, judging from her gasp and the pleasure in her eyes, the man behind thrust deeply into her. "Enjoy this with me."

The man and the woman moved slowly and rhythmi-
cally, her grip on Scratch's throat constricting and then
relaxing with the thrusts, her eyes half lidded, like a
junkie taking a hit. Once she licked at his mouth, presumably for the blood, and a moment later she nibbled
and sucked at his lips, as if suckling them. An obscene
and inexplicable smile possessed her face.

When he started to speak, the smile vanished and her
fingers suddenly dug into his throat with such force that
he froze, knowing she could tear out his larynx before
he could blink. Her position was such, given his weak-
ened state, that he was basically helpless, and that if he
did manage to break free, the kung-fu dude would finish
him off.

The kung-fu dude, incidentally, had his eyes closed
while he was banging the hell out of the woman.

Scratch took a deep breath in an effort to remain
calm, and in that instant the woman's smile returned.

"That's better," she whispered. "Just go with it. . . ."

The pace was picking up. Scratch saw the woman bite
down on her lower lip as she clamped her eyes shut.
Moments later, with a simultaneous shudder of pleasure,
they came, presumably together.

"Let me go," said Scratch, his voice whining.

He felt the woman relax, though she continued to rock
back and forth gently. Her eyes opened and a new smile
appeared, that of someone who had pulled off a prank,
someone who had won the game.

She kissed his forehead, placing her palm on the side
of his face.

"Something to remember me by . . . Scratch."

She spoke his name slowly, and as she did she used
her fingernails to tear three bloody lines into the skin of
his cheek.

He screamed. The man kicked him in the head, and
the blackness consumed him.

He awoke some minutes later to the sensation of
Brian gently slapping his face.

When he got home he discovered that the man's

semen was still on his pants, covering the entire area of his crotch. Rather than wash them, he threw the pants away.

He and Brian did not tell a soul about what happened, and other than a single night of breaking it down over a half-rack of Heineken, they never spoke of it again, though Scratch did refer to him as Sniff whenever he wanted to bust his balls.

And though they would never be missed there, neither one would ever set foot in Birk's again.

16

"That was *so* hot," said Diana. As was their custom, they were making quiet love in the aftermath of the violence and mayhem they had wrought.

"You were," said Damien, "how shall I say it . . . *devastating*. As usual."

"To all parties involved."

"To this party. You make me crazy."

They drew close and moved together, one with the moment and each other.

"I have another idea," said Damien.

"You are insatiable," said Diana.

"A game."

"It's all a game."

"A blood challenge."

After a pause, Diana said, "Ooo . . . how romantic."

She was straddling him as he sat, moving slowly at a well-practiced pace that she knew would allow their coupling to last as long as they desired. As always, she controlled the movement and therefore the moment of its conclusion. Because of this tantric approach, their orgasms were unthinkably potent to the point of losing consciousness. These were her favorite times with him, talking quietly as they made love without the influence of kink, planning their lives and their games, tuning out the world. Once in a while she would pull away just to gaze down upon the moist image of the snake etched in ink around his penis. The snake memorialized an incident from their past, one of their games—two years earlier she'd seduced a married Baptist minister in a small town in Idaho, ultimately causing him to lose his job and his wife. Before the game began, Damien said it couldn't be done, and the tattoo of the snake had been proposed by Diana as the prize if it could. Prize and punishment had become synonymous in their world. She had been there when the tattoo was applied; in fact, it had been her job to keep him erect through the painful process of bringing the serpent to life. She had accomplished this by performing cunnilingus on the female tattoo artist doing the work while Damien watched from the studio chair, helplessly bound and gagged.

She loved the serpent inside her, the way it filled her body and soul, making her delirious with pleasure and a sense of belonging. She owned the serpent, had tamed and mastered it, and now it served her.

"It's been a long time," he said.

She knew he was referring to the blood. "Too long," she replied.

He grasped her hips and urged her to move more urgently. In their evolved state, they understood the power of words in their game. Without the words there was nothing. The games, at first exhilarating in their own right, were now mostly fodder for their words.

The term *blood challenge* required no elaboration. They had performed them several times in their five years together, usually when things became boring, which they did easily. The prize was taken in blood in one form or another. Most of the various tattoos on their bodies represented the culmination of one of these challenges, and they were always together when the image was rendered onto the skin. They had to find a tattoo artist willing to work this way, but that was easy and part of the game. Like the tattoos, the assortment of curious scars also represented victory or defeat, and for this edge-play they required no outside professional—only a sharp scalpel and a bottle of good wine.

They both marveled that the line between winning and

losing had become blurred. Lately, in defiance of even
their own rules, they had begun to take the mark together regardless of who won or lost.

The game was everything. The serpent's dance.

Each of them wore a vial containing the blood of the
other around their necks, with a vow to never remove
it. Admittedly, they'd borrowed the idea from a couple
of eccentric movie stars who'd leaked it as a PR ploy,
but it sounded interesting, so the next blood challenge
was undertaken with this at stake. Diana knew how to
apply the syringe, slowly and deeply at the moment of
their mutual climax.

"Tell me," she said.

"A seduction game."

"Against impossible odds."

"First to the finish line wins."

"In that case you don't stand a chance," she said.

"You're sexist, and you underestimate me."

"Not guilty on both counts. Just being real. I'm a
woman, I don't have to work at it. I just have to ask
and then lie down. You, on the other hand, have millen-
niums of social programming to shatter."

"Too true. Which is why you won't like what I intend
to propose."

She said nothing, slowing the reciprocating movement
of her hips slightly. Finally she said, "Then the stakes
should reflect as much."

"Agreed."

"So tell me."

He smiled, then kissed her cheek. With his lips resting
on her skin he said, "Wesley's new girlfriend."

Diana stopped moving altogether. She leaned back
and looked at him, the dance momentarily suspended.

"You're a pig."

"I told you."

"You just want to seduce that new brunette."

"Before Wesley does."

"Then you better hurry."

"That's not the game I have in mind." He allowed

her to contemplate this for a moment, then continued. "Let me lay it out for you. Wesley's hot for this new project manager, Bernadette something or other. That makes her dangerous, which is what makes her interesting. You, on the other hand, will seduce the unseduceable."

"How about *I* seduce her first?"

"Interesting. But I like this better."

"No doubt."

"The little programmer, Grasvik. You go after him, I go after her, the winner tastes blood."

"Be specific."

"Tell you what. I'll let you define the stakes."

She smiled, pleased with this. "That could be dangerous to your health."

"I'm counting on it."

They moved quietly for a few minutes, watching the world float past. It was night outside, the moon painting the clouds with nuance and shadow.

"She's beautiful."

"That she is."

"And he's a pimple on the ass of masculinity."

"But he's brilliant. I thought you said brilliant was sexy."

"You're brilliant," she said. "That's what I said is sexy."

"So are you in?"

"My stakes?"

"Your stakes."

They rocked back and forth for a moment, then Diana said, "You have to get Wesley out of the way."

"I hate that arrogant little prick."

"I can help with that, you know."

"You want to fuck him, don't you."

"Because you hate him. Wouldn't that be interesting?"

"Are those your stakes?"

"I'm considering it."

"Let's do a blood challenge on his ass sometime."

"Either way, he's mine when it happens."

"I'll be there with a camcorder."

Suddenly a new voice interrupted their exchange. It was a shrill squeal and came from the radio headset that Paul Lampkin—known in these moments to Diana as Damien—had pulled down around his neck.

"Cessna six-zero-two, Albuquerque center, over."

Damien, now Paul Lampkin once again, corporate pilot, pulled the headset back in place. "Cessna six-zero-two, roger."

"Cessna six-zero-two, Albuquerque center. Descend to one-eight thousand, contact Phoenix approach, one-two-zero-point-seven."

"One-two-zero-seven. Cessna six-zero-two, good night."

Paul reached around his lover's torso and punched in an eighteen-thousand-foot setting on the autopilot, causing the nose to lower slightly. He checked the trim and the engine gauges, then switched the radio to the assigned frequency before he once again became Damien, dark lord and lover. Phoenix approach could wait another moment.

"An interesting game," he said, "don't you think?"

"You have no idea how interesting, my sweetness."

She was grinding against him now, well into the home stretch. The lights of Phoenix were illuminating the horizon before them, and she knew there were only minutes remaining. She knew the subtle threat in her words would hasten things. She loved these shuttle flights with no passengers, because she got to be alone with him in the sky.

"You'll never do it," he said. He didn't have to explain what he meant. Both of them knew what he'd accomplished in the past, and they both held it up as the benchmark standard of their debauchery.

"We'll see about that, won't we," she said. To surpass what Damien had achieved, someone would have to die. It had been leading to this, and here it was.

She put her lips on his ear and breathed words into

it: "Maybe him . . . maybe her . . . maybe even you, eh? Maybe it's you whom the spider consumes."

That did it. Damien arched his back and screamed as the serpent spit its venom into her. As a joke, she reached behind and depressed the transmit button on the yoke.

A moment later words could be heard through the headset, another pilot on the same frequency: "Phoenix center . . . what was that sound, over?"

"Don't ask," came an anonymous reply. Those pilots were real cards sometimes.

Diana grinned as Damien descended from his orgasm, caught between laughter and bliss.

He whispered breathlessly through his ecstasy, "You're an exquisite little bitch, you know that?"

She rested her head against his shoulder without responding.

It would have been the moment, had they been normal lovers, in which one would profess their love for the other. But then, there was nothing normal about these two or what they defined as romance, as love itself, and over the course of their five years the words had never been spoken aloud.

What was normal, anyway, except that which the lovers embraced with passion? Who got to say, and who would deny the freedom to love as one chose?

In their own way, each of them knew.

Though one of them didn't know everything.

PART TWO

>><<

And the Lord God said unto the woman,
what is this that thou hast done? And the
woman said, the Serpent beguiled me, and I
did eat.

—Genesis 3:13

PART TWO

> 17 <

*The sickness escalates as I approach the place where
sin was redefined. Even now it remains a sanctuary of
sorts, where the earth moved and where Christ died yet
again, where my universe coalesced, if only for a while.
That pleasure can lead to such pain is one of many les-
sons written here, but there are others—that betrayal can
erase all that was once rationalized as good, that if the
end justifies its means then surely I am the biggest fool
to have walked the face of the planet.*

*At least it got me out of my shit-bag of a marriage. To
deny that truth would only propel me deeper into the
depths of my own shame. A fool, perhaps, but a hypo-
crite, I hope never.*

*But I am a fool no longer. If he touches me I will
amputate his hand. If he tries to excuse himself from
blame, I will laugh and try to find pity for him, and in
doing so perhaps discover a shred of lost humanity. If he
expresses regret I will be strong, though I will stop far
short of forgiveness. I'll leave that to higher powers than
me, because that's who he'll have to answer to in the end.
I am finished with the pain of knowing him. My burden
now is living with the pain of remembering him.*

Frankly, I can't imagine what the hell he wants.

*I check my hair and makeup in the mirror before I get
out of my car. There were things he liked, things had to
be just so, little tricks of femininity that he claimed
dripped onto his libido like erotic morphine. He will like*

*what he sees tonight, and I will enjoy denying him access.
That's what women do, we eviscerate those who have hurt
us with a flagrant display of what can no longer be
possessed.*

*That, I decide, is why I came. To show him I have
moved on.*

And perhaps, to show myself.

*As I go inside, a flash flood of memories washes over
me, and the water, once warm and comforting, is now
cold. I see faces I knew, inhale scents that take me to
another time, not so long ago. I see myself in a reflection,
and I turn away.*

*He is already here, waiting for me, in our special room.
I am sorry that I came.*

Bernadette's father was, and would be until they
pumped him full of embalming fluid, an obsessive fish-
erman. Trout, bass, carp, catfish, walleye, the occasional
flounder, it didn't matter. She couldn't remember a day
in which the latest issue of *Field and Stream* wasn't the
centerpiece of the family coffee table. Once, long before
it was a punch line, her mother had with complete
bourbon-fortified sincerity given her father an ultimatum
disguised as a choice: he could have her, or he could
fish. And with complete seriousness her father had replied, "Well, honey, I'm really going to miss you." Bernie was never sure if her mother drank because he
fished, or he fished because she drank, but in either case
it was the most critical omission on the divorce decree.

Bernie grinned at the memory as she stared into the
mirror, preparing for the evening ahead. She had thrown
out her own line, baited it with all the feminine mystique
she could muster, and today she had received a percepti-
ble nibble. Tonight's mission was to bury the hook so
deeply that the ensuing struggle for freedom would be
an exercise in futility. Those six-hundred-dollar black
leather pants would get their debut—worth every damn
penny, too—paired with a tight black long-sleeved top

and accented by just the right abundance of silver jewelry.

She had been on the project for less than a week, and Wesley Edwards had invited her to meet him for a glass of wine. Those were his exact words, which meant this wasn't about the project. A wide-eyed Wesley had attended Jerry's kickoff briefing, and he had stopped by her new desk more than once to see how she was doing. If this was a *meeting* he wouldn't have asked, he'd have announced. No, this was business of a completely different flavor, preferably a nice merlot.

AZ88 was old-town Scottsdale's hottest place to be seen, located in the pedestrian mall across from the Scottsdale Civic Center. There was a significant gathering of what looked like black-clad mourners just outside the door, awaiting their assigned tables from a list that meant next to nothing in a place where every fifth patron was a local sports celebrity or a friend of the doorman. Two of the walls were eighteen feet of plate glass, as if the brightly lit activities within would be of interest to a less-privileged world, or perhaps simply to show off the art deco appointments. This wasn't the place for a business meeting or a clandestine rendezvous. This was serious cruising.

Wesley was standing in the middle of it all, waving his arms at her from what would be their table for the evening. He was wearing an unstructured sport coat over a rayon T-shirt, all of it the requisite black. The small risk she had taken with the leather pants had just paid off— Wesley had come to troll, too.

It occurred to Bernie that Peggy would have liked the look. The thought gave her strength and perspective in equal doses, anchoring her back to her objective.

The doorman seemed to know who Bernie was, waving her past the scowling crowd already wondering which Phoenix Sun she was there to meet. Indeed, there were three of them inside, along with two Cardinals, a horny Coyote and half the cast from a program on the WB. She could feel the eyes on her back as she approached

Wesley and, sensing his body language, offered her cheek for him to kiss as she arrived.

"I'm glad you came," he said, holding her chair.

"I'm glad you asked."

"Probably shouldn't have."

"I have to work for you before I can sue you."

"Were you a lawyer in another life?"

"Worse. I almost married one in another life."

He was seated by now, taking the lavender chair right next to her at a table for four. The little things were adding up nicely.

The waiter arrived too quickly, a college student who by necessity tolerated this crowd but no doubt preferred the company of lit majors. Wesley was studying the wine list when Bernie gently pulled it from his hands, asking, "May I?"

His surprise quickly gave way to a sheepish grin and, a moment later, a shallow nod. Bernie returned the smile, acknowledging her own brazenness.

She turned to the waiter. "Do you have a Silver Oak cabernet, something before 'ninety-five?"

"We have a few of the 'ninety-four left in stock. And one 'eighty-nine . . . one ninety a bottle, I think." He smiled, but just barely.

"He's paying," she said, "we'll have the 'ninety-four."

The waiter departed with an affirmative nod, unimpressed. He'd seen all manner of first-date icebreakers and creatively inspired flirtations, and he just wanted to score some tips and get back home to his girlfriend.

"I am so upstaged," said Wesley, sipping from a glass of water.

"Gotta watch me that way."

"That's easy. You look very nice tonight."

"I clean up."

"Indeed you do." He took another sip of the water, this one forced. "So here we are, immersed in those awkward moments as the chitchat warms up." He waited for a smile, which she delivered on cue.

"Any ideas?" she offered.

Wesley's body language shifted to something a bit more formal.

"Okay, here's the deal. I like the way you handle yourself. Too early to tell about the project, but you're a pro, that's obvious. I just wanted to get to know you a little better. There'll be more projects, so who knows. We're growing, I need managers."

She pivoted outward and crossed her kid leather legs for his benefit. It worked as planned—his eyes dropped there and then quickly moved away.

"So this *is* a business meeting," she said.

He grinned, almost shyly. "Not my intention, to be honest."

She smiled, proactively trying to take away his discomfort. If things went well she'd have plenty of *that* for him later.

"Tell me about that past life," he said, "including the lawyer. That must have been scary."

And so it began, the ritual of the newly acquainted, interrupted only by the arrival of the wine and his periodic refilling of their glasses. Bernie touched all the appropriate biographical bases with self-deprecating humor: her childhood in Texas, the schools and the parade of boyfriends and all the sports that kept her sane—she purposefully left out the fact that she was ready to test for her black belt in tai-kwon-do—with a few little cynical quips tossed in about her parents and her inability to completely forgive them for being human. She touched on her three primary relationships—"I've been in love three times" was what she said—noting that one of them was an attorney. This, in turn, prompted a short philosophical reverie on the subject of forgiveness, complete with a recitation by Bernie of Don Henley's lyrics on the subject. To Bernie, the song was a hymn.

. . . *it's about forgiveness . . . even if, even if, you don't love me anymore . . .*

While they both loved the song, neither of them were much for the notion of forgiveness, frankly, and they left it at that.

Through it all Bernie was conscious of her posture and the accessibility of his sight line. It was another of those exclusively feminine games that went completely undetected by men, who had no idea they were being played. She made sure to touch his forearm from time to time, and on more than one occasion allowed her eyes to drift over him with the tiniest of approving smiles.

Wesley was proving to be a bit of a surprise. Not only had he willingly recited song lyrics, he seemed in no real hurry to talk about himself, perhaps the first straight man on the planet to combine these two attributes. He actually seemed to prefer listening, even asking questions and calling for elaboration. In Wesley's case it was easy to assign meaning: this man was hiding something. He was a hunter and not a gatherer. A predator, playing a vicious game. A poseur.

Of course he was. He had seduced her sister. He had shattered her life, then taken it from her and walked away clean. And it had all begun by listening to her, so rare and so noble. Something Peggy's husband had no time, inclination or ability to do.

Conscious of the alcohol in her system, Bernie resolved to remember why she was there and who she was with. It would be easy to forget, get swept away in his movie star eyes and soft charm. The trick would be to hide this steely countenance beneath a skin of velvety smooth vulnerability. Alcohol or no alcohol, she was still, above all, a woman on a mission.

She sensuously folded and unfolded her legs as if stretching, running her hands down toward her ankles as she asked him to tell her his life story. Bending this way, her top billowed forward slightly, allowing him a glimpse of her breasts.

"So," she said, seizing a moment of quiet as he poured them both more wine. "Do you fish?"

His eyes widened before he smiled. "Do I what?"

"Fish. You know, rod, reel, worms, bad hygiene?"

"No. I don't fish. Why?"

"Just wondering. What then? What makes Wesley Edwards, CEO, tick?"

"Who's hiring who here?"

"I always believed that interviews are a two-way street."

"This isn't an interview."

"Isn't it?" She smiled coyly over the rim of her glass as she took a sip. There was an art to the zinger, and a glass of wine was a great prop.

Wesley shifted, as if settling in. She couldn't tell if he was uncomfortable with the request or relieved that it was finally his turn.

"I'm pretty easy, really. Born in California, moved here in grade school, graduated ASU. Played baseball, didn't get drafted, hauled my broken heart up to Stanford to learn how to conquer the world, got my money's worth. Mom died in 'ninety-six, Dad's remarried and lives in Florida. I go from problem company to problem company, I chop heads and sell assets, and I get ridiculous stock options and bonuses when I deliver what I said I'd deliver, which I always do because I don't bite off more than I can chew.

"As for what makes me tick, what you see is what you get. I despise bullshit, which is unfortunate because we live in a world fueled by it. Color me a cynic, but I think most people are up to their eyes in bullshit and can no longer recognize the color brown. I'm not married because I don't have time and I don't like kids for more than ten minutes, and frankly I haven't met a woman who can handle me or stand me long enough to know me. I don't have close friends because I don't buy into the it's-all-about-the-beer philosophy of my esteemed peers. I do what I want, when I want, and because I understand the physics of relationships and the synergy of business, I usually *get* what I want, and when I don't I just move on. I have an I.Q. somewhere north of one fifty and a high pain threshold, and my goal in life is to get rich enough to buy an island and get the hell out of Dodge, and I'm closer to it than I care to discuss or you would believe."

He paused, but only for a heartbeat. Long enough for his expression to soften.

"And oh yeah, I think Costner's I-believe-in-the-hanging-curveball speech from *Bull Durham* is the single best soliloquy in the history of motion pictures."

He sat back, bringing the glass up to his mouth, studying her for a reaction, some little tick that would signal success.

Bernie held his gaze for a moment, then said, "Do you do that the same way every time, or do I rate a customization?"

"Know thyself," said Wesley. "I don't apologize."

"I don't imagine that you do."

"Listen, I know how all that sounds. Like more bullshit. But it's *my* bullshit, I've worked hard for it, and it serves me." He ended the sentence with a small grin.

"Like a shell serves a hermit crab."

He looked up to the ceiling, as if impatient with himself for not making his point more clear. Or perhaps impatient with her.

"We're all hiding from something," he said. "Playing games, justifying our crap, copping out. Welcome to the human race. The number of people who really get it are few and far between. I'm just trying to play at a higher level than that."

"So how's it going up there?"

"You think I'm arrogant."

"Do I? What else do I think?" She drew a deep breath, suddenly realizing how close she was to blowing this. So she added, "Listen, I don't like bullshit either. It's just that I believe that the game we're playing—I like to refer to it as *life*—is a team sport."

He raised his glass in a mock salute, with no other response.

She had met men like this before. And usually, when they looked this good on top of it, she found herself interested. Something about the elixir of self-confidence and the opportunity to nurse a spoiled inner child back to health.

Wesley launched again, this time ticking through a lengthy laundry list of his candidates for the bullshit hall of fame. Bernie listened to it all, genuinely fascinated, in no small part because she agreed with much of what he said, and what she didn't she found both amusing and refreshing. Wesley Edwards was nothing if not opinionated.

As he spoke, someone sitting behind Bernie fired up a cigar, thus reminding her of something she had planned for tonight, should the occasion arise. Recalling the cigar magazine in his trash, she had intended to take an unlit cigar from Wesley's hands at the moment it emerged from his pocket, expertly clip one end—with her teeth if need be—hold the other in the flame of his lighter for a few moments before raising it to her mouth and, with gracefully hollow cheeks and glistening lips, suck life into it, twisting it slowly as she did so, and then finally, with a coy smile, rolling her head back and blowing the smoke toward the ceiling with exquisite slowness. All the while, somehow avoiding the urge to throw up.

"That's pleasant," she said as the scent grew stronger, rolling her eyes. "I should ask, you smoke cigars?"

"No. I don't do cheap fads. Ironically, I own shares in a publishing company that puts out a cigar magazine, so I can't be all that pious about it. You?"

She smiled, even laughed a little, though he had no way of knowing it was at her own expense.

"I don't do fads either."

"Good, then I can hire you after all."

"Because I don't do fads?"

"Because you don't smoke. Two rules: never hire a smoker, never hire someone who uses the word 'dude' to start a sentence."

Bernie couldn't help but crack a smile. "So, what, are you a republican or a Mormon or just judgmental?"

"Think of it as CEO prerogative. People have their little flags, little socially acceptable flaws that nonetheless give them away. That's two of them."

"Gives *what* away, exactly? In terms of their job qualifications, I mean."

He shifted, only slightly impatient. "I go with the odds. Just calling it as it is."

Bernie shook her head in an I-can't-believe-this-guy way. Her sister had been a part-time smoker, mostly behind her husband's back. But Peggy certainly didn't qualify as the exception to Wesley's odds on this issue. In fact, Bernie realized she agreed with him more than she didn't. With every sentence Wesley Edwards was hoisting his own flags, and not all of them bearing a skull and crossbones.

On impulse, and just for the hell of it, she suddenly asked if he had any brothers or sisters, something he'd curiously omitted.

"One sister," he said with a sudden smile. "God love her. You?"

Even though she'd opened this can of worms, something sizzled deep in Bernie's stomach. One sister, indeed. She looked at him so severely that he jerked his head back, as if to avoid being tagged.

She turned her head away before responding. "My sister is dead."

Their eyes locked for a moment before Wesley said, "I'm sorry."

"So am I. She killed herself."

Now she looked for a tell, hoping desperately to see something flinch behind his eyes. She knew she was treading a minefield here, but wine always did that to her, made her go straight at things, to hell with the kid gloves.

Wesley pursed his lips. Without looking he said, "That must be . . . I don't know. None of us can know, I suppose."

He was good, genuinely uncomfortable. Remorseful, humiliated, embarrassed. Academy Award time. She wanted to smash the empty bottle of cabernet across his jaw.

She drew a deep breath and said, "I should go."

He looked at his Rolex and nodded. He was supposed to protest, beg for forgiveness, try to extend his time with her. But Wesley wasn't playing by the rules tonight, not allowing her to toy with him. Instead he was playing against type, being considerate and accommodating, and therefore complex and intriguing.

Who is *this guy? And what does he want from me?*

"I'll walk you to your car." He was already up, reaching for the back of her chair.

"I'm sorry," she said.

"It's okay. Let's get some air."

With his hand lightly touching the small of her back, he guided her through the maze of tables toward the door, which still held a sizeable crowd at bay. As they passed through them into the warm Arizona night, he bent to her ear and whispered, "This place is complete bullshit, don't you think?"

There was always the chance that Wesley would try to kiss her when they reached her car. Perhaps this was the cause of their silence as they walked through the velvety desert air under a billion points of light. Or maybe there were simply no unfinished threads of conversation to pick up, no elaboration required. It hadn't been a conversation at all, really, it had been a joust disguised as a preening. Bernie wasn't buying into the Wesley-as-sensitive-man act. For her part, the silence had been a visualization of how she'd deflect the kiss when it came.

"So here's the question," she said, digging into her purse for her keys. She fished them out, hit the button to unlock the door, then looked at him. "What's the price of all this well-cultivated cynicism and self-righteousness?"

He smiled, not remotely jarred, as if he was happy she had been paying attention.

"You do cut straight to the point, don't you?"

"My guess is you like that in a woman."

"You're amazing. You should run my production team."

"You can't afford me."

"Don't be so sure."

"The question stands."

He nodded, seeing that he was on the hook for an answer. She took note of his expression and realized that, while few and far between, Wesley's moments of discomfort were as obvious as his ego in moments of comfort. This discovery alone had made the evening worthwhile. She could read him, know when she had her finger on his pulse, and later, her foot on his throat.

He wetted his lips nervously. "You want me to say it's lonely at the top."

"Just plain lonely would do. I don't give a shit about the elevation."

"I have all the company I need."

She opened the car door, which he held as she got in. This would have been the moment when the kiss should have happened, but she realized Wesley was way too in command of the game to consider it, and she liked the idea of her taking away the prerogative. He who submits first loses, and while that little dance has always been the epitome of bullshit, playing it was sometimes as unavoidable as it was fun.

"I guess," she said thoughtfully, "what I'm really asking is . . . is it worth it? Staying behind those castle walls, keeping all the riffraff out."

"That *is* a better question."

"I'm hoping for a better answer."

He smiled, not completely for her benefit.

"I'll let you know when I get to the island. Good night."

Wesley closed the door, stepping back as he issued a small wave. If he was grieving for the lost prerogative, it didn't show. He turned and headed away, hands pocketed in very expensive linen slacks. *Sexy* linen slacks. After a moment he withdrew something from his jacket pocket, something with wires—his mobile phone head-set. Of course.

Bernie waited until he rounded a corner, wondering if he'd turn for a final look, but it didn't happen. When he was gone she started the car and pulled out.

The fact that he hadn't looked back wasn't what concerned her on the drive up Scottsdale Road to her rented condo. Or the fact that he'd needed to call someone at the first possible moment. No, it was the realization that she wasn't completely sure why she so desperately *wanted* him to look back that would keep her up half the night, or from which side of the fence her desperation was coming.

The perspective with which she'd started the evening was foggy, at best.

And the game, or whatever it was, was definitely on.

18

A Corvette, Diana realized, was not the best vehicle for this job. Observation, undercover work, stalking—whatever you wanted to call it—called for something no one would remember, such as a Taurus or, God forbid, one of those new little Korean cars. It was safe enough tonight, though, sitting here in the neon daylight that illuminated old-town Scottsdale, a place where a tight new 'Vette fit right in with the preponderance of German sedans and luxury SUVs. She was parked across the street from a popular restaurant called Bandera and the smell, mesquite chicken on an open grill, was killing her on a night when she'd eaten a late lunch and no dinner. She'd followed the Volvo from the moment it had pulled out of the condo lot, and was lucky to score a spot just down the block from where the mark had parked his Escalade earlier in the evening. "The mark"—she liked that, very Ludlum. Staying a block behind, she'd followed the woman—love the pants, babe—on foot to her rendezvous with Wesley Edwards at AZ88 and had watched them mess with each other's minds through the glass walls from a bench next to a fountain outside. When she saw that they were getting ready to leave, she'd hightailed it back to her car and was behind the wheel when they arrived back at the Volvo, observing their little song and dance, her avoidance, his couldn't-care-less posing. Knowing Wesley Edwards as she did, he probably really couldn't care less. He'd walked right past the Corvette as he departed, already absorbed in an urgent conversation on his wireless mobile.

Bernadette had remained in the Volvo—she clearly wasn't happy—for nearly a minute before she'd pulled away.

The traffic at this time of night in Scottsdale was brisk, so it was easy to follow her home without the possibility of detection. When they were nearly back at the condo, her mobile phone rang. She didn't need to say hello.

"Where are you?" she asked.

"I'm back," said Damien. "In and out, no problem."

"Have fun?"

"Always. Breaking and entering beats surveillance any day. Where are you?"

"About to tuck her in."

"And?"

"We need to do something about your boss, that's for sure."

"Did he kiss her?"

"Fucked her on the hood of her car."

"You get pictures?"

"I'll take care of Wesley Edwards for you. But the bitch is an iceberg. You don't stand a chance."

"I love it when you underestimate me."

"So how was your evening?"

"Guy needs a mother. Place was a sty."

"And?"

"He's easy. Two computers, a bunch of tech stuff. He's some kind of closet investor, lots of how-to stuff, brokerage brochures, like he's got some cake."

"Probably makes more than you."

"His thing is video games, must have a couple grand worth. Has all the systems—GameCube, PlayStation, Xbox, an old 64. Has three different TVs wired. Fucking fruitcake. Get this, he has a movie poster in his living room of Angelina Jolie as Lara Croft."

"That's interesting. Any porn?"

"Better. He's into comic books. I mean, *serious* comic books."

"And?"

"He doesn't need porn. He gets off on the graphics. You'll like it. I do."

"Supergirl?"

"Better. Darker. No minors allowed."

"Vampirella."

"You wish. But you're close."

"Tell me."

"If you're nice to me."

"How about if I'm *not* nice to you?"

"Then I'll tell you anything."

"How far are you?" she asked.

"I'm on Lincoln."

"I'm there in fifteen. Pour me a sambuca."

"Three beans, sweetheart."

They disconnected simultaneously, neither of them saying good-bye.

Two hours later, Jerry Grasvik arrived home at his Mesa apartment from visiting with friends—pizza and his sixteenth viewing of the *Tron* video, still the visionary standard among real players. He crashed through his door, never turning the lights on as he went into his bathroom, stripped naked, brushed his teeth and flopped into a bed that hadn't been made or even changed in two months. He had no idea that someone had been here, touching his things, assigning meaning, looking for a weakness they would use against him.

Or that one had been found.

Its name—her name—was Lady Death.

19

The door to Wesley Edwards's office had been closed all morning, and Jerry Grasvik was in there with him. The fourth floor was traditional in its layout, with a central bank of elevators opening to a lobby, where the first thing a visitor saw was Nadine Worobey's smiling face. The offices wrapped around the elevator lobby, with a central aisle allowing access to every nook and cranny, which on this floor meant management and their dutiful lieutenants. There were two other floors occupied by Oar Research—Jerry's cubicle was on the second floor with the other byte-heads—but this was where the action was, where Wesley Edwards ruled the world. His was the only enclosed office in the company, a glass-walled chamber built on the southwest corner with a view of the Paradise Valley area and Camelback Mountain beyond, and later in the day, the world-class sunsets that graced the city. Not that Wesley had ever noticed such a thing. More likely, Bernie presumed, he chose this location because of its view of the parking lot. Guys like Wesley liked to keep an eye on their rides.

It wasn't lost on Bernie that her cubicle was also on this floor, rather than down in the trenches where the projects unraveled. Her view was to the east, to the sprawl of Kierland Commons and the airstrip beyond. This placement, she decided, was a very good sign, because she was sure it was Wesley's doing. He was one of those CEOs who thought the terms *hands-on* and *con-*

trol freak were synonymous. He could watch her—which in his mind meant he could control her—and she could watch him.

Shortly before noon on this, the day after their "date" at AZ88, a striking woman emerged from the elevator and announced herself to Nadine. She wore a navy pants suit with a masculine cut, yet she was extremely feminine in her movements, footwear from Donna Karan, and a fortune in understated jewelry. This was a man-loving woman of substance and purpose. Carrying a two-thousand-dollar briefcase, she sure as hell wasn't from the high-tech world. As Bernie looked on, there seemed to be some discussion. She saw the woman give Nadine her card, saw Nadine shake her head as she shrugged, saw the woman's polite but unyielding smile, then saw Nadine go through the motions of punching something into the phone system.

Then the woman took a seat to wait.

Ten minutes later Jerry emerged from Wesley's glass cage. Nadine pointed out Wesley's office, and the woman moved toward it.

Watching the greeting that ensued, Bernie was certain this wasn't competition. But as she kept watching, she was equally certain this was trouble of some kind.

"Sharon Hobbs," said the visitor as she handed Wesley her card. Wesley squinted at it, and without looking back up indicated the chair where he wanted her to sit. "Thank you for seeing me," she continued as she sat in the chair next to the one he'd pointed to. It was uncomfortably warm from its prior occupant.

Wesley continued to stare at the card as he sat back down behind his desk, which was the size of a pool table and littered with files. He wore a crisp white shirt, his necktie tight and neat as it always was. Bernie had observed that he always loosened it on the elevator whenever he was leaving the building, but never inside.

"Torgeson, Barton and Mattern," he said, finally look-

ing up from the card from which he had just read the
name of Sharon Hobbs's firm. "Who's suing me?"

He tossed the card onto the table in front of him,
folded his hands and leaned back in his high pleated
leather chair, which squeaked slightly under his weight.

"You assume you're being sued?" she asked, returning his smug grin. Already there was chemistry
brewing, though fragile as nitroglycerine at this point.
"That's interesting, don't you think? I do."

"I'm glad you're amused. How can I help you?"

"I have a rather delicate matter to discuss with you."

"Do I need an attorney?"

"Depends, I suppose. I'm here in an unofficial capacity, more a representative than an attorney, actually. For
today, that is."

"Now *that's* interesting."

Their eyes locked. Wesley was working very hard at
not showing any expression, while Sharon Hobbs, seated
with her legs delicately crossed and her hands folded in
her lap, sat forward slightly, wearing a little you're-not-
fooling-me smirk.

"Are you warm, Mr. Edwards? May I call you
Wesley?"

"Mr. Edwards is fine."

"Your cheeks are flushed."

"You come here to muck around with me, or do we
have business?"

"My client works for you."

"That's a start. Who is it?"

"I'm not at liberty to say, actually."

Wesley snorted with amusement, almost as if he expected to hear this.

"That's bullshit. It's such bullshit, in fact, that I ought
to throw you out of here on your very exquisite ass. And
if you want to sue me for *that*, go right ahead."

Sharon Hobbs cleared her throat and looked away,
collecting her composure for a moment. When she
looked back her expression was as deadpan as his.

"I'm here as a favor, to be honest."

"See, there's more bullshit. There's never been a lawyer in the history of wing-tip shoes who has ever done a favor for anyone."

"The favor is for you, actually. I'm getting two forty an hour to convey a message. My client is afraid to bring this to you personally. She fears . . . repercussions."

"She?"

"That's right."

"Repercussions for what?"

Sharon shifted in her seat and winced slightly. "My client says you have, in the past, made forward comments that are inappropriate in the workplace."

"Is that right." He didn't frame the words as a question.

"She says you have mistaken her social posture, her attempts to simply be friendly, as flirtation, and that you have on occasion been flirtatious and solicitous toward her, in private and in front of other employees, causing her embarrassment and emotional distress."

"That's bullshit."

"You use that word a lot, don't you."

"So you *are* suing me." He didn't move a muscle as he spoke, and he kept his eyes riveted on hers, his expression straight out of a poker game.

The woman allowed the eye contact, then offered a slight smile. "Not yet. I've been asked to tell you that if your behavior continues in this fashion, she will have no choice but to pursue a legal remedy."

Wesley blinked several times and began chewing on his lower lip.

"Are my cheeks still red?" he asked.

"Is my ass still exquisite?" she asked back.

Now he leaned forward and folded his hands formally on the desktop.

"Let me see if I've got this straight. You represent an employee of mine who says I'm coming on to her, but you can't or won't tell me who it is so that I can cease and desist the inappropriate behavior."

"Perhaps I don't need to tell you who it is."

"Maybe I'm doing four or five of my employees, who's to say?"

Sharon Hobbs licked her lips and turned away momentarily, her smile widening.

"Mr. Edwards, I can appreciate your position, and that you are going to great lengths to show me that you are neither intimidated by me nor troubled by this matter, that in fact you are taking this lightheartedly. I can appreciate all of that. You're an important man, lots of hormones, can't let a little squeal from the peanut gallery get to you, right? Perhaps you can appreciate, then, the position of my client, who fears for her job. She simply wants the behavior to stop. You've got yourself a get-out-of-jail-free card here, Mr. Edwards, and I suggest you stop trying to shove it up my ass."

"There's an idea."

She nodded contemplatively. "I can see this is doing no good whatsoever."

His expression suddenly changed. As if he finally got the joke.

"What's a discrimination claim bringing these days, thirty grand? Fifty? I had a friend, got hit four times in a year, and the poor bastard had only nailed one of the women making the accusations. That's an expensive indulgence, don't you think?"

"My suggestion to you is to look in the mirror and ask yourself which of your employees are worth that kind of money, and decide what you're going to do about it. Seems simple enough . . . just start acting with a little decorum around here, and this will all go away."

"Will *you* go away with it?"

Her smile vanished. "You know, I really hope you screw this up. I'm going to enjoy squeezing six figures out of you, maybe cost you your job."

"Not a chance, lady."

"You cross the line with my client one more time, it's a done deal. Try me. Please."

"That's not a bad idea. Trying you, I mean."

Sharon Hobbs nodded and stood, then reached down for her briefcase. She turned toward the door, stopping as her hand hit the handle.

"My client was wrong," she said. "About one thing, at least."

"And what might that be?"

The smirk returned. "She said you were really good-looking." It then widened into a smile, a full-blown bill-board special with a multitude of implications, as she pushed open the door and walked with purpose through the office toward the elevator lobby. The walk of a woman who knew she was being watched.

Bernie saw that Wesley didn't move as he watched his guest walk away. When she was gone he got up and went to his glass wall, standing there with his hands behind his back, surveying his kingdom. She had to divert her eyes to avoid him noticing her watching.

A moment later she chanced another peek. This time he was standing the same way, only now next to the exterior window, staring out at the parking lot. Bernie stood up so that she could see the lot more clearly her-self. The woman who had just been there was crossing the pavement toward her car. She got into a bright red Corvette, which in itself was an interesting choice of ve-hicle for someone who looked more like Princess Diana than Diana Ross.

Wesley didn't move as he watched the car pull out of the lot and then disappear, and he didn't move for sev-eral more minutes after that.

"Game on," said Diana into her mobile phone. Da-mien was somewhere over Utah in the jet, one of Wes-ley's personal loans of the aircraft that kept Paul Lampkin the pilot busy, while Diana the Huntress tended to the business of their games until he got home. He flew without a copilot for these unfunded trips with their oh-so-needy passengers, and was coming back to Scottsdale now by himself. He usually called her from the airplane, sometimes talking for hours on the company dime, using a secure air-to-ground frequency that was safe from even the most clever of eavesdroppers.

"He bought it then?" said Damien. There was a faint whisper of jet-engine ambiance in the background.

"Swallowed it like bad medicine, and now he's shitting his pants."

"Sounds like you had fun."

"I should have been a lawyer. Get paid for fucking with people like that."

"Some of us, like me for instance, do get paid for doing what we love. And you're right—you'd have been a scary lawyer. Definitely the district attorney type."

"Seeking the death penalty."

Taking the mocking tone of a court official, he said, "Representing the state of Arizona, Lady Death."

"Absolutely."

"So . . . let the games begin. We have an even playing field. The lovely Bernadette Kane has just been declared a free agent."

"As long as you have a penis, love, it'll never be even."

"We'll see about that, won't we, love."

She lowered her voice to a purr. "I want blood, Damien."

Other than his breathing there was silence on the line, and she could visualize him touching the serpent as it grew, alone at thirty-five thousand feet, getting off somewhere over Provo.

She touched the STOP button on her phone and smiled. After a moment the smile faded away, replaced by shadows that reached all the way back to Dallas.

20

She was easy to spot because there was never anybody in this place, especially at this hour. Hell, she would be easy to spot at Bank One Ballpark on opening day, dressed as she was. Jerry tried to be cool about it, but there was no way he wasn't going to get closer. In an otherwise empty showroom, standing shoulder to shoulder tends to invite conversation if you got past the initial go-screw-yourself look.

The Collection Connection was, as Jerry liked to tell his gamer friends, "the shit." This was party central for the real graphic novel enthusiast, with back issues and a computer database that could put your mouse on virtually anything ever published. Toss in the posters and action figures and a bunch of sports and movie memorabilia, and you had nerd nirvana. They even played cool rock music, and loud. The owners had initially put some video games near the door, but that drew the wrong crowd and they were gone after a month. This was a purist haven now. You could spend hours just knocking around. The owners didn't care, and he'd done it many times. Out here in Peoria, there was no way he'd run into someone from work, which was just how he liked it.

It was eight thirty, half an hour before closing. He'd been here for forty-five minutes when she came in, frantically chewing bubble gum, wearing a tight stretch short-sleeve top, black jeans with a thick studded belt, and suspenders that arched directly over her nipples. But it was the hair that got him—long and dark, pulled back and braided into a single thick strand, with one long wisp escaping to the front of her face, causing her to pull or blow it back frequently. Her pants were tucked into midcalf Doc Marten boots, laced in front, with their trademark blocky heels. Her arms and wrists showed traces of ink, which totally turned Jerry on.

After a few minutes of cruising the aisles she looked his way, caught him scoping her out. He glanced down quickly, nerves zapping prickly charges through his skin. The chick looked exactly like—he was embarrassed to think it, it was too freaking good to be true—exactly like Angelina Jolie channeling Lara Croft. His favorite actress in his favorite movie playing his absolute ultimate fantasy woman. Well, second favorite, anyway, but they'd not yet done the movie for his number one. She even had the lips, and while no one on the planet had Angelina lips except Angelina, these weren't bad. Not bad at all, in fact. Didn't hurt that she had a subtle shade of pink lipstick on, either.

As she thumbed through some comics in another aisle, Jerry positioned himself slightly behind so he could watch with more discretion. He'd come here tonight to browse, and while this wasn't what he'd expected, it was a nice bonus. She was older, maybe too old for this place and this look, could be thirty, give or take five years. The clothes and the hair warped the usual benchmarks of age. Those glorious lips were moving slightly to the lyrics of the song of the moment, and her head bobbed slightly as she thumbed through back issues of Marvel comics. The books were categorized by publisher, and Marvel had the most square footage in the store.

It took him fifteen minutes to work up the nerve to say something. The process nearly had him nauseous, his stomach not wanting any part of it. He actually gave it up several times, but there was something about her, and with the way things were going for him these days, now was the time to take a chance. She'd finally caught his eye and even smiled at one point. Definitely the time.

After all, he thought, he was going to be freaking rich in the near future, and a lady like this on his arm would be icing on that cake. Delicious, sweet, black icing.

"Sevendust," he said as he moved to the bin across from hers. All she had to do was look up and there he'd be.

She did, raising her eyebrows as she said, " 'Praise'."

"Excuse me?"

" 'Praise.' The song . . . it's called 'Praise'. Cut two on their third CD."

He whistled silently, nodding his head. "Wow. You're good."

This made her smile as she went back to thumbing through the comics.

An awkward moment came and went. If he didn't climb aboard now, he'd miss the wave.

"You collect?" he said, making sure his voice was loud enough over the music. But not too loud. This was delicate business.

She nodded but didn't look up, still mumbling the Sevendust lyrics, which were as dark as her eyes. She wasn't going to make this easy for him.

"Marvel?" he asked.

She looked up this time and seemed to study him for a moment, as if considering whether to play or send him packing. Her head continued to bob with the music and she still chewed her gum, and from this proximity he was sorry he'd taken the shot. Not because of disappointment—quite the contrary. She was beautiful, not a word often applied to gamer chicks or comic book collectors. In fact, he couldn't remember ever seeing a "beautiful" woman in here, and it was unsettling.

Finally she smiled, and he could breathe again.

"Mostly Marvel," she said. "I collect women characters . . . the antiheroes."

"You mean, like, villainesses?"

"Yeah. Marvel has the most. Not necessarily the best, but the most."

"Chaos has the best," he shot back, a bit too eagerly, he thought. He had just branded himself a comic nerd.

"You got that right," she said just as quickly.

His heart was pounding.

"You collect Lady Death?" he asked.

"Lady Death, Purgatori, Bad Kitty . . . Chaos rocks the bad girls. But Marvel, I mean talk about a sorority of evil . . . Black Cat, Black Widow, Electra . . . you hear they're making a movie with her? That chick from *Alias,* I think."

"I heard that. She rocks."

"Yeah. I do her, Viper, Nightshade, Mantis, Tigra, Valkyrie, Madame Web. . . ."

"You've got all those books?"

"Not all. That's why I'm here, seeing what's come in. You?"

He raised his eyebrows, not sure what she was asking.

"Who do you collect?" she clarified.

"Well, I've got all the Lady Death . . . I'm hoping they do a movie for her, but I haven't heard. I've got all the Dark Horse stuff, Buffy and Angel. . . ."

"Dark Horse did *Barb Wire,*" she offered.

"Got it on video. Pamela rocks." He immediately regretted using the same adjective twice. He was sounding like a fifteen-year-old. An excited one, at that.

The woman—this was no girl, that's for sure—nodded and smiled. It changed her, it was a too-polished smile instead of the shy, awkward smile of the younger chicks who dressed this way—gamers, punks, wannabes. She sounded intelligent, well schooled.

His stomach was still twisting, but for a different reason now. He needed to elevate his game.

"I'm Diana," she said. She reached across the book bins and extended her hand, which were tipped with short black fingernails. He noticed the tattoo of a spider-web on the flesh between her thumb and the base of her forefinger. His heart skipped at the sight.

"Jerry. Live around here?"

"No. You?"

"Mesa."

"Holy shit . . . what are you, lost?" She laughed.

"Dedicated."

"One of Lady Death's slaves."

His stomach knotted as he tried to muster a natural smile. "You could say that."

"You know who her father was?"

"Matthias," he shot back, "six-hundred-sixty-sixth-generation descendant of the fallen angels." He smiled, making sure the next question was taken in good humor. "You know who her mother was?"

Diana snorted an are-you-shitting-me? laugh. "Marion, from an angelic bloodline. Lady Death's name is Hope, she renounced her humanity in a trick by Lucifer and became Death, and when she cast Lucifer through the gates of heaven she became the supreme ruler in hell."

I'm in love, Jerry thought to himself.

She wore a proud little grin; her nodding was no longer to the music.

"What do you do besides read comic books?" she asked.

"You mean, like, for a living?"

"I mean, like, yeah, for a living." She was mocking him, but not with meanness. She was playing along.

"I'm in computers."

"There's a surprise."

"Really. I'm a programming manager for a software company. How about you?"

Her smile turned sly, as if some evil strand of female DNA was preventing her from being quite this easy this quickly.

"I'm a personal trainer. Bally."

Perfect. A passion for fantasy and rock-hard abs. He had died and gone to fantasy heaven. Or perhaps this was hell, ruled by Lady Death herself.

"So, you probably go out with, like, weight lifters and stuff."

This made her chuckle. "Slow down, cowboy."

"No, I mean . . . okay. Busted."

They shared the giggle now. His eyes instinctively lowered to the ground.

"I don't go out. Not much."

He looked back up. "Me neither."

"Hard to find compatible Lady Death aficionados out there, isn't it."

He nodded. "You play video?"

She nodded. "Nailed a Rank A house on Luigi's Mansion on the first night."

"No way. You play GameCube?"

"Not much. I have a PlayStation, but my friend has a Cube."

"First night?"

"You don't believe me? Try me."

"Are you serious?"

"Do I look serious?" She stepped back and opened her arms, as if to display the head-to-toe merchandise. Right on cue, the loud music suddenly snapped off and the house lights flashed on and off.

"You plan that?" he asked. His heart was pounding so hard he was sure his shirt was rippling.

She twirled her fingers in a witchlike manner. "Lady Death has *powers*!"

He tried to chuckle with her, but there was so much overload in his system that he wasn't sure how he sounded.

"Cool," he said. "You want to, like, grab a beer or something? I mean . . ."

"I'd love a beer. There's a steak place next to the ballpark, Texas something or other. . . ."

"I know it."

"Meet you there in ten."

"Deal." He shuffled a moment, still the fifteen-year-old. "Be there in ten."

She smiled, then went back to sorting through the racks of comics.

He walked away, wondering if he should stay, walk

her to her car, and why she wasn't heading out the door
like him. The room seemed eerily empty with the
music off.

He waited for her in the parking lot. The only other
car there was a spanking new red Corvette.

It took an agonizing fifteen minutes for her to arrive
at the bar. He'd considered staying in the lot to watch
the Corvette, but that would have seemed odd, him leaving first and then lingering. Even gamers had to muster
up a little class in situations like this. Now was not the
time for *odd*—he was struggling enough with that issue
as it was. But she seemed to like his eccentricities, indeed, even share a few of them. And she had scored a
Rank A house on Luigi, so what else was there?

It occurred to him that this was too good to be true.
But then, like every guy who had ever sensed a wake-
up call for his mojo, his judgment clouded in the wake
of an invitation from a beautiful lady. Yea, though I
walk smack dab into the valley of death, I shall fear no
evil because I'm blinded by hormones. I go willingly with
my head up my ass, with hope and a hard-on, and promise to be surprised later on when I get freaking scorched.

She arrived with a copy of a Lady Death comic book.
She plunked it down on the table as she slid into the
booth across from him.

He picked it up, checked the date of issue. "*This* is
cool."

"For you," she said. "Don't say you already have it
because it came out today."

"You bought this for me?"

"Got one for me, too. Check out the cover."

He looked down at the book. Lady Death was standing on a pile of skulls, one thigh-booted leg raised upon
the summit, bathed in heavenly light streaming down
through a crack between angry black clouds. Her gloved
arms were raised as if beseeching the gods behind those
clouds, holding a wicked pronged spear in one hand and
a bullwhip in the other. Her long golden hair was thick

and fell to the small of her back, and the wind was whipping it into a frenzy that seemed to meld with the smoke rising around her. Her eyes were black, her lips red, her breasts ridiculously full.

A feminist's worst nightmare. Sure weren't many of those in the comic book trade these days.

"Sexy, isn't it," said Diana, her voice suddenly, deliberately low and full of breath.

Jerry looked up to see that she was staring at him over the rim of her glass of beer, which she had raised to her mouth. Her expression was somewhere between a smile and a challenge, and clearly she was soaking up his reaction, fully engaged in making him squirm.

It was then, in that moment, that he knew he was as good as dead.

They talked and stretched two beers over ninety minutes. She was suddenly interested in hearing about his job, which he described with an honest humility borne of the belief that there was nothing remotely interesting about it, especially to a mysterious woman with one foot in the Twilight Zone. He managed to squeeze out some of her personal details between her probing—she was new in town, her parents had died and left her some money, so she'd moved here from L.A. to pass the time with the Bally thing until she decided what she wanted to do with the rest of her life. Mostly he tried to swing the conversation back to the unreal but familiar world of comic books—"Did you know that the guy who wrote *Vampirilla* claims the CIA made him kill JFK? True story. . . ."—but she was coming down to earth. He sensed he needed to pull it back, at least from his level of obsession, which bordered on religion and occupied far too much of the real estate in his brain for anyone to accept or understand.

For her it was just a thing, a hobby, perhaps even a fascination, and he should be content with that. He'd blown more than one potential sexual relationship by prying open his shell too soon, exposing the dark desires he kept sequestered there, fed by his fantasies and given flight by the comics he read and the games he played. He had to remind himself that this began as her game, it was she who had opened the cover of this unfolding comic book, and it would be her who would write the script.

"So, how about that PlayStation challenge?" she said as she drained what remained of the beer, which was by now almost room temperature. "You up for it?"

"I thought it was a Cube challenge."

"I have a PlayStation. But if you'd rather not . . ."

Her smile was coy, in complete schoolgirl contradiction to the dark persona she was going for when she put on tonight's outfit. In two hours he would be certain of two things about this woman—first, she was a study in complex contradictions, which he found curiously delicious. With an I.Q. as high as his, it was hard to find a connection that didn't force him to slow down. And second, she was perhaps the most sexually compelling female he'd ever met, due in no small part to the first issue.

"Like I'm gonna say no?" he said, trying for a coy grin of his own.

"As long as you're up for it." She nibbled at the tip of her tongue, making sure he understood that the double entendre was deliberate.

"No problem there," he said, feeling his cheeks flush.

"I'm going to whup your ass," she said as she slid out of the booth. And then, with a little wink, she added, "and maybe we'll play some video, too."

"Oh my God," was what Jerry Grasvik said in a barely audible voice as he gazed upon her naked flesh. Diana had purposefully turned around before pulling her top up over her head, and she remained facing the mirrored wall of her bedroom as she slipped out of her pants, allowing him a view she knew he wasn't expecting, one that would either send him flying out the door or into a speechless stupor. It was always the latter, so she

never really considered the former as a possibility. Her
body would have been enough to elicit such a response
from any man with functioning glands, but in Jerry's case
he'd moved on to the exquisite tapestry that covered her
back, and his mind was suddenly engaged in a way his
glands couldn't fathom. She raised a hand behind her
head and pulled the long braid away, allowing him a
clear view of the coiled serpent that rose to become the
hand of a woman grasping an apple. At first he didn't
see the bright red Jagger lips on the cheek of her ass,
but when he did he said it again, even softer this time—
"Oh, my God. . . ."

He didn't see her smile in response.

She turned, glowing in the soft light, and now his eyes
beheld the thin brass rings through both nipples, and the
braided wire tattoo around her biceps was suddenly the
most bewitching sight he'd ever seen.

He was erect, harder than he'd ever been in his life.

She'd attacked him as soon as they entered the house,
pushing him back onto the first couch they encountered
and sucking the confusion out of every orifice in his
skull. He quickly forgot the hundred questions he'd for-
mulated while following her here—who was she calling
on the mobile phone, was this really her two-million-
dollar house with its ten-million-dollar view, how much
freaking money did her parents leave her, what's up with
those movie posters on the walls, and whose BMW was
that parked out front?—all of it filed for later as he
surrendered to her mouth and her hands and the guttural moaning that came from deep in her throat as she
tried to swallow him whole. She'd quickly rendered him
naked, leaving his clothes in the living room as she led
him into her bedroom by the penis—literally—finding it
hilarious that he didn't argue. She'd pushed him into a
plush leather chair in a boudoir sitting area overlooking
all of Scottsdale, and that was when she turned her back
and began to strip, moving sensuously to the music—
soft flutes, suited to an Asian garden—that had been
playing over the house's integrated system from the mo-

ment they arrived. Maybe the place was wired, one of those state-of-the-art mobile phone links where you could dial up your music and air conditioning or whatever else you desired in the way of computer-generated comfort before you hit your driveway, which in this case was as long as your average par four.

She offered her hand, and he stood to accept it. They embraced and kissed as she turned and maneuvered him toward the bed, where she again pushed him, this time to his back. She mounted him immediately, pinning his arms to the mattress as she leaned forward and began her dance.

"You like?" she said, her eyes at half mast as if she were stoned.

"Jerry like," he whispered back.

Fifteen minutes later Jerry not only liked, he was sure he had seen the face of God, because only God could have created such pleasure. She evolved from sensuous to animalistic to something approaching insanity, and he wasn't sure how many times she came, or if she even came at all. It was as if she was trying to crush his pelvis, absorb his very being deeper and deeper into her body. He was certain she didn't notice or even care about the moment of his climax, which arrived with such sudden force that he couldn't stifle a scream that sounded more like torture than release.

She was perfect. He had made love to Lady Death herself. And somehow, he had survived.

The mirrored wall in the bedroom slid back on its tracks before Jerry Grasvik had even reached the end of the driveway, wide-eyed and still unable to believe his good fortune. Behind it was a small enclosed sitting area, furnished with a soft chair and a table just large enough for a glass of wine. This was where Damien had been sitting with a glass of dry Chablis, watching through the one-way glass as Diana showed Jerry Grasvik a new level of feminine hunger. He was naked for this private show . . . the serpent had come out to play.

Damien and Diana had refined their deal somewhat. Rather than a race to the finish, their challenge would be gauged according to attempts, thus eliminating the need to rush things. Seduction was a process of preparation, at least when done properly, and fairness dictated that each of them take the time they needed. But preparation aside, it was, they both knew, still a woman's world when it came to the prerogatives of sex. It wasn't the first bad bet Damien had made with her, and it wouldn't be the last. He was, they both laughingly acknowledged, a glutton for punishment.

Diana would take the first shot.

By noon she had booked an appointment for collagen injections in her lips, with Damien there to hold her hand. By three she'd found just the right brunette wig at the Arizona Mills discount mall, already braided, plus a few new things appropriate to the occasion. By six she'd absorbed everything the Internet had to offer about comic books, Lady Death in particular—it was in these moments that her nearly photographic memory came in quite handy—while Damien went off to see if tonight might be Jerry's lucky night. By seven she'd put on her new things and went out to try her luck on a GameCube demo station at the Fashion Mall, with a helpful Luigi's Mansion tutorial from a wide-eyed clerk who, most conveniently, said she looked a little like Angelina Jolie. *A little* was perfect.

Just before eight, sitting in front of her computer as she continued to bone up on comic book lore, she received the anticipated call from Damien. He had followed Jerry home from work, sat outside his apartment for several hours eating a Quizno's sub, then followed him to the 101 heading north. He'd found several receipts and advertisements for the Collection Connection in Jerry's apartment, so they knew this was where he indulged his fantasies. As soon as Jerry passed the curve at Princess there was only one place he could be going, so that's when Damien placed the call. "Game on," he'd said, and with that she headed to her car. Diana's preparations during the day could have simply been a dress rehearsal had Jerry not headed out, but they got lucky tonight.

As would he.

This was how it worked—despite the competitive nature of their games, they willingly served as each other's second as necessary. For Damien in particular, it didn't matter who won or lost. It was, as they say, how you played the game. And for Damien, how you suffered the consequences later.

And now it was over. It had all gone down just as she'd said it would.

Diana waited for Damien on the bed, legs spread, her sex glistening with the remnants of Jerry Grasvik's visit. This was part of it, sharing the filth, the merging of sins. Damien crawled over her from the foot of the bed, hovered for a moment, then pressed himself down, entering the darkness, drowning in her heat.

She allowed him to move for about a minute before she spoke. A minute was all that was required on nights like this.

"Blood," she whispered, pressing her teeth hard against the cartilage of his ear. "Soon."

Damien moaned as his body suddenly seized, his head thrown back, the veins in his neck standing in stark relief to his skin. He remained absolutely silent as his orgasm overwhelmed time and space itself. Diana knew not to move, to let him take it where he wished, though she watched his face with wide-eyed wonder. He was never more beautiful than this.

Without further words they turned on their sides, still joined, her leg swung over his hip, his thumb gently stroking her temple. Within minutes the thumb stopped and they were asleep, a flute playing softly in the background.

21

The office politics at Oar Research were nothing if not amusing, at least to Bernie. Being a freelancer she had a certain distance from the rules that politics dictated, and she could laugh at what she saw without repercussions. Wesley Edwards, for instance, was both feared and respected among the rank and file, perhaps because he was the only person on the property who wore a tie, perhaps because a stern look from him could set a career back years. There was a set of special engraved coffee cups in the break room that were for Wesley's exclusive use, usually with bankers and clients. There were no signs or placards to that effect, but everyone knew. He had his personal parking spot—hallowed ground. In fact, if an innocent car parked there, Nadine was to be notified immediately and a manhunt for the culprit would soon commence. Many employees referred to him as Mr. Edwards, which was unheard of in a world where Intel folks called their boss Andy and Steve Jobs still wore jeans to Apple board meetings. Some called him Big Ed behind his back, no doubt in reference to his license plate. This morning Bernie walked past the conference room to see that Wesley was holding court, using a laser pointer with the lights dimmed, transferring data from a laptop to a massive LCD flat-screen monitor while wielding a wireless mouse. Rather than missing the old days, which in her case had involved an overhead projector and slides, it made her stomach sour.

They hadn't crossed paths since their drink together two nights earlier, though their eyes had connected through the glass walls of his office, in response to which he nodded ever so slightly without changing his facial expression. She hadn't expected otherwise, and she wondered if he was waiting for her to make a move, which needed to happen outside of the workplace if at all. It never entered her head that this was anything remotely close to a cold shoulder. No, this was posing, decorum, image management. This was Wesley being Wesley, who had a front to put up for the troops.

The anxiety of doing nothing was making her crazy. She had come here for justice, not to put together a Web page for Oar Research. Her ego, her ability to seduce the boss, had only one purpose, and that was to forward her objective. The project itself was kid stuff, actually—she'd approved an initial design template and navigational strategy, and while graphic artists and programmers were assembling the alpha version, Jerry was working with a freelance writer on the content. Or at least that's what she was told, since she hadn't met the writer and still didn't know what the content of the site was to be. That, Jerry had said, was still up in the air. There really wasn't all that much for her to do at this point, which made the waiting game all the more frustrating. The off hours were even worse. She had no one to call and had seen all the movies that were out. She even had trouble concentrating on a book—she'd started the one written by her new neighbor—so she was left with remembering the past, which didn't help.

The phone on her desk at work had yet to be connected—high-tech business, indeed—so she found herself walking around a lot, jumping on phones at empty desks to do her business, reading a lot of company literature. Nadine told her that some guy had called, but that didn't make sense. Eric wouldn't have left a message here, and would have called her condo anyway. She started to e-mail him to see if that was the case, but thought better of it. She knew full well that IT managers could see every keystroke that occurred within their domain, that there was a digital record of it, and she didn't want Eric connected to this in case something went south.

So this morning she left for lunch early, walking over to P.F. Chang's for some take-out lo mein. As she walked back through the parking lot she saw Wesley's Escalade pulling out, and without hesitation decided to seize the moment. She had no idea where he was headed, but she needed data, and when she needed something she prompted the fates to provide it. Instead of going back to her desk she went to her Volvo.

Keeping a healthy distance because he knew her car, she followed him down Paradise behind a massive strip mall, where he connected to Frank Lloyd Wright Boulevard and then the 101. He exited at Shea, stopped at a Fry's, went in, and minutes later came out carrying a bouquet of flowers.

Bingo. Maybe she'd get to see who else saw the sensitive side of Wesley Edwards.

He drove a few more miles east on Shea, curiously close to her condo, actually, then pulled into what she at first thought was a golf course. She parked across the street to allow some time to pass, ate a little lo mein while it was still warm, then drove through the gates, quickly realizing how wrong she had been. This was a cemetery, one-half square mile of dead people and headstones. She could easily spot the white Escalade, then, seeing that no one else was around, realized how easily he could see *her*.

She pulled behind a brick building where the cemetery landscapers kept their implements and turned off the engine. Two Hispanic gentlemen were working inside, getting ready to dispatch the next customer to eternity. They looked up briefly but paid no attention to her after that. Beyond the building, across the expanse of the grass, she saw Wesley get out of his vehicle and walk to the middle of an open space, his white shirt glowing in the midday sun. Even from here, she could see that his necktie was pulled loose, and that he wore sunglasses. He kneeled, putting the flowers on the ground, and arranging them just so. He remained in that posture for two or three minutes, one hand rubbing his chin, head bowed. Then he got back into the Caddy and drove quickly off the property, as if in a great hurry.

Bernie waited for a moment, then made a choice. She drove to where he had parked and got out. There was only one bouquet of flowers on the impeccable grass, which was dimpled with flat grave markers. Looking back to the entrance to ensure her solitude, she got out, leaving the door open and the engine running. She walked over to the flowers, a mixed bouquet typical of what men buy, which were wedged into the dirt next to the marker, keeping them upright.

She bent slightly to read the name: Dorothy Edwards. Under the name was a date of birth, seventy-seven years ago. Next to that was the date of death . . . the seventh anniversary of which was today.

What she had seen really changed nothing, except perhaps the lens through which she now viewed Wesley Edwards. Killers have mothers, too, but this didn't keep them from the gas chamber, didn't make the people who sent them there so much as blink. But she had to admit, there was something tender about what he'd done, alone and for no one else's benefit. She was sure most of the people at Oar would be somewhat surprised to know what their boss had done today at lunch.

Seven years, and his mother still mattered.

If nothing else, it solidified Bernie's next move, made it easier to step into. She would ask Wesley Edwards out to a ballgame.

Her only option was to corner him in his office. But you didn't just stop in for a chat with Wesley Edwards. He was always in a hurry, either on the phone or on his way to or from a meeting. The good news was that everyone in the company knew he was involved with Bernie's project, or at least interested in it, and the two of them having a conversation right here in front of God and the saints would not be alarming.

At least she prayed Wesley and the saints would agree.

The bad news, though, was that his body language had been particularly ominous today. She'd seen him having an unfriendly chat with Nadine in his office earlier, a meeting that ended with her storming off in a huff. Several other employees had been in there as well—all women, come to think of it, none of whom even got to sit down—and upon leaving each looked as if they'd just been diagnosed with breast cancer. The energy was bad today, but she couldn't wait. The energy surrounding Wesley Edwards was bad every day.

She was not without a plan. She borrowed a phone to call the ticket office at Dillard's, an anchor store at the Fashion Mall, putting two box seats at "the BOB"—Bank One Ballpark—in her name for the Diamondbacks game that night.

At around three o'clock an opportunity presented itself. Wesley had been alone in his office for some time now, though constantly on the phone. He used his wireless headset even in his office, pacing behind his desk as he gazed out at the desert and did whatever it was he did all day. But he was out from behind the desk now, the headset abandoned, going through a drawer in a filing cabinet. She hurried over and knocked on the glass door, pushing it open before he had a chance to look up.

"Hey there."

He just raised his eyebrows with no expression at all.

"Offer you can't refuse . . . tonight, two seats behind first base, lower level, on the aisle. How about it?"

He blinked three times in quick succession. As if he couldn't believe his ears. Already she knew this was a mistake, but there was no backing off at this point.

"Come in," he finally said, looking away. He shut the

drawer and went back to his chair, taking a file with him. When he saw that she remained standing next to the door, he motioned for her to sit.

She didn't.

"I need to clarify something," he said. His voice had an unexpected softness to it, similar to the way he'd talked to her the other night.

"Clarify away." Her stomach was suddenly a cesspool of regret.

"It was just a get-to-know-you drink. I never positioned it as anything else. I don't date employees."

She rocked back a little, as if dodging something— probably the urge to call him on the bullshit he claimed he so despised. Heat assaulted her cheeks, which she knew was impossible to hide from the world.

"I'm not your employee, Wesley."

"I beg to differ. In fact, at your day rate you are my highest-paid employee."

She nodded. He wasn't smiling, so she wasn't about to either.

"I'm sorry to have bothered you."

"I appreciate the offer."

"Right."

She turned toward the door.

"Something's come up for me," he said, adding a tone of helplessness to his voice. Of course, his trying to pretend that her invitation was out of school would be an embarrassment, and he was far too cool to get blindsided by anything embarrassing. An explanation was called for, and Wesley had an explanation for everything.

She turned back, cocking her head with just a smidgeon of sarcasm that announced he wasn't going to get away with this. She wanted him to know that she, too, was far too cool for embarrassment.

"Maybe when the project's over," he said. "I'd like that."

She pursed her lips, giving the impression that she was considering it. Her response here was crucial, because it would define their relationship going forward.

With one quick dip of her chin she snatched open the door and got the hell out of there. No words, no tone, no risk.

Besides, she didn't want him to hear the sound of her dark agenda—indeed, her entire world—crashing back to square one.

> **22** <

E—It's all over. W just slammed the door in my face, and if there's a back door I haven't found it. Proximity is everything in this game, and it just went away. I'll probably finish my project here, take the money and run. Then again, I may not. Depends if I can remain civil, knowing what I know. Or if I can live with myself for doing nothing. To be honest, I'm more afraid that I WILL do something. And that I'll regret it later.

You were right. Nothing good can come of this. The past won't go away, and it won't leave me alone. So I must leave while I can.

I know I shouldn't be emailing you, but you said to if it's important. Thank you for helping me. Best to Shannon. Will contact you when I'm back in town.

Love, B.

Bernie sat with her feet up on the windowsill, gazing out at the Scottsdale airport, where a succession of private jets had been approaching from the north and taking off to the south, climbing right outside her window. She wondered if one of them was the Oar jet, but since Wesley was a mere eighty feet away, chatting madly into the mouthpiece of his headset as he waved his hands for unseen emphasis, that was unlikely. She knew that the plane was used for other purposes than Wesley's personal itinerary, and wondered fleetingly if one of the jets out there was carrying the most gorgeous pilot she'd ever met.

Now that she'd e-mailed Eric, which in her mind constituted a decision, she felt a lightness she hadn't known in months. The world would go on. And someday, if there was anything at all to the notion of karma—and she believed that there was—Wesley Edwards would get his head handed to him on a platter. It's just that she desperately wanted to be the server when it happened. But now, that dark pleasure seemed impossible. Short of crossing the line, there was no way to expose Wesley to the consequences of his actions. She needed an angle, some crime to expose, some trap to snap shut. But without access to his life she was finished. Sure, he'd said that perhaps they could get together when her project was over, but that was just a limp male kiss-off.

Peggy would rest in peace either way. That had been Eric's message to Bernie all along.

She felt a hand close around her shoulder. She jumped, then turned to see that Nadine was sitting on the corner of her desk, staring out the window. She could immediately smell her perfume, which she'd already noted Nadine refreshed every day right after lunch. She looked like she'd stepped right out of an issue of *Working Woman*.

Nadine said, "He talk to you, too?"

Bernie furrowed her brow and shook her head.

"Oh, come on, sweetheart. I know you two had a drink downtown."

Bernie's mouth gaped open. "How . . ."

"The night has eyes."

Bernie smiled sadly as she shook her head. "Someone saw us."

"Someone always sees us."

"So what do you mean, did he talk to you, too?"

Nadine smirked, as if being patient. "Well, you don't exactly look happy sitting here, so *something* happened. And I saw you in there with him. . . ."

"Do you miss *anything* around here?"

"Not much. Given what's going on, I just assumed . . . you know . . ."

"No, I don't. *What's* going on?"

Nadine's smile was coy. She looked back out the window as she spoke. "I told you that Wesley and I were once two ships that passed in the night. Bumped, actually . . . swapped a little oil, in fact."

She waited for Bernie to respond, which she did with a nod.

"Well, I got a little talking-to today. Me and Robyn Delemarter and Karen Krager and Barb what's-her-name." She paused, then added, "And you."

They locked eyes, Nadine's smiling, Bernie's confused.

"The big red flag," Nadine continued. "All of us in Wesley Edwards's personal address book had it waved in our faces today. Wesley in CYOA mode."

Bernie shook her head. "You're *way* too far out in left field on this one."

Nadine looked back at the skyline. "Really? He didn't ask you if you had talked to anyone about seeing him . . . socially, I mean?"

"No. That's what he asked you?"

"He didn't imply that it would be for your own good to respect what went on between you, that there were career implications for both of you?"

"That wasn't what we were talking about."

"Really. Maybe you get an exemption as the current woman of the hour."

Bernie felt the heat returning to her face for the second time today. "Is that what I am?"

Nadine leaned down, lowering her voice. She cast a quick look over her shoulder to the office to make sure their privacy was still intact.

"Look, I don't mean to pry. Okay, I do, but that's not the point. This guy is bad news. I like you, okay? Somebody's threatening a lawsuit, and he's scared. So he's hitting some old bases, waving his dick around. I'll tell you this, when an animal like Wesley gets cornered, get out of the cage. Someday somebody's going to nail that bastard, but until that happens . . . I just hope you don't get caught in the cross fire, is all. That's all I'm saying here."

Bernie instinctively checked Wesley's office, just as Nadine had.

"You think he's into something that's, I don't know, illegal?"

"If it isn't illegal then it's unethical, I can tell you that. There's more shit going on than you'd believe, sweet-heart. Some of the people he's talking to are, shall we say, a bit on the shady side. Don't ask me how I know, but I know."

Bernie felt her pulse accelerating. "You don't like him much, do you?"

This wiped all trace of mean-spirited humor from Nadine's expression. She said, "You once accused me of being in love with him."

"They're not always mutually exclusive."

With that, Bernie thought there was an outside chance Nadine was going to cry. A moment passed as Nadine fought for control of her emotions. Then she said, "I'd like to see the bastard get what's coming to him. That's all."

Bernie drew a deep breath, sucking in the fresh air of renewed hope. Now was the time to take a chance. "What if I told you I'd like to help you with that?" she said.

Nadine's head snapped to Bernie, her eyes wide.

"Go on."

"I mean, what if there was something going down, something the authorities would be grateful to know about."

"Count on it."

"What if we could expose it, get close enough to it to understand it, then document it somehow, turn it over to the right people."

Nadine's face evolved from wonder to suspicion.

"I thought you liked the guy? I mean, aren't you two . . . ?"

Bernie was already shaking her head. "Listen, I'm trusting you. You've told me things, so you must trust me, too. We had a drink. That's it."

"Might be dangerous," said Nadine.

Bernie smiled mischievously. "Sounds fun, if you ask me."

Nadine didn't return the smile. "Why would you do this? I mean, you've got a job here, making some good money . . . why would you put all that in jeopardy for no reason?"

Bernie looked hard into Nadine's eyes and said, "Maybe I have a reason."

Nadine held her gaze, then nodded. "Maybe you do."

"We could help each other," offered Bernie. "You monitor calls, keep a log. You see something, I go in, check it out."

"Definitely dangerous," said Nadine.

"How badly do you want his ass in a sling, that's the question."

Nadine pivoted her head, taking in the whole office. She didn't look back as she said, "There are over two hundred people here, decent people, families, a few pricks but mostly people who deserve a shot. It's been good . . . good pay, nice benefits . . . it all goes away if Wesley gets caught with his hand in the cookie jar."

"What are you saying?"

"I'm saying we all go down with him. Who knows, maybe he's planning on cleaning the place out and disappearing. Maybe it's some kind of stock scam, in which case we all get burned. But if we can stop it, get on the right side of the fence . . ."

She looked back at Bernie.

"Not to mention the woman scorned thing," said Bernie. "Let's get real."

Nadine smiled a complex smile. "I knew I liked you. Do the right thing, get a pound of flesh . . . it works for me."

Both women looked across the floor to Wesley's office. He was leaning against the glass with one hand, using his other to gesticulate emphatically. He wore his trademark headset, connected to his desktop telephone with a coiled cord. They watched him for a moment without saying anything. Bernie recalled the scene earlier that day, Wesley bent over his mother's grave, arranging flowers, and something kicked in the depths of her stomach.

No one said right and wrong would be clear, or that either would be easy.

"Somebody's got to do it," said Nadine softly, almost to herself. Then she touched Bernie on the shoulder, precisely how she'd started this discussion. "We'll talk," she said, then she got up and walked back to her station at the front desk.

Bernie watched her go, suddenly sorry that she'd sent the e-mail to Eric, buoyed with a sudden new hope that Peggy would indeed rest in peace after all.

23

It was mid-May, and the heat that assaulted Bernie's face as she walked out of the Oar Research building was nothing short of a hair dryer between the eyes at point-blank range. This wearing all black business was in direct contradiction to common sense—they should leave that little exercise in hipness to the New Yorkers who invented it and the Californians who ripped it off, neither of whom, in her experience, cared much for common or any other type of sense.

It was just after six, and her intention to go home early for a swim had been sabotaged by an impromptu meeting of the project staff, which at this point consisted of four people. Wesley had already gone for the day, thank God—she wasn't sure how that would have worked, given the conversations she had that afternoon. The meeting was to settle a dispute between the graphic designer and the assigned programmer, the former having concocted an idea—*tres cool,* he'd called it—that would have tripled the allotted budget. Besides, animations and a soundtrack on a worm-detection program seemed a bit excessive. The programmer had blown the whistle, and the two were hurling some serious four-letter adjectives at each other by the time Bernie arrived. She listened carefully, with the requisite sensitivity and thick skin where designers were concerned, then made her ruling: budget was king; the design was indeed *tres cool,* but sorry, not on this project, end of discussion.

Being overruled by a freelancer wasn't the designer's idea of *tres cool*, however, and he had bolted from the room uttering a colorful expletive.

Bernie was grinning about this when she came face-to-face with Paul Lampkin in the parking lot. Not exactly face-to-face, because she didn't look up until he spoke.

"I see you got the job," he said as they drew close. When she heard the words she looked closer, and what had been a grin exploded into a smile. A sudden little buzz in her stomach electrified her knees, almost causing them to shake.

"If it isn't Sky King," she said, accepting his handshake, remembering the effect it had had on her before, and was having again.

"Paul Lampkin," he reminded her. That was good, not too assumptive, even though he had every right to be. His smile was as blinding as the sun positioned directly over his shoulder, causing her to squint. He ran his hand back through his thick black hair, parted in the middle and continually falling forward onto his face. He was dressed as if he'd just come off the golf course, olive Tommy Bahama slacks, black polo shirt, Ecco loafers, and the hottest pair of sunglasses she'd ever seen on a man. Those pilots sure knew their shades. It was a job requirement.

"I was thinking of you today," she added, still holding his hand. It appeared he would have held the grip as long as she'd let him, so she pulled it back with the sudden realization that the energy she'd sensed crackling between them the other day was still very much at high wattage.

He said, "I'm glad to hear that."

Her smile changed to acknowledge how this sounded. "I was watching the planes land"—she flicked her eyes in the direction of the nearby airstrip—"and thought maybe one was you."

"Glad they're keeping you busy," he said, laughing softly. "Probably was. Couple of good bounces on impact, dragged a wing. . . . That was me."

She felt silly, and they both giggled in that way that is unique to flirting.

"I was thinking of you today, too," he said.

"No you weren't!" she shot back.

"Really! I actually called to see if you ever ended up working here."

She nodded approvingly. This was getting better by the second.

"Nadine, right?"

"A man should never reveal his sources."

Here came the awkward silence, neither sure whose turn was next. When a guy this hot diverted his eyes at the moment of turning the corner from flirtation to invitation, it was a good sign.

"My source said you were away from your desk, and something about not having a phone yet."

She just nodded. This time, the warmth in her cheeks felt delicious.

"I wanted to see if I could ask you to dinner sometime."

Now it was Bernie who diverted her eyes, a move that required just the right nuance, somewhere between shy and flattered, a move she was very good at.

"Of course Nadine told you all the résumé basics . . . that I'm not married, just got here and didn't know anyone. . . ."

"Actually," he said, "she didn't."

"Then how'd you know?"

"Just a hunch."

Sometimes there was no hiding from the truth. Sometimes the truth hurt, and other times, like now, it felt like a warm caress.

Behind her well-practiced expression of humility, her mind was reeling. While she'd certainly thought about seeing him again—several times, in fact—it was never anything more than a voyeuristic hit, an impending visual hormonal feast. It was no different than hoping to run into one of the city's hunky athletes or a visiting movie star, only this guy was better looking than anyone in either category. The sudden possibility of going out with him was colliding with the entire Wesley proposition, which until a few hours ago had been the only target—romantic and otherwise—on her radar.

He sensed her hesitance. "I'm sorry," he said softly, "I don't mean to be forward."

"No-no-no!" she said reassuringly. "I'm just . . . surprised."

"I can't tell if you're pleasantly surprised or you've-got-to-be-kidding-me surprised."

"Neither can I."

"Listen, I'll call you. Think it over. Better yet, you call me. Unless you're one of those women with *rules*."

"Not sure what *that* means. . . ."

"You know, rules. As in, *I-never-call-men* kind of rules."

"Princess rules," she offered with a smile that exempted her from guilt on this count.

"Exactly."

"I'm not a princess."

"Thank God."

"A queen sometimes, but never a princess."

"So you'll call me then. Nadine has the number."

"Or you'll call me. She'll have mine, too."

"Okay then."

"Okay then." Another awkward moment logged in the books.

He extended his hand, and she was happy to oblige. If they ended up in bed she'd make him shake her hand the entire time.

He continued toward the building, she toward the parking lot. Several steps later she stopped, hit by an idea that may already have come too late.

She turned and called his name. He was just opening the door when he heard her.

She walked toward him. He let the door close and returned to meet her halfway.

"Here's a thought," she offered. "I happen to have Diamondbacks tickets for tonight. My date canceled.

Short notice, I know, but hey, I have no rules about stuff like that."

"Tonight," he said.

"Right. One hundred level, right behind first base."

"Visitor's side."

"I have no idea."

"No way I sit on the visitor's side. Just kidding." He glanced at his watch, which like his sunglasses was pilot-perfect. "We should get going."

"So we're on?"

"Just let me run inside for a moment." An envelope had been in his left hand as they spoke, and he held it up now to indicate this was his business inside. "Fuel report," he said.

"I'll put this in the trunk," she said, holding up her computer bag.

"Be right back," he said. Then he turned and hurried toward the building. When he got to the door he turned, pressing the door open with his buttocks. He wore a huge grin.

"Great idea," he said. "Johnson's pitching."

"Who?"

He shook his head. "You'll see."

For a moment it all went away—her vendetta, Eric, the e-mail she had sent him, Wesley, Nadine, even Peggy. She wasn't even in Scottsdale anymore—she was back in her life, immersed in the world and moving forward, very much at home with herself for the first time in months.

She was going to a baseball game with the best-looking man in Arizona. What could be better than that?

Because of the tinted windows, not to mention the glare of a demon sun, anyone watching them from inside the building would remain unseen.

In this case, most conveniently.

It was, by all standards, a perfect evening. The seats turned out to be ideal—twenty-fifth row, straight back from first base, on the aisle for easy beer and hot dog runs. The ballpark was surreal, with its sliding roof and centerfield swimming pool.

Even the drive to the ballpark had been a delight. They went in his car, a spanking new BMW 745i, which had the interior of a spaceship. Some of the time was spent playing with the electronics, particularly the GPS screen and its many other applications, which in Bernie's voiced opinion required an extra year of grad school to understand. This made him laugh, something he did easily and often. She found her new friend to be utterly delightful, comfortable with the obligatory small talk and quick-witted. He was a bit of a smart-ass, which suited her fine. And just as Wesley had been a few nights ago, he was an easy listener, one who prompted her to talk about her job and her impressions of the area.

Once, as he leaned down to scratch his ankle, she noticed that the sleeve of his shirt rode up slightly, revealing a tattoo encircling a very compelling biceps laced with veins. It was only visible for a moment, but the sight intrigued her, not because she had a fetish or even an interest in body art, but because it opened another can of worms entirely. Paul Lampkin, golden-boy pilot, just might be a bad boy underneath all that charm. And that, in Bernie's unspoken catalog of tastes and preferences in men, was just dandy. A little spice on the main dish made the dining experience all the more rewarding.

It was game time, 7:05, when they arrived at the stadium after a brisk walk from where they'd parked some eight blocks away. In their hurry she noticed that he walked with an easy grace, and she knew she could add athletic to the list of attributes this guy was chalking up.

Women notice the little things men do when their focus is not directly on them. Most men are oblivious to this, since it's easy to be Mr. Charming one-on-one, but when pressure arrives from the flanks, women get a peek at the real character lurking beneath. Bernie didn't have to wait long for this opportunity—someone was in their seats when they arrived. The men in her past would have flashed their tickets with a disapproving grimace and impatient body language, and if resistance had been shown they'd have been quick to belly up to a confrontation. But Paul was utterly nonchalant in this situation—by the time the two young guys squatting in their seats had gathered up their beers and programs, they were all exchanging jokes and best wishes, with no need for an alpha-male demonstration of turf ownership.

She had trouble keeping her eyes on the field. Paul was somewhat of a baseball enthusiast, claiming he'd played in high school but had let it go when he went to college and took up flying in the ROTC. He'd been a pitcher, and he seemed eager to explain what would happen next, where the pitcher would spot the ball on a particular count, and he was right four out of five times, the fifth being only because the pitcher made a mistake. She'd never realized there was so much strategy involved. She'd thought they just threw the damn ball toward the plate as hard as they could. He explained the aerodynamics of the breaking pitch, how the same laws of physics that enabled an airplane to fly—Bernoulli's law, he'd called it—could be applied to the spin of a baseball thrown at sufficient speed, causing the ball to alter its course in flight.

All very interesting, but not nearly as interesting as the way his eyes twinkled as he spoke, or how he used his hands to illustrate the laws of Sir Isaac Newton and this Bernoulli character.

By the fourth inning, after they'd dispensed with the business of hot dogs and beers, she realized she hadn't asked him anything about his life. It was three-zip Diamondbacks, and Gonzo—Luis Gonzalez to the uninitiated, which she no longer was—had already parked one in the swimming pool.

"So tell me *your* life story," she said, making sure to note the timing of his response as she thrust the hot dog into her mouth. Something would have been lost had he jumped at this too quickly, but he didn't, displaying just the right level of hesitance and embarrassment.

"Bernoulli's law is much more interesting."

"I'll be the judge of that."

"If I tell you everything I'll have to kill you."

"I see . . . ex-CIA, eh?"

He wasn't smiling as he said, "Something like that." He kept his eyes on the field as he spoke.

She let a pitch or two go by before pressing the issue. Obviously, she'd hit a nerve, not a pleasant one. At some point she'd want to know, but now was not the time.

"Okay, let's start with that tattoo on your arm."

He pulled up his sleeve and she got her first good look. It appeared to be Asian lettering of some sort, very elaborately rendered. The ink had a shade of gray to it against his tan, as if it had been there a while. Just as impressive were the bands of rigid muscle visible beneath the surface of his skin.

"Vietnam?"

"I look that old to you?"

She realized immediately that she was easily a decade off the mark here. Paul was one of those men who defied age and confounded any attempt at a guess.

"What's it mean?"

"It's ancient Mandarin, means *mind your own business.* I'll tell you right off, I have others. It's a long story."

"But I should mind my own business."

"Maybe someday," he said. His smile was convincing, but she couldn't help but feel it was time to change the subject.

He was far more accommodating on the predictable stuff. He was born and raised in Oregon, where his father was a truck driver and his mother was an alcoholic after a career as a grocery cashier. He'd been a jock in school but his grades were marginal, one of those gifted kids who never applied himself. He'd gone to school in California on an ROTC scholarship, working at a local airport refueling Cessnas to pay room and board. After college he went through OTC and earned his wings, served a hitch flying C-141s after washing out of fighter school like nineteen out of twenty applicants did. He tried to latch on with United Airlines when he got out, and ended up working his way to a flight instructor rating in the civil aviation world. One thing led to another, and here he was flying fat cats around the country in their airborne limos, serving coffee and doing the preflight safety announcements himself. He'd been married in his mid-twenties, was caught with his pants down and that ended that—an interesting admission, she noted—and has been celibate ever since. He winked when he added that footnote, much to her relief.

Nowhere in the narrative had there been any mention of the CIA or the tattoos. She'd leave well enough alone for now. Like he said, maybe someday. She was more appreciative of the way he'd delivered this brief biography, very unimpressed with himself despite what she considered to be a quite impressive résumé, rushing through it because he was certain she'd only been polite in asking, pausing to appreciate a well-placed slider on the black or the turn of a spiffy double play.

Only half of what he'd said was true, of course. He had grown up in Oregon, and his father had indeed been a truck driver, just as his mother had become a dedicated alcoholic by the time he was ten. The trouble started when he came home from high school one day to find his father knocking his mother around the party room. By then he was well into what would become an obsession with the martial arts, and after a shoving match he'd put his father through the plate-glass patio door. That done, he spent the remainder of his high school years living with an aunt, who booted him the day after graduation because her live-in boyfriend was afraid of him. He'd gone to a local junior college, which was where he discovered aviation, which in Oregon was like taking up ski jumping in the Mojave Desert. He did, in fact, work at a local municipal airport refueling and washing Cessnas, taking part of his compensation in

flight time and instruction. He hadn't finished college—
he reasoned he'd rather fly airplanes and seduce older
women with real jobs—which meant that United or any
other airline would never look at him. But he did stay
around airplanes his entire life, finally earning enough
hours to advance his licenses and begin earning a living
as a flight instructor.

He'd never married, though he had lived with several
women who shared his twin obsessions with physical fitness and kinky sex. They were easy to find, and with his
looks even easier to bed. A bar fight in the late eighties
earned him a police record, the circumstances of which
were exacerbated by the fact that he kicked the shit out
of both of the arresting officers, surrendering only to the
six other policemen who arrived simultaneously bran-
dishing billy clubs—*defensive batons,* the judge had
called them—one of which caught him on the forehead,
resulting in eighteen stitches and an authority grudge
that survived to this day. His lawsuit was thrown out of
court, and the resultant police blotter had prevented him
from landing the type of corporate flying job for which
he was now fully qualified.

He moved to the Phoenix area in his mid-twenties to
get away from an ex-girlfriend who knew too much
about him and had taken to calling each and every new
woman who came into his life to explain that he had a
thing about violence and an imagination that bordered
on the psychotic. He'd hooked up with Wesley Edwards
six years later, through a woman he'd met at a college
bar in Tempe. Edwards happened to be shopping for a
pilot for his new jet and didn't want to pay the market
rate or follow all those pesky FAA rules. It was a perfect
union, one of convenience and economics, though what
had begun with a potential for friendship had quickly
found its place in the social order of things—millionaire
golden boy hires hard luck pilot boy, who would be fine
if he didn't rock the airplane. Paul had always suspected
that Wesley resented the fact that Paul was better look-

ing than him, which he wasn't used to and could tolerate only as long as Paul knew his place. Which he did—standing over him one day with his foot on his neck.

The real kicker to Paul Lampkin's story, however, was also omitted tonight. His father had died of prostate cancer when Paul was nineteen, and his mother, who was a dead ringer for Sophia Loren, married a slightly wealthy gentleman two decades her senior. When Paul was thirty his mother and stepfather, whom he'd only met twice, died in a hotel fire in South America. Irregularities in the man's will and the fact that he had no surviving children meant that Paul was the sole heir to a fortune that netted out somewhere just shy of nine million dollars.

For a while, because of his good fortune, Paul believed in God. But then the stock market tanked and it didn't last. Now all Paul believed in was the preservation of his capital and his lifestyle, not necessarily in that order. And, ahead of both, the pursuit of pleasure, the dynamics of which had evolved over the years to a level that most people couldn't comprehend.

Except for one remarkable woman, of course. Diana understood perfectly.

24

The walk back to Paul's car was conducted hand in hand, largely in silence. All was right with the world—the D-Backs had won, Randy Johnson had been brilliant, the beer was cold and the hot dogs were, well, hot. Most remarkable of all was the fact that no gremlins had popped up in these first hours of their new relationship. Everything had been perfect, as if scripted by someone who knew what she liked in a first date with potential. His grip completely enveloped hers in warmth, and she walked with a small grin on her face.

Coming around the side of a building, they immediately saw two men leaning against the side of the Beamer. Bernie felt Paul's grip stiffen just before he pulled his hand away. But they didn't break their stride; in fact, they picked it up a notch.

The men were Hispanic and young. One of them, fairly tall, wore a gray plaid shirt with only the top button fastened, the rest billowing out over the belt of baggy black pants. The other wore a sleeveless T-shirt, untucked, also with baggy black pants, and wore a black string around his head that tied right above his eyes. She could see that neither of them had bothered to tie their shoelaces. One had his arms folded; the big one was smoking a cigarette.

"What's up, guys?" said Paul as he approached. He had already pulled his keys from his pocket and hit the remote button, causing the car to issue a beep and blink its parking lights. The two toughs continued to lean on the car.

Paul and Bernie were eight feet away when they stopped. She didn't want to be here. If she had been with anyone else she would have just kept walking.

"Nice ride, man," said the one who was smoking. He flicked the butt at Paul's feet. "You got any money?"

"Listen guys, let's just call it a night, okay?" Paul actually had a lightness to his voice that Bernie was sure the thugs found offensive, if not simply amusing.

"I said, you got any money, man? You dissing me?"

"No dis. No money. S.O.L., pal. Sorry."

Paul shot a look at Bernie and put his hand out, touching her waist, gently pushing her back.

"Let's not do this, okay, guys?"

The one who hadn't spoken yet took a step forward, uncrossing his arms. He was an inch or two above Paul's six feet. His sleeves were rolled up, revealing forearms covered with multicolored tattoos so dense that they resembled a long-sleeved undershirt, or graffiti-covered ham hocks.

His wrist cocked several times in a move he probably thought was cool and had been practicing since he quit grade school, and at the end of the routine there was a knife, the blade glistening in the streetlamp's pale light.

Paul was done talking. He assumed a defensive pose Bernie recognized as she assumed a similar one herself, though she was a few feet behind Paul so she didn't think he could see that she was ready to support him.

Her support wasn't required. He waited for the big man to advance, and with his first move proceeded to kick the knife out of the guy's hand with a move so quick the other goon jumped in surprise. A moment later the second guy was charging, unable to duck a quick jab from Paul's right hand, which was followed by a spin kick to the knife wielder's head. As he fell back the second guy hesitated, a fatal error because it gave Paul enough time to drop to his hands and swing his legs in an arc, clipping the guy at the knees, leaving him seemingly suspended horizontally in midair for a moment before he crashed to the ground on his hip. Paul was back on his feet like a cat as he proceeded to place a kick worthy of the World Cup finals to the side of the second thug's face. Then, just for insurance, and maybe for fun, Bernie thought, he stomped down on the wrist of the first guy, who was reaching for the knife where it had fallen. Bernie heard a crack and knew that this young tough wouldn't be playing the piano any time soon.

Paul took Bernie's hand and pulled her toward the car.

"Time to go," he said, his eyes darting from side to side. He shoved her toward the front of the car as he opened his door. By the time she got in the engine was running, and seconds later they were pulling away. She pivoted, seeing that both of their new friends were still on the ground, in various stages of trying to get back to their feet to compare broken bones.

She drew a deep breath. Paul had both hands on the steering wheel, his eyes wide, his chest heaving.

"Slow down," she cautioned. Adrenaline was a traffic hazard, even in the best of times, and there were baseball fans still lining both sides of Seventh Avenue. She noticed that his breathing was deep and rhythmic as he lifted off the gas.

"You okay?" he asked, reaching over to put his hand on her knee.

"Hell no," she said, realizing that she was starting to tremble. Her pulse was still racing, and she was having trouble getting a full breath.

"Slow it down," he said, his hand now at the back of her neck, massaging with iron fingers. She closed her eyes and rolled her head from side to side, concentrating on the pace of her breathing, drawing air deeply instead of quickly. In a few seconds she felt a wave of release, and when she looked at him he was smiling.

"Better?"

She nodded.

"That was amazing," she said.

"CIA training . . . you get to keep it when you check out."

"You just might not be kidding."

This made him chuckle. "Up for a drink?" he asked.

They went to the Biltmore Hotel, still Phoenix's most prestigious address after over seventy years. But they weren't looking for prestige; it was simply on the way home. Designed and built in 1929 in the shadow of the Wrigley Mansion—now a private dinner club—by protégés of Frank Lloyd Wright under his strict guidance, the place was a name-dropper's paradise. You either came here for the architecture, which still looked as innovative as anything being built today, or you were scouting for famous faces, because this was where they were.

Bernie and Paul sat outside, overlooking the courtyard and flower garden, nursing cold beers served in crystal flutes. Her eyes drifted, and she nodded to her left.

"Is that Magic Johnson over there?"

Paul snuck a glance. "No, Penny Hardaway."

"Maybe you should go over and compare tattoos."

"Cute."

They both turned away, not wanting to be obvious.

"Look," she said, holding up her hand, which still trembled. She didn't tell him she was even shakier on the inside, despite the half hour since the confrontation.

Paul took the hand, holding it in both of his. Keeping eye contact, he brought it to his mouth and kissed it softly. His lips were shockingly warm to the touch.

"This one, too," she said, holding out the other hand, which didn't shake. He did the same with it, but now it was just a goof.

"I guess you're my hero now," she said.

"I saw you back there," he said. "It's a reflex . . . you'd have done the same thing. How long have you studied?"

"Started in high school, but I've slacked off. Stopped

short of my first-degree dan test, made up all sorts of excuses."

He nodded, as if he'd been there. "After a while you ask yourself, what's the point, right? I mean, if you're not into the spiritual side of it, it gets sort of, I don't know . . . dumb. Monotonous. That was my experience."

"What level are you?"

"Fifth."

"Scary. Shall I call you Master?"

"Only when we play love slave."

He smiled as he took a sip, his eyes riveted on her for any unusual reaction. There wasn't one, her smile just as playful as his.

"So," she said, "you're not into the Zen of it. What *are* you into?"

"You mean Zen-wise? My spiritual persuasion, so to speak?"

She nodded. "Pretty personal, I know. But we almost died tonight. You saved me, now you're responsible for me."

"That's the Zen I'm *not* into," he offered with a grin. "Somebody made that up ten thousand years ago, and some people still believe it today. Just like a lot of what we call religion. We also saw a ball game together, too. Same difference, you ask me."

She just stared at him.

He said, "You want an answer, right?"

"Would be nice."

He allowed his gaze to drift out to the cabanas that surrounded the courtyard. She could tell he was going to give her a serious take on the issue.

"You may be sorry you asked."

"I'll be the judge of that."

"Because I *do* have an answer."

She smiled gently and nodded for him to go on.

"What I'm into is not worrying about it. We live, we die . . . what happens then, happens. It's like physics, how an airplane flies—it flies for one set of reasons, natural laws, and those laws make sense, every time. Doesn't matter if you don't understand them, they still apply to you. Same thing with the universe. How many major religions are there—three? Ten? And within the so-called Christian doctrine, how many contradictory paradigms are there? Three? Ten? Will the Mormons who believe in the same Jesus Christ that the Catholics believe in—and they agree, there was only one Jesus Christ—really be the only ones in a heaven of their own design? They both think so. Will the child of Catholic parents who forgot to have holy water sprinkled on its forehead really go to hell if he dies in an accident before they get around to it? You know how many really smart people buy into that crap? And who invented shit like purgatory and the Pope, anyhow? I mean, try to find the Pope in the Bible—you can't. He's not there. Purgatory either. Somebody with an agenda and a robe made it all up. They're all cults, in my opinion. Look up the definition of a cult and apply it to your favorite church. Then again, don't, it'll make a cynic out of you."

Bernie realized her eyebrows were stuck in the up position.

"Wow," she said.

Paul didn't hear. He took a swallow of beer and went on.

"So what do I believe? Because it's all science—call it spiritual science if that makes it easy to swallow, no difference—I believe there's one truth, and nobody really knows what it is. Nobody's come back to set us straight. We're all grasping at smoke rings, desperate for hope, trying to make sense out of what is actually random freaking chaos, and some of us are ruining our lives in the process. Missing the party, so to speak. Do I believe there is more here than meets the eye? I do. While our experience is random, the physics of it all aren't remotely random. Those physics had to have been created, which means there *is* a Creator. That I believe. That's what turns physicists like Stephen Hawking and Gary Zukav into spiritualists who write bestsellers about

the soul . . . they've pulled back the covers and they
can't explain what they see there. Which in Zukav's case
is interesting, because then he pretends to be explaining
everything. I believe that this Creator, call her or him
what you will, put us here to learn, to experience the
whole enchilada if we can. And I believe that what you
do and what you say you stand for doesn't mean squat,
because in the end it's all dust. The Creator and those
natural laws of his take over from there."

Bernie puckered her lips and blew a silent whistle.
She could tell Paul was uncomfortable having bared his
soul this way.

"My mother the Baptist would want me to run like
hell right about now."

He looked at her over the rim of his glass, which he
was draining. "What do you want to do?"

"What you said is very provocative. But I think you've
ignored a key element."

"And that is?"

"Consequences. You acknowledge a Creator, which
implies order, yet you assign human behavior to random
chaos without consequences for our choices."

"I don't think that's what I said. In any case, all I can
say is . . . who really knows?"

"A few hundred million people believe someone did
come back to set us straight, that it was all written down
for us. They think *they* know."

He grinned, as if she'd just waltzed into a trap. "So
which parts do you believe, and which do you throw
out? And who gets to assign meaning? And which mes-
siah was the real deal, because they all have a few hundred million fans. And where The Book is concerned, is
it all, or is it nothing? Can't have it both ways. And you
can quote me to your mother."

He winked. Bernie pretended to ignore it.

She said, "Maybe what matters is in your heart.
Maybe that defines it."

"Maybe," he said slowly. "But then again, if in the
end there can only be one truth, and if your heart be-

lieves one thing and mine believes another, then one of us, by definition, is wrong. And that same few hundred million would tell you that one of us is going to roast in hell for it. And, by the way, that all this is the mandate of the good and just Lord who wrote it all down for us."

"I don't think we're going to solve this one tonight," she said. "Or that we should try. We haven't even finished our first date and already we're arguing religion."

"You asked. And we're not arguing."

"Actually," said Bernie, "I think you just made a case for blind faith."

"Hear hear. The blinder, the better."

"That, I buy into."

Paul leaned forward. He took one of her hands in both of his.

"So what's in your heart . . . right now?"

She didn't move, knowing what was coming, and when he saw that she wasn't squirming he also relaxed, turning the moment into a slow dance. He touched her chin with his fingertips and drew closer. The touch of his lips on hers was feather light, and he used them to grasp each of hers in turn, pulling slightly, allowing the tip of his tongue to barely caress the skin. After a moment he pressed closer, sealing his mouth with hers, gently parting her lips with his tongue, hesitantly probing, not deeply, but playfully.

He pulled back as slowly as he'd gone in.

"You close your eyes," he said. "When you kiss. That's sweet."

"Doesn't everyone?"

"I wanted to see you from this proximity. You're a very beautiful woman, Bernie. I mean that."

Suddenly her breath caught short. She wanted to respond but there was nothing to say. She put her hand on the back of his neck and pulled him closer, kissing him again.

Paul swung the Beamer into the slot next to her Volvo in the darkened Oar Research parking lot and turned the engine off. He turned in the seat and reached out to touch her shoulder. They hadn't spoken much on the drive back, but they did hold hands.

"Thank you for inviting me. I had a great evening."

"Me too."

They kissed. Nothing heavy, appropriate to the moment.

"I don't want it to end," he whispered during the kiss.

She pulled back, making sure she didn't smile. "What are you saying?"

He, however, smiled coyly. "I'm saying you're a great kisser."

"That's what I was afraid of." She sat back on her seat, breaking contact.

"What's wrong with being a great kisser?"

"You know what," she said, already digging in her purse for her car keys.

"Let's go somewhere. My place, your place, talk about religion some more."

She pivoted, leaning her back against the door. "Maybe we can hit politics, too, really piss each other off. I don't think so, Paul. I'm tired. My brain is on fire."

"Princess rules?"

"Common sense. I stay with you tonight, I'll regret it."

"But you'll have a good time doing it. Common sense isn't always good sense."

"It should be about more than that. But that's just me."

"Maybe it is about more than that." He leaned in for a kiss, but she put a hand on his chest, stopping him.

"Defining moment, Paul. Don't blow it, okay? Please."

Their eyes locked. Finally Paul lowered his chin in resignation. He puffed out his lower lip playfully to show that he wasn't taking her rejection all that seriously.

But it was serious. Diana had won. Though, perhaps not at the cost of his ultimate conquest of this tasty woman and her feisty manner, which he would savor in ways her Baptist mother would shudder to imagine. He had learned that often you had to sacrifice the battle to win the war. He'd pay that price with Diana. He would bleed for her, because this new woman was special in a way that he already found disturbing. That, too, was part of the fun.

Two minutes later both cars pulled out of the Oar Research parking lot onto Butherus, turning toward Scottsdale Road. Once there, the Volvo turned right, the Beamer left.

From a parking lot across the street, a red Corvette pulled out from the shadows, turning in the same direction as the Beamer.

Bernie almost forgot to check her e-mail when she got home. She sat on her balcony with an iced tea for a while as the fire in her brain simmered down, watching the twenty-foot fountains—which lent a name to her complex, The Fountains—directly in front of her unit. They shut off at midnight, so she went back inside, laughed at an infomercial for a strap-on electrical device promising to rid wearers of their love handles, then went to bed.

Half an hour later, the fire not completely quelled, she got up and turned on her computer, where a message from Eric was waiting.

B—sorry to hear you are frustrated. Good news on this end, though—I've been working up a profile on W, looking under rocks, finding ghosts. Am making progress—guy is definitely no boy scout. Be careful. You've come this far, suggest you stick it out. But DO NOT take action. Too dangerous. And too soon. May have something for you before long. Want to check it out before sending you on goose chase. Can you get into his computer files safely? DON'T answer that—yet. This may be bigger than you thought or hoped. Appreciate sensitivity to my situation—will keep you posted. Please don't respond, for God's sake don't call unless urgent, am on a short leash, already pushing the envelope. Will do all

*I can, will keep you posted. Above all, be careful, lay
low. Have faith, we are close.*
    E.

She didn't fall asleep until well after two, and only
then after downing two Excedrin PM tabs. Between the
day she'd just had—Nadine's invitation to take Wesley
down, the unexpected delight of the ball game and its
frightening aftermath, and of course the man who'd
saved her, and now Eric's e-mail and her resurrected
intentions—there was too much to process, all of it immediate and intense.

Be careful. Lay low. Bide her time. What better way
to comply than in the company of a man who looked
like a cross between Antonio Banderas and Antonio Sa-
bato, with Al Pacino hair and the body of an underwear
model? A man with a soft voice and even softer lips
who flew airplanes and kicked serious butt when necessary? A hero, perhaps. One who wanted her, which certainly wasn't all bad, even if he was a little pushy about
it. A man who cared about the nature of the soul instead
of the virtues of the zone defense in passing situations.

What better way to avenge her sister's death, she
thought in her final waking moment of the early morning, than to fully pursue her own life while she waited
for a weakness to show itself?

Was it Wesley keeping her awake, or was it Paul? Or
might it be something else entirely?

25

Time was of the essence now, and Wesley Edwards knew it. Not that time was a problem; indeed, he had been working toward this milestone for months and was well prepared. As long as Jerry Grasvik was healthy, nothing could stop him now. The distributor was coming to town tomorrow, and once that fuse was lit, an avalanche of inevitability would follow. The media would pick it up, someone would give it a cheesy name, and a few million e-mails would begin flying through cyberspace as every propeller-head with an opinion weighed in, all of it hot air. Until someone came forward with an antidote for what would certainly become known as the most significant threat to the technological well-being of corporate America and therefore the country's entire economy—a digital apocalypse, perhaps—chaos would rule.

Once the units were distributed, each and every credit or debit card in the world would be rendered dysfunctional, bringing the economy to its knees within a day or two. But there would be more. Much more. Mission-critical networks would have no choice but to shut down, retail commerce would grind to a halt, all resulting in massive layoffs and a panic on Wall Street. And yet, no one would step up to save us all. At least not right away. Because the little software worm that was the wicked stepchild of Jerry Grasvik's genius would require weeks to isolate, dismember and study, and only then could a program be written to counter the effects and block further entry. Entire technical infrastructures would have to be redesigned, reprogrammed, redeployed and reimplemented by bewildered employees in sudden need of retraining.

The cost would be measured in billions, little of it recoverable.

If a solution could be discovered quickly, it would be priceless.

And then, to quote the song, a hero comes along. Little Oar Research in Scottsdale, Arizona, a virtual nobody in the computer security game, will christen its Web site, which will contain a white paper analyzing the problem and outlining the solution. The paper and the underlying code will be the work of Jerry Grasvik himself, who, because of his background as one of the primary architects of the industry-standard firewall code for remote access commerce—that is, ATMs and other point-of-purchase card-swiping terminals—will be completely credible. Of course, the solution will exist in code form only, and it will be proprietary—it will belong exclusively to Oar Research. To deploy the solution quickly enough, someone will have to either license it from Oar, or buy it outright. Preferably buy the entire company. That someone will, by necessity, be a major player in the high-tech industry, with resources already in place to quickly deploy the solution to a desperate marketplace. Someone to whom price will be no object. Someone whose name is already a household word.

Once Wesley hit the street with Jerry's code, Oar Research would in a heartbeat be worth something on the order of a quarter of a billion dollars, give or take a few million. With his stock options and bonus thresholds, his take would be in excess of twenty-five million, and the people who owned the company would write the check gladly. That's what they'd hired him to do, and they had the good sense to look the other way while he did his job. As for Jerry Grasvik, he'd never have to work another day in his life.

This was why Wesley Edwards was in downtown Phoenix on this day, visiting the law firm of Wustrack, Carlson & Smith. Specialists in corporate transaction law, they bought and sold companies for their clients, or took them public when that was the more lucrative solution. But they did far more than file papers with the corporation commissioner. They would provide the myriad resources required when the shit hit the wires—a grassroots public relations strategy to get the Web site and its content noticed quickly, a press relations package that put the right message into the right media hands almost before it was news, a nifty due diligence portfolio for the wave of salivating buyers for the company, and a negotiating team anchored by the eternally handsome Mike Wustrack himself. The guy had built a reputation as the Leona Helmsley of corporate deal making, as well as a notorious womanizer and a killer tennis player. His cleverest legal eagles, a team headed by JoAnn Smith, a former crackerjack district attorney in another life, would deflect anyone who looked upon the whole process with anything remotely resembling a jaundiced eye. This team had already scripted and seeded a story that explained Jerry's ability to offer a viable solution before anyone else even understood the problem, involving a series of exchanges over the past few months in secret Internet chat rooms frequented by hackers and other shadowy computer players, all with code names and shielded IP addresses that defied identification . . . largely because they didn't exist at all. According to this scenario, when Grasvik caught wind of the impending worm, he began working on a theory. When the worm hit the street he was ready, a reluctant hero who was happy to serve when called.

Wustrack, Carlson & Smith's fee would come straight off the top line, plus what could be thought of as a "tip" originating from somewhere under the table. In Michael Wustrack's mind, this transaction was no more or less ethical than most of the other deals they had authored over the years. They had been involved in similar situations before, where the line between problem and solution was both gray and blurred, and they understood the sensitive nature of business in an industry where secrets were commodities, where he who held the code dictated the rules. In this case Oar Research held the code, and a don't-ask-don't-tell mindset dictated the context of every meeting that occurred between Wesley Edwards and the lawyers who would set him free.

Meanwhile, Wesley was sleeping just fine, thank you. Twenty-five followed by six zeroes buys a lot of peace of mind. And besides, bigger names than his had made significantly larger fortunes executing far more daring, even dastardly strategies. Rather than being looked upon as criminals, those guys had their pictures on the covers of magazines.

Today's meeting had gone well. Michael Wustrack was a consummate pro, and he asked only those questions that kept him on the right side of the fence. Everything was ready to go. In fact, Wustrack was in a bit of a hurry to catch a court time with a Suns cheerleader.

Wesley was in a descending elevator when something caught his eye. In some upscale office towers in this part of town, the elevator buttons were labeled with the names of the tenants of the floors. Wustrack, Carlson & Smith had the top two floors, but on the sixth he noticed the name of Torgeson, Barton & Mattern. A little alarm went off in his stomach, in time to press the button before the car passed it by.

It wasn't that he'd forgotten the visit from the lady lawyer with the attitude and a warning to stop sharpening his pencil in the company Cuisinart. It wasn't even that he'd back-burnered the issue. Rather, he felt he'd dealt with it as best he could, and had moved on. He had other fish to fry, and after having a little chat with the handful of women in his employ with whom he'd exchanged bodily fluids, he went back to the business of making a killing. The last thing he needed right now was legal trouble.

Seeing the Torgeson, Barton & Mattern name, however, triggered an impulse he knew he could not resist.

He was extracting the woman's business card from a card keeper in his pocket when he entered the plush lobby. This wasn't a top-floor law firm, but it had aspirations as such and the décor was over-the-top plush. As was the receptionist, who resembled Loni Anderson—hair the size of a Hyundai, surely working off her law school tuition by putting in, say, forty years at the front desk.

"Good afternoon, may I help you?"

Wesley was tempted to ask her where she got those lips, but instead slapped his Sharon Hobbs business card on the counter and asked if she was in.

"Do you have an appointment?" Her smile today needed some work.

"No. Is she in?"

"Yes, but she's in a meeting. Can I tell her who's waiting?"

"Tell her Wesley Edwards is here, and he's *not* waiting."

"One moment." Rather than handle this one over the intercom, she got up and walked back into the mysterious inner sanctum where these lawyers earned their two fifty an hour. His intention was to tell Sharon Hobbs that the problem had been handled, and that any future reports of misconduct would clearly be motivated by profit, in which case she'd hear from his attorney, who barbequed kittens and puppies on weekends for kicks. The receptionist returned after ninety seconds, about five short of Wesley's limit, followed by a woman who, if she was a day, was pushing fifty-five and looked like Janet Reno. A woman who was definitely *not* Sharon Hobbs.

Her smile was much better. She extended her hand. "Hi, I'm Sharon."

"You're Sharon Hobbs?"

Her smile was unaffected. "I believe I am."

When Wesley narrowed his eyes, a pink hue flooding

his cheeks like wine spilled on a wedding dress, she asked him what was wrong.

"You came to my office and left this," he said. "Someone's having some fun with both of us, I think."

He handed her the card with her name on it. She shook her head and handed it back to him.

"Someone said they were me? Should I be flattered?"

"Oh yeah."

"My guess is you'd be more apt than me to know who would do that."

"Somebody's busting my chops. Sorry to have bothered you."

The two women glanced at each other as Wesley turned for the door. The receptionist had no recollection of an attractive woman with short dark hair who'd come in the week before, asking about the kind of cases they take here, and she certainly hadn't seen the woman palm one of the cards from the dispenser on the counter.

"Listen," said Ms. Hobbs as he reached the door, "you find out who it is and want to have a little fun back, as in upside the head with a lawsuit, give me a call."

She winked, and he couldn't help but smile.

But not because of her great wit. Because he'd already thought of a way to find out who the woman was who'd thoroughly fucked up his week at a time when he really didn't need the distraction.

26

Everything had to be perfect when the blood game was consummated.

There were candles, too many to count, their reflections bouncing and multiplying between the fully mirrored wall and the floor-to-ceiling glass that opened the bedroom to the balcony and the sprawl of the city far below. The double doors were ajar, and it was as if the night itself had blown in on a warm breeze, dancing with the flames. Music played softly from a forty-four-speaker custom sound system that filled the entire house with the soundtrack from a movie Diana thought romantic.

Even when there was blood, there was romance.

They had gone their separate ways during the first part of the evening, Diana to a gay nightclub to dance and Damien to a movie, something with subtitles and real butter on the popcorn. He was to arrive home precisely at ten, disrobe in the hall and enter the bedroom—the chamber, as it was referred to tonight—fully erect. How he achieved that state would be his own business.

She was waiting for him on the bed, the covers thrown back, her tan body with its gallery of erotic ink in stark contrast to black silk sheets. All she wore was a pair of high-heeled Gucci sandals with little straps that drove him mad, and a complicated little smile, which drove him madder. And as always, a vial of his blood around her neck. On the nightstand next to the bed, among the candles, were a box of tissues, a jar of boric acid antiseptic and a surgeon's scalpel.

Damien reclined against a stack of pillows propped against the headboard. Diana rested her head on his shoulder, lying on her side with her knee thrown over his legs. They were still moist from the sweat of their lovemaking, and as they gazed out at an unsuspecting Scottsdale, a soothing midnight breeze wafted in through the open glass. Damien stroked her hip while Diana pressed her hand to his chest, warming the place where she had carved the initial *D* into the skin just above his left nipple. She'd rendered it in cursive script to make it pretty.

"What the hell were you thinking?" she finally said, her voice softer than the words.

"Thought I had a shot," he said just as quietly. "No guts, no glory."

"Next time I'll hire a gang of Mexicans, make you a bigger hero."

"She wasn't going down tonight. Not for the entire cast of *Ocean's Eleven*. What'd that muscle cost you, anyhow?"

"Hundred each. I also gave them head in their car before you got there."

"I don't believe you."

"But you'll think about it, won't you?"

"I mean about the hundred. They'd have done it for twenty and a hand job."

She laughed as she playfully pinched the fresh wound on his chest, causing him to inhale sharply. They snuggled tighter, a new soundtrack kicking in on the stereo.

The obvious questions went unasked tonight because they had come up the last time, though they still remained unanswered. Like this one, that game had been Damien's idea, and like this one it had ended with what was now a small half-moon scar on the back of his right hand. They'd talked it all out then, the part of them that acknowledged the illogic of it, debating the part that embraced the thrill. He'd tried to explain it wasn't that he wanted her blood so badly that he was willing to risk his own to get it—indeed, he assured her that he cared for her too deeply to wish her pain, playful or otherwise—or even that he experienced some textbook masochistic return when he came up short. His addiction was simpler, more elegant, more a gambler's pact with the devil. He simply liked to play. Sure he wanted to win, but the higher the stakes, the greater the kick.

They agreed it was complicated. Some couples created arguments so they could make up and then make love. Others rented videos, some joined swingers clubs, most just closed their eyes and pretended to be humping someone else. To each their own, but those were gradeschool games and this was graduate-level kink. Mind fucking by master mind fuckers. Their blood challenges weren't about the prize, the blood itself, they were about pursuit and conquest. About power. Blood was simply the currency of power, and nothing else would do. And, Damien had to admit, he definitely got off on the way Diana wielded her power, even if he had to bleed for it. That fascination, staring into the blazing eyes of a woman who wanted to consume you, was as old as the Garden of Eden.

Tonight this would all go unsaid, but all would be remembered.

"I think you're lying to me," she said.

He looked down at her, but she didn't return his gaze. This, too, had come up before, and he knew what was coming next. She was accusing him of being too attracted to Bernadette. The challenge and the surrender of his blood gave him license to pursue that attraction without breaking a covenant with Diana. Without the guilt of betrayal.

Interesting, he thought, how even in her moment of conquest she was no match for the little green monster. This, too, was as old as Eden.

"That's not it," he said, knowing she'd already accurately labeled it a lie.

"I notice you weren't suggesting I take Wesley Edwards to bed. No, I get Pee-wee Herman and you get Julia Roberts. I wonder who really won, after all."

"I think she looks more like Sandra Bullock, actually."

"Fuck you, Paul."

"You want to seduce Wesley Edwards, sweetheart, you go for it."

"And meanwhile, you get to finish what you just started. Have some balls, admit it! You want her, and you're manipulating the situation and me to get what you want."

This was the old cake-and-eat-it-too can of worms, and it had proven to be explosive. Every once in a while Diana would pry open the lid and inhale the fumes, and in the ensuing swoon she would talk out of both sides of her mouth. She loved their little games because she got to command her power like a fierce goddess, unattainable and omnipotent, having her way with men and discarding them like so many unsolicited love letters. It rang her bell, validated her femininity. And like him—or at least so she claimed—she had no interest in a traditional relationship and the rules of sexual conduct that would constrain and ultimately doom it to failure. And yet, she wanted more from him than she was willing to come out and ask for—a pliable sense of commitment, a one-way ticket that prescribed different rules for him than for her. He could play, but he couldn't *like* it too much. The solution, he had quietly concluded, was easy—if he stuck to women less attractive than her, she was fine, she was even amused. But if his end of the playing field was threatening, something akin to PMS reared its head during the postgame analysis, which was supposed to be titillating instead of frustrating.

And here they were again. Julia Roberts and Sandra Bullock, whomever you preferred, were both *very* threatening.

Diana swung her legs to the floor, sitting on the bed with her back to Damien. He reached out and lightly began tracing the tapestry that covered her back with his forefinger.

"You're being unfair." His voice was thick and slow, careful to avoid any hint of defensiveness. "Okay, the game's fixed, that's the kick. For both of us. You get to win because you *should* win . . . you get your pound of flesh, and I pay the price for my sins. We both get something out of it, and then we get each other. That's the dance, sweetheart. What, suddenly you don't like the music? It's just foreplay . . . always has been . . . it's about us, not them. It's about tonight, the rest has always been hot talk, that's all. They don't exist. *We* exist."

He paused, giving her a chance to respond. When she didn't, he added, "What is it that *you* want?"

She turned, her eyes narrow, burning into his.

"I want what you have."

Her real name was Vicki Garlington. She grew up in Pacific Palisades in a house overlooking the ocean and had lost her virginity at the age of fifteen to the groundskeeper, whom she thought looked like the baseball player Jose Conseco. She told her father about it the next day and was relieved when the groundskeeper was summarily fired, thus eliminating any sticky complications born of proximity. Her father was a type-A studio executive who lived with his third trophy wife, who'd once worked on a soap opera. Vicki's mother died when Vicki was five due to an anesthesia fuck-up during plastic surgery, a procedure she'd undertaken after Vicki's father had urged her to keep up with the times. The ensuing settlement had been for eleven million, three of which went into a trust fund that would become Vicki's when she turned twenty-five, provided she had earned a college degree and was gainfully employed.

She happily attended UCLA, earned a degree in psychology and, like most psych grads, took a job as a bartender. She worked at a hot Sunset Strip rock club—a veritable laboratory of flagrant psychology at play— where she began collecting touring rock stars and acquired a fleeting taste for recreational drugs. That lasted until she was twenty-five, when it was time to collect.

The day after her twenty-fifth birthday she went to the bank and withdrew all the money, now about seven million dollars. With the help of a tax attorney she set up some annuities so she'd never have to work again, then ended up marrying the guy a few months later. He even wrote his own prenuptial agreement—she'd had the presence of mind to run it by another lawyer on the side—which she rammed up his ass eight months later when she caught him having an affair with an IRS auditor named Aileen. She hadn't spoken to him or her father since.

Later that year a friend tipped her off to an Internet site for singles, with unedited personal ads. One of them, as her friend put it, "sounds just like you."

Dark god, late 20s, seeks evil queen to conquer the world. Okay, I'm a little over-the-top, but I'm also rich and much too handsome and tired of vanilla women who can't or won't understand my hedonistic ways and sinister fantasies. If you'd like to discover your potential and your power, face your fears and explore your dark side with a man seeking and offering honesty, courage and the willingness to be outrageous, then this may be an opportunity to change your life and mine. You must be beautiful, intelligent, philosophically-minded, fit, fashionable, slightly dangerous, look hot in black, like to travel, read, laugh, drink fine wine, despise rules, love children as long as they belong to someone else, and generally live every day to the max. If you are into romance and ritual and are ready to embrace the absurd with utter conviction, with a man who has no limits to his imagination, call Box 40877.

That had been five years ago. She'd kept the ad for a few weeks before responding, but she couldn't get it out of her head. It was the "romance and ritual" line that got her, though the entire context was intriguing. The friend had been right—it sounded like her. So she called the box and left her name and number on the recording, adding that she'd never met a man who could keep up with her, so this could be interesting, if he had the balls for it.

He certainly did, and it certainly was. Their relationship began on the telephone—he lived in Arizona—with several of their conversations lasting well over an hour, touching every base hinted at in his ad. His questions tested their compatibility to the point at which she challenged his sincerity, and perhaps those balls she'd mentioned earlier. Maybe he really looked like Danny DeVito and wasn't ready to come out from behind the Zorro façade. But he was articulate and funny, considerate and charming, a young Sean Connery without the accent or the chauvinism. She couldn't believe that a man walked the earth with this much concern for emotional and intellectual chemistry without the influence of sight and touch. By the time they met they were already infatuated with each other and well down the road to being in serious heat. In hindsight she realized it was a brilliant strategy of seduction, implemented by a master at it, one who loved women to the point of worship, second only to his love of himself and the fulfillment of his desires, twists and all.

Their first meeting lived up to the telephonic foreplay. He told her to be at the Santa Monica airport, that he was sending an airplane to pick her up. The "airplane" turned out to be a thirty-million-dollar Gulfsteam IV, with champagne on ice and music already playing. But there were only the two pilots, one of whom was gorgeous beyond belief, who had come to fetch her for a rendezvous with the mysterious Damien—he had provided just his first name at this point—at an undisclosed location. Normally such an adventure would be far across the line of common sense, but from the beginning he'd promised mystery and intrigue, and by God he was delivering. She'd gone out and bought a black leather pants suit for the evening, which turned out to be a perfect match to the jet's interior. Somewhere over Palm Springs the pilot came back to the cabin and introduced himself as Damien . . . and after penetrating three of her orifices and bringing her to eight otherworldly orgasms before they ran low on fuel, the rest was exquisite history.

Both had the marks and the body art to prove it.

Diana rotated her shoulders slightly and, using her eyes, drew his attention to her back. This was all the clarification Damien needed to explain what she meant when she said *I want what you have*. What she wanted was to be his equal, to match what he had achieved the year before, the conquest that had been the inspiration for the magnificent fresco etched with diabolical brilliance across the skin of her back.

Temptation had become sin . . . sin had become flesh, rendered unto death.

"Seduction is easy," she said. "But what you did to that woman . . . that was dark. That was power."

"It was also dangerous."

She leaned in and kissed him. "All the better."

Suddenly everything had changed. The tone, the words, the implications . . . they were playing again. This, too, was Diana's thing, resolution of conflict by diversion from it. It was her way of demonstrating that he had a point.

"I can make him fall in love with me," she whispered through her kiss.

"Are we talking about Wesley or the little programmer?"

Her tongue burrowed deeply in his mouth, then pulled back as she playfully said, "I'll destroy Wesley later. I'm talking about Jerry."

"Ah, Lady Death lives."

Her tongue was tracing the outline of his lips now. "Precisely."

"He's probably already in love with you," he breathed into her hair the way a connoisseur inhales a fine vintage. "And who wouldn't be?"

Nibbling at his lips now, she said, "I can take him all the way."

Damien felt his breath getting short, as it always did when his body responded. He positioned himself so that her reaching hand could more easily find his emerging hardness.

"Tell me," he said, clamping his eyes tightly closed. "Say it."

She purred, nipping at his throat now, her hand fully engaged in the resurrection of the serpent.

"You'll have to pay," she said, her voice playful now. "Something . . . eternal."

She swung her leg over his hips and eased herself onto him, throwing her head back in pleasure at the moment of penetration. Then, moving with a quick rhythm, she put her hand on his chest and slowly raked a fingernail across the oozing outline of the *D*.

"Say it," he said, his face contorting with the pain, masking a strange smile.

She watched him a moment without altering her movements, then pressed her mouth against his ear just prior to the inevitable moment of release.

"I can make him die," she whispered.

27

It was the sum of seemingly disconnected little things that made Nadine think this was an opportunity to pounce. Important people were flying in today, people without names or itineraries. They weren't customers or investors, or Wesley would have sent the airplane to fetch them. Because it was her job to schedule the conference rooms, she knew they weren't coming to the office for their meeting, which was odd because there were plenty of rooms available. Wesley had told Nadine to block out his afternoon, but didn't respond when she asked him where he'd be, which he normally volunteered. If he was planning on playing golf or some other form of hooky he'd have asked her to cover for him, something she had done many times before. No, this was secret stuff. He spent the morning with his telephone on mute and the door locked, head down in paperwork, which never happened. And he'd skipped his noon workout, highly unusual unless the situation was critical.

Most of all, Nadine just had a gut feeling, and she trusted her gut when it came to her boss. She could be wrong, but they were risking little by covering the bases.

They were ready for something like this. Just the day before Bernadette had acquired a digital camera with a hefty telephoto lens, and had it with her today. She'd parked her car in the back of the building so she could exit the area without being noticed. Following Wesley would be risky, but if she stayed well back in Scottsdale's

notoriously manic traffic—these people drove like co-
caine addicts—she could see without being seen.

At one thirty Nadine noticed Wesley hurriedly stuffing
the papers that had covered his desk into his briefcase.

"Get ready to fly," she said softly as Bernadette
picked up her call, her phone having been connected
that morning.

Bernie hung up, grabbed her purse and the camera
and headed for the stairway, which was on the opposite
side of the building. She'd be in her car first, then hook
up with Nadine using her mobile phone. Nadine would
ensure that Wesley did, in fact, depart in his own vehicle
instead of being picked up, then tell Bernie which way
he was heading.

As Bernie rushed past the front desk, she suddenly
whirled and snapped a photo of Nadine, grinning mischievously. It was meant as a joke, but Nadine didn't
seem to appreciate the humor. If she were a cop or a
bodyguard Nadine would have demanded the film. But
there was no time for that now, and thanks to digital
technology there was no film. Bernie could feel the heat
of Nadine's glare on her back as she rounded the corner
toward the stairwell.

The departure went according to plan. The Escalade
was heading toward Scottsdale Road. Bernie waited until
Nadine told her which direction it was turning before she
drove out of the lot. He was heading south, toward town.

"Why'd you do that?" she asked.

"Do what?"

"Take my picture."

"You sound paranoid."

"You should be paranoid, too. This isn't a game."

"Sorry," said Bernie, shaking her head privately. "No
harm, no foul."

A moment passed. "Call me when he gets wherever
he's going." Then the line went dead.

She'd e-mail Nadine the photo later and tell her to
lighten up.

The Escalade was easy to follow at a distance, though

there was no shortage of high-profile SUVs in this neighborhood. Suddenly Wesley swerved into the turn lane and hung a left onto Doubletree at the swanky new Gainey Village strip mall, the most expensive floor space in town. Bernie didn't make the light. As she waited she called Nadine.

"I'm stuck." She told her where she was.

"Shit." A moment passed, then Nadine came back, her voice urgent. "There's only one place he could be going. Turn into the Hyatt, half mile on the left. But be careful—unless he uses valet he'll park in the lot on the left, and he'll be on foot heading inside when you drive by."

"What should I do?"

"Turn in, then go right, park in the employee lot. You can walk in from the other direction. Check the lot. He'll be there."

"What if he's not there?"

"Then try the athletic club across the street. That's where he works out. But I doubt that'll happen. If he's there I'm buying lunch for the next year."

"Okay. Let's hope."

"Let me know if you see anything."

There was no sign of Wesley on the walkway leading into the front of the hotel, or near the entrance courtyard with its huge glass cinder-block fountain. She did see the Escalade, though, parked near the door where the valets stored the showier rides.

She called Nadine quickly.

"He used valet. He's inside."

"Not good. If he was hiding his tracks he wouldn't have done that."

"What should I do?" Bernie immediately felt stupid asking the question, not because of its nature, but because she had allowed Nadine to be the air traffic controller in this little game.

Bernie spoke before Nadine had a chance to answer. "I'll check out the lobby. If he's not there I'll hang around, see if someone walks him out."

"It's a long shot."

"He's probably meeting some woman." Two days ago this thought would have gnawed at her. But since she'd met Paul, Wesley didn't seem half as intriguing.

"Get a picture so we can blackmail his ass."

"I'll let you know."

Just like that she was back in control.

The Hyatt Regency's plush lobby was on two levels. Beyond the front doors were stairs leading down to the piano bar, then out to a patio bar and the courtyard beyond. In the distance was the hotel's fabled swimming pool, and beyond that, a man-made lake surrounded by homes occupied by pro jocks, retired CEOs and, rumor had it, a former vice president of the United States.

She was so taken by the view that she almost gave herself away. After checking the front-desk area and the rest of the upper lobby, she stood at the top of the stairway and noticed Wesley sitting at one of the tables at the patio bar, checking his watch. She tucked herself behind a planter full of decorative cacti, hoping no one saw the move.

One of the valets, dressed in a white pants suit that made him look like a gay mechanic, did indeed notice. But he just grinned and shook his head, as if he saw stuff like this all the time. No doubt he did. She smiled back and he turned away.

Wesley was now on his feet, shaking hands with two men who were now arriving at his table. They had just passed her, in fact, as they came from the elevators and descended the stairs. They wore pastel golf attire, one of them bulky and dark, probably Italian, the other somewhat older, balding, and very thin.

She raised the camera to her eyes, adjusted the lens for a nice close-up, and began clicking.

But she stopped, not believing what she saw next. Arriving from the other direction, joining them at the table after handshakes and smiles, was Jerry Grasvik. He was carrying a small cardboard box, which he placed on the table in front of them.

*   *   *

Nadine had no explanation. In fact she was disappointed, concluding that if Grasvik was there it must have been a client or consultant meeting after all. Grasvik had been out of the office all morning, which meant nothing other than he was an eccentric little prick who did what he pleased most of the time.

Nadine suggested that Bernie give it up and come on back to work where they could plot their next move. Bernie agreed, then proceeded to take a few more shots.

But instead of returning to the office, she went to her condo, which was only a few miles away. She had been up half the previous night trying to make sense out of the directions that came with the camera for connecting it to a personal computer. Whoever wrote this shit had obviously never been near a PC in his or her life—nothing worked as it was supposed to according to the instructions. She had finally jury-rigged the connection by intuitively changing the order of the prescribed sequence, and had sent a blistering e-mail about it to the customer service department listed in the booklet.

Today, though, it took her only a few minutes to connect the camera and successfully download the pictures she had just taken into her PC. That done, she opened her e-mail, wrote an apologetic note to Eric explaining what this was about, and that she was going to attach the shots as a file. Eric worked miracles with raw information, and she badly needed a miracle.

Before she went out to the pool to relax, she e-mailed Nadine's picture to her, with a note saying she'd be back in the next day, and to keep smiling.

When she came in from the pool two hours later, there was a phone message from Paul Lampkin, asking if she was free that evening for dinner. The curious thing about this was the sudden realization that she'd not given him her home number.

It never occurred to Wesley Edwards that this meeting needed to take place behind closed doors. There was no reason for anyone to notice them, and anything that was said was spoken in cryptic terms that would bore anyone desperate enough to eavesdrop. Besides, there was a certain kick to doing this in the sun, and there was no point in spooking Jerry Grasvik more than he already was. The guy was a nervous wreck, and he seemed to be distracted for a couple of days now. Besides, these guys were professional thugs, who had to be on their best behavior in public to avoid notice.

Grasvik had delivered a box containing one hundred plastic credit and debit cards, representing thirty different banks, a variety of major retailers, service stations, airlines, and other institutions that utilized swipe-card technology. They were bootlegged copies of actual working cards, with codes easily hacked and duplicated by Grasvik very early in the preparation phase of the project. He'd actually opened phony accounts at each of these institutions so that it would be impossible to link access to anyone who could be identified. Imbedded on the magnetic strip on the back of each card was the most potentially lethal software worm the world had ever known, giving Jerry or anyone else the ability to penetrate the firewall of the target organization's servers and wreak whatever havoc they desired. Extortion, vandalism, account manipulation, covert alteration of data . . . it was all just a few keystrokes away for anyone with one of these cards and the know-how to manipulate the server, something Jerry had provided on a master CD inside the box with the cards. The only solution, at least at first, would be to shut down the systems entirely, effectively bringing business to a complete standstill within a day or two.

After that, it was a question of what it was worth to solve the problem.

A few minutes after Bernie had departed the Hyatt, one of the strangers used his mobile phone to call an associate, who verified that an agreed-upon sum had been deposited in an appropriate offshore account. This money had virtually disappeared from the Oar Research financial statements—not being publicly traded had its advantages these days—and with Grasvik's creative and invisible access to their bank's account servers, the transfer was masked under the name of a dummy corporation.

Having been duly paid and the logistics having been thoroughly reviewed, the two strangers said their farewells, taking the precious cardboard box with them. Later that afternoon they boarded a United flight that connected to New York, and by the end of the next day the cards had been distributed via FedEx to a team of operatives dispersed around the country, none of whom had the slightest idea what this was really about. Their instructions were simply to use the cards, call in, then go back under the rock from whence they came.

In a few days, as soon as Jerry confirmed and transferred the IP addresses and protocols of the target companies, all hell would break loose. By then the new Oar Research Web site being created by Bernadette Kane would be ready to launch, and Jerry would complete the job by downloading his little white paper, which included a situation analysis, a pro forma worst-case scenario, and enough of the remedying code to convince the most skeptical of egotistical programmers that this was their only salvation.

Jerry had even decided on a name. He would call his worm the Serpent.

In the meantime, Wesley Edwards would continue to prepare to put the company up for sale.

Dallas, Texas

Eric's little boy, Max, was having the time of his life spreading applesauce across the surface of his baby chair tray. He was in a rare mood, so Eric hesitated to apply any negative energy to the situation, but he was the designated mop-up man in these situations, and tonight would be a doozy. He'd arrived home to the news of a broken water heater, an eight-hundred-dollar nonbudgeted item, and Shannon was in a bad mood for any of a number of possible reasons, most of which he'd ceased inquiring about because the response was almost always, "Nothing, why do you ask?"

Because you're about as warm and friendly as a county clerk, that's why.

Just another day in paradise.

"Heard from Bernie lately?" asked Shannon, completely out of the blue. She was standing at the sink rinsing dishes.

Eric's stomach gave a little tug, warning him to be careful here.

"No," he said.

"Really. I would have thought you'd have heard from her by now."

Eric raised his eyebrows. "Nope. Probably embarrassed because it's a waste of time."

Shannon stopped what she was doing and looked at him.

"You'd tell me if you heard from her, right?"

Eric took a deep breath, steadying his nerves. Time to change the subject.

"You'll be the first to know," he said, leaning in to wipe Max's mouth as he spoke.

28

Scottsdale, Arizona

The offices of Paradise Valley Security were just across Scottsdale Road from one of their newest clients, Oar Research. It struck no one as either ironic or odd that a computer security company would utilize an outside security firm to patrol their parking lot, but the software program had yet to be written that could keep an ardent burglar out of the building of their choice. In addition to video monitors and digital lock management systems connected to PVS's twenty-four-hour monitoring and response service, one of their video cameras was mounted on the roof overlooking the Oar parking lot.

After Wesley said farewell to the people who would light the fuse of his master plan, he drove directly to the PVS offices. There was something eating at him, and he wouldn't rest until he'd discovered who was doing the chewing.

He sat in a darkened room full of electronic equipment, not unlike a sound studio's control room. He was staring at a large video monitor, operated by John Foley, the resident video rent-a-cop here at PVS. Foley was from the Midwest, long and lean, possessing a dry wit. He had moved here from Minnesota after his career in the animal nutrition business collided with the realities of working for a family-owned business when you weren't family. He took his new job very seriously, which on more than one occasion had endeared him to

Wesley Edwards, who used this technology to keep tabs on the comings and goings of certain employees. He and Foley wouldn't be having a sleep over any time soon, but each man respected the abilities of the other, and when Foley did these little under-the-table favors for Wesley, Suns or D-Backs tickets had a tendency to show up in his mailbox.

"Time code eleven forty-eight and change," said Foley, slowing the frame speed of the image on the screen, which encompassed the entire parking lot. Wesley's white Escalade was in its anointed stall, and many other familiar employee cars were easily recognizable. Were it not for the movement of the palm trees in the breeze, the picture looked like a still shot.

Until, moving in slow motion, a car appeared and parked in one of the spaces near the door that were reserved for visitors. Wesley had phoned ahead to give Foley a bracketed time frame to scan, and Foley was ready with the tape when Wesley arrived.

The car was a late-model red Corvette. The door opened and a figure emerged, immediately discernible as a woman. After checking her hair in the reflection off the driver's side window, she began walking toward the building.

"Bingo," said Foley, freezing the frame here. The visitor was attractive, wearing a dark pants suit, carrying a briefcase. Her sunglasses gave her a mysterious, federal agent type of look.

Foley leaned back and looked at Wesley with raised eyebrows.

Wesley smiled. "You're good," he said, keeping his eyes on the screen.

"Let me show you how good," said Foley, his fingers already poking at the keys on the control panel in front of him. One hand went to a mouse, and a dot that had appeared on the screen suddenly became a box. As Foley worked the mouse the box began to move, growing slightly as it surrounded the image of the Corvette. With a few more keystrokes the image inside the box

filled the entire screen, and they were looking at an en-
larged close-up of the car. Without hesitating, Foley
punched in the command for another box to appear,
which he now positioned over the back of the car, surrounding the lower middle portion. With a flourish he
struck a key, and the screen filled with a slightly grainy
close-up of the car's license plate, still large and clear
enough to read.

Wesley was still smiling as he nodded. "Gotcha," he
said softly.

Foley pivoted in his chair, reaching into his shirt
pocket to fish out a folded piece of paper, which he held
out toward Wesley.

"Me and Garth," he said, leaving it at that.

"You and who?" Wesley wasn't getting it.

"Me and Garth . . . we have friends in low places?
The song?"

Wesley shook his head.

"Forget it," said Foley, shaking his head as well. "This
never happened."

He shook Wesley's hand and left the room. Wesley
unfolded the paper and saw that Foley had written a
name and address under the Corvette's license number.
The name was Vicki Garlington, and he recognized the
general vicinity of the address as somewhere in the hills
off of Lincoln. Mummy Mountain or the north side of
Camelback, very high rent.

"Gotcha," he said again, though this time he wasn't
smiling.

29

*In the elevator it hits me once again, as it has in the
middle of so many nights and so many conversations and
otherwise innocently occupied moments—the panic attack, the overwhelming guilt and its accompanying trem-
ors, all of it reduced to four simple words expressed as a
question, asked so many times, answered in so many
ways.*

What have I done?

*I certainly can't say I wasn't warned. Not so much
about him, as about the door we were opening. Of course
she didn't know him, I took great care with that issue. I
told my sister just enough to justify myself, how handsome he was, how wealthy and successful, the jet-set rich-
and-famous lifestyle. Things that would seduce her, as
well. She would never give her approval, always so precious to me, but she would give her support, always so
unconditional. She knew my husband, so she would understand. If she didn't know my lover there would be
nothing to judge, and I would remain somehow noble in
my deceit.*

As it turned out, I didn't know him either.

*We walked through that dark door together, hand in
hand. Passion blinds us to consequence, and we are consumed by it, body and soul. Only later does the latter
become of issue, because the former heals itself with time.
But the soul waits for absolution that eludes the human
grasp, and the best we can offer is our own forgiveness.*

The elevator opens and I am drawn toward my fate. I cannot feel my feet, and as I look down, my head spins from the height. I turn a corner, and as I walk down the corridor of my life, I see that, once again, the door is ajar. And once again I ask myself, what have I done?

This, thought Bernadette, was irrefutable proof of the existence of God. Nothing this beautiful could be written off as a molecular coincidence or an academically explicable confluence of atmospheric gases and refracted light. Here was the purest essence of the Divine, a glimpse of heaven, as if some celestial door had cracked open to allow the liquid brilliance of it to explode forth into our realm, if only for a few minutes. It was humbling, and to deny its source was the worst kind of ignorance.

Below her was where God had drawn a line in the sand with one magnificent slash of Her holy claw—Bernie enjoyed regarding the Creator in the feminine person—though now we called it the Grand Canyon and explained it away as a hundred centuries of simple erosion. Above her was the purest crystal blue, bottomless as it dissolved into a deeper azure to the east. And ahead, spread before her like some cosmic Sistine ceiling, was the most spectacular sunset she had ever seen. These moments were unique to Arizona, at least that's what Arizonans said, where glowing clouds lined with electric pink cradled the setting sun and cast bolts of creamy pastel brilliance across the sky.

For a moment, looking over at Paul, sitting here with his jet-jockey sunglasses and his cute little pilot headset and his Greek statue jaw, his face bathing in the mauve hue of the sunset, she was certain she was in love. At least for tonight. If ever a girl had a right to a temporary swoon of romantic surrender, this was the night.

He had called again at six, asking if she could meet him at the Oar hangar at the Scottsdale field. She assumed he had something he had to finish up, and that they'd head to dinner from there. She asked how he got her home phone, and he reminded her that they worked for the same company, which was full of eager mouth-pieces. Nadine, of course, being the most prolific. This wasn't exactly accurate—Bernie was just a contractor—but she let it go. She was glad he'd used whatever lever-age necessary to arrange the call.

The jet was sitting on the tarmac in front of the han-gar, glistening in the bright sun. She wished she'd brought the digital camera, since this was a story she just might want for a scrapbook someday. Eric would get a kick out of it, too. Paul was checking the flaps when she walked up. He was wearing beige shorts and leather sandals, revealing interesting tattoos on both ankles, which she'd ask him about later. His shirt was a burgundy rayon, flowing like thick velvet as he moved, showing off a sculpted physique beneath.

It was a nice start. The jet, the shirt, the warm sun . . . she deserved this. Her life might not be so picturesque before too long.

"Your chariot, my lady," he said, actually kissing her hand when she arrived next to the airplane. She was grinning too widely to respond, so she accepted his hand and stepped up into the tiny cabin, remembering the new-car smell of polished leather from her earlier trip. Sitting on the nearest seat was a plastic bag, and she recognized the AJ's logo, the gourmet grocery store that just happened to be kitty-corner to her condo.

"Where are we going?" she asked.

Paul climbed in after her and pulled the hatch up, enclosing them in the cabin. There was an immediate shift in the ambient sound, the airport and the traffic suddenly gone, replaced with a muted nothingness that made the space seem even smaller.

"Out to dinner," he said. He looked at his hand, as if he was holding an imaginary ticket. "Let's see . . . you're sitting in seat 1-F. Right this way, ma'am."

He motioned to his left, toward the cockpit.

"You're kidding," she said, wide-eyed as a child.

"I'm not. What, I'm gonna leave you back here by yourself?"

He guided her forward and helped her into what would normally be the copilot's seat. He quickly climbed into his own seat, stepping over the center console with practiced grace. Then he put on his headset, the mouthpiece of which barely reached the corner of his smile. Even that looked appealing, in the same way that some men look hot in uniform. Something about authority and purpose, the accoutrements of command.

"I can't believe this," she said, taking in the array of gauges and digital readouts in front of her. "Don't you need a copilot or something?"

He smiled at the comment, but kept his attention on his work. His lips were quietly reciting what she concluded was a preflight checklist. His hand reached out to touch the settings and levers and readouts that the list entailed, as if his eyes alone couldn't be trusted. She was stricken with a sudden sense of comfort, his competence and confidence most apparent. It was something a man can't fake, the command of the moment, the protective assumption of responsibility. It was sexy as hell.

He flipped a few switches, and suddenly the whine of one of the engines was audible behind them. He shot her a quick glance and smiled when he saw that she was studying him.

"I'll explain everything once we're airborne. Buckled in?" He leaned close to check her harness, which in the cockpit included straps than came down over the shoulder to connect to a traditional belt around the waist. She could smell his cologne, perfectly understated, a woodsy musk scent that reminded her of her father.

If he'd wanted to take her right then, she'd have given in.

But that, she had a feeling, was coming later on in the evening.

*   *   *

They took off to the south, and once again she could see the Oar building on the right as they banked to the west. Paul wore sunglasses now, and as he spoke into the headset she could hear nothing, the engines drowning whatever exchange was required with the control tower. He tapped her knee and pointed to his right, wanting her to look at the hills, where Pinnacle Peak and her cousins were aglow in the early-evening sun.

"I never get tired of this," he said, louder now. She watched his smile, saw the little boy who had once flown paper airplanes from the top of an old garage, had sat next to some runway in an old car with his father to watch the jets come and go. At least she hoped it was like that for him, that the dream had come early and that his life was now the fulfillment of it, one of the few who get to live their deepest desires.

If she only knew how true that was where Damien was concerned.

They flew a northerly course. She wanted to ask about their destination, but since he hadn't volunteered it she assumed this was part of the intrigue. Once they leveled at eighteen thousand feet—they had to stay well below the commercial air lanes, he explained—he seemed to relax and turn more of his attention to her. He seemed to know which questions were burning in her mind, so he launched into what would have been a nice little speech for a Civil Air Patrol graduation party. She didn't mind, but she was more interested in studying the landscape of his face as he spoke, one of the things women do when they are regarding a man in a sexual context, wearing the mask of great interest while stripping him of his clothing in their minds.

The jet was a Cessna Citation, one of the older models, and had been in service since 1975. As if he realized this might make her nervous, he quickly assured her that he was personally in charge of the airplane's maintenance, and was planning on living a long and rewarding life. He asked if she remembered Thurman Munson, the

old Yankee catcher who'd crashed his Citation performing touch-and-go landings—she didn't—saying that
this was the exact same model. Then, again as if realizing
this wasn't the most comforting of thoughts, he reminded
her that he had logged nine thousand flight hours to
Munson's two hundred, and that this plane had been
rebuilt from the nuts up, pardon the pun, several times
in fact, that it was on its seventh set of engines, that the
avionics—the electronic control and navigation instruments—were brand-new and state-of-the-art, and that
the investment that had been made in this airplane's
integrity and safety was about ten times the original pur-
chase price. She had to agree, the airplane looked and
smelled brand-new.

Without much prompting he went on to tell her about
his arrangement with Wesley. Because the plane was privately owned and operated, and because of its size, it
was perfectly okay to operate with one pilot, though he
often hired a copilot for client runs and longer flights.
Wesley had given Paul complete control over the management of the company's entire aircraft program, which
meant that in addition to flying, Paul managed the budget and oversaw maintenance and safety issues. Wesley
often loaned the airplane to other parties, so it had to
be flight-ready on a moment's notice. As for his taking
it out on little personal flings like tonight, Paul said that
Wesley didn't mind a certain amount of use, and that
he always offered to reimburse the company for fuel,
which unless it was a long trip Wesley never accepted.
This was a perk, he said, one that only contributed to
Paul's belief that he had the best job in the world short
of flying an F-18 for the military, something he'd never
done and would always regret missing.

Bernie decided not to pursue that one—she sensed
there was a story attached—assuming Paul would tell
her if he wanted her to know. Chatty as he was, she
didn't have time to change or develop the direction of
the conversation anyway. But it was charming, really,

seeing him so enthused, and he'd delivered all this information without the slightest hint of misplaced ego, for which she had a keen sensitivity in men.

So far, he continued to be just about perfect. Then again, she hadn't yet heard much about those tattoos.

Twenty minutes into the flight he announced that they were about to arrive over the Grand Canyon. He pulled back on the throttles, and she could feel the nose dip slightly.

"Are we landing?" she asked.

"No. Just visiting. If you've never seen it from the air, you haven't seen it."

He reached for a switch, looking up and smiling at her as he did so. Suddenly the cabin was full of music, grand and sweeping, something Bernie thought she recognized from a movie.

His smile was soft as he put his hand on top of hers. Looking down, she noticed the tattoo of a spiderweb at the base of his thumb. And a crescent white scar in the middle of the back of his hand.

He wasn't finished with his surprises. They turned and flew east over the canyon, at one point descending to an altitude that was lower than the lip of the canyon itself. Back at altitude a few minutes later and without explanation, he cut the power and the plane began to descend. Shortly thereafter she saw a landing strip ahead of them, situated only a few hundred yards from the edge of the canyon itself. She remained quiet as he worked the throttle, letting the little plane feather downward, lowering the flaps a third at a time as they drew closer, releasing the gear, easing back on the power . . . until the tires nudged the pavement and the plane glided to a stop.

They were in the middle of nowhere. Not a single structure could be seen.

"I love this place," he said, turning off the runway as it ended. "Old military field, built in the fifties when they put in all the Titan sites, then abandoned when they shut 'em down in the early seventies."

"You can just land here?"

"Nobody here but us snakes," he said as he climbed out of the seat, offering his hand as she did the same. It was deathly quiet, adding to the sense of isolation. He lowered the hatch, and as they stepped out she felt as if they were in another time, even on another planet. The air enveloped them with a humid warmth, thicker than Scottsdale air. In the distance the horizon was aglow and the entire sky had turned pink, as if in a dream.

He handed her the plastic bag from AJ's and extracted a blanket and a duffle bag from under one of the seats.

He took her hand, and they began walking toward the canyon.

Bernie estimated the drop from where they spread their blanket to be around six hundred feet to the river below. There was no trace of civilization as far as she could see, just them and the canyon and the setting sun, which quickly evolved in color and brightness. He put his arm around her shoulder as they watched it in silence, riveted to the spectacle as the last of the white fire blinked away, leaving the sky a shade of orange filtered with a pink haze, the color of marbled rainbow sherbet.

A few minutes later the light began to diminish. Shadows played off the walls across the canyon, and she laughed that she'd seen this on postcards and on hotel lobby murals since she was a little girl.

Paul withdrew four large candles, placing one at each corner of the blanket. As he lit them he said, "I'm a romantic fool. You might as well know that about me right off."

"Gee, I hadn't noticed," she said.

But there was another thought in her mind, a dark one that she wouldn't mention. She tried to quiet it, but she'd always been this way, finding a crack in what seemed perfect, unable to completely surrender her trust. She visualized him suddenly turning on her and tossing her over the edge to the Colorado River far below. Why he might do this wasn't a part of the imagining, she just saw him move, felt herself flying. It could be months before anyone found her. She hadn't told a soul where she was going, or with whom.

Enough. It was foolish paranoia. And it may well be part of the reason no man had completely penetrated her shell. So far, if ever a man was going to poke his head through her armor, it was this romantic fool, tattoos and all.

He didn't disappoint in the food department, either. Most guys would have stopped at Subway and called it a meal. He'd brought huge Mexican shrimp the size of lobsters, and a cup of spicy sauce. There was brie and Carr's crackers, and fresh grapes, which she hoped would be hand-fed, one by one. For dessert he'd brought a small strawberry cheesecake and two plastic forks. Just so he didn't fall too far out of the realm of masculine credibility, he forgot the napkins. There was also sparkling water in what appeared to be a wine bottle.

"Sorry, I don't drink when I fly," he said. "I hope you don't mind."

He just kept getting better and better.

It was completely dark now. She could barely see the Cessna parked less than a quarter mile behind them. The stars were just now coming out, a spectacular mural as divinely convincing as the sunset had been. Big bang molecular accident, my ass, she thought.

"You're very sweet," she said, feeling a buzz just as real as if they'd just finished a bottle of merlot.

It was a surreal moment, a movie moment in which the script called for their first real kiss. She didn't count the mashing of the other night, where the beer and the aftermath of violence had made them vulnerable. This was the real deal, prepared and presented with the craftsmanship of a master, and she wasn't about to turn away.

They kissed for several minutes, in no hurry . . . seemingly, confusingly, without destination.

"This isn't happening," she whispered through the

kiss. She wanted more, but she couldn't be sure he was in the space. She'd never met a man like this, never could have imagined one could exist.

"Romance and ritual," he said, burying his face into her neck. She could sense him inhaling the scent of her. She understood what he meant by romance—God, did she understand—but the ritual part eluded her for now. She concluded that he meant going slow, making a dance of it, rather than the traditional manly cut-and-thrust approach.

She was the one who reclined first, gently easing back to the blanket, pulling him with her. Everything she needed to say, everything he needed to hear, was in her eyes.

His reference to ritual began to make sense. Each article of her clothing was removed with reverence, and he took his time to worship the newly exposed skin with soft kisses. She'd never been with a man who progressed so gradually, yet filled each moment with a thrilling surprise. It was as if he had fallen into a trance, bewitched by her, and the power of it was intoxicating. Somehow, without her noticing or participating, he had rid himself of his own clothing, and soon they lay naked together under the stars. The candles still burned, but the light seemed to diffuse into shadow, leaving them afloat on a tide of milky blackness.

He pulled back, sitting on his knees and haunches. Grasping her legs under her calves, he pulled her to him, wrapping her around his torso, entering gradually yet firmly. He controlled all movement, holding her under her buttocks as if she were weightless, arching his back to beseech the stars. Suddenly he was part animal, submitting to a craving beyond his understanding, yet he didn't disappear in the act like most men did, always mindful that this was a dance for two, and that while he was leading, it was she who created the music. He filled her completely, brought her to ecstasy not once, but three times before he lost himself in her.

Moments later he was leaning over her, breathless in

her hair, stroking her face with his fingertips. They remained joined for many minutes, listening to the night.

It was perfect. He was perfect.

In the darkness she never saw the storyboards of triumphs and defeats that were etched into his flesh.

The Citation's landing beams lit up the entire length of the deserted runway before lifting off into a perfect licorice sky. They had left the candles behind to burn out on their own, and he circled back, executing a low pass so that she could see where they had been. Then, with a shove of the throttles, he set the airplane on its tail, ascending at an almost vertical angle for nearly a minute.

"This is how you make me feel," he said loudly as the engines screamed under them. "Powerful . . . invincible."

They leveled off, the engines pulled back, and he could speak normally again.

"This is why I fly," he said, not looking to see if she'd heard, or what her reaction to the comment might be. But she did hear, and it made her smile.

They landed in Scottsdale just before midnight. He walked her to her car, saying he had to put the airplane away and that it would take some time. He kissed her gently, not the kiss of lovers, but the kiss of friends on the verge of love, which imparted a certain promise.

"I'll see you soon?" he said, the question mark at the end very clear.

"I'm not going anywhere," she said. They squeezed their hands together a final time before she got into her car.

As she drove off she checked the rearview mirror. He was still standing there, his hand raised in the air in farewell.

It was, without the slightest inclination toward doubt, the most wonderful evening of her life.

At the moment the wheels of the Citation carrying
Bernadette and Paul lifted off the runway at Scottsdale
Municipal Airport, Jerry Grasvik walked through the
door of a bar and grill near Gainey Ranch called Zipps,
which would have one believe they served the best burgers in town. Sitting at a booth near the back, already
working on a glass of beer the size of a bowling pin, was
the woman he knew as Diana, whom in his dark and
secret heart he liked to think of as his own personal
incarnation of Lady Death. Hell, it was his fantasy, and
he'd cast it any way he pleased.

To his great delight, she had dressed the part. She
wore a leather miniskirt over dark nylon leggings that
were too solid to be traditional nylons. They were
tucked into nasty little short-heeled, pointy-toed boots
with a retro kick to them. Her top was low cut, with
sequins that looked like studs spelling out the word *Bitch*
across her breasts. Nice touch, that. Over it she wore a
short black leather jacket, tucked in at the waist, the
collar turned high. But he saw none of that right away.
In fact, he almost didn't recognize her. Because her hair,
which had been long and dark and braided very Croft-
esque, was now blond and full. No, this full lion's mane
was, without coincidence, straight off the cover of the
Lady Death comic book she had given him the other
night. This was all for him, which meant something
wonderful.

He was hard before his butt hit the bench of the booth.

"You like?" she asked, running her black-nailed fingers through the blond mass.

He nodded, trying to be cool, but failing miserably. She smiled to let him know he wasn't fooling her.

"I'm into wigs . . . what can I say."

"Suddenly I am, too," he said, reaching across the table to touch it. It felt real, as well it should—it was human hair, something she'd owned for two years, when she and Damien had worked a little game one night in Chicago. A commodities trader somewhere in the Windy City would never be the same.

"So how's your cock?" she asked, her expression as mundane as if she'd inquired about his day.

"Happy to see you," he said, signaling the apathetic waitress that he wanted the same beer Diana was drinking.

"We're going to have some fun tonight," she announced, picking up the menu as she spoke. "Let's eat . . . you're going to need your strength."

She looked up and winked, delighted to see that he was already squirming.

They had burgers and onion rings and another pair of those stupendously tall beers. She tried to get him to talk about his job, but he was evasive, reluctant to bore her with what he called "tech shit" despite her assurance that she was interested. She had to be careful here—he'd alluded to a "big project" the other night, and if she pressed the issue now it could backfire. She'd get him to tell her eventually, of that she had no doubt.

To deflect her curiosity he asked personal questions of his own, going over the old ground of her job as a trainer, her inherited fortune, her knowledge of contemporary hard rock and her tastes in dark fantasy comics. He was especially interested in the house, and she fed him a story that now included the admission that she had a male roommate—good to cover this contingency in case he saw an electric shaver and some boxer shorts somewhere in the house—adding that he was gorgeous but gay, so don't even go there.

"I saw your house today," he said, dabbing at his mouth with a napkin.

She tried not to react, but inside an alarm was triggered. It had been a risk taking him home, but Damien had insisted, wanting to do the closet voyeur thing again. But there was always the chance that Jerry would come back unannounced, or drive by. Diana had that effect on men, possessing them quickly, and because she preyed on the weak the risk of this was even higher. If he somehow got inside or crashed the wrong party, so be it. What the hell, it was all just fucking around anyway. Nonetheless, her adrenaline level was suddenly elevated, because this time out there might be something more than kicks at stake.

"I thought you lived in Bumfuck. What was it—Mesa?"

"I do. I climb Camelback most days before work. It's how I get my exercise . . . instead of those pukes in the gym . . . sorry." He remembered she was a trainer at Bally's, though she'd not mentioned which one. "It's just that it's not only a better workout, but it's freaking beautiful, man. You can see everything from up there."

"Including my house?" she asked. As often as she'd sat out on her deck, she'd never looked close enough at Camelback to notice any hikers. Then again, they probably weren't visible from that distance.

"Yeah. I thought it was kinda cool. I was imagining what you were doing."

"Sleeping, I guarantee it."

"That's what I thought. You should climb with me some morning. If you wait too long it gets too hot. Takes about two hours if you bust. Killer workout."

"I'll think about it." Her trainer story was about to bite her on the ass.

As they were preparing to leave she pulled out her purse and began digging. Then her hand came out, balled in a fist, which she extended toward him across the table.

"I want you to take this," she said. She opened her hand, revealing a diamond-shaped blue pill.

He stared at it, and with a sheepish voice said, "I don't do drugs."

"It's not a drug, silly," she said, putting some humor in her tone. "Well, not like you mean."

"What is it then?"

She leaned across the table and whispered, "Viagra."

His head began shaking immediately. "I don't need Viagra," he said.

"Believe me, I know. That was me on top of you, remember? Just take it."

His expression darkened. "I don't get it. What's up with this?"

Her free hand reached for his, grasping it tenderly. She leaned across the table and spoke quietly. "It's a hundred milligrams. Which means, dear little Jerry, that there's nothing short of Lorena Bobbitt that will keep you from your appointed rounds tonight."

She paused, checking to see if anyone was listening in. Jerry was still frowning, but good-naturedly now. More skepticism than disapproval.

"Trust me. I have plans for you. I have six or seven plans for you, in fact. Believe me, you want this."

He looked down at the pill.

"Will it make me sick? I've heard that."

"It'll make you hard. Until-next-week kind of hard."

He smiled, took it from her and swished it down with the last of his beer.

"Good boy," she said, leaning back. "Because if you don't satisfy me in every way that I ask, I'm going to have to punish you."

"And we certainly wouldn't want that," he said as he slid out of the booth, beholding Diana in full leathered glory for the first time since his arrival. He looked her up and down and said, "Am I crazy, or is that pill working already?"

She kissed him, right here in front of God and every-body, then walked toward the door, correctly assuming he would follow.

She had him now. He would do anything she asked.

At the moment the Cessna touched down back at Scottsdale airport, Jerry and Diana were at her house, lying on the stripped bed, gazing out at the lights. She had put one of his CDs in; Jerry Cantrell never sounded so good, drugs or no drugs.

"You should go," she said. Nothing had been spoken between them since he'd rolled off of her fifteen minutes earlier, after his sixth successful orgasm of the evening. The first had been in the parking lot at Zipps, in the back of his car because her Corvette wasn't designed for copulation. The second had been in a public park at Fountain Hills twelve miles to the east—she'd made him wait until the world's largest fountain spouted its three-hundred-foot tower of water, saying she loved the sym-bolism of it. It wasn't quite dark and they'd found a grassy area out of the line of sight of the parking lot. Afterward they'd driven back to Scottsdale for another drink, at Barcelona this time, the hot new bar near Jer-ry's office, where they laughed at the BMW boys and the Virginia Slims girls crowding the place, parading their goods in an ages-old dance of egos and 1040s. After much protest he'd allowed her to sneak him into the women's bathroom off the restaurant—the one at the bar was too crowded with women trying to out-primp each other—and he'd penetrated her in one of the stalls after she promised not to make a sound when she came. She had lied, and they were summarily asked to leave the premises. By now they were well on their way to legally certifiable intoxication, so for their fourth act she'd asked him to take her across the street to his of-fice, which he again protested mightily and unsuccess-fully. He'd fucked her on the glass table of the main conference room, in full view of the executive floor thanks to the glass walls. Of course the building was empty tonight, though she assured him that wouldn't have changed anything, they'd have simply drawn the blinds. The fifth round went down in her hot tub—Diana said her roommate would get off on knowing that another man had made a deposit there. And the sixth and final chapter had been in her bed as Jerry Cantrell sang, with a surprisingly soft energy between them. She even lost the wig for this one, making it somehow more genuine, less recreational than real.

Then again, he was drunk. He could assign meaning to anything in this state.

Which he did. All in all, Jerry was certain that his world had changed. He couldn't deny a certain sense of pride—a stud was something he'd legitimately never considered himself. Couldn't have been the pill alone. Hell, he'd only masturbated three times in a single night once before, after which it got sort of boring no matter which comic book villainess was on the pillow next to him. Diana had shown him many faces tonight, they had laughed together—until tonight he'd not considered himself all that funny, either—they'd made fun of all the pretentious assholes to whom they were invisible, they'd pushed through fears and broken rules, they'd been evicted as a team, and generally made each other delirious with sexual pleasure.

Best of all, tonight they had become *friends*.

And now she was kicking him out on the street.

"Have I done something?" he asked, sitting upright. "It's not even midnight."

"I have to be at the gym at five," she lied. "And you have to work, too. Unless you're climbing some mountain first. And no, you haven't done something."

She smiled now. For a moment he thought the illusion had been shattered.

As he dressed he took a moment to appreciate his surroundings. The house was huge, two stucco levels tucked seamlessly into the rocks, something on the order of six thousand square feet, with the requisite pool and spa, the latter built into an outcropping in the patio deck

that made it seem to float in space. It was impossible
not to notice these kinds of places as you drove through
Scottsdale, but to him they had always been like the
rocks themselves, far removed from his life, inhabited
by another species.

But all that was about to change for Jerry Grasvik.
This was his first time on the hill, so to speak, and he
was surprised and even elated to admit that he liked
it here.

"You ever think about getting, you know, married
or something?"

"Is that a proposal?"

"No. Give me a week on that. You'd never marry
someone like me, anyhow."

She propped her head up with a hand. She was still
on the bed, watching him dress. "What's that supposed
to mean?"

"Look at this place. I live in a dump. Woman like you,
you don't marry downhill. But all that's gonna change, I
can guarantee you that."

Another alarm sounded deep in her mind.

"So I *am* going to marry beneath my station?" she
offered.

"Maybe you won't have to. At least, if you fall in love
with me."

"Don't tell me," she said. "You guys are going public
and you've got options. Close?"

He stopped dressing and stared at her. The smile, his
entire countenance of a little boy in Disneyland, was
suddenly gone.

"What?" she asked in alarm. She knew she had hit
a nerve.

"Something like that," he said. Then he returned to
pulling on his pants, moving quickly now.

"Tell me," she said, touching his shoulder.

He didn't answer. Everything about his aura now
screamed that he was angry.

She said, "What the hell are you pissed off at me
for?" Her tone was incredulous. She was taking a risk,

but she was nothing if not a master in deceptive little moments like this. It was why she was so good at the game, almost as good as Damien.

He froze, raising his chin, his lips set firmly. Got him.

"I'm sorry. It's just . . . money intimidates me. *People* with money intimidate me, like I'm not good enough to talk to them. But that's gonna change. And soon, too. Sometimes things just turn out good . . . that's what's gonna happen."

"Jerry, that's wonderful! I'm ecstatic for you!"

She waited, but he didn't take the bait.

"Are you going to tell me?"

He was buckling his belt, she only had a few more seconds.

"I can't."

"Can't, or won't?"

He sat on the bed, taking her shoulders in his hands. "Listen, I'll tell you everything. But not now, okay? Just trust me. When this goes down, I'll buy you two houses like this. I'll buy you a freaking island if that's what you want."

She summoned the softest expression she had in her arsenal, then said, "Only if you're on it."

His face cracked into a smile. "You're amazing," he said.

She pulled him to her, commencing a long embrace. She had just stumbled upon a new game, deliciously exciting because it was bigger than anything they'd tried before. To win it she had to do exactly what she'd told Damien she could do—she had to make Jerry Grasvik fall in love with her.

It was working already. Jerry was trembling as he held her, as if all his dreams and fantasies had just come true. As if he was no longer alone.

Only now, there was more at stake than matching Damien's dark powers of seduction, more to it than putting him in his place and evening the score. This was beyond ego and vanity, more than Diana the Huntress and Damien the Demon Lover hunting prey for fun and bragging rights. The game was about to go to a whole new level—now it was fun *and* profit—and if things worked as she planned, perhaps somewhere down the road she'd still deliver on her boast to Damien.

Lady Death, indeed. When she had all his new money, Jerry Grasvik might just end up dead after all.

> 31 <

By the next morning Bernie's old insecurities were kicking in like sore hamstrings after a marathon. She wasn't naïve, she wasn't a schoolgirl, and she certainly wasn't about to make up stories about it. As she liked to say, her mama didn't raise no fool. But hot damn, that was one kick-ass, straight-out-of-a-storybook night, with a guy who, if she were to describe him to her friends back home, they wouldn't believe it for a minute. Too good to be true. In each of her three previous relationship meltdowns, wallowing in the anxiety of being alone and the certainty of dying a childless spinster, those same friends had told her to let it be, time heals all wounds, and for God's sake don't go looking for love. Never happens when you're desperate for it. Look for a good lay instead—she reluctantly passed on that piece of advice—maybe a gold card to tide you over, but the love thing has its own timing, and it won't show if you're impatient. So maybe that's what this was about, she was here for something else entirely. Love, which liked to drop in unexpectedly, might just be crashing this little revenge party.

On the morning after the dream date of a lifetime, that's how it felt. It was a wonderful sensation, and while she felt silly considering the possibilities, she was certainly open to them. She'd let it be, as advised, go about her business, see what transpired on both counts. Even if Wesley came to nothing and her time in Scottsdale proved fruitless, at least she had last night.

With that in mind, she made her coffee and opened her e-mail.

B—don't know if this is good news or bad, but here goes. Ran the photos through one of my police contacts. Got a hit, a big one. The young dude is Brandon Nelson, your basic Brooklyn street tough. Long list of priors, assault, dealing, extortion, suspicion of murder. Line on the guy is he's muscle for bigger fish. Which brings me to the other guy. Name is Bobby "the Twin" Pellitier, and I'll sum it up for you in two words: organized crime. The guy is a mid-level goombah in the mob, which means you've stumbled onto something bigger than you thought. Like I said, don't know if this is good or bad. But I do know this— you need to watch your ass. Stay in the game, but don't get too close. You may not like this, but my friend has notified the FBI, and they may contact you. Just stay cool. This is what you came for. I hope, in the end, it's what you really want.

As for the other photo, the pissed-off woman, nothing came up. Nice-looking lady though, if she'd smile.

Thanks for respecting my safe zone. I'll explain later. I'm all over this, Bernadette.

Love, E.

Suddenly the knot in her stomach had nothing to do with Paul. Be careful what you ask for—her friends were always telling her that, too—and she'd asked for Eric's help. Eric, who had never backed down, never failed her when she needed him. He must indeed be under pressure, because his tone in the e-mail was odd. As if he was hurried, under the gun. And he'd used her full name, something he hadn't done in the twenty-five years she'd known him. She wasn't sure how she felt about the FBI involvement, either, but if Eric was right and she had tapped into something huge, then this was how it had to be. This was, she reminded herself, what she'd come to do.

Suddenly on the cusp of breaking Wesley, she realized she'd never really believed it could happen. She'd worm her way into his life, maybe throw a metaphoric pie in his face and expose him to his constituents as the lowlife that he is. Maybe all she wanted was for him to know that *she* knew, that he didn't get away scot-free. But she'd never dared hope for this, and the magnitude of it made her question her motives and her ability to see it through. In fact it made her uneasy, in need of a spiritual shower.

Maybe Eric had been right from the beginning. Leave the revenge business to higher powers. Negative energy, the lifeblood of her agenda, had a way of quietly seeping into your soul, the osmosis of bad karma, and before you knew it you became what you despised.

Now, after Eric's e-mail and the reflective beating she gave herself, she was more grateful than ever that the prospect of an intimate new friend, even a protector, was front and center in her life. Eric was a thousand miles away, but Paul, if she needed him, was just a telephone call away.

No one on Mummy Mountain noticed the nondescript white van with the ladder lashed to its roof appear sometime before dawn, and which was now parked a hundred yards down from the gate to Diana and Damien's house. Service vehicles were common on this road, and as invisible as the domestic help that arrived in them—pool cleaners, dog walkers, personal trainers, house cleaners. They were part of life here on the hill. At six thirty a gate swung open and Damien's BMW pulled out, heading as if by instinct to the airport, where Paul Lampkin would meet two Oar Research marketing managers and fly them to San Jose for a lunch meeting. Ten minutes after that a red Corvette appeared, heading across the valley to the Echo Canyon Park lot at the base of Camelback Mountain, where Diana would wait with hot coffee and bagels for Jerry Grasvik to come down from his thrice-weekly assault on the summit.

The man in the van knew nothing of the airport or of Diana's plans for Jerry. This morning he only knew that the house was now empty, and he would roll the dice that it would remain that way. At least for fifteen minutes, which was all he needed.

The van pulled up to the gate. The man who got out was tall and portly, wearing coveralls with a logo on the back that no one would read. He carried a small electronic device, which he pressed against the gate's control box, holding it in place. There were 9,999 possible configurations for a four-digit code, and the little machine ran through them all within forty-five seconds. Not that it ever took that long, since the laws of probability said that it would randomly stumble across the target code long before it reached the 9,999th alternative.

This morning it took only seventeen seconds.

The gate swung open. The fat guy in the overalls got back in the van, the gate closed behind him, and life on the hill was back to normal again.

Life at Oar Research, on the other hand, was anything but normal on this particular morning for Bernie. When she arrived at her desk just after nine there was a note on her chair. She assumed it was from Nadine, who had given her a conspiratorial wink when she passed the front desk on the way in. Then again, Nadine wouldn't compromise their new partnership with a note.

Bernie picked it up with apprehension that proved to be well-founded. It was from Wesley, asking her to come to his office as soon as she got in.

Wesley was on the phone—using his headset, of course, pacing in front of the window. When she knocked, he motioned for her to come in and sit, and when she left the door open he motioned for her to go back and shut it. He held up one finger, indicating he'd be done momentarily. He nodded as he listened, something that always amused her when observing people using the phone.

"I know, I know . . . but I already told you, we might not *need* a prospectus . . . of course I do . . . because it's a waste of money if we place privately . . . I hope within two weeks, but there's no way . . . I know that. . . ."

She sensed it was a lawyer on the other end. Something about the way Wesley kept getting interrupted and the look of angst on his face.

Finally Wesley nodded, said "Okay," then pushed a button as he tore the headset away and flung it onto his desk.

"Lawyer?" she asked with a smile. She hadn't exchanged good humor with Wesley in days, and she wanted to test the water this morning.

He actually grinned, though she thought she could hear the cracking of atrophied tendons as he did so. "What, you clairvoyant, too?"

"I've been told."

"So you already know what I want."

He was actually being playful, prompting her to take a chance. "You want a project update. There's a deadline approaching, and you're worried."

His grin faded into something she had more trouble reading.

"Not worried," he said, no longer playful. "Where are we?"

She rattled off a status report—the templates were done, the programming was close, the designer was an egotistical baby who couldn't take no for an answer, and the beta, the initial test version of the Web page, was still a week away.

Wesley chewed on his lower lip as he listened, perched on the corner of his desk. She wondered what it would take to get him to sit down, something she'd rarely seen in her days of observing him through his glass office walls.

"You need anything from me?" he asked.

"Yeah, actually. I keep asking Jerry for the content, and he keeps dodging me."

Wesley looked away. "Jerry's done with the content."

"So when do I get it?"

"You don't."

"Excuse me? How do I finish the damn—?"

He held up a hand for her to stop, that feeble little grin back in place, though a bit forced this time.

"When's the beta?" he asked.

"Schedule says a week from Friday. I can make that. *If* Jerry delivers."

Wesley nodded, rubbing his chin now. "Let's say you turn the finished programming over to Jerry and he dumps in the content. When then?"

"Depends on what he has. With a Web page you design first, program second, write third. It's like coloring in between the lines. If he's done, as you say, it may or may not fit together."

"Let's say that's Jerry's problem. When can I—*we*—have it?"

"You need it sooner than a week from Friday?"

"Let's say I do."

"Well . . ."

"I need it Monday."

Bernie whistled silently and raised her eyebrows.

"That's tight. My programmer—"

"What if you program it yourself? Bust your designer for templates by Friday, you program over the weekend, drop in dummy copy to test the navigation, tweak it yourself, turn it in by end of day Monday. Can do?"

"I don't know, I've never worked that way."

"I didn't ask if you'd done it like that before, I asked if you could do it now."

Ah, the old Wesley was back. Maintaining direct eye contact as he issued ultimatums and spewed rhetoric.

When she didn't answer, he opened a drawer in his credenza and withdrew a piece of paper. He glanced at it, then handed it to Bernie.

It was a check for five thousand dollars, payable to her.

"I don't understand," she said, staring at it.

"It's a bonus. Five now, for your weekend, five more on Monday when you deliver. On top of your contract, of course."

She allowed a moment to pass, processing what this could mean.

"You're giving me a bonus to do what I'm already being paid to do?"

"No. I'm giving you a bonus for getting me out of a jam. One with a lot riding on it. Believe me, I'm happy to pay you to make this happen. Are we good?"

Suddenly it dawned on her, crashing through the gates of her awareness like a football fan arriving with the beer . . . the realization that her project was involved with Wesley's little scam, whatever it was. It should have been obvious, but she had been going through the motions on the Web page, looking for sinister shades elsewhere. She hoped it didn't show in her expression.

"What's wrong?" he asked.

She met his eyes, forcing her mindset from fear to amazement. Wesley was too good not to read her like a balance sheet.

"I'm just, I don't know . . . blown away."

"Can you do it?"

She nodded, eyebrows raised. "Yeah. I can do it."

She picked up the check and took it back to her desk. Once there, she opened her laptop and did what she should have been doing from the get-go. She e-mailed Eric, telling him about what had just happened. If he was talking to the authorities, if he was bringing in the FBI for God's sake, he needed to know everything.

They would both just have to deal with the consequences later on.

Bernie had found that the drive home at the end of the workday, if undertaken an hour on either side of five o'clock, qualified for television coverage as an extreme sport. There was something in the air down here that made people drive with complete disregard for

safety and common sense, much less something as unnecessary as courtesy. People weaving in and out of
lanes, flagrant tailgating, the blaring of horns, everyone
on a cell phone . . . if you reached the next stoplight
first, you won. Not only that, every fourth car was a
Cadillac the size of a small barge, driven by a color-
blind octogenarian with wraparound sunglasses that
looked like they were popped out of a welding helmet.
If you responded to being cut off or tailgated with a
questioning look, or God forbid a middle finger, you got
a *what's-your-problem-pal?* glare in response, like *you*
were the asshole. This was why Bernie usually left early
or hung out in the neighborhood after work to shop or
catch a light dinner.

Tonight she worked until seven, already pushing the
schedule to accommodate Wesley's demands and earn
her ten-grand bonus for delivering by Monday. After
grabbing a burger at In-N-Out—a phenomenon beyond
the ability of sociologists to explain—she took the long
way home, staying on Frank Lloyd Wright Boulevard all
the way to Via Linda, where she turned to angle back
toward Scottsdale Ranch and her little condo.

Once on Via Linda she realized someone was following her.

She'd noticed a white van on her ass back on Frank
Lloyd Wright. That was certainly normal, but when she'd
changed lanes—hey, if the guy wanted to blast by her
in the right lane, she was happy to move—the van did
the same, staying right on her tail. When she turned onto
Via Linda, catching a yellow light to do it, she noticed
that the van turned as well, actually running the red to
stay with her.

A physical reaction swept over her, a familiar fight-
or-flight tongue of ice across her spine that hadn't
changed since childhood, when it had been a frequent
visitor. Tonight she would opt for flight, so she sped up
suddenly, expecting—hoping—to see the van drop back.

But that didn't happen. The van barely lost distance.
Quickly she perceived a new problem. A quarter mile

ahead was the only stoplight on the street. It was at Shea, which bore traffic as if the governor had ordered an evacuation of the city. She prayed the light would be green, because running a red at this intersection was suicide.

She saw the yellow, then saw it turn to red. She was two hundred yards away.

Think fast. She could wheel to the right on Shea without having to stop, but only if the traffic had a timely hole. The road was too wide to stop in the middle and block both lanes. Either way she played it, the guy in the van would have time to jump out and get to her, if that was his game. Then again, maybe he was just another schmuck trying to get home in time to watch *Survivor*.

She chose the right lane, waiting until the last moment to hit the brake. Looking left, she saw that there was no way she could turn, but an opening was seconds away.

The van pulled up next to her on the left. Not in the lane, but inches away. She'd have to slide over the center console and bolt out the passenger door.

But not without looking first.

The man wore a baseball cap and sunglasses. That's all she saw, because her eyes were drawn to something else. He was holding up his hand, extending it toward her, as if he were holding a gun. But it wasn't a gun. It was his finger—not his middle finger, but his forefinger pointing right at her, his thumb pointing straight up. Just like you'd do if you were pantomiming shooting a pistol. As she looked he crooked his thumb down and up, a finger-gun.

Bang. You're dead.

He smiled broadly.

The opening arrived. Bernie wheeled the Volvo hard to the right, swinging into the curb lane, narrowly missing a car in the middle lane. She floored it, quickly matching the traffic flow. Only then did she look in her rearview.

The van hadn't turned.

32

Damien picked up on the second ring.

"Paul?"

A pause, then, "Bernie, hello!" He almost asked how she got his number, but he quickly remembered he'd used his mobile phone to call her the night before, and she probably had caller I.D.

"I'm sorry to call. . . ."

"It's okay! I thought of you today. A lot."

"I thought of you, too. Listen . . ."

"Are you okay? You don't sound okay."

She hesitated, struggling to keep the emotion out of her voice. "No," was all she said.

His voice was very soft as he said, "What is it? Talk to me."

"It's not you, nothing about last night. Someone . . . I just need to see you. Now before you answer, just listen . . . this isn't me being clingy or overreacting to last night, okay? Don't get the wrong idea. It's just . . . someone followed me home. I don't want to be alone tonight."

Damien shot Diana an inquisitive look. They were in their bedroom, Damien having just stepped out of the shower, Diana putting away some new clothes she'd purchased that afternoon—a few little black ditties that Jerry would love. She responded with a confused look of her own, having already deduced that it was Bernie on the line.

Damien mouthed *she wants to come over* without making a sound.

Diana smiled and slowly nodded. The way she smiled reminded Damien of why he was with her—the promise of mischief, a hint of darkness.

"Come see me," he said.

"I could meet you somewhere. . . ."

"I want you to see where I live. Please."

A pause, then, "If you're sure that's okay . . . I feel funny inviting myself. . . ."

"Stop that. You need a hug. I'm the guy."

He gave her directions and hung up. Diana already had her arms around him, waiting for his full attention.

"What *shall* I ever wear?" she said, just as she kissed him deeply.

Paul Lampkin met Bernie at the door forty-five minutes later, taking her face into his hands as he kissed her. The house had been Diana-proofed, as they called it—Bernie would have to start digging around in closets and drawers to sense that a woman lived here. If she found something suspicious, he'd explain that he had female decorators, female housekeepers, a sister who visited frequently, whatever it took. But that was the least of his concerns tonight. Bernie wouldn't be poking her nose anywhere it wasn't supposed to be. Diana had seen to that.

She was predictably blown away by the house. She was, in fact, speechless for a minute because it wasn't at all what she'd expected.

They were still in the foyer, and from here she could see into several rooms, as well as out through the glass walls toward the expanse of Scottsdale and the mountains beyond. The entry was actually to the side of the main house, so that when visitors entered they beheld the grandeur of the interior and the exterior simultaneously. The double front doors were ten feet high and arched at the top, made of black metal accented with crossing bands of brass. The foyer floor was of creamy marble laced with tan and pink, as were two thick columns that set it off from the rest of the house. Two steps brought you down into the living room, with a stone-surfaced fireplace the size of a small garage, also flanked by smaller columns. The ceiling here reached two stories, at the center of which was a rounded dome housing a leaded glass skylight. A mezzanine walkway was visible to one side, looking down into the sitting area. A wide hallway beckoned from her right, leading to guest bedrooms and other special-purpose areas. To the left through one of the high arched doorways she could see a family room, and beyond that the kitchen area, outfitted with more granite and marble than the local cemetery. Also visible was a magnificent curving staircase, the railing to which matched the metal detail of the front door.

As she took it all in, she remembered some of the specifics of his background, as related to her at the ball game a few nights earlier. Nothing about that little bio would have led one to believe that he was rolling in dough.

"I know what you're thinking," he said, reading her eyes. "How does a lowly pilot live like the president of an airline, right?"

"Crossed my mind," she said, her head pivoting back and forth to take it all in.

"I'll tell you sometime," he said, urging her into the family room area with a gentle hand at the small of her back. "Let's just say I invested foolishly in the late nineties, got lucky, then sold early."

"Very lucky," she said, her eyes even wider now when they arrived at the informal living area, which included a family room with a flat-screen television the size of a small billboard, another massive fireplace, floor-to-ceiling teak bookshelves, and a view out to a horizon-edge swimming pool and a hot tub that seemed to hang out over the city.

"Cisco options," he said. "My broker said sell, I held. Amazing what happens to fifty thousand dollars over eight years with a company like that, especially when you're in and out of options instead of the stock. Then he said hold, so I sold. Good timing, too. Parlayed it with a couple of crazy telecom plays he said not to buy . . . what can I say."

"Guy's good," she said, appreciating the way he kept his ego out of the story. She knew enough about Cisco to know that, if what he'd just said was true, he'd scored four or five million dollars on the deal. Maybe more. She pegged the house at two to three million, so it was possible if he decided not to let the IRS in on his secret.

The saddle leather couch was oversized, and as she sank into it she concluded that it was without a doubt the most comfortable piece of furniture she'd ever surrendered to. This was when she noticed the music, which she recognized as the soundtrack from *The Cider House Rules*.

"I do the best margaritas in Arizona," he said, already at the bar, starting to slice into a pile of limes. "Blended or rocks?"

"Rocks," she said. "No salt."

"A purist. My kind of girl." As he began pouring ingredients into a blender he said, "Tell me what happened today."

She replayed the incident, demonstrating the feigned handgun with her hand.

"Don't suppose you got a license number."

"Damn, I knew I forgot something."

The blender came on. To pass the moment, he came to her, bent over the couch and hugged her from behind. She closed her eyes, releasing herself and her anxiety to the safety of his embrace.

A minute later he returned to the bar. He poured the drinks into two large glasses and came back. Before sitting down he picked up a remote control from the coffee table. When he hit a button, fire appeared in the fireplace.

"What a boy scout," she said.

He sat next to her, putting a hand on her shoulder.

"Cheers," he said, clicking his glass against hers, then taking a drink.

"Now I want you to tell me *why* someone would do that to you."

"If I said I didn't know . . ."

"I wouldn't believe you." He took another sip, his eyes communicating an earnest concern, or at least a determination to get an answer.

"How well do you know your boss?" she asked.

She didn't tell him about Peggy or why she'd moved to Scottsdale. Nor did she tell him about Nadine or their plans to follow the slime trail and see where it led. She simply said she'd stumbled onto something that she thought suspicious, and when she confronted Wesley about it—she was making this up as she went along, realizing she'd opened a can of worms that didn't need opening right now—he seemed defensive.

"Did he threaten you?" Paul asked. "Directly or indirectly?"

"No. He was just pissed. I'm probably imagining all of this . . . it was probably some crazy guy who gets off on scaring women."

"It's amazing what gets some guys off," said Paul, draining the final drops of his margarita from his glass. Without asking he got up, then returned with the pitcher, refilling her glass. His was already full from the trip to the bar.

"These are strong," she said, already feeling a heaviness in her eyes, and mere moments later, in her chest.

"Is there any other kind?" he quipped, again touching her shoulder. "You're tense. Here . . ."

And with that, he set down his drink and spun her away from him, massaging the muscles of her neck and shoulders.

"That's nice," she said, not sure if she'd spoken loudly enough for him to hear.

"Finish your drink," he said, his voice blending into the music now, surrounding her. She took a long swallow, loving the sour sweetness of it, the coldness as it slid down her throat.

His face was at her neck now, kissing under her collar.

"I'm glad you're here," he said.

Her eyes remained closed, and her head began to sway. The music was thicker now, the fire somehow warmer, and she felt sleepy. Too much margarita, too soon.

"Drink," he said, holding her glass to her lips for her. She swallowed, the ice of the drink welcome in the sudden warm air of the room.

"You look tired," he said. "You can sleep, if you want to. I don't mind."

She swam in his touch for a few moments, realizing that opening her eyes would take incredible effort, and that she didn't want to try it anyway. Sleep was a good idea. Perfect, in fact.

"You're sure? Maybe for just a minute. I'm so . . . tired. . . ."

"You have a right to be tired," he said gently, whispering in her ear. He was stroking her hair now, and after a few seconds he eased her down onto the cushions, taking the drink from her hand.

A moment later he stood, lifting her feet from the floor onto the couch. He placed her hands gently over her stomach, then picked up his drink and took a long swallow.

He didn't look over as Diana walked into the room. She stood next to him, putting her arm around his waist, and together they watched Bernie sleep.

The dream was delicious, unlike any she'd ever known. At times she thought she was awake because Paul was with her, his voice reassuring and his touch warm, telling her it was all right, to let it be . . . that she was beautiful . . . she was in a huge bed that looked out over the city, which was dark now, the horizon a swirl of stars and streaking light . . . but then, as it is in dreams, the world was black again, the music fading in

and out . . . rising and falling in the night sky, riding in
the jet next to Paul, touching his face . . . diving into a
lake of sparkling water, twisting in depths of soothing
moisture . . . she was on the blanket now, overlooking the
canyon as candles twirled overhead, her skin sensing the
thick night air, wrapped in its caress . . . Paul stroking
her face, licking her nipples, speaking her name over
and over, spreading her legs with tender hands, his kisses
descending . . . inside her now, urgent fingers, probing,
first one then two, now many, rhythmic and demanding . . . somehow still suckling at her breasts, lips pulling
at them . . . while other lips and then his tongue probe
and play at her wetness, teasing with electric pleasure . . .
his voice at her ear, whispering her name, urging her to
come for him, come with him . . . the face between her
thighs twisting with passion . . . a finger pressing into
her backside, intruding through forbidden gates . . . the
sky opening to swallow her whole . . . a dark silhouette
of his face against the clouds, melting into them, changing shape . . . two clouds, two faces dissolving . . . a
mounting need, the burning promise, the loss of will . . .
the screaming of the engines as they went vertical . . . a
shudder and a whimper she thought was hers . . . blind
ecstasy, bordering on madness . . . and then, as the madness subsided like a wave washing back to sea, soft lips
covering her mouth, a hungry tongue, the taste of her
own salt, the smell of jasmine. . . .

The chemical Damien slipped into Bernie's margarita
was known on the street as GHB—gammahydroxybuty-
rate—though more commonly as the date rape drug. A
few capfuls and you made someone sick; ten to fifteen
and you put them in a semi-conscious, dreamlike state
such as Bernadette's; twenty capfuls and you had yourself a full-fledged gang bang. Diana had purchased a
bottle of GHB a year earlier to use in one of their out-
of-town scenes, and though it never went down she hung
on to it, trusting that something would eventually come
up. And sure enough, it did, when she was told that

Bernie was on her way over to swaddle herself in Paul Lampkin's comfort.

Damien and Diana stood arm in arm the next morning, watching Bernie drive through the gates on her way home to shower and go to work. She awoke at dawn with a splitting headache, her face buried in Paul's shoulder. Explaining that she seemed to have had a bad reaction to the margaritas, he was falling all over himself with apologies, offering to make her breakfast, to nurse her back to normal. She thought it was sweet, but all she wanted was to go home and clean up. She couldn't remember anything about what had happened, and he assured her that nothing had, other than his holding her in the night, keeping the demons at bay. She vaguely remembered demons, a dream where they came to devour her, but she didn't mention this to Paul. No point in sounding like a hysterical schoolgirl this early in their budding relationship.

Diana pulled Damien down to her, kissing him playfully. "She was fun," she said.

"I can still taste her on you," he said. He could also smell the faint trace of her jasmine perfume, something he'd bought for her on a trip to Japan.

"Maybe we should do that with Jerry . . . I'll taste *him* on you."

"Not in this lifetime," he said, pulling away.

They walked back into the kitchen, where he poured them both a cup of coffee. In the ritual of their life together, this was one of his.

"So, did you sleep on it?" he asked, not needing to frame the question any further. While Bernie slept they had retired to the deck to discuss what Diana had learned about Jerry's impending wealth. They explored her next move, how to get Jerry to reveal the source of that wealth, and once he did, how to get their hands on it. She said she'd sleep on it, thus inspiring the question.

Damien signed up right away, delighted that the game was suddenly different from before. They had also discussed the tantalizing proposition that Bernie had stum-

bled upon something dirty in Wesley Edwards's Day
Planner, and the prospect of using it to watch Wesley
squirm. This kept Bernie in the game, too, much to Damien's delight. Diana took careful note of this.

They agreed on both counts that it would be refreshing to have something more at stake than blood and
ink. A good week for gamesmanship, indeed. Without
acknowledging it, both knew there would be no going
backward from this point on. The game, the stakes, their
partnership, all of it hung in the balance now, with Jerry
and Bernadette playing the role of pawns. They had yet
to discuss what might become of them when the game
was over.

"I did," she said, smiling coyly at him over the rim of
her cup.

"You have a plan, then."

She sipped, taking her time, making him wait.

"Foolproof."

He opened his palms, wanting to hear more. "If you
tell me you'll have to kill me?"

Her little smile disappeared behind the cup. "Something like that," she mumbled, just loud enough for him
to hear.

"Give me a hint."

She summoned the grin again. "Let's just say it's
something women have been doing to men since the
dawn of time. The natural order of things, you might
say."

"Really. Have you pulled it on me?"

"More than you know, my dear. More than you
know."

33

Bernie couldn't remember ever feeling like this. It wasn't just that her head throbbed and her stomach felt like she'd swallowed the Great Salt Lake. Bad as all that was, she was what her mother had always claimed as her own personal malady—a nervous wreck. Between Wesley and his scam and Paul and his sexual chemistry, she was blinded to reason, on a speeding train with no stops until the end of the line. Good and evil had an iron grip on each arm, tugging with the force of her own conflicted desires. She was somewhere she shouldn't be, doing what she shouldn't be doing, frightened of failure, terrified of the consequences of success. She was completely alone with what she had created. Eric was lost to her, swimming in his own problems. It was suddenly all bigger than she'd imagined, with risks and consequences beyond her control.

And worst of all, none of it would bring Peggy back. This was all an exercise in cynicism and foolish pride, in the ego of outrage. She had been warned that nothing good could come of it. She was supposed to be setting the world straight, but instead she was setting it on its ear.

And then there was Paul. Beautiful, strong, charmingly witty, darkly provocative Paul. Could love spring from the pursuit of hate? Or was the relationship doomed because the seed had been planted in false soil? How many times had she seen this movie—the hero is

forced to lie to get what she wants . . . she falls in love
in spite of her desperate mission . . . the lie and the love
both promulgate, one for the sake of her intentions, the
other in spite of them. Then the lie is exposed, and while
the mission is won, the love has been forever compromised. In those movies forgiveness prevails, the deceived
lover conquers pride and bitterness and meets her at the
airport with flowers and a ring. The audience weeps and
cheers, the critics simply puke and the film goes to video
in a month.

There was something else, too. Something disturbing
in a way she couldn't explain away. It was the dream
last night, the experience of it not sitting well, or still.
The line between dream and reality, so unimportant in
the moment, was now an incoherent question that kept
tugging at her sense of propriety. What had she really
done, and more frightening to consider, what had Paul
done? Worse yet was knowing that in the darkest re-
cesses of her mind she had enjoyed the surrender. She'd
actually been sore this morning, as if it had happened
in this world instead of in her head.

She didn't know what or who to believe. Not even
herself anymore, perhaps the most troubling thing of all.

This was going to be fun. Entering into a process in
which the outcome is a given frees one of restraint,
allowing for creative license and, especially in this case,
a leisurely pace. This was Diana's favorite sport, and she
was its Wayne Gretzky.

Today she was going to completely and, as they say
in the law, with malice aforethought, mess with Jerry
Grasvik's head.

Damien would be at the airport all day participating
in a mandatory FAA shakedown flight on the Cessna
after an all-night overhaul on the landing gear, one of
the parts you don't want getting temperamental on you
as it reaches old age. The old bird was the Dorian Gray
of aviation, it just got younger and younger with each
new part they put on it. Diana dressed in a little black

sundress with sandals, feeling very femme fatale as she set out to torture Jerry for the day. She forwarded the phone to her mobile, which meant she could be there to watch as he came unglued.

First stop was the Echo Canyon parking lot, where she'd been the previous morning. Jerry was stepping up his routine to a daily climb, the by-product of a sudden concern for his physical appearance. She saw his little Nissan pickup in one of the stalls, meaning he was still on the mountain, which in turn meant his cell phone would be in the car. He'd told her he never took it with him on the climb, which would be like taking a CD player into church.

Just to be sure, she got out and went over to the pickup. Sitting on the passenger seat was his cell phone, on top of a stack of computer geek magazines.

This was where she'd place the first call. He'd see that she'd called him as soon as he got back to his car. He'd get her message, and the first little arrow through his heart will have drawn blood.

She cleared her throat and tested her voice. She was going for a subdued tone, like she really didn't want to have to say what was coming.

"Hi, it's me. Listen . . . we need to talk. I've been thinking and . . . we just need to talk. Call me."

No good-bye. Just a click.

Twenty minutes later he appeared at the head of the trail, barely breathing hard. He wore a backpack full of books and water bottles, his form of resistance training. His goal, he'd said, was seventy minutes round-trip, and he was within ten minutes of it.

She watched him fish out some water, kill the entire bottle, then make his way to his car. She had parked on the street and walked in, and was standing at the opposite end of the lot behind the stone fence.

He got in. His head lowered. He picked up the phone, looked at it. Head back up, as if thinking. Back down, punching in numbers.

Her mobile phone rang in her hand. The caller ID confirmed it was Jerry.

She let it ring until her message kicked in. He'd have to wait to see what this was all about, each minute an eternity of stomach acid and doubt.

Diana smiled as she cut across a patch of dirt to her car.

She followed him to the Oar building, staying far enough behind to remain unseen. As Jerry got out of the car she dialed his work extension. Normally he'd shower first in the employee facility, but she had a feeling he'd forgo that today.

"Hey. I was hoping I'd catch you." She let a long pause help set the stage. Her tone was that of someone who'd just been told a close friend had died. "I need to talk to you. Please call me."

Click.

She watched him go inside, walking quickly.

Four minutes later her mobile phone rang. She closed her eyes, placing the phone against her cheek, feeling the vibration.

Then she went to the Great Indoors across the street and sat at Starbucks for an hour, smiling as she looked out at the parking lot. Her mobile phone rang four times during the hour she was there, none of them answered.

A little after ten Diana got in her car and drove north, up past The Boulders resort and into Cave Creek. She did this for one reason—she knew the mobile phone reception here was terrible, that calls were most often disconnected within the first minute, that is if you could get through at all.

"Hello? Can you hear me?"

"Diana . . . God, I've been calling you all morning!"

"Hello?"

"Diana, I'm here. Can you hear me now?"

Silence. There was static on the line and she wanted to take full advantage of it. Finally she said, "Hello? Jerry?"

"I'm here. I've been calling you . . . can you hear me?"

"I can hear you." Silence. As if she wasn't sure where to start.

"Hello?" he said urgently.

"I'm here, Jerry. Listen . . . I've been thinking about the other night."

"So have I. You don't sound happy . . . what's going on?"

"It's just . . . I don't know, it's stupid."

"If you're feeling something then it's not stupid."

She could hear the anxiety in his voice. She took a deep breath to make sure he could hear the angst in hers.

"I think we need to talk."

"We *are* talking."

"I mean, really talk. Can you meet me?"

"Of course I can meet you. . . ."

The line was quiet now, so she scraped her fingernails across the tiny holes at the bottom on her phone. "Hello?" she said, sounding breathless. "Jerry?"

"Diana, I'm here. Where are you? I'm here. . . ."

She clicked the phone dead, and then she laughed out loud.

Her phone rang eight more times before noon while she browsed the Cave Creek shops. When she got to The Boulders hotel bar, she put it on the table next to her as she sipped a glass of Chablis with her shrimp Louis. It rang four more times during the hour she was there, and she smiled at the bartender, who gave her a quizzical look each time it did, wondering why she didn't answer. She thought about telling him, saying that she was torturing her lover just for the fun of it, seeing how the news would hit him. But she decided against it, finding it more fun to make him wonder. It was always more fun when they didn't have a clue they were being played.

She called Jerry again at ten after one. She was hoping

he'd be gone to lunch, that he'd take a late break to stay by the phone. But this was working better than she'd expected. He was probably too upset to eat.

He picked up on one ring.

"Why haven't you called me?" she said, very pissed now.

"I *have* been calling you, every freaking ten minutes! Where are you, Mexico?"

She let a long moment pass, her way of scolding his insolence.

"I'm sorry," he said, right on cue. "What's going on with you?"

"Can you meet me? It won't take long."

"Of course I can meet you. And what won't take long? You can take all day with me, you know that. . . ."

"Brokers Grill, at five." It was only a few blocks from his office.

"How about now?" he asked. She could hear in his voice that he was in agony, and that this would be the longest afternoon of his life. Perfect.

"I can't. Five." Then, a long moment of quiet.

"I'll be there," he said. "Listen, are we okay?"

An even longer pause now. Then, "I'll see you there, Jerry." Her voice this time was resigned to something final.

"This is a mistake," she said. He'd been waiting at the Brokers Grill for twenty minutes, and his face was actually red when she walked in. He was sitting at one of the outdoor tables under the mister, presumably because of the smoke inside. The Brokers Grill was "cigar friendly," in her mind a laughable contradiction in terms. He'd tried to kiss her hello, but she'd turned her head to offer her cheek.

As they sat down he took her hand, but she gently pulled it away from his grasp. She saw that he had taken in her appearance, and that in spite of her torment it pleased him, perhaps because it was a glimpse of what

he was about to lose. The sleeveless dress showed off
the tattoos on her arms in a way that said *kiss my ass*
to judgmental eyes.

He glanced from side to side before speaking. "What's
a mistake?"

She burned her eyes into his and said, "We are."

Then she sat back and watched the show. It was all
very subtle, but she could see it happening, the gloss
washing over his eyes, the slight blush to his cheeks, the
body language, him fighting it off, trying to remain cool.
She fought back the desire to grin and just watched,
sipping her water.

"I don't understand," he said, shaking his head.

She drew a deep breath and blew it out with a flourish.
"Okay," she began. "Let me see if I can do this."

The waitress made a timely appearance, so Diana ordered a glass of wine. Jerry didn't want anything other
than for her to get on with it.

Finally she turned in her seat and leaned forward, putting her hands on his knees.

"We started fast. Too fast. That alone isn't what's
wrong, but it makes things complicated because we don't
have a history. We're feeling each other out, and I liked
what I was feeling. That's the problem, Jerry, I *liked*
how I felt. And then . . ."

Emotion caught in her throat.

"Go on," said Jerry, barely audible. "And then . . ."

"I can't be intimate with a man who won't be intimate
with me. I'm sorry."

His jaw fell open. "I don't know . . . what the hell are
you talking about?"

"Of course you don't know. You're a man. By definition, you don't know."

"I'm not like other men."

"That's what I thought. Until . . ."

"Until *what*, for shit's sake? You're driving me crazy
here!"

She pulled away. She manufactured a look that was
the product of many years of development and practice,

something that danced between affection and regret. The eyes of a father who has to put down his son's rabid dog, the brave smile of good-bye on the face of a wife at her husband's deathbed. If she wasn't the Wayne Gretzky of this game, then she certainly was its Meryl Streep.

"It's none of my business," she said. "You made that perfectly clear."

His face froze, then evolved toward understanding tinged with disbelief.

"You have all these big plans," she went on, "but you won't let me in. They don't include me. Not that they should. I'm not a fool, Jerry . . . but I thought we had, you know, connected, found something in each other. After you left . . . I don't know, I just felt so . . . alone. You going on with your life, and me . . ."

He was shaking his head. "We just freaking *met* each other, Diana! What do you want from me?"

Her eyes clouded, right on cue.

"I want you to follow your heart. Like I follow mine. I want to *be* with you, Jerry . . . I want to play with you, make all your dreams come true."

She leaned in for the kill, her voice low, just for him.

"I want to be your Lady Death, and you to be my slave forever. I thought we could do that, be something special together, you know? But when you couldn't let me in . . . I felt cheap, like you were using me. I'm sorry, I know how that sounds. But I don't just fuck guys I meet in comic book stores, okay? It's just that I . . . that I was beginning to really care. I was beginning to hope."

She sat back, like a surgeon who had just sutured a ragged incision. Now let's see if the patient lives or dies.

"I didn't know," he said, his voice matching hers. "If I'd have known . . . of course I wanted that, felt that way . . . but how could I know?"

"Well, now you know."

"And you want to break it off."

"Before I get hurt."

Now he shifted in his seat and set his jaw.

"Stop. Right here, right now. Listen to me. Are you listening closely?"

She nodded, her eyes wide.

"You were, you *are,* too much to hope for. You've been in my dreams since forever, okay? When I saw you I about swallowed my tongue. When you talked to me I couldn't believe what I was seeing and hearing. And then, who you turned out to be . . . you were perfect. Perfect for *me.* But I couldn't assume anything, okay? I mean, here I am, this techno comic book freak, and here you are, this rich and gorgeous goth chick who knows everything I'm thinking and feeling . . . who actually *digs* me. Me! How could I take that chance? I *wanted* to tell you everything—but I didn't want to blow it, you know? But now . . . let me tell you. Please. It's not too late, okay? That's all I can do, be honest with you now, open up to you."

She couldn't wait to tell Damien about this.

Diana closed her eyes, as if going backward from her decision was painful, as if she was about to compromise the very thing that made her strong. But she would do it for him, because it was that important, she felt that strongly. All of this screamed at him from behind her closed eyes and trembling lips, which he leaned in and kissed softly.

"I'll tell you everything," he whispered reassuringly. "Right now."

She opened her eyes and smiled through a complicated little pout.

He said, "But there's something you should know." He lowered his eyes. "What we're doing . . . it's not what you'd call legal. I mean, nobody's gonna really get hurt or anything, but sometimes you gotta cut some corners to play this big."

A nasty little smile spread across her face as she put her arms around him and drew him close. She put her lips to his ear and whispered, "That's perfect."

At that moment, Jerry knew he had a new partner in crime.

* * *

Diana didn't know where Damien was. This wasn't unusual—they didn't keep tabs and impose expectations, which meant they both came and went without question. He had stayed away overnight before, several times in fact, and sometimes he'd call, sometimes he wouldn't. She kept that scorecard to herself, in a place that was rapidly filling up with documentation.

She had so much to tell him tonight. This was not the time to piss her off.

It was nearly seven o'clock when she heard the door-bell ring. Something pinged in her stomach, because no one had buzzed in from the gate, and the gate alarm had not sounded. Damien wouldn't ring the bell, he'd just pull his car into the garage and come in through the utility room.

She kept a gun in her closet. She was in the family room watching Bob Golan on *Entertainment Tonight* when the doorbell sounded, and she was tempted to run for it, especially after looking down toward the gate and seeing it was still closed. But that was premature, even rash—it could be Jerry, could be a neighbor kid, even the Seventh-day Adventists, all of whom were capable of jumping a fence.

She looked through the security peephole in the door, but nothing was there. The bell rang a third time while her face was pressed against the metal surface.

Irritated, she yanked open the door, her breath catching in her throat.

It wasn't Jerry, it wasn't a neighbor kid, and it wasn't some fence-jumping jackass in a suit and a crew cut handing out pamphlets. It was Wesley Edwards, a Cheshire cat smirk on his face.

Using a bad Cuban dialect, he crooned, "Lucy, you have some 'splaining to do. . . ."

> **34** <

Dallas, Texas

Eric Killen was fed up. His wife had adopted PMS as
a second career, and his job was not one in which grati-
fication was either instant or all that common. His son's
health was stable, but the doctors said you could never
take it for granted, that you could wake up one day to
a whole new plate of enchiladas that wasn't on the menu
the day before. On top of all that, it had been several
weeks since Bernie had taken off for Scottsdale to
launch her little crusade, and he was worried. Not only
for her, but for the people who got in her way, God
help them. He had promised her he'd be there when she
needed him, and that he'd do what he could on this end
in the meantime. Since the day she left town, he had
been working toward that end.

And now, for the first time, something promising had
come up. He had called in many favors, cast out many
lines, and this morning his telephone rang. Being in the
crime and punishment business may not play to the ego,
but it created contacts and situations that were useful to
someone who needed to peek behind the curtain, even
if it meant bending a few rules. One of the administrators at Da Slamma, the home where Eric knocked heads
with the juvies sent there for serious attitude adjustment,
was aware of Eric's involvement with Bernie's situation.
He also knew someone at the security firm that had the
Embassy Suites account, the same Embassy Suites where

Bernie's sister had leapt to her death from a sixth-floor landing.

The guy called Eric this morning to offer his services. He was skeptical, since he'd made all his files and videos available to the police at the time of the investigation. But things were different now. They didn't know the name of Peggy's lover then, and because of the suicide verdict there was no reason for them to be interested now. Without the slightest evidence of foul play, the fact that Peggy had been involved with someone besides her husband was no longer of interest to the police beyond it being a motivating factor in her suicide. They couldn't exactly arrest the guy for being a cad. She had jumped, she was alone when it happened, and that was that. But now that Eric had determined who the lover was and had a picture of the guy for his trouble, maybe there was something that could be done.

The security guy, who rather liked the idea that he might be able to one-up the cops in uncovering foul play, was happy to take another look. He'd go through the video captures of the front desk one more time—the camera clicked a still shot every thirty seconds, twenty-four seven—even going back a few weeks just to be sure. He'd already checked the registration records, and there were indeed a handful of Wesley Edwards registrations in the months preceding the suicide. None of that proved anything to the police, since there was no way to connect Peggy to Wesley Edwards, at the hotel or anywhere else. But there had been no Wesley Edwards registration on the day of the suicide—Peggy had booked a room under her own name, and according to the police had gone there to get high, write her suicide note and take a header over the railing. But if Eric could prove that Edwards was there, if there was video that showed this to be true . . . it was worth a look. It would be a start. And the guy at the security firm was willing to give it a go.

Eric was driving the license photo over to him after work that day. He also had a picture of Peggy, which he'd borrowed from Bernie's mother, who had not heard a word from her daughter since she'd left town.

This didn't surprise Eric at all, given Bernie's rocky relationship with her mother. But it did alarm him, because he hadn't heard from Bernie himself. Not a call, not an e-mail, nothing. And his calls to her cell phone had gone unanswered, which was odd since Bernie had voice mail on that line. The phone company wouldn't give out any information about her account, so they were, as usual, of no help. He'd called Oar Research several times asking for her, but was told that a Bernadette Kane did not work there, and there was no way for the operator to know if she was in the building as a contractor. He'd been forwarded to the HR department, and was again assured by a very helpful fellow that no one named Bernadette Kane was employed by Oar Research, and that there was no record of a subcontractor by that name, either. He'd stopped calling after the first few days, leaving a message to have her call him if she showed up. For all Eric knew, Bernie had yet to penetrate the walls of Wesley Edwards's fortress.

He'd considered flying out there to check on her, but Shannon would have none of it, and he'd be paying a price for his friendship for years to come. Bernie was a big girl, and if she were in trouble she'd call. She had disappeared before, vanished from his life for months at a time, in fact. Maybe she'd given it up, met some guy with a convertible and a tan, taken up golf with him. But until he knew, Eric would continue to worry, and he'd continue to seek answers on his end. That was what friends did. That's what Bernie would do for him if the roles were reversed.

And if anything happened to her, Eric would deal with Wesley Edwards himself, wife or no wife, price or no price, law or no law. That's what friends did for friends, too.

He just wished to God she'd call.

Later that Friday night, the eleven o'clock news ran a story of dubious interest to a public more concerned with the continuing search for cowardly terrorists, the recovery of the economy, and whether the Kings would beat the Lakers. The report came in the second half of the broadcast, long after well over sixty percent of the viewing audience had called it a night.

In Arizona, however, Wesley Edwards and Jerry Grasvik, in separate bedrooms at different ends of the city, were breathless with anticipation. They were not disappointed in what they saw.

One of the largest banks in the nation had been forced to shut down its entire system that day due to a computer malfunction. There was suspicion that the problem had been caused by the introduction of a foreign element into the bank's computing infrastructure, a virus commonly known as a software worm. The extent of the damage or the duration of the outage was not known, and other banks were put on alert to heighten computer security until the source had been identified. Other notorious software menaces were mentioned, like Code Red, Nimda and LoveLetter, with a comforting reminder that these problems were usually contained in short order and rendered harmless through easily implemented countermeasures.

At opposite ends of the city, Wesley Edwards and Jerry Grasvik both laughed.

At the time of the broadcast, the name of the worm had not yet been released to the press. But the technicians beating their collective heads against the walls of the target bank knew, because the worm itself had told them.

The Serpent was here, and it was hunting for prey.

PART THREE

The wolf and the lamb shall feed together,
and the lion shall eat straw like the bullock:
and dust shall be the serpent's meat.
                                    —Isaiah 65:25

35

They had sex before they talked about his impending riches. Jerry wanted it the other way around, but Diana was so turned on by the prospect of his criminality that she couldn't wait, proving it in the car by going down on him during rush hour on the 101, much to the delight of a bus full of retirees heading for a nearby casino. Now they were in his apartment in Mesa, shades drawn, a pissed-off but muted Static-X clamoring about anarchy in the background. And to think, they used to actually *sing* on the radio.

Before Jerry's chest stopped heaving—she had wanted some "jungle fucking" today—Diana asked Jerry to explain everything to her, from the beginning.

Jerry said, "I don't like to brag."

She offered a tender smile and a little squeeze of her hand, which was cupping his testicles at the moment. She thought it a metaphorically perfect pose, given what she had in mind for him.

"I can't concentrate," he said, sliding off the bed. "You want a beer?"

"Sure." She didn't, but it was time to go with the cash flow.

He walked naked to the refrigerator, the centerpiece of a tiny kitchen tucked into a corner of the living area. She thought of Damien and his finely honed physique, like an Olympic vaulter with a tattoo of a snake on his pole, and told herself this was an investment of her time that would pay big dividends, hopefully soon.

"What would you say," he began, handing over the beer and sitting at the foot of the bed, out of her playful reach, "if I told you I was the best-kept secret in the history of computer security? You know, the guy they never caught, the one that got away, the Carlos the Jackal of all things silicon, a master of disguise and deception who basically taught all the other assholes who *did* get caught everything they know?"

"Well," she said, "I'd wonder why you're not a VP at Microsoft or Intel, or working for the CIA, something like that."

He smiled, nodding as if he knew this was coming. "That's like asking Kid Rock why he isn't a record company executive."

"Thought you didn't like to brag?" Her smile assured him she was just kidding around. He blushed anyway. "I'm sorry. Please . . . tell me everything." She pulled her knees up under her chin and wrapped her arms around them, settling in.

He had two résumés, he said, that ran in parallel and couldn't be shown during the same employment interview. The first began when he was in high school, and was the foundation of the second, his "straight" career as one of the youngest and brightest software architects in the security sector of the computer industry. By fifteen he knew more about personal computers than the lab teacher at school, and was already bored with the off-the-shelf software applications that made them useful. He taught himself how to create his own programs, you name the language, and soon thereafter, how to steal them from others, which was far more fun. Quickly, though, he realized that nothing about the industry appealed to him. He knew several guys who worked at hardware and software firms, and basically they were selling their souls for stock options and the right to have squirt-gun fights in the office on Fridays. Were it not for the existence of the computer world's seamy hacker underground, he'd have moved on to something more intellectually stimulating, like neurosurgery or perhaps producing pornography. He had always, he confessed here, had a weakness for the dark drug of the forbidden.

Those really were, he told Diana with a wistful smirk, the good old days. Hacking was nothing more than gaining root access to another computer, using a stolen point-to-point protocol account, then something called telnet—a terminal emulation program that allows a system to connect to a server—to connect to a target. From there you could hack into password files and login IDs, and basically, if you could write script, play God from there on out. In those days hackers were more like cowboys than criminals, plying their trade to spread awareness of the need for stronger security measures rather than profit or mischief. Not to mention bragging rights. That boasting took place in highly secret chat rooms, most of them invitation only, buried deep in the backstreets of the Internet, and if you were a poseur you were quickly exposed and exiled. It was here that clever techniques and new programs were exchanged freely between brilliant players who knew more about Unix code than they did about shaving. Initially, much of their genius was applied to defacing Web sites—including the Department of Defense—and tinkering with private e-mail and financial accounts. Gangs of hackers sprang up—Genocide 2600, the Cult of the Dead Cow, Legion of Doom, and one called TNT, where Jerry spent a lot of his time and learned much of what would become his trade. There was even a hacker convention in Las Vegas, called DefCon, which was frequented by undercover Feds who wore spanking new clothes from the Gap that, in a laughable effort to look cool, were two sizes too big.

Meanwhile, Jerry had enrolled at UC Santa Barbara with a major in computer science that would lead him to a sterling career in computer security, his employers completely unaware that he was rapidly becoming the Don Corleone of the digital underground. But unlike some, he wasn't interested in ruining the Internet, he was interested in owning it, and that meant the preservation of the major institutions and corporations who invested in it. It was this perspective that drove Jerry toward an understanding of the nature of computer security and the software that would protect Web sites and companies from people just like him. Hacking was like religion, it was pure and misunderstood, and ruined by bogus opportunists who, in their hearts, were simply delinquents. One guy, a committed Satanist named Pr0metheus, was still out there, hacking into any Web site with a Christian agenda for the purposes of promoting his whacked point of view. There were vandals who sought the destruction of proprietary programs and commercial sites. And there were thieves, who often cut their teeth by learning how to alter grades in their schools' student databases, who now sought to covertly divert data and funds from the digital files of major financial institutions. But the most notorious of them all was a fourteen-year-old kid who called himself Mafiaboy, who was now in prison. Because of his monumental ego, he would never admit to anyone, even to ingratiate himself to his captors, that he'd learned almost everything he knew in a chat room from a player known as the Randomizer. While his cyber-name had become legend, the Randomizer's real name, Jerry Grasvik, had never been discovered.

Mafiaboy was nothing if not audacious. On February 7, 2000, he used a program called Barbed Wire—a variant of a dangerous Tribal Flood Network program that swarms a target system with data, overloading it until it simply breaks—to completely shutdown Yahoo!, one of the primary portals on the Internet. After bragging about it in the chat rooms—something that really pissed the Randomizer off—he struck Buy.com, eBay.com and Amazon.com within days of each other, and then hit CNN's global online news operation. The next day he hit Datek and E*Trade, two mainstays of the online brokerage industry, virtually bringing them all to their collective digital knees. Also hit were several major universities—including the University of California at Santa Barbara—for a total of seventy-five high-volume systems worldwide. Microsoft was next on his list, and he'd have pulled it off if he hadn't been stopped.

By now Jerry was already the leading analyst at one of the nation's largest telecommunications companies, landing the job before he'd even graduated. By day he was designing, testing and implementing network security protocols—known as firewalls—and by night he was the brains behind at least four of the most clever player-handles in the IRC chat rooms. When the Yahoo! hack became what President Clinton called a "technological Pearl Harbor," a task force was summoned to Washington, which included a distinguished roster of specialists from the Computer Emergency Response Team at Carnegie Mellon University, MCI WorldCom, Sun Microsystems, and others, including Jerry's company. As one of the pioneers of firewall programming, Jerry was asked to attend, sitting two chairs down from Attorney General Janet Reno and right next to National Security Advisor Sandy Berger.

Not long after the conference, the FBI received an anonymous tip that led them to an ISP in Montreal. By analyzing data packets in a unique way described by the informant, it led them to an address and to the arrest of Mafiaboy. The informant was never identified because he had routed his communications through a network of sixteen e-mail servers in nine countries—including Buckingham Palace, just for kicks—each with a stolen password and login ID. They would never know that after showing Mafiaboy the Barbed Wire code he had created, it was the Randomizer who had ratted out Mafiaboy, an irresponsible and dangerous youth and therefore not worthy of protection.

This, rationalized Jerry, was his karmic penance, his way of wiping the slate clean. He needed to move forward in the straight world with a somewhat clear conscience.

When he was laid off two years later, his company's stock was worth eighteen cents a share, down from thirty-two dollars. Jerry's once-promising options were redeemable at four dollars a share. And oh by the way, he took the specifications for the nation's swipe-card firewall technology with him.

And now an old problem had returned from the dead—he was getting bored again. Others far less skilled than he had founded companies and cashed out with hundreds of millions, if not billions of dollars. A few of those pukes had been hanging in the very same chat rooms in those early years, learning their trade from teenagers who didn't give a rat's ass about Michael Jordan or Michael Jackson or Michelangelo. It was time to cash in on what he had learned over the years, grab his piece of the cake and disappear. After all, he was nearing his mid-thirties and it was high time he retired.

Since the dawn of creation—that is to say, the day somebody slapped a computer on a desktop—there hasn't been a propeller-head worth his salt who could describe in repeatable layman's terms the nature and intention of a specific piece of technology. Jerry was no exception, but Diana didn't interrupt him as he explained the software worm he had recently dubbed the Serpent in her honor. She would clarify what was beyond comprehension when he was finished, since all she needed were the high points to take back to Damien to devise a hijacking strategy. So she listened with a furrowed brow and regular nods of her head, as if any of this techno-babble made the slightest sense to her. She thought a server was someone to whom you gave your lunch order, and Pascal was the name of the short-order cook.

The upshot of it was this: the harmless-looking little laptop computer on his desk in this pigsty of an apartment held a digital time bomb of apocalyptic proportions. Jerry had unleashed upon an unsuspecting retail economy a completely incomprehensible and unsolvable software worm that made their computer systems vulnerable to penetration. The worm was in the process of being distributed across the country via otherwise normal-appearing credit and debit cards whose magnetic strips had been programmed with Jerry's code. Once the cards were used, Jerry was able to enter the operating systems of his victims and do whatever he pleased with their data, anything from playfully switching decimals and balances to complete and unrecoverable obliteration. These companies would pay whatever price necessary to kill the worm and prevent reinfection, and the company who brought forth this salvation could write their own ticket. And best of all, because Jerry-the-former-telecommunications-security-guru was a master at encrypting and cloaking the digital pathways that connected him to these corporations, he would remain invisible, as well as invincible.

Jerry would be both antichrist and savior as the Serpent unleashed its venom on the digital world.

And Diana would be his Judas.

Right there in front of her, on that fourteen-by-ten-inch slab of plastic and silicon, was the source code for the Serpent itself, the database of IP addresses for each of the target companies, a list of protocols to manipulate and generally fuck with the data in those servers, and a program that would restore a penetrated firewall to pristine condition and forever patch the hole through which the worm entered. The device that had imprinted the Serpent code onto the cards was in his office at Oar Research. And while the code itself had already been released into the wild, so to speak, the only means of controlling and then killing it was right here in front of them.

Jerry sat back and folded his arms. Like most engineers who had just unveiled their technology, he looked confident that there would be few, if any, questions forthcoming. His expression was at once proud and humble, knowing that it was too much to comprehend, perhaps too frightening to accept from a Jimmy Olson–meets–Bill

Gates character such as himself. Perhaps this was what the good Lord had meant when he had promised that the meek would inherit the earth . . . right after they learned how to program in Unix.

"I don't know what to say," she said, staring at the laptop.

"You can start by telling me how impressed you are."

"You're not doing this alone."

"No. My boss is handling the distribution side. And all the stock bullshit."

"So basically . . . you're rich."

"Not rich. Well-off. You get greedy, you get caught. You get screwed by your partners. I take my cut, then I'm gone. Let's just say I won't have to work again for a while. Like about four hundred years."

During the lecture she had moved behind his chair, lightly touching his shoulders as he sat before the computer monitor and keyboard, both of which were wired remotely to the laptop sitting at the side. Now she bent over him, wrapping her arms around his upper chest, and pressed her face into the nape of his neck.

"Who knew," she said, more a growl than an utterance, her teeth playfully nipping at the skin covering his jugular vein. "Mild-mannered comic book nerd masks alter ego of brilliantly diabolical, and therefore extraordinarily sexy, extortionist."

"It's okay then?" he said, his head thrown back and his eyes closed.

She suddenly pivoted him in his swivel chair. He was still naked, and her words and perhaps her teeth had resurrected his interest in further exploring their impending partnership.

She looked down approvingly, smiling as she sunk to her knees before him.

"Are you afraid I'll run?" she said. "Or that I'll make you fall in love with me and I'll take you to the cleaners once I have you in my wicked clutches?"

She lowered her head to his lap.

He said, "Whatever happened to living happily ever after?"

She pleasured him for a moment, then looked up and said, "My thought exactly."

36

The telescope was pointed directly at Camelback Mountain. It had been purchased the night before by Damien, seven bills plus tax for something just this side of lab quality. Liquid morning light poured over the hills that dropped to the Indian reservation land to the east of Scottsdale, and the shadows were long and sharp, lined with shades of gold. It was already in the lower eighties, very pleasant here on the deck of Damien and Diana's house, with its view of Camelback and the entire east side of the metroplex. They had been up for an hour, sharing a run down to Lincoln and back, followed by a protein drink out of the blender and English muffins soaked in honey. Diana had positioned a padded bench in front of the telescope, and she was kneeling on it now with her knees wide apart, wearing a T-shirt but no pants, scanning the north side of Camelback for any sign of Jerry on his morning climb. Damien was behind her, his hands grasping both sides of her pelvis as he drove the serpent in and out of her with casual indifference.

"Anything?"

"If I tell you you'll stop."

"Hope he takes his time, actually." His fingertip traced the tattoo of the tongue on her left butt cheek.

"I had a thought," she said.

"One of your charms."

"He's not going to step back from their plan, then

stab his boss in the back, no matter how much I get in his head."

"You push too hard, he gets spooked." He thrust with a little extra emphasis as he added, "Unlike you . . . the harder I push, the better *you* like it."

She allowed the moment of demonstration to pass without comment. Sometimes their sex was more confrontation than conjugation, her ability to remain unmoved by his ministrations quietly affirming her dominance over him. When, that is, she could pull it off. It was bullshit, of course, but it made her feel better to hold something back.

Finally she said, "So what if we give him a way to make a little money on the side, before the big payday?"

"God, I love it when you talk that way."

"I mean, the guy can set up an offshore account, have money deposited, make it look like he's e-mailing them from the White House if he wants to."

"Must be nice to be so fucking brilliant." It wasn't the first snide comment he'd made about Jerry since this started, something she noted with interest—he'd never shown an attitude about the bit players in their games. Perhaps this little breeze between them was the first wisp of the winds of change.

"We hit a few companies," she said, "for, say, ten or fifteen million, then shut it down. I take half and disappear, he runs back to Wesley and finishes what he starts."

"With a broken heart, don't forget." He added, "I like *whole* a lot better that half, don't you?"

"I don't know how I'd manage that."

"You'll think of something."

A few moments passed, his pace accelerating slightly.

"Meanwhile," she said, "you continue to pillage and plunder the lovely Miss Bernadette." She would return the jealous tone, try to draw him out on his end and see what was under his skin where Jerry was concerned.

They had come to this—they could no longer just fuck. There was always something else now, a parallel agenda, unspoken and unshared. And it was ruining the sex.

"I didn't notice you complaining the other night," he said. Then he added with an angry thrust of his hips, "Only fair, sweetheart, only fair."

She had agreed to his continued dalliance with Bernadette, rationalized as a potentially useful connection to Wesley and the company. But Diana knew Damien's interest was far more carnal than strategic, and she would draw him out on this issue, as well.

They moved for a moment, Diana still pressed to the eyepiece, though she was losing her focus as she started to succumb to Damien's rhythmic talents. To regain it she pivoted the telescope to the right, to the west end of Camelback where the trail began. Having been there she knew the rocks would likely obscure a view of the path, but it was worth a try. If it were later in the day she'd see real rock climbers ascending Praying Monk, an eighty-foot rock that actually looked more like a praying johnson, but this morning there was nobody home.

She moved the scope's line of sight back to the summit, noticing immediately that something was moving in the circular frame. A quick focus revealed it was Jerry, standing on a rock, chest heaving, arms held to the sky. His eyes were closed as he inhaled the rarified air; either that or he was about to faint from exhaustion. He was alone, the first climber of the day to arrive.

"There he is," she said, thankful for his timing.

They changed places, Damien mumbling something lewd as he pulled away and knelt on the bench, pressing his eye to the lens.

"Little fart, isn't he."

Diana had already walked back into the house.

After nearly a minute he felt her cool hands on his hips, just as he had touched her earlier. She was spreading his buttocks in a way that made him freeze. The cold tip of something hard touched him, then began pressing into him with a gradual force that was at once cruel and perversely compelling. He'd bought her this toy at a lesbian shop in south Miami on a whim, with its belts and buckles and a Schwarzeneggeresque unit in black latex, but it had thus far remained in the box. This, he suddenly realized with some measure of regret, wasn't what he'd had in mind at the time.

"You little bitch," he said quietly, closing his eyes as she went where no man had gone before. But he didn't move, allowing her the prerogative. He'd once promised her he would deny her nothing, and because he demanded the same in return, this was no time to compromise their little carnal covenant.

"Only fair, *sweetheart*," she said, her voice uttering this last word with a distinct tone of menace and an emphatic thrust that would go undiscussed, though acknowledged with an involuntary groan from the receiving party.

When it was over, and after there had been plenty of time for Jerry to go back to the office, shower, and reach his desk, Diana called to suggest they meet after work for a drink and some serious conversation. She had a proposition she wanted to discuss, something she assured him would be well worth his time. He didn't hesitate—he offered to take the afternoon off if she could make it earlier—due in no small part to the fact that she allowed him to believe there was a sexual aspect to the idea.

Upon reflection, she decided that would indeed be a good way to make him more receptive to what she really had in mind. Money and sex had always been compatible cell mates.

Damien had a short flight to Colorado Springs today— this made her laugh, since he said that always involved a rough landing, and he would perhaps feel today's touchdown and think of her. It would also give her plenty of uncluttered time to come up with just the right thing to wear.

37

Bernie almost forgot to check her e-mail before leaving for work. She had taken a long swim this morning, then relaxed in one of the lounge chairs to warm herself in the sun with a chilled can of V8 and the newspaper. It was a perfect moment, the pool framed by swooning palm trees and surrounded by gentle waterfalls, and like the preponderance of perfect moments here in paradise, it reminded her of how isolated she was. Not *alone,* perhaps, but definitely lonely. Even with Paul on the horizon—literally, in his case—there was still something about her deception that separated her from the real world, living in the shadow of her own duplicity. She thought of Wesley, how she was almost drawn into what most women would acknowledge was a magnetic aura of power and raw sensuality. Peggy hadn't been weak, she had simply been human, seizing at something she thought had passed her by, rationalizing it away with the rigor mortis of her marriage.

Thank God for Paul and the perspective he now offered.

She went back in to shower, quickly realizing she was behind her intended schedule. If she were to meet Wesley's accelerated project deadline she couldn't afford mornings like this, and if she wanted to stay in the loop she couldn't afford to screw up. Once dressed and made up, she began shutting down her laptop, then remem-

bered to open Outlook Express to see if there was anything for her.

There was.

> *B—moving forward, but need your help. May be risky,*
> *but this could put us over the top. I need you to send*
> *me something with W's fingerprints on it. Metal or plastic*
> *would be best, paper will do. Something flat, rather than*
> *a pen. Also—this will be tougher—if you can get in his*
> *computer and snoop around his email and Word files,*
> *that would be helpful. He has protected access—user*
> *name is "WesEd," password is "Snake." Don't ask me*
> *how I know—let's just say I continue to have friends*
> *who owe me, one of whom works at an ISP. There are*
> *no secrets in cyberspace. Send what you can, but not to*
> *my house. Be sure to mark it "Personal" but do not,*
> *I repeat, do NOT include a note. Hang in there. We*
> *will win.*
>
> *E.*

God love Eric, even if she couldn't. At least, in the
manner she preferred.

Bernie printed the e-mail before she left. Nadine
would not only want to see it, she might be just the one
to help make it happen.

Nadine stared at the printout of the e-mail for nearly
a minute, her eyes narrow.

"Who is this guy?" she asked when she finally looked
up, the narrow eyes now suspicious as well.

"Old friend. Good friend."

"If he's such a good friend, why isn't he here?"

"It's complicated. He's married, for starters."

Nadine looked down at the e-mail again. "Why is
he—?"

"Because he knew my sister," said Bernie.

Nadine had never pressed Bernie to explain why she
was so interested in Wesley Edwards, or more accu-

rately, in pinning him to the wall. It had struck Bernie as sort of odd, especially since they had taken significant risks together toward this end. If it were Bernie, she'd want to know.

Nadine blinked rapidly, her mind processing what she'd just heard.

"Wesley had something to do with your sister," Nadine said, as if reading the mental telegram that had just landed in front of her. "Something . . . bad."

Bernie nodded.

"You said your sister was dead."

Bernie continued to nod.

Nadine closed her eyes as she blew out a chest full of air, her cheeks billowing as her eyebrows arched. Watching her, Bernie felt an unexpected wave of emotion, her eyes welling up as her throat constricted. She had cloaked her grief with such righteous anger, fueled with the hope of justice, and it had fortified her. It had kept Peggy alive. As long as her quest was in full raging motion she could hide from the inevitable, facing the vacuum in her life that had once been her sister. And suddenly, in this moment, she was no longer alone with her secret, already united with a woman who instinctively understood why she was here. A woman who shared her point of view.

Nadine looked up to see Bernie wiping the first tear away.

"I had no idea. I thought . . . I don't know what I thought."

"It doesn't matter," said Bernie, putting her hand on Nadine's shoulder when she noticed that she, too, was welling up. "Getting this done matters."

Nadine was behind the front counter as they talked, sitting in her chair, Bernie standing in front. As fate would have it, the elevator door opened and Wesley Edwards emerged, walking straight toward them. He was reading a *Wall Street Journal,* and as he passed he didn't look up or otherwise acknowledge their presence.

They watched him come and go, both women shaking their heads.

Then Nadine looked down at the e-mail in her hands.

Without glancing back up, she asked, "What are you doing tonight?"

Darkness had finally come to the valley of the sun. The Oar Research parking lot was vacant, illuminated by landscaping lights lining the perimeter. The last employee, a graphic designer who frankly needed to get a life, had departed a half hour earlier. Bernie was parked illegally along the nearby thoroughfare that bordered Kierland Commons, which, as usual, was crowded with people still waiting for a table at The Cheesecake Factory, or to get in the door at P.F. Chang's, where the bar was the equivalent of a spawning run on the first day of salmon season.

She couldn't wait around in the parking lot. The fewer people who knew she was there, the better.

Bernie's mobile phone rang, right on schedule.

"You there?" asked Nadine.

"I'm here."

"Still inside," said Nadine, referring to Wesley's patronage at Barcelona, the packed bar located just across the street. Nadine had followed him when he left the building just before eight, and he'd driven straight to the bar, meeting with two other men who, based on how they toasted their bottles of Heineken, were facsimiles for friends. Men didn't meet with their real friends in places like this, they met with guys who made them look good, important. Bernie could have made her move as soon as he placed his drink order, but there were still people laboring in the Oar building, and Wesley was known to return after an evening meeting. Prudence dictated that she wait until the office was dark, and only then if Wesley was safely preoccupied, preferably at home.

"I don't like it," said Nadine. Bernie knew she was

bivouacked in the Barcelona lot, with a straight line of sight on Wesley's Escalade.

"It won't take me long," said Bernie. Her stomach, however, was siding with Nadine.

"Won't take him long to change his mind, either."

Bernie checked her watch. "I'm going in," she announced, already putting the Volvo in gear.

"Keep your mobile on," Nadine said.

"No shit," said Bernie, "just don't fall asleep on me."

Nadine closed the flap of her mobile phone. But instead of setting it down, she started tapping it on her chin, squinting toward the entrance to Barcelona, which was crowded with hopeful singles and couples who had been single when they arrived.

Suddenly she opened her car door and walked toward them. She adjusted the waist of her skirt, a slim black linen with a white satin blouse tucked into it, over nice little business heels that conveyed that she was more than met the eye. Before she reached the door she also attended to her hair, and out of habit took a little swipe at both corners of her mouth in case any lipstick had accumulated in an unattractive manner.

She pushed through the crowd, exchanging a smile or two, thinking she should come back when she could relax, have a drink, tell a few lies to someone half her age. She made her way into the bar, which at first glance was a rolling sea of razored hair and black-clad shoulders. She spotted Wesley and his two friends at a small table next to the wall, leaning close as if speaking of things no one else would understand.

She brought her mobile phone, which had been in her hand all this time, up to eye level. She punched in a number, pressed the SEND button and held it to her ear. As she waited for an answer, she counted seven other patrons holding phones, and heard another ringing. She also noticed that the crowd wasn't quite as young and stupid as she'd initially thought. She decided that she might come back here when this thing was finally over.

Then again, maybe not.

"Edwards," answered Wesley.

"Someone's poking around in your office," said Nadine.

Bernie had her story down. There was a deadline, and her ass was on the line for it. She had the code to the front door, knew where the light switches were, and if anybody asked, she had nowhere else to be. She'd open her laptop on her desk, boot up the project, spread some notes around, kick off her shoes. Maybe turn on the radio, make some strong tea. Then wait, see if anyone came out of the woodwork. See if her phone rang. See if she could keep her dinner down as she mustered the courage to act.

She was motionless, waiting for the right moment, surveying the office. Light danced with shadow, screen savers blinked, digital clocks waited, all of it breathing life into the silence. Hollywood's highest-paid cinematographer could never reproduce this diversity of angles and shades, all of it creating a surreal stage for her spy games. A nova of electric illumination from Kierland Commons and Scottsdale Road's retail centers lit up the desert sky, combining with a full moon to splash the glass walls of the building with a false dawn, filling the room with ghosts.

Tonight she would become one of them.

Wesley's office door was open. Once inside she would be instantly visible to anyone who entered the floor, and if they did it quietly and without turning on the lights, she wouldn't know they were there.

She got up and quietly crossed the carpet in her bare feet.

Wesley's desk was as clean as if it had just been delivered. All of his drawers were locked. Short of schlepping his chair out to her car, she couldn't find a thing that might have his fingerprints on it.

A light flashed. She froze, then realized it was just headlight beams two blocks away as a car turned a corner. Her heart was slamming against her rib cage, and in the office beyond, the ghosts softly laughed.

Wesley's computer monitor and keyboard rested on a credenza by the wall. The computer itself, a customized generic box stocked and maintained by the IT geeks downstairs, was on the floor next to it. Bernie pushed the high-backed leather chair to the monitor and sat down. Like almost everyone in every office in the land, Wesley never turned his computer completely off. It was a bad idea, actually, quite against the religion of real computer people because it burned out circuits before their time. No one could prove it, but it was a widely held urban legend among byte-heads. So instead of a blank screen, Wesley's monitor displayed the image of a screen saver, and an odd one at that—a silver snake slithering across a background resembling sand. All she had to do was touch the mouse and the machine would spring to life, showing her a screen full of icons, the infamous desktop, none of which would welcome her in until she slapped down his user ID and password, which Eric had so conveniently supplied.

Wesley, the snake. Maybe he had a sense of humor after all.

She reached for the mouse, then stopped. There it was, right in front of her, the one thing in the office that Wesley touched each and every day, a million thumbprints on the left side, a million more forefinger prints on both top buttons. It was a Logitech mouse, a common generic brand, and the office was full of them. All she had to do was replace it with someone else's and stash it in her purse.

She spun in the chair and stood up. Then her heart stopped and her stomach exploded.

A man was standing at the door.

He was tall, built like an old Buick, bald on the top with the hair on either side resembling a pair of brown slippers she'd once owned. She'd never seen him before, but she hadn't seen half the people who worked here.

They stared at each other, still as statues.

Finally she said, "Can I help you?"

He blinked, but that was his only movement. Oddly, his eyes remained fixed on hers rather than scanning the room for more information, such as a burglar's bag, or perhaps a weapon.

"Can I help you?" she repeated.

"Who are you?" he asked, his voice a little too calm to be credible.

"Who are *you*?" she answered, narrowing her eyes, going for the proverbial good offense as her best defense.

He said, "This is Wesley's office."

She said, "No shit, Sherlock," adding a little giggle for effect.

"You don't look like Wesley."

"Thank God for that."

The stare down once again commenced. At this point it occurred to Bernie that this wasn't what it seemed, not a comforting thought. She'd rather have to explain herself than sit here and wait to be nailed to a cross. She ran through the options—he was a burglar, maybe an ex-employee who still had the door code, maybe a security guy, or someone from Wesley's past—nothing clicked, just as nothing comforted.

Without taking her eyes off the stranger, she reached down and unplugged the mouse from Wesley's computer. She wound the cord into a ball and stood up.

"Computer trouble. Just switching out a part. You?"

The man blinked again, then nodded slowly, his face expressionless. She decided to take a chance. She reached for Wesley's phone.

"I'm calling security."

No response. She had to punch in a number fast or her bluff would be called.

She punched in ten digits from memory. It was Nadine's mobile phone. Then she put the receiver to her ear and looked back at the man.

It was then that he smiled.

As she listened to the ringing, the man turned and

walked calmly through the office, blending into the shadows as he navigated toward the lobby area and disappeared.

"Tell me you're out of there," was how Nadine answered.

Bernie started to speak, but was alarmed at the strength of her beating heart. She took a deep breath, fighting back a sudden light-headedness.

"Bernie?"

"I'm here. Give me a second."

"Are you okay? Talk to me!"

"I'm fine. I just had some company."

"Who was it?"

"No clue. Some big bald guy."

"Jesus."

"I don't think so."

"Sounds like the security guy. What did he say?"

"Absolutely nothing. He just stared at me, then left. It was too weird."

"You get the prints?"

"Oh yeah."

"Any files?"

"Didn't get that far. Not sure I should now."

"I agree. Get the hell out of there. Meet me at Earl's. You know where that is?"

"Yeah. I'm out of here."

The line went dead.

Bernie went back to her desk, scanning the office for any sign of her fellow intruder. If he was there, he was hiding under a desk somewhere, which wouldn't surprise her. Her intention had been to actually access Wesley's hard drive, see what surprises were there. But there was no time for that now. The fingerprints would have to do.

Bernie quickly packed her computer and slipped into her shoes, all in one motion.

A few paces away she stopped next to a cubicle, its walls lined with vacation photographs. She had no idea who sat there, but when they arrived the next morning the occupant would wonder where her mouse had gone.

It was identical to Wesley's, which was why Bernie unplugged it and quickly took it back to Wesley's workstation.

That done, she headed toward the elevator. As she
passed the front desk she stopped. Sitting on the counter
was a card. Bernie had noticed it earlier that day—it
was from Wesley, commemorating National Secretary's
Day, which had come and gone a few weeks earlier.
Nadine had commented at the time that she wasn't a
secretary, and Bernie thought it a callous sentiment in
return for Wesley's attempt at showing at least some
cursory appreciation. Nadine kept it around as a sort
of gag.

Suddenly, like a shot of ice to the heart, she froze.
The elevator bell rang, like a shotgun blast in a nursery
at nap time.

Bernie grabbed the card and stuffed it into her purse
with Wesley's mouse. A little backup wouldn't hurt, in
case the janitors had wiped down the mouse earlier in
the evening. Unlikely, but possible. Bernie had always
been good at contingencies.

Wesley walked into the lobby.

Bernie had less than a second to look calm, knowing
she'd fail at it. Instead she put her hand over her heart
and breathed deeply.

"God, you scared the shit out of me!" she said.

Wesley didn't smile. "I saw your car."

She gulped down some air, not entirely acting now.

"What are you doing here?" he asked.

"Programming," she shot back. "What are *you* doing
here?" The old offense-defense thing worked before,
might as well give it another go. After a moment she
cracked a smile, a good-natured challenge for him to
continue this little third degree.

"Checking my e-mail," he said.

"Sounds like both of us should get a life."

Wesley narrowed his eyes, focusing them on the computer case slung over her shoulder. Her heart spun in
its cage, the moment lasting an eternity.

"So how's it coming along?" he asked.

"You'll have it on Monday."

He nodded, looking back at her. "You don't like me all that much," he said, and only now could Bernie perceive the effects of alcohol in his demeanor.

"It was just a get-to-know-you drink," she said, parroting what he'd once said to her. "I never positioned it as anything else."

He nodded, cracking a tiny grin. "I deserved that." Smiling wasn't easy for Wesley Edwards, and it showed. "I'm not that bad a guy."

She returned the grin. "A little schizoid, if you ask me."

Suddenly the smile vanished, as it does on people who've just come from a bar.

"Probably right," he said. "Have a good night."

He walked past her, and now she could smell everything Barcelona had to offer, booze and smoke and perfume and bullshit, something Wesley once claimed he detested.

In the parking lot, with her pulse finally under control, she chanced a glance up to the fourth floor. She could see Wesley standing in his office, a dark silhouette pressed against the glass, watching her with his hands on his hips, the way her father used to stand when he disapproved of the world.

She fired up the Volvo and got out of there as fast as she could, anxious to get to Earl's to tell Nadine what had just happened.

But strangely, Nadine never showed. When Bernie called her mobile phone, there was no answer. She waited an hour, then went home, unsure whether she was more confused or frightened by the events of the evening.

In either case, things were certainly heating up.

Understandably, Bernie was unable to sleep, her body still wired on adrenaline. More than that, her mind was on fire, confused by the bald man in the office, excited by the proximity of victory, grateful for Eric, alarmed at Nadine's sudden disappearing act. Worst of all, she could do nothing about it, at least not now, not here.

There was something else, too. It was just an idea, but Bernie no longer believed in coincidence, and this one was a whopper. Wesley's computer password was "snake," and his screen saver was the squirming image of a snake. He was in bed with thugs, perpetrating a software scam that just happened to coincide with the national outbreak of a badass worm the press was calling "the Serpent." A sure thing? Hardly. But worth a hefty bet. She wished Nadine was reachable, because this was worth kicking around.

After two hours of wrestling with it, losing the bout miserably at that, she got up to do the only proactive thing available at the moment. She wrapped the mouse and card in a Ziploc sandwich bag, which was then inserted into a padded envelope she'd purchased that afternoon. Though she desperately wanted to include a note, she honored Eric's request. Under the address— thank goodness she had his business card in her purse— she printed "PERSONAL" in large block letters.

Then, on a whim, she fished her lipstick out of her purse—Fetish by MAC, the *it* brand these days. She spread some over her index finger and stared at it. Years ago, when she and Eric had given their romantic potential an honest but ill-fated spin around the block, she used to send him notes with a lipstick imprint of her puckered lips on the outside. That wouldn't fly now, of course, and she had far too much respect for his comfort zone to try it as a joke. So instead of lips, she pressed her lipsticked finger onto the envelope, right next to the word *PERSONAL,* leaving a textbook perfect "Fetish-by-MAC" fingerprint.

Just so he'd know she hadn't lost her edge. Just so he'd know she remembered.

> **38** <

From the outset it was clear that the pick of the evening would be Diana's. She selected the place to meet Jerry for their drink, a meat market called Buzz FunBar, which it was if you were twenty-two and regarded your frat-house experience as the high point of your life. She opened by announcing that she'd have a little surprise for him at midnight, a ploy she knew would create an energized context for everything to follow. From there she picked the restaurant—she had him follow her to El Chorro, which was visible from the balcony of her house, meaning his car would be nearby the next morning—then she chose the itinerary for the rest of the evening. At each place they went she picked up the tab. At one point she even promised that she would pick *him* up, literally, and throw him into her bed.

But it didn't get that far. In Jerry's view, it was Diana who also picked the fight.

From El Chorro they went to Caspers and giggled at the Bon Jovi crowd shaking their booties, clad in Dockers and leather minis. She, on the other hand, wore tight black vinyl pants and a matching vinyl halter top, which, combined with the tattoos on her arms, thoroughly pissed off every woman in the place. The bartender even comped their first round, saying he hadn't seen a woman that hot since Madonna stopped in with her dancers after a show one night. Jerry asked her three times what the surprise was, and three times he was teasingly denied access to her thoughts.

From there it was off to Martini Ranch for a little chemical infusion, then to Axis-Radius for some serious dancing and more alcohol. In a blurry-eyed moment of intimacy, Jerry confessed he'd never been with a woman like her, a woman every man in the place would go home and whack off to later. After thanking him for this strange compliment she told him she never thought she'd be with a man this brilliant, and very possibly, this dark.

By now it was eleven and Jerry was swimming in anticipation. Time to culminate the evening in a place where her outfit and her attitude would fit right in, because every conceivable demographic and taste was represented here except poverty. This was Sanctuary, which had been receiving national press for its celebrity clientele and upscale aspirations, which were delivered in five separate theme rooms. They skipped the Moroccan Room, which was the least crowded, full of smashed conventioneers. They had cosmopolitans in the Martini Room, where the host from the *Fear Factor* television program was holding court. They sipped sambuca in the Voodoo Lounge, which was where those who had paired off elsewhere ended up, and after peeking in the Divine Lounge, reserved for the loud and obnoxious, they had their final drink of the night in the VIP Room, in the company of NBA players and visiting Hollywood luminaries and at least one chain-smoking supermodel.

Also present, though they only said hello in passing, was the pilot of the Oar jet, whose name Jerry couldn't recall. He was drinking alone at the bar—must have the day off tomorrow. Jerry got a little quiet when Diana commented that the pilot was probably—no, certainly—the best-looking guy in the place.

"Jerry's jealous," she said, puffing out her lower lip sarcastically.

"I know him, actually. I can introduce you."

"I thought you said you can't remember his name?"

"A nit. You want to meet him? I'll do that." There was no humor in his eyes. It was a challenge, one he hoped she would back away from.

Rather than reassure or offer comfort, she laughed. It was a cruel little chuckle not meant to draw him into the joke.

"You think this is funny?" he asked.

She ran her tongue over the rim of her glass. "It's hilarious. What say we take him home . . . I'll tie you to a chair and make you watch me fuck him blind."

The tip of her tongue appeared like a crimson wisp, playing along her upper lip.

"You'd do that," he said.

Her eyes were dark bullets of promise.

Suddenly he grabbed her behind the neck and pulled her in. Holding her jaw with his other hand, he kissed her urgently, pushing her back against the rear of the booth in which they sat. This was a common posture in the room, so no one cared. He could have stuffed her between his legs under the table and no one would have noticed. Something close to that was going down across the room anyway.

"You make me crazy," he breathed into her mouth. In response she reached under his shirt and began to tweak one of his nipples.

Jerry looked up to see that the pilot was still at the bar, the only person in the room who seemed to be watching them. He smiled and raised his glass in a little salute.

"You want me," she hissed as her teeth found his ear. "Right here, right now."

"You'd freaking do it, too, wouldn't you. . . ."

"No. I want you fresh and strong when I get you home."

He liked that one. They kissed for a while, trading cute little guttural noises, perhaps disgusting if you were in the next booth.

"Almost midnight," he said. "Time for my nasty little surprise."

She pulled away, wiping her mouth with her fingers, smiling as if she'd just won a bet. Then she looked at her watch.

"I didn't say it was nasty."

"No? Could have sworn—"

"If you like what you hear, then we'll go home and be nasty."

"What I *hear*?"

"I have a proposition for you," she said, straightening herself as she sat upright, adjusting her top, which, much to the delight of two guys lurking nearby, had slid to the side. "I've been thinking."

He nodded, remembering that this was how she'd put it when she called him earlier about getting together— a *proposition*.

She leaned close, putting her hand on his shoulder. She pulled him in so that her lips were barely touching his. She spoke in bullets, each punctuated with a short kiss.

"About you. About us. About our future. About our *financial* future."

Something tugged at a part of his brain that hadn't made noise in a long time. He recognized it as hope, a glimpse of a dream coming true. He had been expecting her surprise to involve velvet ropes and unspeakable little toys, things he had whispered in her ear as the Absolut and the sambuca turned the pages of the comic book in his mind. He had expected Lady Death, but this was better. As least for now.

"Tell me," he said.

She looked at her watch, as if to ensure that midnight had indeed arrived. Then he saw her glance toward the bar. He did the same—thankfully, Pilot Boy had gone home.

She laid it out for him, careful to avoid presumption or a perception of naïveté. She also wanted to convey a sense of purpose and experience, as if she was comfortable talking in eight-figure sums and dropping the names of secure offshore depositories. She wanted Jerry to believe that she had been looking for an opportunity just like this one—and the brilliant man who could pull it off—for a long time.

She began by saying how impressed she was by what he'd created. She understood its power, and how he would wield that power to bring the most arrogant of corporations to their knees. That, she assured him, was sexy. Power and sex were interchangeable to her, and she knew enough about him to understand that women like her were what he'd been dreaming about all his life. This was a perfect situation for both of them, she said, and they had to find a way to make it work.

At this point Jerry assured Diana that he had every intention of making it work. She took his hand and looked in his eyes as if the rest of the bar had disappeared.

"Listen to me. I know you've got people in this with you . . . your boss, maybe others. I wouldn't screw that up. I know there's been a lot of work done, things put in place. And I know you'll be taken care of, you'll get what you deserve. But whatever it is, you deserve more. This is *your* software, your golden goose, and it doesn't lay the egg if you don't make it sing. You get what I'm saying?"

"No."

She squeezed his hands tighter. He already sensed his world, or at least his hope for it, was about to change.

"I believe in the win-win. Just like you. But what if you could put them off a while, even for a week . . . and we put your little golden goose to work for *us* first? Without their cut, without compromising what you've already got going."

"Delaying the schedule a week compromises the project."

"Okay, then what if we squeeze the goose on the side. Run our plan and your plan simultaneously. Nobody gets hurt, nobody knows, we take out ten, twenty million without anyone knowing."

He narrowed his eyes. "I don't know what the hell you're talking about. And neither do you."

"Listen to me . . . you crack into the server, or whatever you call it, at a major corporation, grab them by the balls and squeeze. Every minute you hold up their business costs them millions of dollars. I liked what you said the other day about greed, about how it can kill you . . . that was a wise man talking. So here's the deal, Jerry—you set up an offshore account, do whatever it is you do to shield it from identification by the authorities, okay? You tell the company that they deposit two million into the account, all cash, no strings, and you turn their business back on. You go away, like you were never there. Nobody can find you because you're the fucking Houdini of e-mail. We hit five, eight, ten companies and give them twenty-four hours to make the deposit. Meanwhile, you go on with your other plan. We pick different targets, there's no crossover, nobody gets their pants in a wad about this. It'll be cheaper for them to pay you than to hunt you down."

She paused to gauge how she was doing. Jerry wasn't moving, not even blinking as he stared at her.

She waved her hand in front of his face, smiled sweetly and said, "Hello?"

He lowered his eyes. "That's your proposition?"

"It'll work. Tell me why it wouldn't."

Jerry glanced to the side, suddenly interested to see if they were being watched, which of course they weren't. He turned back to her, his forehead carved with doubt.

"For starters, it's just plain freaking *wrong*. I could give you ten other reasons it won't work, but that's a deal killer for me. It's amoral."

Now it was her good humor that bled away into a confrontational glare.

She said, "You need to explain to me the moral landscape of your original plan, Jerry. Because frankly I don't see the *freaking* difference."

He fidgeted, as if what he was about to say was either too obvious or too complex to put into words. Or per-

haps that he was disappointed that he had to say it. His
voice was soft, as if patiently speaking to a child, and
his eyes remained on the floor.

"This isn't about the money, okay? It's about evolu-
tion. Not power, not ramming it up someone's ass and
laughing all the way to the bank. It's about change, and
I'd have to lay out the entire socioeconomic matrix of
the industry to make that remotely clear to you. Let me
put it this way—the people who run the system need a
wake-up call, they need to understand just how *vulnerable* they are. If we don't attach a price tag to it then it
won't mean anything to them . . . they have to *feel* the
pain of their own shortsightedness. That's how it's been
since the beginning—you have freedom fighters who believe in an open and equal system, and you have the
profiteers, who eventually corrupt it. Everything I've
done in my career has been pointing to this. This is my
time, my shot . . . my chance to make a difference."

"Oh please," she said, "spare me the Abraham Lincoln bullshit."

This made him smile and look at her, though sadly.
She wasn't getting it.

"I don't expect you to understand. What you propose
is very close to what we're already doing, okay? Scary
close. Except your plan comes from a different place, it
doesn't deliver a solution. It doesn't create *change*."

"I wonder if your boss shares your position on that."

"I believe he does. After we hit them, the infrastructure of digital commerce—the very heart and soul of the
future economy, by the way—will move in a different
direction. Vulnerability will disappear, theft and risk will
minimize . . . costs will go down, the technology will
explode into the mainstream in a way that it can't
right now."

"Do you know how much you sound like a fucking
terrorist?"

"Terrorist, criminal . . . which of us is worse, eh?
That's not fair, Diana."

"You take, what, a couple million away for your efforts? Which are *you*?"

He looked down, pursing his lips as if frustrated. "When this is over I'm history. I need—no, I freaking *deserve*—enough to cash out, disappear, leave the war to the new soldiers. I'm done. I helped invent the movement, and this is my swan song. If you don't like that, don't believe that, then I'm sorry. I'll sleep just fine when this is over."

Diana stared at her empty glass for a long, awkward moment. Then she closed her eyes and summoned the tears that she knew would soften him.

He put his arm around her, placing his chin on her shoulder.

"There was no way for you to know any of that," he whispered.

Through her tears, she said, "I just wanted us to, you know . . . *be* together."

"We *can* be together. It's more than a couple million, okay? More than enough for two lifetimes. Yours and mine . . . we can still do this."

He paused, putting his fingers under her chin. "Hey . . . how's that sound?"

She looked up, offering a brave little smile. "I'm sorry," she said. Then she embraced him tightly, her tears returning as she shuddered and wept into his shoulder.

She watched him drive out of the El Chorro parking lot, offering a final wave as he turned in front of her. He'd wanted to continue their evening in the manner she had led him to believe it would progress, but she seized the eternal loophole of sexual escape—her headache was throbbing, she said, and emotionally she was too confused to be intimate. She needed to be alone, work it out, get herself right. Think about all that he'd said to her. She told him that she was suddenly confronted with an even more complex man than she'd thought, which meant her feelings and intentions were more complicated, too.

She needed time to work it out. To come to grips with herself. Not much, just the night. She asked him to forgive her, which he did readily and enthusiastically. He told her that her predatory instinct was a part of her that appealed to his most secret desire, a woman who would always challenge and provoke him to the limits of his intellect. A woman who embraced his fantasies with the same zeal with which she appreciated his mind. And now, his heart.

She told him not to worry. That she would be fine in the morning, after a good night's sleep, maybe another good cry. She was so ashamed, and she had to deal with that on her own. She said she would call him and they would go from there.

As Jerry turned the little Nissan truck out onto Lincoln, Diana picked up her mobile phone and punched in a number.

Damien answered on the first ring.

"You alone?" he asked.

"I'm not coming home."

"So you're not alone."

"I am. But I won't be."

"Ask me if I'm surprised. Don't hurt him."

"I'll call you in the morning. Early. Be up."

"I'm always up."

"That you are. We need to talk."

"Ooo, sounds scary."

"More than you know."

"I'll miss you."

"You're sweet. Just picture me . . . hurting him."

She clicked the phone off and pulled out onto Lincoln. She drove past the street leading up the hill to their house, noticing that the lights were still on.

Then she drove back into the dark heart of Scottsdale.

Camelback Mountain rises some sixteen hundred feet over the dead center of Phoenix, with a fifty-mile, three-sixty view that money can't buy, no matter who you are. A few million will get you a killer view from, say, three hundred feet—and that's just for the lot—but thanks to county building restrictions dating back to the Depression era, the only way to the top is on foot. From there you can look down on the rich and famous, since the mountain is entirely surrounded by estates that are easily mistaken for country clubs or luxury hotels, a few of which approach fifty thousand square feet, with private lakes, multiple tennis courts and even a few short par fours.

Few of these homeowners had availed themselves of the two trails that ascend to the top of Camelback, though some have undoubtedly sent the help up with cameras to snap a few aerials of their layout. The Cholla trail begins at the east foot, and while it is the longer of the two, it is known to be the easier trek—Lady Bird Johnson once walked it in high heels. The last few hundred yards, though, are no picnic for anyone with a fear of falling to their death onto sharp rocks. The preferred route, usually crowded with fitness freaks and those who'd read the online raves—this hike being touted as the primo urban ascent in the nation—is the Echo Canyon trail, originating at the northwest corner of the mountain. From here one passes the landmark eighty-

foot monolith known as the Praying Monk, so named
for a legendary friar whose camel collapsed in the heat,
prompting him to kneel in prayer for both of their well-
beings, and perhaps a bottle of Aquafina. Legend holds
that the tableau was so moving that they were turned to
stone—by the Chamber of Commerce, perhaps—for us
to appreciate for all time, and for a hardy few to hone
their rock-climbing chops. The trail goes pretty much
straight up from there, a thigh burner of the highest
order, and for those who endure, the summit rewards
them with a staggering visual feast. And punishes them
the next day with quads too sore to touch.

To the north is Mummy Mountain, where there was
at least one powerful telescope through which one could
read the logo on your backpack.

Jerry Grasvik had been clamboring to the top of Camelback Mountain nearly every morning for the past two
years, always taking the tougher trail. He created little
games to make it more challenging, such as wearing a
twenty-pound backpack, or trying to avoid using his
hands as he hopped from rock to rock. Each ascent was
timed, and despite his performance he always took a few
minutes to appreciate the vista and down a quart of
water. On some days he'd hop the fence at Echo Canyon
Park before dawn and do the climb in the dark so he
could watch the sun come up over the McDowell Mountains. It was as close to religion as he'd ever get.

This was such a morning, the stars still out and the
parking lot fenced off when he arrived. He made the
climb in forty-one minutes—he had to slow down even
under the brightest moon—but was happy he'd done it
because the sun hadn't yet broken the horizon. Jerry
was often the first climber of the day to summit—it was
a private source of pride, actually—so he was disappointed to see someone already standing at the east
edge, his back toward Jerry as he watched a ribbon of
gold light spread across the rim of the mountains.

Climbers aren't often the friendliest lot, and Jerry,

being typical of them, gave the guy his space as he sat on a rock drinking his water. He had a lot to think about this morning while partaking of this celestial drama. Diana had rocked his boat in a way he hadn't expected, and he'd reacted in a way he would have never guessed. Surprise, yes, outrage, perhaps, but immediate capitulation . . . where'd *that* come from? The woman was under his skin, to be sure, and while he didn't approve of her exploitive ideas, her dark instincts and her playful fashion were fascinating. As strong as his fantasies had always been, he'd never really thought he'd meet a woman who would embrace them, much less exemplify them, and he knew he had to proceed with caution.

If you accept a dance with the devil, be sure to bring the right shoes.

Lost in thought, he was surprised to hear the other man speak without turning to face him. Several minutes had passed without the slightest acknowledgment, and he'd nearly forgotten the guy was still there. The sun had broken the seal now, filling the valley with long shadows as it colored the sky a bright harvest gold.

"What a fine line it is," said the man, "between the first day of the rest of your life, and the last day of your life."

Jerry looked up, unsure he'd heard right.

"Pardon me?"

"The difference between them defines the man, don't you think?"

Jerry stared at the guy's back. He was silhouetted against the rising sun, perfectly framed, and it flashed through his mind that this was a true movie moment. He wished he had a camera, in fact.

Then the man turned, already smiling. This wasn't the face of God at all.

It was the pilot. The best-looking guy at the bar last night. He wore baggy black pants and a black workout shirt, his muscular arms laced with tattoos. Every time Jerry had seen the guy he'd been wearing a white shirt and tie, and his hair was always greased back, Wall Street style. Today his hair fell to the side of his face, whipping in the wind.

Jerry cracked a little smile, not because he was glad to see the guy, but because it was the expected thing to do.

"Hey, I know you," he said, realizing he was stating the obvious. He got up and took a few steps forward. He couldn't remember the pilot's name as he extended his hand. "Jerry Grasvik . . . I'm with Oar. You flew me to Sacramento a while ago."

Paul Lampkin accepted the handshake, but instead of offering his name, he said, "Ever wonder what it's like to die, Jerry?"

Paul was staring hard at Jerry, a disturbing smile on his face. Like an animal caught near the water with his back to the forest, Jerry sensed immediate danger. He began to slowly inch backward.

Paul shifted his gaze to the sunrise. "I always wondered about that. About murder. About the moment right before something like that goes down. There's an intimacy about it, a connection between the killer and the condemned."

His head suddenly snapped back to Jerry. "Is this making sense?"

"No."

"You ever kill anyone, Jerry?"

Jerry squinted, frozen by the question.

Paul looked down and rubbed his eyes.

"Listen to me," he said. "This isn't about you. I mean, it's about *you,* but it's not personal or anything. I'm not interested in watching you squirm or chasing you around the mountain, okay? I just want you to know . . . I'm not enjoying this. It's just business. That's it. Business. If there was any other way . . ."

Suddenly it struck Jerry. His mind went back to last night, at the bar.

"Diana," he said.

Paul shook his head, the smile returning. "Piece of work, isn't she?"

"What is this, man?"

"It's what you think it is, Jerry. I'm sorry."

They locked eyes. Paul was as calm as if he was waiting for his morning coffee. Jerry, however, was already trembling, weighing his options.

Suddenly he bolted, heading back toward the trail head. He knew that if he could reach it he'd have a chance, each stone an old friend. No way Paul could catch him once he started down.

As he was about to leap over the first edge he felt his legs fly to the side and he landed hard on his hip. Paul had kicked his feet out from under him from behind, moving with astounding agility.

In that moment Jerry Grasvik knew he was already dead.

Paul grabbed Jerry by the belt and began dragging him toward the other side of the summit. The drop-off was abrupt, a solid rock face descending some two hundred feet to a plateau of jagged boulders, and from there the hill tumbled in a series of ravines to the backyards of the most expensive homes on the north side. Jerry fought with all he had, but without footing he had no leverage, and without leverage he had no chance.

Near the edge Paul suddenly let him go. He stood back, but Jerry only rose to one knee, his other knee throbbing in agony.

Paul had been right—he didn't look like he was enjoying this at all.

"Remember that scene in *Butch Cassidy*," said Paul, "when they were being chased and—"

"What are you, a movie critic?" interrupted Jerry with a justifiably impatient tone.

"Remember what Newman said?"

"Fuck you."

"No. He said *the fall'll probably kill ya*."

Jerry knew that his screaming knee was useless, that

the initial kick had probably broken it. His chest heaved, and his heart was pounding with a ferocity he'd never experienced.

"Bad way to go," said Paul. "If it were me, I'd rather go out swinging."

Paul glanced down, but it was a diversion. In an instant his foot shot out, connecting with Jerry's jaw, cracking his head back and sending his shoulders slamming to the ground. Paul was on him instantly, gripping his head, then snapping it to the side, shattering several cervical vertebrae and severing the spinal cord.

Jerry never felt a thing, which was Paul's intent after all.

Thirty minutes later, Paul was jogging along one of the side streets between McDonald and Lincoln, passing several of those fifty-thousand-square-foot obscenities visible from the summit. He'd taken the longer Cholla trail off the mountain, which he knew was less likely to be occupied, and thankfully wasn't this morning. Now, safely away from the mountain and one of several joggers already on the streets, he slowed to a walk and pulled his mobile phone out of his pocket.

Diana picked up on the first ring. She was sitting on the patio in a black silk robe, legs crossed, watching the aftermath of the sunrise on the first day of the rest of her life.

"How is your run going?" she asked.

"Almost fell," he said. They had agreed to this cryptic mode of conversation, knowing that mobile calls can be easily monitored. Attention to detail would be their salvation, as it always had been.

"But you're okay?"

"I'm good."

"How was it?"

"Harder than I thought."

"Really? I'm surprised."

"I got through it."

"I'm so very proud of you."

"I went the distance, did what I said I'd do."

"You deserve a reward."

"I'm counting on it."

"Tonight. If you're up for it."

"You'll see how up I am. How about you?"

"I'm done with my exercises."

On the table next to her was Jerry's laptop computer, which she'd taken from his car at Echo Canyon earlier that morning, right after he'd started his climb. She'd used a jimmy device on the lock, something Damien had shown her how to do, and it had taken her only four seconds to get in and out.

"Come home to me," she said.

After she hung up, Diana went to the telescope, which she'd used to watch the two men stand toe-to-toe at the summit, seen Jerry trying to run, Damien's pursuit and takedown, Damien dragging Jerry to the edge, a flurry of movement, followed by stillness.

Then Jerry Grasvik's quiet flight to the bottom of the summit's east ridge.

Diana unplugged the jacks that connected the telescope to a digital video camera. She ejected the disk and took the camera back inside.

Damien would be home soon, and there was much to do.

Bernie knew something was wrong as soon as she stepped off the elevator. It was the first time since her arrival at Oar Research that Nadine was not already at her post, sipping from a paper coffee cup, madly transferring calls. Given her no-show the night before, this could not be a coincidence. Sitting in her chair this morning was a young woman Bernie had seen wandering the halls downstairs. She looked like Cyndi Lauper from those god-awful eighties videos, and from the expression of frustration on her face it was easy to discern that she wished she were somewhere else.

"Hi," said Bernie as she approached the desk.

"Help you?" said the woman, with all the charm of a bored Midtown Manhattan retail clerk. Like those clerks, she refused to look up at her customer.

"I think I work here," Bernie said through a forced smile. She didn't like this little twit already.

"Lucky you."

"Where's Nadine this morning?"

"Not a clue."

"She didn't call in?"

"Wouldn't know. They say jump, I say how high."

Bernie wandered off, her mind wrestling with this non-coincidence, when she barely heard Cyndi Lauper sarcastically wish her a nice day from behind.

Sitting on Bernie's desk was a bouquet of flowers. The

card read simply: "Fly me." She smiled, then turned her attention back to the current emergency.

Bernie tried Nadine's home and mobile numbers, with no answer. She opened her computer and failed at appearing busy; she'd never been good at looking cool when her nerves were having seizures. Too much was happening too fast. She needed answers but there was no one to call. Eric had erected a wall behind which he was supposedly pulling strings, but he wouldn't know about Nadine in any case. Nadine didn't seem to have any close friends on the floor—it suddenly occurred to Bernie that she had assumed that role by default—so there was no one to ask about her whereabouts. The only other person who might know something would be Wesley, who coincidentally hadn't arrived for work, either.

Maybe the two of them were off having one of their little performance reviews. Nadine had certainly been a nosy parker of late, and Wesley was too sharp not to notice.

Bernie was too upset to work. The elements of her Web site were in place. All she had to do was implement the final programming, which she could do in her sleep over the weekend. To pass the time, she began to search the Internet for anything about the so-called Serpent worm. While there were plenty of Web addresses devoted to computer security and virus protection—Yahoo! yielded five hundred ninety-nine computer virus update links—she confined her search to the major virus software players, McAfee, Norton and Microsoft, all of whom had at one time or another been suspected of creating the very plagues their products were designed to prevent. None of these pages, however, had been updated to acknowledge the sudden threat of the Serpent, which thus far was a single blip on the vast radar of digital wellness. She imagined the cheeses at those companies sitting in boardrooms wondering who had beaten them to the punch with this next big opportunity.

Whatever Wesley and Jerry were doing to keep this under wraps, it was working. The initial release of a few days ago was a PR ploy, seeding the market with awareness for the moment the Serpent was unleashed for real.

Wesley arrived shortly before ten. As soon as he entered his office he closed the door and plugged in his headset. Bernie watched from her desk as he listened to his voice messages then hurriedly dialed his next call. It must have been a doozie, too, because his face went slack just before it went pale. He paced a moment, then threw the headset onto the floor and sat at his desk. He placed both of his hands behind his neck, lowering his forehead to the desktop, remaining that way for two motionless minutes.

The day was certainly shaping up to be a killer.

Bernie considered an approach to inquire if anything was wrong. But this was not her place, not in an office in which she was the outsider among people who had known their boss much longer, though perhaps not as well, as she.

Wesley suddenly snapped back to life, grabbing the telephone and punching in a number.

Bernie jumped out of her already electrostatic skin when her telephone rang. As she picked it up, Wesley was looking right at her.

"Can you come in here?" His voice was uncharacteristically subdued.

"I'll be right in."

"Please." And then he hung up.

"Close the door."

The tone of Wesley's voice said this wasn't going to be pretty. She feared the news would be of Nadine's sudden termination, followed by questions about what she was really doing here last night.

"Jerry Grasvik is dead."

Bernie inhaled sharply, yet another jolt of nature's best defensive chemicals assaulting her system. Strangely, she felt a rush of emotion tightening in her throat. She

covered her open mouth with a fist and fought for
control.

Wesley spoke quietly. "Climbing accident, this morning on Camelback. They found him at the bottom of the
summit ridge."

"My God. . . ."

"I need your help, Bernie."

"Excuse me?"

"With the project. I need you to finish it."

The room had started to spin, so Bernie eased herself
into one of the chairs in front of Wesley's desk. She
drew a few deep breaths, gripping the armrests firmly
until the sensation passed.

"You want some water?"

"I'm fine." Her eyes bored into him. "You were his
friend."

"I wouldn't say that. We worked well together."

His expression said he seemed to know what was coming next.

She said, "You're one cold-blooded bastard, you
know that?"

"I'm afraid I do."

"Guy's dead for, what, three hours? And all you want
to know, all you have to say, is that you need someone
to finish the damn project?"

Wesley slammed his palm onto his desktop and sprung
to his feet. "What the hell do you want from me? A
speech?"

"A little fucking humanity would suffice."

"I don't have *time* for humanity, lady, fucking or otherwise. You think I don't hurt right now? It's none of
your business how I feel! But it is your business to get
this project launched. You have no idea what's at stake."

She looked away. As soon as she did it she knew it
was a mistake.

With a much calmer tone he said, "Or maybe you do."

There was no response that made sense, so she just
stared at him.

"You were here last night," he said. "Someone was

in my office. I don't believe in coincidences, and I don't underestimate the power of your curiosity."

"You think I was messing with your computer?"

He grinned slightly. "I didn't say anything about my computer."

Another syringe of battery acid pierced her stomach wall.

Wesley put his hands on his desk and leaned in, casting a quick glance out to the office to see if they'd drawn undue attention.

"Listen," he said, "I don't blame you. I'd want to know, too. All this secrecy, designing a site without content or copy. Maybe that's what you were looking for, or maybe you just wanted a peek at my tax return. Right now I don't give a shit. What I give a serious shit about is the survival of this company, and if that makes me a cold-blooded bastard, talk to the two hundred people whose paychecks depend on whether I pull this off or not. So you can sit here on your lovely but self-righteous ass and judge me, or you can save the tearful eulogy for later and step up."

Her chest was heaving, and from the look in her eyes it was obvious she was considering coming out of her chair to drop-kick him through the plate glass. He had little doubt that she could pull it off.

Sensing this, he added, "I'll make it worth your time."

"I don't have the HTML. Jerry hasn't—"

"I've got his files."

A moment passed in which she could feel the power shift. After weeks of waiting on Eric's e-mails and Nadine's tips, after fantasizing and strategizing, she was finally in the catbird seat. This was what she came here to do. But how could Wesley have Jerry's files if his death that morning had been an accident? There were several good answers to this question, but she'd save that inquiry for a better time.

A little hard-to-get was in order now. It was, in fact, instinctual.

"I'll give you the template," she said. "Have one of your flunkies drop in the HTML, it'll practically program itself."

Wesley's eyes dropped as he turned away. She'd just hit a nerve—Wesley needed more from Bernie than programming. He may have Jerry's files, but chances are he didn't have a clue what to do with them. He was upper management, after all. More likely, he couldn't trust the project to anyone on staff because it was illegal as all hell.

"It's not that simple," he said.

"Sure it is. It's grade school."

"I need someone to . . . operate the system."

"What system?"

Wesley was visibly nervous now. She'd seen this before, almost always in men who were hiding something.

"There's a customer demo," he said. "Tomorrow. I need you to run it."

"I'm programming tomorrow." Her smirk was a little too familiar.

"Don't fuck with me," he said.

"Is that a threat?"

"Why would I threaten you, Bernie? Because you're here under false pretenses? That you aren't really who you say you are? I wonder what *your* game is?" He leaned even closer and lowered his voice. "I told you I detest bullshit. Which means I can smell it a mile away. And you, little lady, aren't smelling so good right now."

Bernie stood and smoothed the hem of her blazer. "I don't have to listen to this."

With that she walked out of the office, knowing that the open door would prevent him from yelling after her.

He didn't exactly yell, but she did hear him say "Tomorrow" one more time.

One of two things had just occurred: he was bluffing about his suspicion that she had a hidden agenda, or the recently missing Nadine had changed uniforms in the past twenty-four hours.

Bernie was betting on the bluff. Either way, Wesley Edwards was on the precipice of a long, hard fall, because Bernie had nothing to lose by staying in the game.

She tried not to grin, knowing that most of the floor was observing her exit from Wesley's office. But damn, those balls felt good in the palm of her hand.

That, too, was instinctual.

Just to make him squirm, Bernie left the office within minutes. She caught an early lunch at The Cheesecake Factory, reasoning she would beat the crowd. After that she went home, changed into her brown-belted gi and went across the street for some sweat and a little release of her well-earned tension. In the middle of her workout she remembered that she'd left Paul's flowers on her desk, and the thought imparted a little extra juice to her kicks.

When she got home she did what she'd been wanting to do all day.

Eric—imperative that you call me immediately. Wesley's partner was killed this morning, supposedly an accident, but I don't buy it. He's asked me to step in and demo the software tomorrow, which means I'll have access to everything we need to finish this. You've asked me not to call you, and I've respected that, but I MUST hear from you today or I will have no choice. I need to know what to do with the proof, and where to go. It's not safe.

I need you.

B.

A swim and a shower helped calm her nerves. She dressed and drove to the Scottsdale airport to see if Paul was at the Oar hangar. She'd called him at home earlier to thank him for the flowers, twice in fact, but there was no answer. Not surprisingly, his BMW was in the lot and the jet was gone, which meant Paul might as well be on another planet, because the only two people she could ask about its whereabouts, Nadine and Wesley, weren't options at the moment.

She drove back to the office, intending to tell Wesley with a good deal of visible reticence that she would help him with the demo the next day. Of course she'd need the software tonight in order to familiarize herself with its operation—this would be the moment of truth. She knew enough about customer demos to assume that she'd be simulating the Serpent worm on a system model, then showing how the application of Jerry Grasvik's radical remedying code made the problem disappear. The so-called customer in question might even be an infected company, and she might be asked to actually implement the code in real time.

Which meant she'd suddenly be an accessory to the crime of extortion. Unwitting, perhaps, unless Wesley came clean with her first.

That infamous and often referenced line between good and evil was suddenly a vague and moving target. The rules were now hers to define, as were the consequences.

However it turned out, she'd have the Serpent and its antidote code on the same disk. What she would *do* with it, though, was another matter entirely. Perhaps she could covertly duplicate it to her hard drive without Wesley knowing. Or if she was doing the demo on Jerry's computer, a high likelihood, she might be able to sneak an e-mail attachment out to her own computer. She wondered what Wesley would tell her about it, because she would have to understand the context of the demo in order to implement it.

But she would have to wait for this answer. Little Miss Pissy Pants at the front desk informed Bernie that Wesley had left the office shortly before lunch, with no word as to where he was going or when he might return. She'd already tried his mobile phone, but it was forwarding his calls back to the office.

Wesley was gone. Nadine was gone. Jerry Grasvik was dead. Eric was doing the CYOA thing while playing undercover hero. And Paul was eight miles high, somewhere over the rainbow.

For the time being, at least, Bernie was in this alone.

That afternoon, CNN broke the story that at least four major corporations were reporting attacks on their servers during the night. At least one said an undisclosed extortion demand had been made in return for the removal of the crippling viruslike code, known as Serpent. The other three had no comment, but did confirm that at this time they had no remedy for the problem, and that their primary systems were inoperable. Some business functions were online thanks to redundant or auxiliary computers, but the implications of further attacks could be devastating. The reports came in after the stock market had closed, but analysts predicted a major selloff in the tech sector and perhaps elsewhere on Monday. The Federal Computer Crimes Unit was in the process of dispatching teams to each company, and would not speculate that the source of the worm had been linked to terrorist activities.

41

Paul urged the little Citation onto the runway at
Scottsdale airport, the tires kissing the pavement with a
minimum of friction. The run today had been to a small
civic airstrip outside of Minneapolis, delivering a snow-
bird friend of a friend of an acquaintance of Wesley's
back home because the man was too sick from chemo-
therapy to fly commercial. Paul loved these types of runs
because he got to make them solo, and the flight back
allowed him to indulge in such unlawful diversions as
barrel rolls and power dives and other adrenaline-
inducing violations of the Cessna Corporation's technical
manual. According to Cessna, the plane was incapable
of doing what Paul made it do on a regular basis.

He taxied to the hangar, shutting the engines down
just outside the large doors as it rolled to a silent stop.
The airport guys would pull it inside and lock up—all
Paul had to do was complete the flight log and fuel report and mop up a bit of bourbon that the wife of the
patient had spilled on takeoff that morning. The woman
never once stopped talking, and Paul had to wonder if
the poor bastard in the pajamas wasn't looking forward
to a few hundred centuries of quiet.

Waiting on the seat of his car was a single red rose,
tied with a black ribbon.

Diana. Tonight would be his reward.

Paul was not unaffected by what he'd done that morning, when he had been Damien, when he had snapped

Jerry Grasvik's neck. He'd had a physical response that remained with him all day, a tingling of the skin and a rumbling stomach, and when he replayed the confrontation, a sense of light-headedness. If there was anxiety at all it was for the possibility, however remote, that he had been seen or that he'd left some forensic clue behind that would later bite him on the ass. But he had always been good at separating paranoia and probability, and the more he recounted his steps, the more confident he became. As for Jerry, there was just the slightest hint of remorse, mostly because of the expression on the dumb shit's face when he realized he'd been betrayed by Diana. Oh, the things men allow themselves to believe when their darkest fantasy invites herself in. Damien was glad he did it the way he did, quick and without pain, and with a minimum of fear. There was a time he would have gone the Torquemada route—the infamous torturer during the Spanish Inquisition—and found a way to get off on it, or at least allowed Diana to get off on it for him. Funny how things had changed, how what was once a recreational drug was now a business decision. The thrill had become tepid, if not altogether dead.

He wondered how tonight would turn out. Diana had been distant lately, at once demanding and apathetic. There was nowhere for them to go now, they had crossed the line from dark games to capital crime, and if the kick was gone there was no point. It had always been about the kick, and despite a few laughs here and there, little else.

Depending on tonight, he would reconsider his options going forward. Tonight, he had a feeling, might just bring yet one more rush to tide him over until the next crossroads.

It was as if he were an insurance salesman who had just been promoted to district manager, with an adoring wife who in congratulatory celebration had cooked his favorite dish and put on that old red dress she used to wear when life wasn't so complicated. The Diana and

Damien version of this suburban myth involved seduction and murder, with millions of dollars still at stake, grilled lobster tails and red wine and a formal-length black rubber dress bought in a fetish shop during a lost weekend in SoHo. She met him at the door with his wine, asked him how his day was as she unbuttoned his shirt, and led him by the hand to the patio, where he could smell the lobster and hear the soundtrack from *Somewhere in Time* playing on the stereo.

The first glass of wine was consumed by the time they sat together. They watched the sun go down over Camelback and talked of things that hadn't come up between them before. Words like *guilt* and *God* and *retribution* were used, but they agreed it was all hogwash, made up by obese Italian monks on a primeval power trip. They toasted their good fortune.

"You seem okay," she said.

"I've had my moments. You?"

"It's been an interesting day. Amazing, really."

"How so?" he asked.

"How one part of you gets caught up in all this drama and fear, and how the other part, the part that reminds you what you do and don't believe in, makes you feel foolish for listening to the first voice."

"So have you decided what you believe in?"

With a distant expression she said, "I believe in nothing."

"So you're okay. You feel, basically, nothing at all."

She eyed him over the rim of her glass. "More wine?"

Without waiting for a response, she took his glass and disappeared into the house. Damien stretched, the weight of the day and the second glass of seven-year-old cabernet thickening his blood, making the evening air thick and even warmer than usual.

She returned, refilling his glass.

"No turning back from this one, is there," she said, reassuming her seat.

"I know."

"It means we have to get real, get serious."

"I was thinking it means we should get some new ink."

"I don't think a skull and crossbones on my other ass cheek would be all that sophisticated, do you?"

"Ah, we are getting older, aren't we."

She was staring at him with an odd sort of detachment. When he saw that she was heading in a heavier direction than his, he shifted his body language to an earnest pose.

"I'd say two million is pretty serious," he said.

"I'm not talking about the money."

"You're talking about *this*." He reached under his collar and pulled out the red vial on the thin silver chain. "You and me. The blood pact."

"Whole new meaning now," she said.

He again shifted in his chair, uncomfortably warm all of a sudden. He didn't like the way she was looking at him, didn't like where this was headed.

"We have to talk," she said.

"I'm listening."

"You've killed for me. That's huge."

He issued a disgusted little snort. "*I've* killed? Check your program, dear. I think this case has two defendants."

He gulped down his wine, in a hurry to catch the buzz that would make this conversation easier to stomach.

He said, "They say when you save someone's life, you're responsible for them. Wonder what it means when you've killed *for* someone."

He expected a response, but she just sat there, the rim of her glass against her lip, staring.

He stood slowly, his legs thick and strangely unresponsive.

That's when the wave hit him, the open patio doors yawning like a black cave, the mountain behind the house shifting as if the Big One had just arrived. He reached down to steady himself with a grip on the chair, but the chair was no longer there.

As he fell, he saw that Diana was watching him over

the rim of her glass, a smile toying with the corners of her mouth.

Behold, I stand at the door and knock.

I am alone on a landing on the sixth floor in this, our very special hotel. It is midnight, the appointed hour of my summons. The door is already ajar. I push it open and step inside. This was our room, our very special place, alpha and omega, where the world of dark pleasure was unveiled to me, and where it was shattered in a nightmare of even darker betrayal. They are, I have since concluded, two sides of the same coin.

There are many candles, just like then. He was romantic, my lover. The room was always prepared with candles and incense, wine and fresh flowers, the warm oils, soft music, wicked toys arranged on the sheets, already turned down. My stomach erupts and my tears cause the candles to glow with an elliptical fluttering. I fear this signals his intention, and for all my resolve I already hear the whispering demons, urging me to submit to the pleasure I had once known, and would never know again.

But this is different. Because now I am truly free, there is no deceit in my presence.

Except, perhaps, the betrayal of my own pride.

I tell myself yet again, I am here to set him free.

What have I done?

I step into the room, a heartbeat is all that separates us now. I sense movement to the side, the rushing of a ghost, the swinging arm, a white flash of impact, the room spinning as I fall without sound.

In the instant before the shadows descend, I see a face.

And it is not his.

As if rustled from an afternoon snooze in the backyard cot, Damien summoned an awareness of his surroundings to the surface of his emerging consciousness. And as in such a nap, he was never sure what was real and what was imagined, or how much time had passed since he'd nodded off. He had dreamed of Diana, of dancing with her across the floor of their bedroom, the music stuttering like a scratched CD, of her undressing and then dressing him again, fitting him with a new tie, a new game, her smile and soft voice coaxing him to play along. And now, as the fog lifted and time slowed to a standstill, he suddenly realized where he was, and what the game would be.

The endgame, as it were.

He was in his bedroom, standing at the foot of his bed. He remembered standing on the bed itself, and then stepping off, stepping up, actually . . . and now he understood what the dream had prevented him from comprehending. He was standing on a tall bar stool, completely naked. His hands were bound behind his back, and something was wrapped tightly around his throat. His feet were unbound, but they were going nowhere.

"Careful, sweetheart," said Diana. The voice came from behind him, where she was just emerging from the closet. She had changed from the clingy black rubber gown to jeans and a sweatshirt, an odd choice given his predicament at the moment. As he pivoted he realized that what was constricting his neck was a thin rope that extended up to the ceiling beam, tied off securely to an eyebolt placed there for other tasty little diversions that involved one or more ropes.

A new game was suddenly in play. If he moved, if he inadvertently kicked the stool out from under him or simply lost his balance, he would hang himself. The stool had a high center of gravity, and it wouldn't take much for this to conclude badly.

"I liked the dress better," he said, already wearing his game face. They had done some serious kink in their years together, drawn blood and seduced strangers, tied and twisted each other in all manner of configurations, penetrated places the good Lord had never intended with objects meant for anything but, yet this was something diabolically new. That alone, and the fact that Diana still had the dark capacity to surprise him, was exquisitely exciting.

She came to his side, reaching up to stroke his penis. Her smile was detached. Oddly, he saw that she was wearing gloves, which like the dark smile would have been more suited to the dominatrix dress.

"What is this?" he said, unsure whether to infuse his voice with playfulness or outrage.

She held the gloves in front of her face. "Did you know they can lift fingerprints from human flesh? Saw it on *CSI*. I never knew that."

She playfully pinched the skin on this thigh, then pulled at the hair there. His reaction was involuntary, and it almost cost him his life.

"Whoa," she said, helping to steady him. "We have a lot to talk about before we get to the fun part."

Damien was suddenly and genuinely frightened. The three-legged stool had gone to two legs, and had she not been there to stop his momentum he would have lost it. His heart was thumping loud enough for him to actually hear it echoing in his body cavities.

"What, not up for this?" she asked, flicking his penis, which was now at parade rest.

Everything in his nature was in conflict. He was a warrior, and when threatened the warrior lashed out. But if he moved he would fall, and for the first time he wasn't sure what her game was, if she would quickly slice the rope or stand there and watch him twirl. She might even go that far—once, just for fun, she'd strangled him to the point of unconsciousness with her bathrobe belt—then cut the rope at the last possible moment. He didn't know how to respond, whether to show his appreciation for her creativity or express his concern for the safety of this little ill-conceived experiment.

It occurred to him that fear, chased with a stiff dose of outrage, was precisely what this little game was all about.

"I take it this is my reward," he said, trying to stifle the part of him that wanted to scream. She was standing close enough to wrap his legs around her head, but that would leave them both suspended, and the thought passed quickly.

"You could say that," she said, walking slowly in a circle, her fingers trailing over his legs. "Remember those old movies, when the bad guy shoots at the feet of the local sheriff and tells him to dance? You want to dance, Damien?"

If she was playing after all, then she was setting the bar at a whole new level.

"You're crazy," he said quietly, a lover's compliment.

She smiled, then went to the nightstand and opened the drawer. She returned with something in her hand.

She held up the scalpel that she had used to carve her initial into his chest. The smile she wore was as confusing as it was compelling.

"What a mind fuck," she said, tracing the edge across the tender flesh just behind his knee joint. "A blade, a lit cigarette, a harsh fingernail, the lash . . . what would it take to make you dance . . . how much can you take, Damien, eh? How much do you love me?"

A little alarm went off in his head. *How much do you love me?* This wasn't part of any of their previous games. And yet it had always been a point of contention, the unspoken word, her subtle lobbying for it, his refusal to let it become part of their lexicon. Now that she had spoken it, he knew that this wasn't a game at all.

"What's this about?" he asked, letting her know that he was onto her. His tone was sincere, as if to say he wanted to get serious in the midst of this insanity.

"Well," she said, now tracing the point of the blade over the tender part of his insole, "first we're going to get a few things out in the open, you and I. Clear the air. That'll be nice, won't it? No more lies? No more wondering what's up, what's next."

"I'd be a lot more open to this conversation if you'd let me down."

This made her laugh. It occurred to him that she was acting as if she were high, which wasn't like her. She was in a zone, and it was not of this world.

"That would ruin the second part," she said, tossing the blade onto the bed behind her.

"Which is?"

Her smile widened.

"The second part is where you kill yourself."

She is wearing my clothes. It is my favorite casual sweat suit, gray with embroidered black designs. She also wears one of my old Dallas Mavericks caps, which I hadn't seen in a year or two. In my delirium this makes no sense, but this is what I see. She wears gloves, and yet it is the dead of summer. Tape covers my mouth, and I taste something bitter, the burning of smoke in my throat. I try to move, but my limbs are thick, and the air hisses in my ears. It is better to lie still, she says, and when I struggle she pins me back to the bed until I agree that she is right. The room revolves, pitches and dives, and I cannot wake myself, bring myself completely back to the moment. I am caught between a very real dream and a very vague reality, and she watches me, smiling approvingly as she brings something up to my eyes. It is a pipe, and now I smell the drug in the air and know that somehow in the dream I have been made to partake of it. I am high, stoned out of my mind, and I cannot move.

We need to talk, she says. We need to understand. He belongs to her, she says, and while I was not the first of his playthings, I was the first to make him turn away from her. To threaten. The game had gotten out of hand somehow, and it was my doing.

And for that, I must pay.

She begins to undress me, and though I try to struggle, I cannot resist.

"Look at me!" demanded Diana, leaning on the bed as if she were about to be frisked. She had suddenly ripped her sweatshirt over her head as she turned her back to him, exposing the exquisite fresco of temptation and feminine evil that now defined her body. This was all she had to say to Damien to trigger his awareness of her agenda.

Look at me!

He beheld her skin, and suddenly understood.

"Look at what I gave to you," she went on, adding, "at how I *loved* you!"

There it was. It all boiled down to what they had done to that married woman back in Dallas. He was in serious, irretrievable trouble.

When Diana turned back her face was streaked with angry tears. She kept the sweatshirt off, a vision of B-movie insanity in her jeans and black gloves and tattooed torso.

"How I loved you," she repeated, touching his legs again, feigning tenderness. "It was all for you, Damien, everything we did . . . always *about* you, *your* fantasies, *your* needs. . . . I gave everything to you, didn't I . . . my heart, my soul, my life . . . but it was never enough . . . *I* was never enough. . . ."

"Diana, listen to me. . . ."

"No!" The calm face exploded into a red mask of anguish, fresh tears running from her eyes. "You listen to *me*! I gave and I gave and I gave . . . and you took and took and took . . . and it was never enough! Not even this. . . ."

She stepped back, grasped the locket around her neck and tore it free. She looked at it somewhat longingly, then let it slip through her fingers as it dropped to the floor.

"Blood, Damien . . . you always wanted my blood. And now you have it."

It was over. Whatever happened now would not be about clearing the air so they could go forward, not about the unloading of her heavy heart. It would be about revenge.

His legs began to tremble. This martial artist who could sustain the splits for an hour, who could run up Camelback Mountain in twenty minutes to do her bidding . . . now those warrior legs were betraying him.

"I was everything you wanted," she said in a voice that was suddenly barely audible. "I was *more* than you wanted because I knew more about your needs that you did. I thought maybe, when we had been there and done it all, that you would see what was left, that you and I were all that remained, all that mattered. That we were forging a bond bound by our blood, something we could never deny. . . ."

Damien shifted his feet ever so slightly, challenging the stability of the stool.

"Diana, stop this shit! You have to listen to me!"

She didn't hear. She was suddenly busy embedding the tip of the scalpel in her own forearm, the blood already pooling at her feet, covering the vial she had dropped there.

In a voice more appropriate to a young girl confessing her first heartbreak, she said, "I just wanted you to love me, Damien . . . to love me . . . just me . . . I wanted you to love me. . . ."

"I do love you, Diana . . . I swear it. . . ."

"No! I've seen her, you son of a bitch, your pretty little Bernadette, so perky and so fucking smart. . . ."

"It's just a game! *Our* game! I *killed* a man . . . and it was for *you*!"

She sneered at him through her anguish, finding some private humor in what he'd said. Her expression stopped him from saying anything more.

"You don't even understand your own game," she said. "You think Dallas was about you . . . that I gave you my skin and my soul because of what *you* achieved . . . but you don't even know. . . ."

Her voice trailed off, as if she'd betrayed some ancient and sacred trust.

"What are you talking about?" he asked quietly, afraid of the answer.

Her eyes blazed, about to thrust the sword.

"Dallas. That was never you. It wasn't even about you. That was me, Damien, it was my doing. I took the woman in Dallas . . . it was *me* who won the game. . . ."

She dresses me in the clothes she had been wearing. My clothes. Now I notice that she also has my bag, but the clothes she takes out of it aren't mine at all. Those are what she puts on now.

You'd be surprised how easy it is to get into someone's place if you know what you're doing, she tells me. That's how she took my clothes, my bag. That's how she got in to leave the note they would find, written on my computer. It wouldn't mention him by name, but they would know. They wouldn't find him because I'd never told anyone how to find him, I'd never told anyone his name. Except my sister, and then only his first name.

Wesley.

It would all be written off as a broken heart, she says. And I know she is right.

She washes my mouth with a wet cloth. Wouldn't want traces of tape to be found there. The dope in the room, which is registered in my name, this is all good. The front-desk clerk will remember the woman in my clothes with my hair, wearing my sunglasses. He'll remember me checking in because the woman checking in was very sad, paying cash, leaving a credit card number because she left the card at home. He'd check the number, and it would be fine. Did I remember when I'd bought him that dinner, and did I know the man I thought was Wesley had a photographic memory, at least where numbers were concerned, and that his name wasn't really even Wesley at all? His name was Damien.

This is how it will work, she says.

Because he loves me and not her. She appears angry as she says this, and I know she is going to kill me.

I try to struggle, but there is no strength, no will to move. I can't scream, I can only listen and watch as she prepares.

She opens the door and peeks into the hall. It is the middle of the night, so it is quiet. Then she comes for me. Lifts me under my arms. Incredibly strong. Drags me backward toward the door. Into the hall. Stops at the railing, balancing me there. Lifts my feet.

Again I try to struggle, but I cannot. I scream, but only I hear the sound.

And then, she is gone.

No more fear. There is only light, bathing me in its warmth. And there is a voice, softly saying my name . . . and I must go.

It had all been a lie. The woman in Dallas, the Wesley charade, the great challenge, the glorious victory. It had always been Diana's game. Diana, the temptress, the true and only serpent.

She was smiling like Satan herself as she watched him process what she'd just confessed, the realization destroying all that he thought was real between them, all that he thought was powerful about himself. He had been played, seduced, and now destroyed, and she was savoring every second of his suffering.

And somehow, in the midst of her pleasure, she was dying along with him. The duplicity of her love infused her pleasure with regret.

Vengeance, like love itself—always somehow less than perfect.

His legs had stopped trembling, but now numbness was setting in. He was being so careful about his movement that his circulation had been compromised. He shifted slightly in an effort to bring them back to life, and in doing so caused the stool to pitch and yaw.

When he yelped involuntarily, Diana covered her mouth with her hand as she giggled.

She put her gloved hands on his legs, massaging them back to life.

"Here are your options," she said. "They aren't pretty."

"I *killed* him for you," he said, his voice now weak.

"That you did. As I killed her for you. So we're even, you and I. The difference is I have you on tape doing it. That telescope brings it right into your living room. I'll leave a copy for your collection. You try to find me, you implicate me, I show the tape. I tell them you were jealous, that I'd tried to break things off with you, but you went nuts, swore you'd kill my new lover and then me, and that when you stormed off to find him that morning I was so scared. So I turned on the tape and saw you do it. I was recording it for Jerry anyway—he wanted a tape of his climb. How convenient and ironic. Then you came back here, attacked me with a knife, tried to kill me, but I ran, barely got out of here with my life. Look, there's my blood on your carpet."

"All of that presupposes I don't fall off this fucking stool," he offered.

"Well, there's the other option. In your office they'll find a suicide note on your computer. You couldn't handle what you'd done, you'd snapped when I told you it was over, that I'd found Jerry, and you killed him in a fit of jealous rage."

"I don't think so," he said.

"Really? Maybe you fall off this stool sometime in the night, the old legs just give out, and down you go. Who would know the difference? What are you going to do, scream? The note's already there, Damien."

She smiled at that. But she was fighting off something rising from behind the sadistic bravado. His hope was that it would surface, and that it would save him.

"Or," she continued, "you can think about it after I've gone, think about how nothing in your life means a thing anymore, how you've just lost the one chance you had, the one woman who truly wanted to give you everything you've ever dreamed. Think about the shit that's down the road when they connect you to Jerry, which they will, especially if you breathe my name to anyone. Maybe you just take that last step, make it all stop. They'll find the locket, see the blood . . . I'll tell them I gave it back to you, like a ring . . . that apparently Paul Lampkin just lost it."

He was breathing hard now, the rope around his throat slightly constricting his ability to draw air. The more anxious he became, the more oxygen he needed, the more the veins in his throat expanded and throbbed.

"I've got his laptop, with the program," she said. "I may even have Wesley. Isn't that a hoot? Me and Jerry's boss? *Your* boss? You'll never know, because either way it goes down, you'll never see me again. But I want you to think about it."

She disappeared into the closet. A moment later she returned, lugging a suitcase behind her, which she'd packed earlier in the day. She pulled it into the hall, then stepped back into the room. She stood in front of him, hands on her hips.

"Whatever you decide, know this—I loved you. I hung on to that as long as I could, and then I snapped. Women do that. We snap quietly, and then we look for our chance to get out. It's gone before you even have a clue it's in trouble."

Her face suddenly went slack, the anger yielding. She stayed with it for a moment, then lowered her eyes and walked to the door.

Paul Lampkin knew this had been his last chance, and that it was gone.

"I always knew this would end ugly," he said after her.

When she turned, her face was sad in an innocent way. "I know you did," she said. "That was the problem all along, wasn't it."

She proceeded to the door, then turned a final time and said, "Cleaning lady comes at eight, in case you decide to stick it out. I'd give anything to see her face when she walks in here."

From somewhere down the hall he heard her add, "Personally, I hope you break your fucking neck."

42

There was no way he'd last until eight in the morning. He had perfected a method of shifting his weight from one foot to the other without disturbing the precarious balance of the bar stool, but that technique could only last as long as his concentration held out. Being the fifth-degree black belt that he was, concentration was his forte, but eight o'clock was more than eight hours into an unreliable future, and Bruce Lee himself would have trouble holding this pose. During the three hours since Diana's departure, his thoughts had landed on many things, some quite surprising, in fact. He thought of one of the *Survivor* television programs, in which the three finalists were made to stand perched on sticks with one hand touching a central pole, the first to fall losing immunity. He'd laughed at the time, considering it a piece of cake, and had actually thought of sending in a tape to get on the show—hell, they'd had a tattooed control freak on the show once, why not another? He thought of his beloved airplane, what they would think in the morning when he was a no-show for a flight to San Diego with Wesley, some big-deal customer demo that was positioned as a "must-fly" priority, which meant if the Citation was down he was to rent whatever airplane was available, no matter what the cost. They'd call Scottsdale flight services and round up a pilot on short notice, and Wesley wouldn't think to be concerned about his missing pilot for more than a minute. He'd hear about it from that bitch Nadine, who had to be fucking the boss. He thought of his parents but could barely remember their faces. He thought of the mountain and Jerry—he was sorry he'd done that one—and of the woman in Dallas who had taken her own life because of how he'd betrayed her. At least, that's what he had thought until tonight.

A friend in the ambulance business had once told him that of the hundreds of people he'd seen pass away before his eyes, he'd never seen an atheist die, that everyone always gets humble when the trumpet sounds. The thought of it made him nauseous, and for a moment he sensed he was no longer alone in his bedroom, standing on a chair with a noose around his neck, struggling to keep his balance.

Time toyed with perception. Minutes passed like hours, yet the hours flew like the fleeting memories that were raining in his thoughts. Somewhere after what he guessed was midnight, fighting now not only to keep his balance but to keep from falling asleep on his feet, he heard a sound. It came from the lower level, probably the garage. Most likely a door, perhaps a coyote picking through the garbage. He froze, focusing his entire awareness through his ears.

Another sound, soft, but definite. Someone was in the house.

Diana was coming back for him. His punishment was over, she had made her point, and she was returning to gloat. Or perhaps she'd reconsidered and would walk into the room and promptly kick the stool out from under him. There was a slim chance it was Bernie, who only had his mobile number, and that phone was down in his car. She might come, find him like this, and though he'd have some quick explaining ahead of him, he'd be saved.

Someone was at the door to the bedroom, lingering for a moment. Then the intruder walked in.

It was a man, tall and thickly built. He wore black overalls, like those worn by the mechanics at the airport.

Strangely, he also wore those latex gloves the detectives used on all the forensic cop shows. That alone made Paul believe he was being visited by a burglar, a happy coincidence at best, more likely the kiss of death. This would be the talk of cell-block six someday.

The man's eyes darted about the room with a surprising lack of interest in Paul.

"Who the fuck are you?" asked Paul, surprised at his own hostility.

The man ignored him. He went to the patio door, slid it open and stepped outside. Paul watched as he went to the rail and looked down at the driveway for a few seconds, then returned to the room, sliding the door closed behind him.

"I'd appreciate it if you'd help me out here," said Paul. "There's a knife on the bed . . . cut me down, man. You want money, I'll give you what you want."

The man stopped in front of him, looking down at the blood on the floor. He bent, touched it with his gloved fingertips, then picked up Diana's locket containing his blood.

He withdrew a rag from his pocket, wiped down the locket and put it in another pocket. Then he turned to the bed and used the rag to pick up the scalpel that Diana had left there. He wrapped the rag around the handle, then turned to face Paul.

"What is this?" pleaded Paul, not believing his eyes. "She put you up to this, man? Talk to me . . . cut me down and we'll talk money . . . please. . . ."

Paul froze as the man reached up and grabbed the vial of blood still hanging from his neck by a silver chain. He gave it a yank to break it free, then put it in his pocket with Diana's locket.

Paul started to protest, but stopped when the guy touched him on the leg, on the upper thigh actually, frighteningly close to no-man's-land.

"Listen, dude. . . ."

The man pulled the blade back, tossing it onto the

bed. He knelt at the base of the stool supporting Paul's weight. He looked up at Paul and smiled.

"Have a nice flight," he said.

Then he yanked the stool out from under him.

The man jumped back to avoid being kicked in the face as Paul thrashed at the end of the rope. It hadn't come close to breaking his neck, but it did the intended job of constricting his windpipe, and it was only a matter of time before unconsciousness set in.

It took two minutes for Paul's awareness to wane, the struggle subsiding in proportion to the sapping of his strength. The man simply stood back and watched, no expression at all on his face.

In the final seconds of his life, behind a curtain of strobing lights and the sound of screaming wind in his ears, Paul once again sensed that he was not alone, and in that moment he understood that he had been wrong about everything he thought to be true.

And that there was a price for his misunderstanding.

The man allowed Paul to hang for another five minutes, during which he went into Paul's closet and gathered up some clothes, his wallet and his car keys. He also retrieved a sophisticated listening device he'd covertly installed in a potted plant days earlier, as well as six more devices from other rooms in the house. The bugs were CIA issue, with a broadcast radius of twelve miles.

Returning to the bedroom, he used the scalpel to cut Paul down, coaxing the body to fall onto the bedspread, which he had arranged just behind the axis of where he hung. He rolled the body into a makeshift mummy, which he hoisted onto his shoulder.

Before he left he wiped off the scalpel and put it into the drawer of the nightstand.

At eight the next morning, the maid would clean the entire lower level before going upstairs. She would quickly notice the spattering of blood on the carpet at the foot of the bed, and spend twenty minutes trying to get it up. But she would fail, leaving a healthy stain that looked more like spilled wine than the blood of lovers who knew no limits.

She would think nothing more of it, at least not that day. It wasn't the first time she'd seen blood in this room, and compared with some of the other sights that had greeted her here, this was child's play.

43

Dallas, Texas

Eric Killen leaned forward and squinted at the thirteen-inch video monitor with its built-in VCR. It was resting on a case of toilet paper in a storage room at the Embassy Suites near DFW, the hotel in which Bernie's sister had plunged to her death some eight months earlier. The security guard, who in the tradition of many who chose the rent-a-cop industry as a career following an apprenticeship at the toll booth, was all of five-five and weighed about as much as a husky German shepherd. His name was Roger Davis, and someone needed to remind him that the mustache thing went out when Tom Selleck decided to shave his, or at least that his CHiPs sunglasses were vintage kitsch of the first order. Roger had asked Eric to meet him here at the hotel, since he'd done his research on the sly and would be in a world of hurt if someone caught him showing this stuff to Eric.

"Here she comes," said Roger, slowing the tape to frame advance. On the screen a woman appeared, wearing a gray warm-up suit and a baseball cap, with her ponytail emerging from the back. She also wore sunglasses. The camera, which shot grainy black-and-white footage, was fixed on the wall behind the front desk, framing the registration area from an angle that looked at the back of the clerk's head and down on the head of the person registering for a room. If that person happened to be wearing a cap, the face was hidden.

Roger had already shown Eric the label on the tape—
this was shot on the evening of the night Peggy killed
herself.

"Peggy," said Eric, mumbling it to himself. An unexpected block of unresolved pain lodged in his throat.

"Okay," said Roger. "Check this out."

The footage went black, then blinked back to life. It
was a close-up this time, even grainier than before,
showing her hands as she signed the registration card.
Roger had already explained how he used the Kmart
editing system at work to do some zooms on specific
scenes of interest.

As Eric watched, Roger froze the frame.

"So?"

"Check out the watch," said Roger. He was dead serious about this. Eric correctly assumed this was the cool-
est thing Roger had done in the security game since
holding a door open for Chelsea Clinton.

The hands in the frame wore a watch with a black
face and a black leather wristband.

"Got it?" asked Roger.

Roger ejected the tape before he got an answer. He
took another tape from the pile he'd brought with him,
checked the label, then slid it into the machine.

"I know this guy, works at the county coroner. Smug-
gled this out to me."

The blue screen turned to scratchy white, then sharply
cut to the image of a still photograph lying on a table.
The point of view vibrated slightly, indicating that this
was handheld camera footage, probably Roger's personal Sony eight millimeter. It zoomed slowly toward
the picture.

It was Peggy's body. She was lying in a pool of water
in the hotel's foyer fountain, sharing the frame with several pairs of feet, all wearing police-issue shoes.

"See anything?" said Roger.

Eric fought off a confrontive answer as he shook his
head, keeping his eyes on the television. It was suddenly

hot in here, which contributed to a sudden sensation of nausea.

Roger froze the frame.

"Look closer."

He put his finger on the tube, pointing at Peggy's left wrist, the same one that had worn the watch when she'd checked in.

"No watch," said Eric.

"No watch," repeated Roger. "They find a watch in the room or at the scene?"

"No."

Eric now looked at Roger, whose eyebrows were raised with an unmistakable air of self-satisfaction. "Wasn't her who checked in. You got a poseur on your hands."

"Maybe," said Eric, not wanting to give the possibility too much credence this soon. There were any number of possible explanations. "No hat, either."

"Interesting."

"Smart lady. She puts the hat on the vic, could leave a hair."

"DNA," said Roger, happy to be swapping cop talk.

Eric just nodded, keeping his eyes on the screen.

Roger ejected the tape. Moving quickly, as if he'd rehearsed the sequence of this presentation, he grabbed another cassette and inserted it into the machine.

"Cut to three months earlier," said Roger.

On the screen a well-dressed man with shoulders like a dump truck walked into frame. A suit bag was slung over his shoulder and his tie was loosened.

"October nine," said Roger. "Meet Wesley Edwards. Paid for two rooms, American Express."

Eric recognized the face from the driver's license mug shot he'd provided to Bernie.

"Two rooms?"

"Data don't lie," said Roger.

He fast-forwarded the tape. Now another man walked into the frame, wearing a sport coat over a tight T-shirt, his dark hair hanging loose over his eyes and brushed back behind his ears. He looked like a model from a Ralph Lauren magazine spread.

"October eighteen," said Roger. "According to the registration database, which correlated to the time code on this video, this guy checked in as Wesley Edwards. Paid with a Visa."

"Freeze that," said Eric. He leaned closer, studying the new young buck. Even from this angle, he could see an indistinguishable tattoo on the back of his thumb as he signed in.

When Eric leaned back, Roger fast-forwarded for a quick moment. When he stopped, the same man walked into frame, dressed this time in jeans, cowboy boots and a leather bomber jacket.

"October twenty-seven," said Roger. "Same deal, same card, same name."

He fast-forwarded yet again. This time the man had his hair slicked back and wore a double-breasted business suit, the kind favored by motivational speakers and game-show hosts.

"November third," said Roger. "I've got six more. Same M.O."

Eric stifled an excited grin and focused on the screen. He watched several more check-in sequences of the mystery man.

"Best for last," said Roger, changing tapes quickly. "December first."

This time, the Latin lover type approached the desk to sign in, only someone was with him. It was a woman, lagging behind, but they had approached together, hand in hand.

Roger froze the frame. "He shoots, he scores," he muttered.

The woman was Peggy. There was no doubt, because she was wearing the same two-piece gray warm-up suit that the woman who had impersonated her had worn months later, on the night her body ended up in the lobby fountain.

"So what do we have?" said Roger, now leaning dangerously back in his chair. "We got a guy keeps checking in using Wesley Edwards's credit card, and he ain't Wesley Edwards. We got a woman checks in as Peggy Hopkins and she ain't Peggy Hopkins. Later that night, the real Peggy Hopkins jumps off the sixth-floor landing in the same clothes, but without the watch she wore when she checked in, because it wasn't her who checked in."

Eric didn't answer. He was still staring at the screen, which was now blank.

"We got us a homicide, you ask me," said Roger, trying to look grim but unable to hide a smug pleasure with his own powers of deduction.

Eric extended his hand in congratulations. "You willing to testify, tell the court how you got all this?"

"Name the date, counselor, I'm there."

"Possible to get hard copy of this? Both imposters?"

Roger offered a *what-took-you-so-long?* smirk. He snatched a manila folder from the table next to him, from which he withdrew two five-by-seven glossies, handing them to Eric.

Eric's eyes were wide as he looked down at the treasure in his hands. He slapped Roger on the back as he got up to leave.

"Shoulda been a cop, Rog. Would have made detective before you were thirty."

"Woulda shoulda coulda," replied Roger.

"I'll call you. Keep this between you and me for a while, okay, partner?"

Roger offered a thumbs-up and a weighty nod as Eric bolted out of the room.

Eric sliced through the rush-hour traffic en route back to Da Slamma and the pile of paperwork he'd back-burnered in favor of Roger's private showing. One of the new student-guests had coldcocked an English teacher, who in addition to being half his size was a fifty-five-year-old woman, and had then attempted to do the same to Eric as he arrived on the scene. Big mistake.

The kid now had a broken nose and a sprained arm, the latter thanks to Eric's respondent takedown and enthusiastic restraining hold, and nothing says paperwork like an injured inmate.

But the word processor would have to wait. He should have bought a lottery ticket on the way in that morning, because he was hitting numbers right and left. In addition to Roger's earthshaking clips, he had a message from his fraternity-brother-turned-air-traffic-controller saying he'd done a little digging on that jet Eric had asked about, and had an update. But before he could pick up the phone, he noticed a padded envelope on his desk. It was addressed to him, and next to his name was a red fingerprint. But even that wasn't what raised his pulse past the fat-burning zone.

The return address had Bernie's name and address in Scottsdale, Arizona.

It took less time to interpret her intention than it did to tear open the envelope. After all this time with no calls or e-mails, it seemed strange that there was no note accompanying the computer mouse and the card, which confused him at first. Both were wrapped in Ziploc sandwich bags.

Instead of calling his ATC mole, he called another college friend who worked for the Dallas Police Department, who had been in contact several times over the years in connection with a few new customers at Da Slamma. He told Eric that if he got the sandwich bags over there before six, he could have any results by nine that night. No promises, but he might even be able to hide the three-hundred-dollar interdepartmental charge in his budget. Eric owed him a dinner and a ball game, and they had a deal.

Then, after one more call to hear what the air traffic guy had to say, Eric made up his mind.

Shannon was going to kill him. But whether she liked it or not, he was leaving for Scottsdale in the morning.

PART FOUR

Judge not, that ye be not judged. For with what judgment ye judge, ye shall be judged: and with what measure ye mete, it shall be measured to you again.

—Matthew 7:1–2

44

Nothing says heart failure quite like bolting upright in the middle of the night to the sound of someone pounding on your front door. Especially when nobody is supposed to know where you live. Bernie glanced at the digital clock as she weighed her options. It was a little before two, which was the number of options she had: get up and see who it was, or pretend she wasn't home and spend the rest of the night a nervous wreck. She'd been asleep all of thirty minutes, so this simple choice seemed extraordinarily complex.

She chose the coy route. She put on a robe, went out to the entry hall and pressed her face against the backside of the door.

"Who is it?"

"Wes," was the answer. "Sorry about the hour. Please."

It was, as the tough guys say, go time. If she opens the door, she's locked into finishing this. Perhaps perpetrating a crime, maybe even signing her own death warrant in the process. If she denies him, he'll either kick it in and force her to comply—despite what the movies would have you believe, her martial arts weren't all that great a safeguard against a pissed-off jock who benches two twenty-five—or, after protestations and threats, he'll reluctantly go away, eliminating her only shot at taking him down. Naïvely, she had assumed this would all come to a head in the morning, and by midnight she had not yet made up her mind how it would all turn out. The more she thought about Nadine going AWOL and Jerry going into the next world, the better going back to Dallas was beginning to sound.

She opened the door.

Wesley still had on his tan suit, which looked surprisingly fresh after a twenty-hour day. A quick mental snapshot had him madly making calls to New York consiglieres while sitting in front of a computer displaying Jerry's program, trying to make heads or tails out of what used to be his meal ticket. Like most bosses, Wesley could talk a good game, but when it came to connecting the ones and zeroes, chances are he knew only enough to be dangerous. If Jerry's code was as valuable as everyone thought, nothing about it would be easy to understand.

He carried a small leather notebook case, the size of a Filofax.

"We have work to do," he said, stepping inside as she moved back.

Outside, parked a hundred yards away behind a row of mailboxes, lights off, engine running, was the battered white utility van with a metal ladder lashed to the roof. If asked, the man in the driver's seat, now wearing a clean set of overalls, was looking for the address of an insomniac client with an air conditioning problem. In the back of the van lay what looked like a statue wrapped in a bedspread, now wrapped in a clear plastic tarp.

But no one would ask tonight. So he'd wait, and when the time came, he'd move forward with his instructions.

Wesley went straight to Bernie's dining room table. He placed the Filofax on the glass surface and unzipped it with what she thought was a touch of ceremonial flourish.

Then he withdrew what she quickly saw was a stack of bills wrapped with a rubber band. Not quite as

quickly, she saw that the bills were all hundreds, and
that the stack was two inches thick.

"Fifty grand," he said.

"I'd have taken a check."

"Trust me, you don't want a check. This project is
under the table."

"I got that feeling."

"There's fifty more when we're done."

"Which is?"

"Two, three days. Depends on you, actually."

"And it's illegal."

"Depends on who you ask."

"Or who your attorney is."

"This is how it's done, Bernie. From Bezos to Ellison
to Bill Gates himself, we all started with cash and a
handshake and something we'd rather not talk about."

"I like how you use *we*. Heavy company."

"The people who made it happen for those guys count
their net worth in nine digits."

"Counting the decimal?"

"Don't fuck with me. I'm offering you the chance of a
lifetime. Are you in, or are you just another pretty face?"

He stared with the intensity of a priest talking a
jumper down off the ledge. For all her history with him,
and despite the unexpected presence of Paul in her life,
part of her still marveled at his chiseled jaw, the piercing
blue eyes, the David Hasselhoff hair. He was, in a way
Paul wasn't, the poster boy for brilliant and decidedly
rogue machismo.

"Convince me."

"The fifty doesn't convince you? What are you, a nun?
Take the money, Bernie. Do the work. There're no victims here, it's just business. You manipulate the winds
of fate and it looks like a happy accident of nature.
That's how it's done. And the world gets a whole new
level of security for their digital secrets. We don't do it,
someone else will, and they'll get a magazine cover for
their time."

She thought he actually looked scared. In reading his face, she knew the opportunity to get what she wanted was still wide open.

"Fifty now, a hundred later," she said.

"Done."

"And a new car, out of your cut. Something German. Just between us girls."

A tiny grin appeared on his face, as if he now knew he'd get what *he* wanted.

"I knew it was a good idea to hire you."

She returned the smile. For a moment a familiar spark lit up the room.

She said, "Tell me what you want me to do."

"For starters," he replied, "I want you to come back to the office with me. Now."

El Paso, Texas

Snap decisions had never been a problem for Eric Killen, though more than one had landed him in trouble thus far. This decision was no exception—Shannon had been livid when he'd announced that he was leaving for Phoenix right after dinner. She'd come right out with it this time, accusing him of being in love with Bernie, of running off to her under the guise of heroism. There was no reasoning with the green monster—it fed on reason and consumed intellect, and he was tired of the old banter, which never allowed him to win.

He told her he loved her, then left the house. As he drove off, he saw her standing in the open doorway, her hands held straight at her sides, no expression whatsoever on her face.

The morning flights were booked, and the only one available landed just after noon and cost over six hundred dollars on short notice. A few minutes on the Internet had revealed the driving distance to be just over a thousand miles, downtown to downtown, and after a quick bout with a calculator, he determined that he could drive it in twelve hours if he kept it above eighty.

So without her blessing or packing so much as a tooth-brush, he'd kissed little Max on the forehead and steered the Avalon toward the I-20 entrance ramp, where 420 miles later it would intersect with I-10, 587 miles from Phoenix.

At the moment Bernie was opening her door to Wesley just before two in the morning, Eric was passing through El Paso, listening to Garth Brooks and eating from a bag of Cheetos. He'd been on the mobile phone with Shannon for a good part of the drive—thank the telecom gods for those no-roaming plans—and she'd calmed down some, though when another woman is involved, concepts such as friendship, loyalty and doing the right thing all take a backseat to groveling for forgiveness and the assurance of noble purpose.

The details helped pitch his case, as well. Shannon already knew about Bernie's journey of discovery—she thought it was a waste of time, actually—and had expressed the right degree of obligatory alarm over the previous weeks that Eric hadn't heard a thing from her. When he shared what he'd learned from the video clips that afternoon—that it hadn't been Wesley who had seduced Peggy, but rather some guy using his name and credit card, and that there was a distinct possibility that someone other than Peggy had checked into the hotel under her name on the night she died—Shannon had no choice but to agree that this all sounded sinister indeed.

He'd neglected to tell her the final piece of news, which had arrived via mobile phone somewhere east of Abilene. Yes, there were fingerprints on both the mouse and the greeting card Bernie had sent him, including Wesley's on both samples. How those prints got into the FBI fingerprint database was not disclosed, and it didn't matter seeing as there was no corresponding criminal record to be found. More interesting, however, were two other sets of prints found on the greeting card. They hadn't exactly been criminal, but they had interesting and possibly dangerous pedigrees that just might have some bearing on this case. He'd have to talk to Bernie to see if those two individuals had crossed her path in the pursuit of her goal. Chances are that they had.

He decided not to share the fingerprint news with Shannon. She was already worried about Eric's emotional connections, no sense bringing darker elements into the hormonal mix.

So here he was, singing a prophetic "Thunder Rolls" with Garth and the boys at the top of his lungs—*three thirty in the morning, not a soul in sight*—fighting to stay awake and wondering how long until the two quarts of bad coffee he'd consumed would force him to pull over. He hadn't really given much thought to how he'd proceed once he got to Scottsdale, though heading straight for the return address shown on the envelope seemed like a logical start. From there he'd go to the Oar Research facility, since the fingerprints at last confirmed that Bernie had, in fact, penetrated those walls, perhaps even Wesley Edwards's inner sanctum. Chances are she had no idea who she was dealing with, and since her focus was on Wesley, she was wide open to getting blindsided.

In his pocket was a number to call in the morning. His friend at DPD was going to unearth some head shots of the aforementioned title holders to those fingerprints, ready to fax to whatever location Eric was calling from. This was why God put up the venture capital for Kinko's, as a way to bail out the innocent before and after business hours.

He wished he had thought to bring his gun. Because of his job at Da Slamma he was licensed to carry a sidearm, which he kept in his briefcase, now sitting in the den at home. He was dealing with criminals and ex-government security personnel, and he wasn't sure which would be the more dangerous. The gun might have come in handy.

But knowing what he knew about those fingerprints and the backgrounds of the people who had left them, he just might need more than a gun to keep Bernie out of harm's way. He'd need a massive dose of luck, and if he didn't deserve it, Bernie certainly did.

When Eric had left the house earlier that evening, Shannon had remained at the door for many minutes after the taillights of his new Avalon disappeared around a corner. She was listening to the silence, hating herself for sending him away with the yoke of her insecurity around his neck. He was so good to her and little Max, undeserving of her wrath, and yet she was helpless before her own rage. She *chose* it, wrapped it around her like an alcoholic embracing the bottle, blurring the line between hate and love.

When she closed the front door she went directly into Eric's study. Max was sleeping upstairs, and she only thought of him for a moment. Such was the selfishness of the addict, alone at last with the monkey. She sat behind his desk, reaching to the floor where Eric's briefcase was resting. She opened it, knowing what was inside.

She brought the gun to the desktop, setting it there. It was heavy, much larger than she'd remembered. She stared at it for half an hour, considering all the ways it could change her world. She picked it up, popped out the clip like Eric had shown her, saw that it was full. She inserted the clip back in place, smacking the butt of it with the palm of her hand. She'd seen that little move on television a million times, and it made her smile.

She clicked off the safety and put her finger on the trigger. She tingled with the sensation, so close to death, so close to ending it once and for all.

And then it came to her. She knew what would happen tonight. And it was good. At the end of it, when the pain had subsided and the tears dried, there would be peace at last.

45

Scottsdale, Arizona

They took Wesley's Escalade to the Oar building. He used the ten-minute ride to explain the basics of the project—the *real* project—opening with his favorite ice-breaker: "A little context." She'd seen more than one Oar staffer roll their eyes at this, but Wesley, who was too sharp not to notice, always pretended not to.

He asked if she was aware of the recent outbreak of a vicious new computer malady known as the Serpent. She felt her cheeks flush as her pulse suddenly exploded, hoping he wouldn't notice as she professed to know nothing about it. As if he were unveiling some secret-handshake covenant among the fraternity of computer security geeks, he explained that part of the process of staying ahead of a frightening array of potential digital predators was to actually develop and model them yourself, so that when some variation of your prototype descended into the marketplace you were ready with a viable solution. Such was the case with this Serpent worm. Jerry was well into the modeling of an invasive software worm that demonstrated the same capabilities as the one that was terrorizing the market now, particularly its propensity to penetrate corporate firewalls. Part of the process, of course, was to simultaneously mirror the prototype virus or worm with an antidotal code, one that rendered the predator useless and even corrected the damage it had inflicted. Jerry had done just that, and his code could be the quick fix the marketplace was demanding now.

And, though it went unsaid, one that they would pay just about anything to access.

Bernie didn't let on that she knew the darker, more entrepreneurial side of this story: That he and Jerry were actually the ones who had subcontracted the distribution of the Serpent, which was in fact Jerry's concoction, and that they were using organized crime resources to get it done. She knew that when Oar Research stepped forward as the savior of the technological world with Jerry's miraculous antidotal program, the value of the company would skyrocket, in all likelihood coinciding with the sudden decision to put the company on the block and cash out.

Wesley wanted Bernie to get into the program so that she could run a customer demo in the morning. Jerry had been very possessive about his work, showing it to no one else. Wesley said he wanted Bernie on this in case it didn't work—if a staff programmer was involved and things went south, it would disrupt other projects and employee morale in general. Using Bernie was a containment strategy, he said. She knew this was more of the bullshit Wesley was so proud to denounce.

There were no cars in the lot when they arrived at two fifteen.

On the walk into the building, which only had a smattering of lights on at this hour, he explained what would be required of her during the demo. They would take the jet to San Diego, drive straight to the customer's facility. Bernie would have about half an hour to prepare, using their workstation and wide-screen audiovisual feed, which meant the entire program would need to be transferred to compact disc. A laptop with the program on the hard drive would be brought along as backup.

"Why their workstation?" she asked, wondering if this was just typical CEO cluelessness or, in fact, a clue in its own right.

Wesley said, "So they can use their boardroom AV."

"Which you can easily wire to my laptop. We don't need their system. A third grader could do it."

"That's what they want, Bernie." A flick of his eyes told her not to press the issue.

"They're infected, aren't they."

He didn't look at her as he inserted a key into the elevator.

"Demo, my ass," she went on. "They've been hit by the worm, and we're going to use Jerry's program to bail them out. What's that worth, Wesley? How much are *you* getting tonight?"

Without looking at her he said, "It's complicated."

"We may need to renegotiate," she said.

As the elevator door closed he shot her a look that said she had crossed the line.

"Just run the program. This works, I'll take care of you. You have to trust me. One fifty and a new Beamer isn't a bad night's work, so don't press your luck."

They rode to the second floor in silence. She would take his advice. She didn't need to press her luck or anything else right now. She was close to achieving everything on her Scottsdale agenda. Tonight she would get her hands on the real Serpent, which in her mind equated to wrapping them around Wesley Edwards's throat.

And, she would get to see Paul in a few hours. She wondered how it would be between them, masquerading as strangers in front of Wesley while they were on the plane.

They went straight to Jerry Grasvik's workstation on the second floor, located in a large room housing four senior programmer cubicles. Wesley held the chair for her as if they were being seated at a fine restaurant. He took off his suit jacket and slid another chair next to hers. He leaned in to the keyboard to enter Jerry's user name and password from memory, which unveiled a desktop full of icons, one of which was the doorway into the Serpent's lair.

Wesley walked her through what he knew, which in typical upper-management fashion wasn't much. There were three major subfiles, one for the prototype worm, one for the antidotal program, the third being Jerry's HTML white paper for her Web page, which she'd been waiting on so she could drop it into her template. She recognized a basic firewall code in the worm file—it was a complex beast that had become the standard for the industry, which had never recognized Jerry Grasvik as the primary architect—but she would have to dig around a while to see what congruent code had been written to either override or alter it. Once she was on top of that, she could go into the antidotal file and see how it integrated with the worm to render it functionless.

"I'll need a couple of hours," she said.

"You can do this, then?"

"You better hope so."

He glanced at his watch. "You have five hours."

"I could use some coffee. And some privacy."

His expression was frozen for a moment, and she knew he was judging her, wondering if he could trust her, or why he should consider it.

She smiled and said, "I like the seven series, in black."

He nodded, though he didn't smile.

"Of course you do. I'll be upstairs. I'll check in on you."

"I'll hold my breath."

He started to go, grabbing his jacket from the chair.

"What about my coffee?" she asked.

"Break room's at the end of the hall. Help yourself, but fair warning." Now he smiled. As he went through the door, he added, "I want a dry run by six."

46

Bernie worked for half an hour before yielding to temptation. She would have succumbed sooner, but she wanted to make sure Wesley would actually leave her alone. She was relieved to see that demoing Jerry's program, while not exactly a piece of cake, was something well within her capabilities, especially since she had several hours of one-on-one with the software. Jerry had indeed been brilliant—driving this vehicle was one thing, but designing it was quite another.

After going to the hall to ensure her solitude, she rooted through her purse for a piece of paper with a telephone number on it. If the elevator door opened she'd hear the ring. This was a chance she had to take, because it might not come again.

It was time to call Eric, regardless of the consequences. She picked up the phone on Jerry Grasvik's desk and punched in Eric's home number in Dallas.

She got his machine. Of course—it was the middle of the night. But if she called again, he just might hear it. If no one answered this time, she'd leave a message, which would have to do.

Shannon picked up on the fourth ring, obviously having just been awakened.

"Eric?" she said.

"No . . . Shannon?" Bernie kept her voice low.

"Who is this?"

"Shannon, it's Bernie. I'm sorry to call at this hour. . . ."

"Bernie! Eric's been worried sick about you!"

Bernie felt something twist in her stomach. Based on how Shannon answered the phone, Eric obviously wasn't home. Could be a business trip, but his business rarely took him out of town. And why would he be worried when he was driving the ship from his end, identifying bad guys and asking for fingerprints and encouraging her to hang in there because he was close to a break-through? Then again, the results of those fingerprints might just be the cause of his big-brotherly anxiety.

"Where are you?" Shannon asked. "Are you in Scottsdale?"

An odd inquiry. "Uh . . . of course. Is everything okay? Is Eric there?"

"No . . . he's driving to Scottsdale as we speak . . . to find *you*!"

"*Find* me? What are you talking—"

"Your mobile phone disconnected, no e-mails, no response to his attempts to contact you . . . he's been out of his mind! He didn't know where you lived, they said they never heard of you at that company . . . Bernie, what the *hell* is going on out there?"

A moment of quiet, then Bernie asked, "Eric never received any of my e-mails?"

"He said he didn't."

"I answered every e-mail he sent, did everything he asked me to do. He said—"

"Eric never heard from you, Bernie. Not once. He never asked you to *do* anything because he didn't know how to contact you."

"I sent him the stuff with the prints. . . ."

"He got that. That's how he got your address, that's where he's heading. He should be there by midmorning."

Bernie's stomach was now on full alert. She was glad she hadn't made that coffee, because she would be wearing it now.

She said, "Midmorning will be too late."

A pause, then, "You have his cell number, right?"

Woman to woman, Bernie could smell a baited question when she heard one. "I don't, Shannon," she said reassuringly.

Shannon gave her the number. Bernie repeated it back to be sure. Then Shannon's voice suddenly took on a motherly rather than a suspicious tone.

"Are you all right, Bernie?"

"I will be. Listen, if I don't reach him, and if I'm gone when he gets here, tell him I'm on the company plane with Wesley, going to San Diego. Tell him to wait, okay? We'll be back in the afternoon."

"Be careful, Bernie."

The elevator bell rang.

Bernie whispered, "I have to go. Tell him to be ready."

And she hung up, mere seconds before Wesley walked into the room.

It was well after three, and Wesley's Escalade was still the sole occupant of the Oar Research parking lot. The only light from the fourth floor emanated from his office, where he was hunched over his computer, a hand on either temple, motionless as if reading. On the second floor lights illuminated a corner suite of cubicles, in which a woman also sat in front of a computer. She was on the telephone, her head turning from side to side quickly, as if she was afraid someone might walk in on her.

All of this was observed through field glasses from the empty parking lot of the Kierland Commons shopping complex a quarter mile away, where a white van with a ladder strapped to its top was the sole vehicle in attendance.

The man inside the vehicle saw Wesley get up from his desk and disappear into the black depth of the office. A few moments later he saw the woman quickly hang up the phone, just in time to see him enter the room in which she worked.

The man in the van picked up his own mobile phone and punched in a two-digit auto-dial number, keeping the field glasses at eye level as he did so.

"Give up on that coffee?" said Wesley as he walked in. Without waiting for an answer he added, "Good move."

He slid the same chair he'd used before up next to her and sat.

"Show me what you've got."

Bernie punched a few keys, resulting in a screen full of separate windows, each depicting a different corporate function, as if the data were streaming from the stores back to this, the company's central system server. It was all dummied data, of course, simulating a major retail operation, with real-time inventory and cash databases, a store security status frame, a store environmental control system—you could turn up the air conditioning from the head office if you wanted—and a roster of store locations that allowed the operator to select which specific store he or she wanted to monitor.

"Welcome to Acme Stores," she said, using the name Jerry had given to his victim in this simulation. "Twelve hardware stores, regional chain, very high end. What you're looking at is a real-time systems snapshot. They don't know it yet, but someone has introduced a worm into their main server using, say, an infected debit card at a check stand. At a glance nothing seems to be happening—that's because someone has to in effect open the door, just walk in and kick ass."

She pointed to a window on the screen. "This represents the system used by the invader, or hacker, if you will. In this case, me. From here I can talk to the victim server as if I were on one of its own terminals, accessing whatever program I want, changing whatever the hell pleases me. Party time."

"So shut it down," he says.

Bernie stroked a few keys, accessing a preprogrammed simulation function that, if she were asked to do it herself from scratch, she would have no clue where to begin. She hoped the folks in San Diego had one of their techheads handy, or they were screwed. A few seconds after she hit the proper keys, the data flow on the cash and inventory databases ground to a halt. Acme Stores was out of business, just like that.

"What did you do?"

"Disabled all their checkout functions system-wide. Nobody buys anything until I let go of their balls." A moment later she added, "Your friend Jerry was scary."

Wesley managed a tiny smile. "You like this shit. Admit it, you're turned on."

"I like German cars, is all."

"So now what?"

"So now you get the hell out of here and let me figure out how Jerry configured the remedy code."

"That would be good." He looked at his watch. "You have three hours."

"This is the hard part. He didn't exactly leave me a technical manual to work from."

"He didn't exactly expect to take a header off Camelback, either."

"All heart, aren't you."

"Spare me the platitudes. Just get it done."

"Don't count your chickens, jack."

She turned her attention back to the screen in a way that signaled she was done talking. Wesley got up, pushed the chair back and walked from the room.

She waited until she heard the elevator door alarm. Then she got up and stuck her head into the hall to make sure he'd really left the floor. She even walked the length of the floor, just to be certain.

When she got back to Jerry's workstation she moved quickly. She picked up the phone and punched in the number to Eric's mobile. If her geography was right, he was somewhere in New Mexico right about now, fighting to keep his eyes open.

The answer she received was not the one she wanted. It was the AT&T guy with his cheeseball recorded voice, telling her that the AT&T customer she was calling was not available, yada yada yada.

She slammed the phone down much too hard.

She was still very much alone, with only her rusty programming skills to keep her in the game. And possibly, alive.

She worked for another half hour, plowing through the maze of code that comprised Jerry's ingenious antidote program, which would slam the door in the face of the Serpent. Suddenly she froze, a thought entering her head like a bullet fired from the top of Camelback Mountain.

Much like Microsoft's Windows operating system, the Unix software that had created the Serpent allowed you to access the program at the root level. Which meant you could see when the application itself was created, when it was last used, and going backward from there, the entire history of program access. She'd never tried it in Unix before, but her experience informed her intuition with a certain savvy that enabled her to get what she needed in less than a minute.

It must have taken Jerry many weeks, if not months, to breathe life into the Serpent. And yet, the application on his workstation had been installed that very afternoon. Which meant it was probably developed elsewhere. Or more likely, Jerry took his work home with him every night on a disk, maybe even e-mailed it to himself, erasing the files on his machine on a daily basis to prevent prying eyes. Chances are he didn't trust his partner and knew his control of the project was tied up in the sovereignty of his program. In a security software company like Oar Research, passwords and encryptions were as easy to circumvent as railroad crossings.

But poor Jerry was wrong. Control had been wrested from him in the most severe of ways.

Somehow, Wesley had retrieved the program from Jerry's laptop or home system and installed it here so she could work on it now. He wanted her to believe she was simply filling in, a mid-inning relief pitcher, of sorts. The time frame supported that—the software had been installed that afternoon, and Wesley had arrived at the office mid-to-late-morning. But she also remembered watching him take the call that, judging from his body language, conveyed the news of Jerry's accident. He was either a pretty fine actor or there was more going on here than met the eye.

Something was indeed rotten in Scottsdale.

Bernie began rooting through Jerry's desk drawers. Not finding what she was looking for, she went to a central cabinet that served all four cubicles in the room, finding it there—blank writeable CD-ROMs, Mitsui, the best in the business. A package was already open, so she withdrew a few and went back to the workstation.

Time was critical, but she would make time for this.

Within a few minutes she had copied the entire application to disk, both the Serpent and the antidote code. It required two CDs, since the program was much larger than the 650-megabyte capacity of a single disk. She popped them into clear plastic jewel cases and put them in her purse, wishing she had a more secure hiding place. If he found them, she'd say they were the Web site templates and pray he wouldn't demand a demo to prove it.

Chances were she wouldn't return to this room after tonight, so this would have to do.

47

The precursors of dawn arrive early in the desert. At a quarter to five the jagged horizon over the looming McDowell Mountains had taken on a pinkish glow, dividing the earth and sky with a surreal neon etching. It was Bernie's first indication that her time was drawing to a close, since she had lost herself in the nuances of Jerry's diabolical program design. Her second indication was a light head and heavy legs, the result of no sleep as she descended from what had been an adrenaline high for most of the night.

But she was getting it. It was almost fun, as most intellectual challenges are when—aren't you just the smart one—you realize you're going to solve the riddle.

Forty-five minutes earlier Wesley had graced her with one more visit, and had left confident that Bernie would represent him well in San Diego. She'd shown him how the antidotal code, when introduced to the infected server, initiated a reprogramming of the firewall, almost as if it were regenerating itself after a tank had plowed straight through its strongest seam. Only someone who understood the firewall code itself could write such an application, the same being true of the Serpent code, as well. Jerry's—make that Wesley's—cover story that Jerry had coincidentally been tinkering with a simulation at the time of the attacks was the only thing that would save him from self-incrimination, since there were only

a few programmers on the planet who possessed this
level of firewall expertise.

All she had to do now, she told Wesley, was practice
the demo integration process to make it seamless and
smooth, which required another hour, minimum. He left
her to it, this time with a wide smile and another promise to "take care of her" when it was over.

As she worked, she couldn't help but wonder what
that could mean.

It was while staring at the impending sunrise at a quarter to five that she first heard the noise. It wasn't the
elevator bell this time, but rather the sounds of muted
shuffling in an empty hallway. Having nothing to hide,
her tired nerves spared her another jolt of adrenalized
stomach acid. She assumed it was Wesley, so she didn't
even lift her fingers from the keyboard as she pivoted
slightly toward the door.

The hormone hit came when she saw who was standing there.

Nadine stepped into the doorway, quickly putting a
finger to her lips. Next to her was a large man with
an immediately familiar face—it was the guy who had
surprised her at Wesley's computer the other night, the
one Nadine pretended to have no clue about.

Bernie's mouth was already forming its first question
when Nadine held up both hands for silence. As she
walked into the room, her companion remained by the
door, his eyes scanning the hallway. He was wearing a
nondescript gray suit, ready for work, while Nadine was
dressed in a one-piece black jumper. If she'd have been
wearing gloves and a mask she'd have been ripe for a
little cat burglary.

Nadine came next to Bernie's chair and sank to one
knee, placing a hand on her shoulder. She spoke in a
whisper.

"You all right?"

Bernie ignored the question and instead asked,
"Who's he?"

"Listen to me," said Nadine with urgency in her soft voice, "there's more to this than you know."

"What happened to you?"

Nadine bit her lip before answering. "That's not important. People died today . . . I wasn't going to be on that bus. What's important is that you've done it." Her eyes went to the screen. "Is this it?"

"Who the hell is he?" demanded Bernie.

Nadine nodded at the man, who had been listening from his post by the door. He approached, pulling something from his jacket pocket. By the time he arrived his wallet was open in front of her eyes, displaying the badge of an FBI agent named Craig Meuser.

Bernie stared at it for several long, very quiet moments. There was nothing here to question, but she'd never seen these credentials before.

Bernie looked at the same face that had toyed with her in Wesley's office. He nodded slightly and flipped the wallet closed.

Then she looked at Nadine. "What the *hell* is this?"

"It's simple," said Nadine. "You've just done what I couldn't—you've cracked the Serpent code."

"You're a Fed?" asked Bernie.

"Who I am doesn't matter," Nadine shot back. "What matters is that you did it, we've got the bastard dead to rights. Not only for this, but for the murder of Jerry Grasvik."

Bernie narrowed her eyes, a sudden rage burning behind them.

"You've been *playing* me!"

"I helped you get what you wanted, Bernie. That's all. We needed what you brought to the party. You didn't need to know what team you were on. You might have backed out, got scared."

Bernie shifted her eyes from Nadine to the supposed Agent Meuser and back again, unsure of what was expected of her now, unsure of her own instincts anymore. Of course Nadine was right, this was precisely what she'd wanted, but now it was as if the kill was being snatched away from her, and with its proximity she had been salivating for it. In a strange way she had been actually looking forward to sitting in front of Wesley's so-called clients and making the Serpent hiss for them. Not only would she conquer Wesley Edwards, she'd beat his code, too.

The man said, "Please back away from the computer, ma'am."

Nadine nodded in encouragement of Bernie's compliance.

When she hesitated, the agent produced an envelope and tossed it onto the table. "Federal search and seizure warrant, signed last night at eleven oh-nine by Judge Marcus Cramer, U.S. District Court, District of Arizona. Please move away."

Rather than stand, Bernie simply rolled back from the workstation. With an impatient roll of his eyes, Agent Meuser grabbed the nearby chair that Wesley had been using and planted himself in front of the workstation. Working with the confidence of someone who had spent many years fingering a mouse, he slapped a CD into the drive and promptly copied the open file Bernie had been working on. When that was done, in a matter of seconds, he closed the window, inserted another CD and copied the rest of the application folder.

Nadine glanced down at Bernie with a reassuring little nod that promised everything would turn out just fine.

"Are there any other files?" asked the man.

Bernie shook her head. He had copied them all.

He ejected the second CD and slipped both of them into jewel cases, putting them in his pocket. Then he once again opened the application and began to enter data.

"What are you doing?" Bernie blurted out, as if he were messing around with her own precious work.

"Stealth code," he said without interrupting the entry of data. "Allows us to track the program . . . like a paper trail, only the scent is digital."

As she watched the screen, not really recognizing anything that was going on, she didn't notice that Nadine had taken something out of a pocket in her pants suit. She knelt next to Bernie and held up a small round black device for her to see. It looked like a watch or camera battery.

"Put this in your bra. If there's a chance he'll find it there, just drop it in your purse. The bra is better."

"What is it?"

Nadine forced it into Bernie's hand. "Listening device. For the meeting tomorrow."

"You know about that?"

With something close to a smirk, Nadine reached to the side of the computer monitor and tapped her finger against a container of paper clips.

"We know everything."

Bernie poured the clips out onto the desk. Among them was a small black disk, identical to the one Nadine had just given her.

"Then you know we'll be on an airplane. You can't bug an airplane . . . can you?"

"No. But we know where the meeting is, and we'll be within range when you're there. You pull this off, we get the body with the head."

"Wait a minute . . . we're just pitching a customer tomorrow, a server that's already been invaded by . . ."

Bernie abandoned her sentence when she saw that Nadine was already shaking her head.

"That's his story, what you need to hear. If you knew who you were demoing tomorrow, you wouldn't play. Who do you think is funding this little masterpiece theater? Whose fifty grand is waiting for you in your drawer at home?"

Bernie's mouth fell open.

"You've given us Wesley, we've got what we need on Jerry . . . now give us the money behind the brains. We need you to see this through, take it all the way. You do the demo, you walk out of there, we meet you at the door."

The man was on his feet now, standing next to Nadine. Bernie's pulse had accelerated into full anaerobic stress, and as they stared down at her she sensed her first whiff of fear. She hadn't feared Wesley, even in the shadow of Jerry's death. But these two, federal badges and signed warrants and bugs and all, were intimidating as hell.

Agent Meuser said, "Make the trip, Miss Kane. We need you to help us stop this before it hurts a lot of people."

When Bernie didn't respond, Nadine added, "This could get complicated if you don't."

"What's that supposed to mean?"

"You've accepted money to help criminals further their acts of aggression against the United States. You're not working for anyone but yourself. It can swing either way, legally speaking. You get to decide. Right now."

That did it. Not that she was considering backing away, or certainly not that she was actually swinging her legs over to Wesley's side of the fence. They were doing fine until this little threat. But now, she knew precisely what had to be done.

She nodded slowly. "Okay."

She would go. She would stash the bug in her bra and hope Wesley didn't try to get amorous on the airplane. But she would do it on *her* terms, not theirs.

They got what they came for. They had Wesley. They had the Serpent code.

And, unbeknownst to them, so did she.

By six thirty the eastern sky was losing its warm mauve, melding into an already brilliant blue. Joggers were crisscrossing the Kierland Commons parking lot, taking advantage of the only time during the day when the temperature hovered close to eighty degrees. By nine it would be in the high eighties, and by noon it would pass a hundred.

Bernie was done. She sat watching the sky, wondering what the morning would bring. It was one of those days

that defined your life, everything before and everything
after separated into discrete chapters.

She waited until seven twenty for Wesley to call.

At seven thirty, two people emerged from the Oar Research building. The man carried a briefcase, the woman
a computer bag and a purse. They got into a pearl Cadillac Escalade and drove out of the lot, turning right onto
Butherus as they began their short ride across the street
to the Scottsdale airport, where a tiny jet was readying
to take them to San Diego for their morning meeting.

The white van that had been parked in the Kierland
Commons lot on the north side of Butherus was gone.

And the red Corvette that had been farther up Butherus to the west was now pulling out to follow them.

Wesley's mobile phone rang as the Escalade stopped
for a traffic light at Scottsdale Road. He and Bernie
hadn't spoken since they'd entered the vehicle, riding
in silence like married people two years out from their
inevitable day in court. Everything they had to say was
spoken back in Jerry's lab at the office, where Bernie
had run him through a demo of how Jerry's antidote
code worked magic on a server infected with the Serpent
worm. He'd watched in silence, and had no questions
afterward. He just told her to back it up on the zip drive,
copy it to disk and bring it along, and meet him at the
front of the building when he called, which had been
over an hour later.

Now he seemed even more nervous, which was why he
dropped the phone as he reached for it on the console.
Bernie picked it up for him, and he snatched it from her
hand rudely. She was tempted to suggest he stick to the
headset, but refrained. Now was not the time.

"Yeah." His typical cheery telephone greeting.

He listened for about thirty seconds, then said "fine"
as he clicked off, looking none too happy about what
he'd just heard.

"Problem?" asked Bernie.

"That was Nadine."

"Nadine called you?"

"She schedules the plane." He shot her a quick, stab-
bing glance. "It's her *job* to call me."

Panic was starting to hyperventilate just beneath the
surface of her calm demeanor. Whatever Nadine was
up to, it could lead to nothing good where Wesley was
concerned. Wesley seemed not to notice that Nadine had
gone AWOL when the heat cranked up. Whatever this
was about, they were linked at the hip, at least until the
time came to plunge the dagger deep into his back. Until
then Nadine was in line to go down with him, which
meant Bernie had best keep the blade within arm's
reach.

"I thought she was missing in action?"

"No. Working from home. Does that once in a while,
crazy bitch."

"Is something wrong with the plane?"

"The fucking pilot. Said he called her, claims he's sick.
Can't fly this morning."

"So what does—"

"So she gets me another pilot. It's like changing a
lightbulb. No big thing."

They returned to an uncomfortable silence for what
remained of the ride to the airport. Which was fine with
Bernie, whose head was spinning with options, none of
them particularly clear or compelling.

As they turned through the airport gate and headed
down the service road toward the hangar, he spoke with
a softer voice than before.

"Whatever happens," he began, "I want you to know
a couple of things. How much I appreciate you stepping
in, getting the job done."

"You made it pretty easy," she said, referring to the
money and the car. "And?"

"And . . . this isn't what you think it is."

"You don't know what I think."

"I know what you think of *me*."

"Do you?"

"What were you doing in my office the other night?"

Bernie tried not to react, but there was no hiding the guilt that swept into her cheeks.

"Nadine, right?"

Wesley smiled, but just barely.

"Don't judge me, Bernie. Not yet. Until you know."

Emotion joined panic in the cheap seats of her pent-up feelings, and the grandstands were getting crowded. She could sense the line ahead, wondering when one of them would cross it. She hoped there would come a time when she would be alone with Nadine for a little Q and A.

"There's something I want you to know, too," she said.

He looked at her, eyebrows raised expectantly.

"You remember me mentioning my sister?"

He nodded, the eyebrows not coming down, awaiting her point. She made sure to look him directly in the eye, even if he wasn't looking at her.

"Her name was Peggy. Peggy Hopkins."

He drove on, eyes straight ahead. Then he simply nodded, as if this made all the sense in the world.

Or perhaps, as if it made no sense at all.

48

As the early-morning drive-time jocks came on at five, Eric was passing abreast of Tucson on I-10, just under two hours short of his goal. He was bored with the CDs in his changer—too much Garth, too much Brooks & Dunn, not enough Aerosmith. He was thankful for some local radio color to assure him that he really was in Arizona. He noted the signs for the Pima Air Museum *(note to self: find an afternoon and get your boring ass back here for that)* and soon thereafter passed the ball fields on the right that he knew were the spring-training sites for the Arizona Diamondbacks and the Colorado Rockies *(addendum to note to self: make the trip in March)*. He was punch-drunk from the drive, having averaged close to eighty, stopping only twice for gas and to relieve himself of bodily fluids and a screaming sciatic nerve still pissed off ten years later about his decision to play college football.

Every time he felt like slowing down, he simply had to picture Bernie's face and imagine her in trouble, very alone with what she'd created. It was more effective than caffeine, which gave him heartburn, and more motivating than Shannon's reluctant permission to come, which also gave him heartburn because he knew she was angry.

He covered the next one hundred miles in seventy-nine minutes. It was just before seven in the morning when he took the Highway 60 exit off of I-10, then five miles to the 101 North junction. Scottsdale was less than ten minutes away.

Scottsdale, he quickly realized, was no ordinary sleepy, sun-drenched, pool-infested suburb, which, being adjacent to greater Phoenix, the rest of the country seemed to consider it. In terms of square miles it warranted nine zip codes, and as far as population goes it was bigger than a few NBA towns, not to mention blowing away *all* the major-league cities in terms of the average gross personal income of its residents.

He took the Indian School exit and stopped at the first gas station he could find. Within a few minutes Eric had a piece of paper in his hand listing a sequence of only four turns and eight miles to go.

Twelve minutes later he was standing at Bernie's front door.

He rang the bell several times. If she was still asleep, the ringing should have done the trick, since it was surprisingly loud even outside the door. He added a few significant bangs to the door itself before concluding she wasn't there.

He'd expected this. She was probably at the office, or possibly working out. He could wait, chance the latter option, but that might cost him time they couldn't afford.

He'd set out for Oar Research. If she hadn't arrived, he'd wait there, rather than here.

But first he had another stop to make.

A gas station attendant across from The Fountains told him where the nearest Kinko's was, only a mile down Shea Boulevard. He found it easily, nestled between a vacant grocery store and a crowded deli called Chompie's, which despite the name reminded him he was starving.

His friend at DPD had come through. He faxed Eric two mug shots of the people whose fingerprints had been on the greeting card, a man and a woman. She was attractive, late thirties, he was thick-chinned and beady-eyed. Both had worked for separate branches of the federal government, which accounted for their fingerprints and photo identification being on record. Both had been involved with security functions, the man for the FBI, Internal Affairs, the woman in an undisclosed department at the Pentagon. Both had left their jobs for private industry, whereabouts unknown.

Interesting. Beyond interesting—it was ominous. Bernie had sent him these fingerprints for a reason. He had to reach her quickly and find out why.

Photos in hand, he then looked up Oar Research on one of the rental PCs, hoping a map might be included on their site. There wasn't, but one of the clerks—one out of five Kinko's clerks who, on average, were actually helpful to customers—knew where it was and gave him the directions he needed.

As he made the last turn off of Scottsdale Road onto Butherus, a private jet screamed over his car, only a few hundred feet high and climbing.

"I'm looking for Bernadette Kane."

"Who?"

"Bernadette Kane."

The receptionist blew out a chest full of air and, with equal disgust, began looking through some drawers for what Eric assumed was an employee roster. It was obvious she'd just arrived for her shift, her purse still on the desk next to a workout bag, a radio headset and her car keys. The directory in the lobby had indicated that the main reception desk was on the fourth floor, which Eric thought was odd. But hey, he was a Texas boy in another state, and from all that he'd heard, another culture, so who knew. Maybe this woman's disposition was par for the course in these parts, too.

"I don't work this desk," she muttered, as if her cluelessness called for an explanation. She looked as if she'd be more comfortable working in a record store, and Eric was just about to suggest this when she found what she was searching for. She skimmed down several pages, then looked back up at him.

"No Kane, Bernadette or any other."

"She's a contractor, I think."

"You didn't say that."

"You didn't ask."

He smiled back at her dagger eyes. He worked with young people who tried to maim their relatives, so she couldn't get to him if she tried.

"Which department?"

It was time to take a shot. "I think she works with Wesley Edwards."

"He's the CEO," she offered, as if he'd certainly made a mistake.

"No kidding," said Eric, still smiling. "That's what she said—Wesley Edwards."

"He's not here."

"Yeah, but is *she* here, that's the question."

"We're not getting along, are we."

"We're doing fine. It's just me. Can you help me out?"

"Well, I can tell you this . . . Wesley's on a trip today."

"That's a start. Any idea where?"

"They don't exactly tell me stuff like that. But I do know the plane's leaving"—she glanced down at her watch—"right about now."

"Which airport?"

"What are you, writing a book?"

"IRS auditor, but don't tell anyone. C'mon, I've been nice . . . which airport?"

She finally smiled. "Scottsdale. Right across the street."

"Cool." He withdrew the faxed head shots from his pocket and held them for her to see. "These folks work here?"

She squinted at the photos, then looked back at him. "Who are you?"

"They do, right?"

She smiled, though she was shaking her head. Not so much to say no, but to indicate that even she wouldn't rat out a coworker.

If they didn't work here she'd have said so.

He waved a thank-you, already halfway to the elevator door.

49

The normal procedure, and the entire point of owning your own corporate airplane, is to park your luxury car, walk across the tarmac to the plane in your Bruno Maglis, greet the pilot with blasé charm as you climb aboard and settle into your plush leather seat, your favorite malted beverage already poured and waiting on the armrest. And if you're so inclined, raise your middle finger in salute to the commercial terminal in the distance. Unless, of course, you're sitting on the runway at Scottsdale Municipal Airport, in which case you could flip off the schmuck commuters clogging Frank Lloyd Wright Boulevard. The door closes behind you, the engines spool up and you're taxiing to the runway before you remember that it's okay to loosen your pretentious four-hundred-dollar tie and kick back.

What throws a wrench into the works is when your hotshot staff pilot calls your assistant in the middle of the night and bails, forcing her to scramble to find a rent-a-pilot for the day.

You never know who's going to show up.

The Escalade pulled into the hangar, which had the singular word *Oar* imprinted on it. Bernie noticed a red Corvette pulling into a space outside, next to the doors. As they got out of the car Bernie's eyes met those of a woman wearing an expensive linen suit the color of the Cadillac, a textured off-white. All business, with a generous dollop of sex tossed in to grease the negotiations.

She carried a leather briefcase and wore expensive jewelry, and her hair was very rock star, though the car might have had something to do with the latter assessment. Everything about you is radical when you get out of a Corvette.

Wesley met the woman as she stepped into the hangar. She offered her cheek, and he kissed her there, putting his arm around her affectionately. Bernie approached, and Wesley smiled at her sheepishly.

"Vicki, Bernie. Bernie, Vicki."

The two women shook hands. Vicki's smile was clearly an acknowledgment of Bernie's confusion—woman to woman, no words were necessary in these moments—and though Bernie tried to be polite this was no match for her confusion. Besides, the new woman's handshake was as warm as a wet gym sock left overnight in the driveway.

"Friend of mine," said Wesley. "She's coming along."

Thoughts crashed into Bernie's mind like radiation. The woman was part of this, maybe from the money side of things, an investment banker, perhaps a lawyer. Maybe she was a New York mob connection and it had become personal. Or, she was simply fucking him, as he'd just implied.

All Bernie said was, "Hey, it's a party."

"Let's do it," said Wesley, leading the three of them to the office door.

Once inside, Bernie saw the airplane sitting out front, basking in the morning sun. No matter how one viewed a small jet, it always looked like a photo layout, with no bad angles possible. A man wearing a white shirt was inspecting the wings, most certainly the replacement pilot.

Bernie wished she had a way to call Paul and check in. It was odd that he was sick and hadn't at least phoned to say good morning, as he'd done so often lately. In a way she was glad he wasn't here today, since it would have complicated her already challenged emotional veneer.

"Go on out," said Wesley, holding the door for the women. "I'll be right there."

As they walked toward the plane, the pilot disappeared to the far side to inspect the other wing. A "walkaround," Paul had called it, the aeronautical equivalent of kicking tires.

"So, do you work with Wesley?" asked Bernie.

"I work *on* him, mostly," said the woman without breaking stride.

"I see. You're a masseuse, then? Pegged you for a lawyer."

"Gets fucked either way, doesn't he?"

Bernie had met women like this before, and wasn't about to let the bitch put a dent in her composure this early in the itinerary. The woman had yet to look over at Bernie as a polite way of engaging in this little battle of barbs, which in its own right was dismissive. Most women did this with some measure of subtlety, usually with their eyes, and it was sort of refreshing to see her paranoia worn so openly. Bernie threatened her, and because they both knew it, this little game was already over—game, set and match to the challenger, which in this case was Bernie.

By now they had reached the Citation. Bernie stood back, allowing her traveling companion to enter first, not hiding a dismissive little head shake of her own. Then she climbed aboard. The other woman assumed a rear-facing seat on the right, leaving the first two forward-facing seats open. Bernie claimed one of them so they wouldn't have to deal with the awkward avoidance of eye contact during the trip. It would be interesting to see where Wesley sat when he arrived.

As Bernie looked up after buckling in, she saw that the pilot was walking back toward the hangar office. She hoped they would hurry, because it was already warm in here, and, given the volatile chemistry of the passenger list, things could heat up fast.

Eric had planned to stop at the airport flight services office to ask about the Oar airplane, but didn't have to. He could see the large Oar logo on the side of one of the hangars farther down the service road, and he sped there, not sure what he'd find or what he'd do about it, only that he had to get Bernie away from these people as fast as he could.

He saw a car parked in front, a red Corvette that he mistakenly assumed belonged to Wesley. Had to be his, with all those jokes about Corvette drivers (*The difference between a porcupine and a Corvette? Porcupine has its pricks on the outside . . .*). He parked in a stall twenty yards shy of the building. From here he had a clear view of the Cessna Citation in front of the hangar, hatch open, stairs down.

The only other vehicle nearby was parked a hundred yards beyond the building, a white van with a ladder affixed to the top.

Eric got out of the car and cautiously approached the building. As he neared the door, he saw that it opened into a small lobby, beyond which was the flight and hangar operations office. Silhouetted against the bright glass wall beyond were two men, standing face-to-face, having a conversation.

Eric stopped short of the door, ducking around the side of the hangar next to a fence that separated the tarmac from the service road. His heart was pounding, a familiar rush of adrenaline that surprised him, since there was nothing overtly threatening about the situation thus far.

His back leaned against the sheet-metal wall of the building. As he gathered his thoughts, he felt a distinct vibration—a door closing from just beyond the wall.

To his left, looking toward the jet, he saw that one of the men, the smaller of the two, was walking out toward the aircraft. And while he had only a driver's license photo to go by, he could tell by the swagger and the context of the moment that this was Wesley Edwards.

He had to hurry now.

Eric took a deep breath and stepped out from behind the corner to face the office door. The larger man was still inside, leaning over a table, writing something.

He went in. The man looked up, and Eric's heart froze in place. It was the man whose face had been faxed to him that very morning. The man who used to work for the Federal Bureau of Investigation, and who had left their employ to pursue opportunities in private enterprise. Such as, perhaps, corporate theft and espionage.

"Help you?" asked the man, whose name on the mug shot was Craig Meuser.

"Yeah, you can. I'm looking for someone. This is the Oar hangar?"

The man stood upright. He was huge, six six at least, and built like a retired outside linebacker. Which, coincidentally, was exactly the position Eric had played. The two men sized each other up in an instant, both heeding quiet alarms blaring in their adrenal glands. Meuser wore slacks and a white shirt, sporting the striped cuffs of a pilot's uniform. Nothing about the fax and fingerprint report had stated he was also a pilot, but this was not out of the question for an FBI-trained operative.

"My friend was scheduled to fly out with you this morning. There's been a family emergency. Bernadette Kane? Is she on board?"

Meuser's response took a moment too long. Eric read it clearly. He knew.

"Don't know the names, I just fly 'em where they want to go."

"Brunette? Gorgeous? Like a young Liz Taylor, only smart?"

The bigger man stared at Eric as if he hadn't spoken, obviously weighing his own options. Finally he said, "Nope."

Eric drew a deep breath, holding the man's eye contact. With a low, measured voice he said, "She's on that plane, isn't she."

The man nodded, but not in affirmation. More like realization.

"I'm afraid I have to ask you to leave."

"Will you just tell her I'm here? It's important . . . I need to talk to her . . . *now*."

"I'll mention the name. Now if you'll excuse me. . . ."

He nodded toward the street-side door for Eric's benefit.

Eric eyed the airplane. "Do you mind if I have a look?"

"That's not possible."

Eric nodded. The charade was getting stale. When he made the slightest shift in his body language, favoring the door, Meuser quickly picked up his leather bomber jacket and produced a handgun. Rather than pointing it at Eric, though, he just held it up for him to see.

"Security and all," he said, smiling for the first time.

Options. Decisions. Knock him on his ass and run for the plane. Back away and hope Bernie wasn't on board after all. Call someone, get this on record now.

"What was your name again?" asked Eric.

"Didn't say," said the big man.

That did it. Bernie was here, about to fly away with people who would bring her nothing but harm. He could take this guy, but only with a quick and unexpected move.

It didn't work. Meuser was expecting it, or he was good enough to respond with a defensive move that felt an awful lot like an offensive chop to the side of Eric's neck. In the moment of Eric's reaction, a fist came crashing straight into his face, sending him spinning to the floor, landing with his back against the far wall.

When Eric recovered enough to realize he wasn't quite knocked out, but wished that he was, he saw that Meuser was locking the glass door to the tarmac from the outside.

The angle of the parked airplane was such that Bernie could look out through the open left-side hatch and clearly see the hangar office and door. She had watched Wesley emerge, and focused her attention on him as he approached the airplane, briefcase in hand, his suit jacket draped over his arm. He was a study in self-absorbed confidence, the kind of guy who knew he drew attention but no longer cared because he had bigger fish to fry. Like Kobe Bryant strutting to the locker room at halftime, too cool to care.

"You ladies getting along?" he asked as he climbed aboard, quickly taking note of the seating configuration.

"Just talking programming," said Bernie, "debating the virtues of C-plus-plus efficiencies versus the intuitive attributes of Visual Basic."

"Actually," shot back Vicki Garlington, "we were debating the nutritional merits of swallowing or not swallowing, but she's never swallowed so she had to defer to my years of experience."

Wesley shook his head, an amused smile signaling his tolerance of the impending catfight. He took the seat behind Bernie, his back to hers, across the aisle from Vicki. Choice made. Which was fine by Bernie. She wouldn't have to look at either one of them.

Something suddenly caught her eye. Movement, chaos and mayhem, coming from the office. It was behind the glass wall, distorted by reflection, but it was there.

Violence. It has its own special, unmistakable choreography.

What happened then registered in her mind as a series of flash frames, each with a caption, each frozen and therefore clear. The man locking the office door as he came out from the office. Turning, walking toward them, his expression alarmed. His face familiar—Nadine's FBI guy from a few hours earlier. Now posing as their pilot. Couldn't be, but here he was, wearing pilot clothes. Someone still inside the office, trying the locked door. Something familiar about the form and movement of that silhouette. A car, wasn't there before, now parked next to the hangar. Familiar Texas plates. A sudden recollection—Eric's Avalon. Eric was *here*. Inside the office. Trying to save her. Fighting with the FBI agent who now approached the airplane as its pilot. The contraband code in her purse. The trip to sell it to the highest bidder. Her sister's killer sitting just behind her. His bimbo blow job specialist. His undisclosed plans for her when this was over.

Bernie's stomach spun in twisted concert with her head. Her hands were already trembling, her limbs infused with sudden liquid fear.

The pilot had reached the cockpit door. As he climbed aboard he immediately caught Bernie's eye. He nodded slightly, a conspiratorial signal—this is good, stay calm and quiet, go with this. We are on the same team here.

Which he couldn't be if he'd just coldcocked Eric in the office.

She waited. Not because of some stroke of timing genius. But because she was frozen with indecision. The FBI-agent-turned-pilot was strapping himself into the left seat of the cockpit. In a moment he would reach behind and hit the switch that closed and sealed the hatch, just as Paul had done on her earlier flights.

Outside, the Avalon with the Texas plates was flashing its headlights on and off, on and off. Honking its horn madly, clamoring for her attention.

One moment left to decide. He was reaching for the hatch control. Hitting it. The hatch starting to close. It was now or never.

Now.

With a single movement she unlatched her seatbelt and dove for the doorway. Her shoulder slammed into it, returning it along its hinges to the fuselage outside. The FBI agent in the pilot's seat spun in it, reaching for her arm, his iron fingers grazing her. Wesley was slower to react, but managed to grab the strap of the computer bag. As she fell forward through the hatch, her momentum stopped, the strap still slung around her shoulder. With a twisting motion she let it slip away, over her elbow, gone.

She fell onto the hot pavement, clutching her purse strap in the other hand. Voices screamed from inside, there was motion in the pilot's window, flashes of refracted light coming from the cabin as Wesley and the pilot scrambled to their feet.

Bernie stumbled toward the building, then veered left. In an echo chamber she heard the Avalon's engine fire, saw the car back up a few feet before lurching forward as the passenger-side door was thrown open. She ran, then leapt, the toe of her shoe catching in the wire mesh of the fence. She tossed the purse over, swung a leg to the top before vaulting over.

She dropped to the ground and snatched up her purse. She stood upright, hesitated. They were standing at the doorway to the airplane, squinting toward her.

They were not giving chase.

"Get in!" yelled Eric, leaning to his right to offer a hand.

But there was no hurry now. She brushed her knees, catching her breath. As she watched, the figures disappeared from the doorway. Moments later the hatch was pulled up from the inside.

Bernie hurried into the car, immediately embracing Eric. A tide of emotion erupted as she wept into his shoulder. She could see that his eyes remained fixed on the airplane as he held her. She heard the first engine start, then the second, the sound of a thousand fans, followed moments later by a roar of power as the airplane inched forward, quickly pivoting toward the north end of the runway.

The Serpent had left the building, and she had lived to tell the tale.

As the Avalon sped away, another vehicle that had been parked at the far end of the service road started its engine. It was a white van with a ladder affixed to its top. After a moment it moved off, too far back to be detected by the occupants of the Avalon, who had other things on their minds at the moment.

50

Eric looked up from the computer screen and said, "None of these e-mails are from me, Bernie. Not one of them."

He had told her this already, several times, in fact. They had traded perspectives during the drive back to her condo after the airport rescue, between his breathless explanation of why he had come and her attempt to explain the chain of events that had resulted in her being on that airplane. But there was too much to absorb, all of it without a sequential context. He feared for her safety, so he came. She smelled Wesley's blood, so she set the trap, crawling inside of it herself to make sure it did its job. They would go over it again and again in the hope that it would gel, and later, make some sort of mad sense.

But it all boiled down to one unacceptable yet undeniable truth: he had heard nothing from her since she'd left Dallas. Not one e-mail, not one phone call.

The first thing she'd wanted to do when they arrived at her condo was show him the e-mails she had received from him. The ones encouraging her to be careful. To stay in the game. Identifying the people in the digital photographs she had sent. Asking for fingerprints he could run through the system. Promising that he was close to a breakthrough.

"But why?" Bernie kept asking. "If someone was

counterfeiting my e-mail, why would they have me send you fingerprint samples?"

The were sitting at her dining room table, the computer and a bagel in front of Eric, a cup of coffee in front of Bernie.

"Theory," said Eric. "They were playing you from day one."

"Obviously."

"Whoever it was, they understand human motivation. You needed to sense that you were getting somewhere so you wouldn't be discouraged, maybe back off."

"So they invent e-mails from you," she chimed in, "to make that happen. But how did they even *know* about you in the first place?"

Eric punched a few keys, bringing up Outlook Express, her e-mail program, then clicking on the Sent Items file. A roster of e-mails appeared under the headings To and Subject, showing everything Bernie had sent out since she'd last purged the file. He scanned down until finding the earliest one with his name, dated shortly after she left Dallas.

He opened the e-mail, then pivoted the machine so she could read it.

"Here's how," he said.

"That's the first e-mail I sent you," she said. "Day I moved in here. You answered, telling me how awkward it is for you to get e-mails from me, that things were touchy at home. You asked me not to respond, that you'd stay in close touch."

"Never got it." He tapped the screen with his finger. "That wasn't me. They hijacked your e-mail before you sent this."

"Spoofing," she mumbled, still staring at the screen.

"Pardon me?"

"They call it spoofing, when someone intercepts your e-mail, then replies, impersonating the recipient. Unless you suspect something is wrong and tear into the machine, you'd never know."

"They can do that?"

"It's actually pretty easy if you know what you're doing. You send someone an executable file—a Trojan, it's called, like the horse—or an instant message online. Little digital men sneak into your system, redirect what comes and goes. It's a lot easier if you can get your hands on the machine itself. Either way, you're spoofed."

"Someone spoofed your laptop."

Her gaze elevated, seeing nothing. She was thinking back, trying to remember the moment when it might have happened. There were days, especially at first, when she didn't take the laptop with her to the office. There were many days and many more evenings when she went out, leaving the computer right here on the table, without even turning it off. She rarely locked the deck door—it was on the second floor, providing a false sense of security—because she liked the evening breeze, so it would have been easy to get in. And there were ample opportunities to access it at the office when she went for lunch or attended a meeting down on the second floor.

She nodded slowly.

"Doesn't explain the fingerprint samples," she said.

Eric stopped biting his lower lip, however thoughtfully, to reply, "Maybe it does."

She looked at him sharply.

"They didn't expect me to hightail it out here. They didn't give a rat's ass what I thought when the package arrived, or what I'd do about it. Why? Because they were going to feed you an answer anyway, something to put you over the top where Wesley was concerned. They wanted you to finish strong, go all the way by making you believe you had Wesley by the balls. Most of all, it means they were ready to close the deal. Time was up."

Bernie pulled the machine to her. She clicked on her inbox and opened the most recent e-mail she'd received from Eric, which had arrived the previous evening just before she went to bed.

She pivoted it back toward Eric and said, "Something like this."

B—prints came back positive. W. is the real deal, full metal jacket. Indicted twice on fraud, once for extortion. Served eighteen months at Chino Federal farm. Supposed mob connections. Very dangerous guy, so be careful. When you get something, call me, whenever, wherever. I will call in the big dogs. You've done it, Bernie. Peggy would be so proud of you. As I am.
E.

Bernie watched Eric's eyes as he read the e-mail, supposedly sent by him. When he was finished, she said, "I never mentioned Peggy by name in any of the e-mails I sent you."

"Whoa. But the spoofer knows her name."

"Which means I know the spoofer."

"You confided in someone," said Eric. "Someone you thought you could trust."

There were, in fact, several candidates. Three, to be exact. But only two could be mentioned in the same breath with the word *trust,* however misplaced.

She nodded, and with a quiet voice said, "Nadine."

There was, of course, much more to talk about than Nadine and the hijacking of Bernie's e-mail. But like the good friend that he was, Eric listened quietly as she explained how it all unfolded, knowing that when she was finished he would shatter her illusions about everything, especially Wesley Edwards. Indeed, what he would tell her would rock the very foundation of her belief in herself and her reasons for coming here. But these truths would also set her free, and he had the pictures to prove it. It would begin a new phase in the search for justice in the matter of her sister's death, and this time it would involve the police.

As he watched her tell the story of her time in Scottsdale, he was stricken by emotions with roots that were decades old. The rules of friendship were often harsh. There would be no sugar to coat the bitter pill of the

truth, and no stay of execution for its delivery. He would
tell her, and he would hold her as she crumbled under
its weight.

But just as he was patiently sitting on what would
become the Great Curveball of Bernie's life, she, too,
was withholding something from Eric. She explained
how Nadine had befriended her and then, preying upon
her pain, manipulated her into doing Wesley's bidding,
all with the intention of stealing the Serpent code that
she would decipher in the process.

But through it all she never once mentioned her new
friend and lover, the pilot she knew as Paul Lampkin.
For the moment, in her mind at least, he was irrelevant
and certainly distracting to the story.

She wished he were here now. She could use a hug,
and despite Eric's great friendship and courage, his embrace wasn't enough this morning.

Neither could have known that their secrets would
collide.

After a few moments of reflective quiet, Eric said,
"We have to talk, Bernie."

"I thought we were talking," she said, her expression
suddenly perplexed.

"I haven't told you everything."

"About . . . ?"

"About Peggy. About that night."

They had moved to the balcony, their feet propped
up on the railing, the music of the fountains providing
a soothing ambiance as the story emerged. But now,
hearing Eric's preamble for what was to come, Bernie
sat straight up, sliding to the edge of her white plastic
deck chair. He was visibly nervous, adding to her sudden
sense of unease.

"Peggy didn't jump off that balcony," he said gently.

"We know that," she offered, her voice submitting to
the onslaught of emotions the visual image resurrected.
But she sensed he wasn't simply reiterating their common belief, and it was causing her stomach to roil.

Eric put a hand on her knee and turned to face her. With his other hand he reached down for the folder propped against the leg of his chair.

The train wreck was at hand.

"It wasn't Wesley," he said. "It was someone else."

Awareness dawned on her with an audible gasp. There was a white plastic table between their chairs, upon which he'd spread the pictures in the order of their appearance. There was the shot of Wesley checking into the hotel the first—and only—time he was there. Then there was the leaner, darker man, gloriously handsome, with his tattooed hand and wildly divergent hair and wardrobe, checking in using Wesley's name. One of them showed Peggy standing nearby. And finally, there was the shot of the woman wearing Peggy's clothes, wearing a watch and a hat that were never accounted for on Peggy's body or in her room.

Eric patiently explained each frame, from its origins in the tape vaults of the security firm, to the time-coded correlation to the computer registration logs. He didn't need to elaborate or state the obvious, and he allowed Bernie long moments of quiet to process each piece of the puzzle. She said nothing the entire time, alternating her hands between her mouth and her eyes, occasionally turning away to compose herself.

Finally, after drawing several deep breaths, she quietly said, "Oh my God. . . ."

He allowed her to continue without interruption, watching her face contort under the impact of her realization.

"Oh shit. . . ." she added.

"Precisely."

"No, not precisely. I mean, *oh shit,* as in I know who it is."

Eric's eyes shot down to the pictures. "Which? The man or the woman?"

"Both of them."

Eric's expression was as if Jesus Himself had just

landed on the pool deck and was calling him to paradise. Shock, terror, and a discernible element of hope.

He shook his head, shrugging while holding his hands palms up.

"You won't believe me when I tell you. I don't believe it myself."

"Try me."

She looked down at the pictures, pointing to each as she called them out.

"That woman is on the airplane with Wesley as we speak. She's his lover, I think, but who knows, maybe something else, too. Never saw her before today."

"Whoa. The guy?"

She looked away, smiling sadly, though her eyes were welling up.

"Actually," she said, looking up at Eric, "he's *my* lover."

It took her a while before she could talk about it. An old paradigm kicked into high gear, the tendency to push everyone away when she was hurting, even lashing out at anyone who would dare enter her space, and while Eric was nowhere on the map of her suffering, he was witness to it and therefore subjected to her wrath. She sat on the deck alone for twenty minutes, leaving him inside to go back over the e-mails assigned to his name, hoping to find some clue that would tie it all together. Finally she came back into the room and embraced him.

He said, "Don't shoot the messenger, sweetheart," speaking the words into her hair as she held him tightly.

"Then find me somebody to shoot," she said in return, and he knew that she would be fine. "I'm sorry," she added.

She told him everything. How she'd first met Paul on the flight to Sacramento with Wesley. How she'd accepted his dinner invitation, which turned out to be a fantasy date on the rim of the Grand Canyon. How he'd seduced her there, and later at his house, and the dream that still haunted her. How he'd call to ask about her day, the flowers, all of it. How she thought she might be falling in love again. There was no immediate connection to Peggy, and the reality of it was too incomprehensible to embrace.

It couldn't be coincidence, but what was it? They left it unsaid for the moment, another part of the puzzle spread before them.

"So what do we do now?" she asked.

"We hand it off," said Eric. "Time to back away, let the professionals have the evidence, see what happens."

"They missed it last time."

"They didn't have these." He tapped the hard copy video frames, now resting on the dining table.

Bernie was staring out toward the pool.

"I don't think so."

"I hate it when you get that look."

"Not before I talk to Paul."

It was then that the telephone rang. They looked at each other, somehow already knowing it would commence the next act.

"Hello?"

"Bernie, thank God."

She pointed at the receiver while mouthing the word *Nadine* for Eric's benefit. In return, he signaled with a rolling hand motion, urging her to keep it going.

Bernie said, "What the *hell* was that all about at the airport?"

"I might ask you the same question. And who was the cowboy in the car? Christ, Bernie, we *had* him where we wanted him. What were you thinking?"

What were you *thinking when you hijacked my e-mail, bitch?*

Instead she said, "I'm done. I saw your overgrown FBI guy playing pilot, and I freaked, okay? I'm just *done*! It is what it is . . . you've got the program, your guy knows where they're going . . . what do you want from me?"

"Don't go all Bill Clinton on me, kiddo. You got what you came for, too. So who's the Lone Ranger?"

"A friend, okay? I can't handle this anymore . . . I needed someone."

There was a moment of quiet on the line.

"Bernie, something's happened to Paul."

She'd heard the expression, but this time her heart *literally* skipped a beat.

"How do you know about Paul?"

"You mean *you* and Paul? After all that's happened, I can't believe you'd question my resources."

Got me there.

"What's wrong?" Bernie asked.

"You need to get over here. I'm at his house."

"Tell me what's happened."

"When you get here."

"I won't come alone."

"Doesn't matter. Just hurry. If you care about him."

Then Nadine hung up. Bernie slowly replaced the receiver in its cradle, her face suddenly pale.

"Tell me," said Eric.

She turned to face him. "We're going to Paul's."

"I'm not so sure that's a good idea, Bernie."

"Sure it is. I want to see his face when his driveway fills up with police cars."

Eric grinned. Bernie was back.

Justice might just stand a chance after all.

51

The Cessna took off to the south, banking over the Oar Research building to fly a northerly course until they were clear of Phoenix airspace, at which time they would bank left and fly a southwesterly heading toward San Diego. A car would be waiting, and after a thirty-minute drive up 101 they would be in La Jolla, parked in a Reserved for Visitors slot at the corporate head-quarters of one of the largest virus protection firms in the computer industry. Wesley had been only partially forthcoming with Bernie when he told her she would be conducting a customer demo today—in truth it was a prospective buyer, the demo being part of a due diligence process that was already nearing completion. Wesley was peddling the company, and having the antidote to the Serpent worm in his pocket would make his asking price seem like a blue-light special. Despite Bernie's inexplicable bolt from the airplane at the last minute, he still had the laptop and a backup disk with the program, and while he certainly wasn't capable of making it sing, someone at the other end would be. Hell, these guys had invented and distributed more viruses than the FDA had ever seen.

Their fill-in pilot for the day, however, had another agenda entirely. If he was successful, none of that would happen.

Wesley hadn't questioned his pilot's credentials when the man introduced himself as Rob Corley. They were all military washouts and commercial wannabes, and frankly he had no more reason to care than he did to concern himself with his tailor's résumé. That was Nadine's job, and he paid her well for it. Paul Lampkin had been a reliable employee from day one, but if he pulled another middle-of-the-night stunt like this he'd be back teaching stockbrokers how to fly Cessna 172s.

Wesley had drawn the curtain that separated the cockpit from the cabin before takeoff. The pilot, whose real name was neither Rob Corley nor Craig Meuser, had chanced a quick peek somewhere over the Mojave Desert, not at all surprised to see his female passenger on her knees in the aisle, perhaps resting her head in the boss's lap to relieve her motion sickness. Yeah, that was it.

He used this little oral diversion to set his plan in motion. From under the copilot's seat he withdrew a canister similar to a propane tank. From his flight bag he took out a gas mask and put it on, then opened the valve on the tank, positioning the outlet on the floor at the base of the curtain. He waited ten minutes, or forty-six nautical miles, before he parted the curtain and checked on his passengers. The woman was still on the floor, only now she was fully reclined, having fallen to the floorboard at Wesley's feet. Wesley's hand dangled over the armrest into the aisle, motionless.

The pilot grinned. It would be interesting if they found the man's body with his slacks down around his knees, but the likelihood of that was negligible. More likely they'd find his pants and the legs they were covering several dozen yards from the rest of him, all of it charred beyond recognition.

His next step was to call San Diego control and request a change in flight plan. Rather than landing at Lindbergh Field, he requested clearance to the Tijuana Airport. His request was immediately approved, along with a new altitude, and he turned the doomed plane slightly to the left.

He had twenty-two minutes to wait until he made his

next move. He thought about going back to the cabin and seeing to the comfort of his lovely female passenger, but contented himself with the mental picture of it instead. Better to remain here to handle the unexpected, which in the air could happen at any time. He did, however, quickly step back into the cabin long enough to grab Wesley's briefcase from under his seat—he had been right about the pants—as well as the woman's purse from her seat. They would no longer be needing them, but he certainly did.

Sixty miles out from the Tijuana Airport he called Tijuana control and requested approach instructions. After making the requisite left turn, he waited until he was in Mexican airspace to break the pattern. Rather than turning again to vector for the pattern, he banked to the west and descended rapidly. Had this occurred in U.S. airspace there would have been a flurry of controller calls, and if nothing came of them he would soon find himself in the company of a couple of F-18s with trigger-happy flyboys still pissed off about 9-11. But this was Mexico, and all he had to do to placate the bored approach controller was tell him he was diverting for a little low-level sightseeing, and that he'd get back to him in a few minutes.

It took nine minutes to reach the coastline some sixty miles south of the Mexico-U.S. border. Pushing the power to maximum thrust, he guided the jet to a position over a hundred miles out to sea, skimming over the water at a height of sixty feet, scaring the living shit out of a couple of Mexican fishing boats, who no doubt thought they were being buzzed by the DEA.

Satisfied with his position, he pulled back on the power, and when the airplane had slowed, extended the flaps and the gear. When his airspeed slowed to 160— flying *dirty,* it was called—and at the risky altitude of only ninety feet, he opened the pilot window vent, allowing a hurricane into the cockpit along with a deafening roar. Soon after takeoff he had prepared for this moment by removing all the pages of the flight log from

its spiral notebook. Moving quickly to create the effect
of an impact, he stuffed the pile of separated papers out
the window. Then he dumped the contents of the woman's purse, as well as any loose papers he was able to
harvest from Wesley's briefcase. Then he closed the
vent, withdrawing the gear and the flaps as he fed power
to the engines.

He remained at wave-top level until landfall, at which
time he banked south, paralleling the coastline, which
was as deserted as another planet, at over four hundred
miles per hour.

He flew for thirty-three more minutes, some two hundred twenty miles down the coast of Baja. He was almost home.

Just aft of the cockpit was a small closet. From it he
pulled a jumping rig, complete with competition parachute, helmet, survival gear and the all-important radio
transmitter, which would signal his ground team to his
whereabouts. He worked it over his shoulders, breaking
a sweat in the confines of the small plane, which wasn't
designed for men his size to change out their equipment.

All that remained was the checklist. The passengers
were still unconscious. The autopilot was programmed
for a course that paralleled the Baja coast, with a seven-
hundred-foot-per-minute rate of climb. In sixteen more
minutes the airplane would bank to the west, just before
it ran out of fuel at an altitude of nearly eleven thousand
feet, at which time it would stall before spiraling nose-
down into the sea.

The final item on the checklist was the unaccounted
for passenger. He didn't need to check on this, since he
had personally placed the body of Paul Lampkin, wearing his flight uniform, in the aft storage compartment
just minutes before his other passengers had arrived. All
he had to do now was remove the partition that separated that compartment from the cabin. The laws of
physics would do the rest of the arranging upon impact.
In all likelihood the plane and the bodies would never
be found, and if they were there would be little forensic

evidence remaining. They'd find the shreds of paper floating hundreds of miles to the north, and they'd never think to search the waters where the airplane would actually crash. But it was a contingency, and his anal handling of contingencies was what had kept him alive thus far.

With any luck he will have accomplished all of this without being seen by anyone who cared, and the folks at the National Transportation Safety Board, in concert with the Scottsdale Police Department, would conclude that Paul Lampkin snapped—they would find plenty of evidence as to why—flying the airplane and its passengers to a watery grave a hundred miles off the coast of Baja.

That done, he returned to the cockpit. With his parachute on he had to kneel behind the seat rather that sit in it, but he could reach the throttles from there, which was all that he needed. He pulled them back to idle, and the little plane seemed to skid in the air, slowing rapidly. He watched the airspeed carefully, since the timing had to be fairly precise. Too fast and he'd be pulled apart. Too slow and it wouldn't recover from an inevitable stall.

He pulled the nose back, slowing the airplane even more.

One seventy, one sixty, one fifty-five—stall speed for the Cessna Citation was listed at one fifty-seven. But what did they know.

It was time to go.

He reached behind the bulkhead, feeling for and then finding the button that would open the hatch. With a slight push it caught the airslip and irretrievably slammed to the full open position.

He jammed the throttles back to the cruise setting—full power would cause the airplane to climb and then stall before the appointed time—before diving headfirst through the door into the lovely Baja afternoon sky.

Wesley threw up in his lap. Given that his pants were around his ankles, it was not the most comfortable of

sensations, and it jarred his thickened mind into a struggle for control. The open hatch at three hundred miles
per hour had completely cleansed the cabin of noxious
gas, and the wind factor—something along the order of
water skiing behind a superfuel dragster—was actually
stimulating, further resurrecting his awareness. He could
hear nothing, contributing to the suspicion that he was
dreaming, or perhaps dead. His first coherent thought—
other than puking on one's privates is indeed disgusting—was that he was freezing. His second thought
was confusion, wondering why Vicki was lying on the
floor in front of him, and why she looked as if she were
in a coma.

His third thought was the realization that something
was terribly, terribly wrong.

The one thing the imposter pilot hadn't counted on
was Wesley Edwards's lungs. That he was an athlete who
once tried to blow up an enema bag to the bursting
point on a dare, and while that hadn't worked—he'd
hyperventilated and nearly passed out—it did speak to
his capacity to process oxygen and toxic chemicals in his
system. Now, sitting in a pool of his own bile, half naked
in an airplane programmed to flame out and die, he was
coming around.

It had been just over sixteen minutes since the pilot
had bailed.

Wesley turned in his seat, quickly realizing two things
that, in his still half-anesthetized mind, made little or no
sense. The hatch was wide open, and through it he could
see brown hills in the distance sliding gently across the
horizon, and the perfect blue of the sea below. And,
there was no one in the cockpit.

Some combination of reflex and survival instinct summoned the will to move. He rolled from the seat to his
hands and knees. As he did, he pitched forward, not so
much from his state of intoxication as from the sudden
loss of the airplane's thrust as the last drop of fuel
burned away in the turbine engines. After a moment the
airplane seemingly stopped in midair—this thanks to the

climb angle the pilot had programmed into the autopilot—accompanied by a strange and sudden reduction in the level of the ambient roar. He used this moment of seeming weightlessness to propel himself forward, scrambling up the aisle with his pants constricting his ankles, using the seats as handholds, fighting against the typhoon meeting him full in the face. He reached the cockpit door, when suddenly the nose dropped drastically and the blue horizon in front of him began to twirl. With all his strength he leapt forward, hugging the back of the pilot's seat, dragging his bound feet in behind him, then under him. He threw his upper body into the chair, invisible hands pulling him back as their hosts screamed madly in his ears.

Wesley was no pilot, but he'd seen a lot of flying in his days as a corporate turnaround specialist, and he had always hung on to a little-boy fascination for the craft. He understood basic instrumentation and the aerodynamic fundamentals of control surfaces. He knew that the stall had been caused by a lack of airspeed, so instinctively he pushed the throttles forward, actually using his bare knee because the best position he could achieve was a half-in, half-out-of-the-seat posture with his legs draped over the center console.

Nothing happened. There was a strange quiet to the sound of the rushing air, and after a moment he realized what it was—the engines were dead. He was in a free fall, only there was no ripcord.

Gradually he worked his legs under the steering yoke. The instruments in front of him, now operating on auxiliary battery power, were spinning rapidly, the artificial horizon making no sense, the altitude readout a blur.

All he could do, all he could muster in this moment of complete mental and physical disorientation, was to grab the steering column and pull it back. He pulled with all he had, closing his eyes as if this somehow squeezed more strength into his arms. But the control surfaces on this aircraft were computer controlled rather

than manual hydraulics, meaning the batteries now feeding the avionics allowed the yoke to respond as com-
manded.

The airplane's descent slowed, its roll decreasing as
the spinning horizon now merely pitched from side to
side. Unlike a full power dive, the airplane had slowed
to a near stop in midair at the point of the stall, meaning
that all of its momentum now was due to gravity, which
only had so much capacity to generate velocity. The
speed of a free fall was barely greater than that of the
aircraft on final approach, so the control surfaces were
more than capable of compressing the air under their
relative angle to the wing, as Bernoulli had so aptly described. In the seconds that remained Wesley sensed
this, the subtle response to his touch, his ability to affect
the angle and speed of descent . . . the distinct possibility
that he could level the airplane before it slammed into
the sand.

He managed to turn the airplane toward the shore.
He would try for a beach landing, though he had no
idea what the coastline here would offer.

He came so close. The Cessna hit the sand in three
feet of water at a downward angle of less than ten degrees, the nose slamming hard, catching and spinning the
airplane to the side, which caused it to roll. The wings
splintered off in the first revolution, leaving a cylinder
of metal to flip over and over no less than forty times,
coming to rest against an outcropping of rocks. What
remained of the tail was the stubs of the stabilizers, now
sticking into the air like a knife left in the back of a
cadaver.

Wesley felt little of it, and he actually experienced
even less. When the nose hit it sent him flying upward,
his head impacting the ceiling panel, causing two cabin
pressure control knobs to imbed themselves to the hilt
into his skull.

As the airplane began to spin he was already somewhere else, wishing he were dead, no longer sure what
that might mean. He was aware of the darkness, in which

he floated for a measureless time, sensing nothing other than his own being, which was no longer anchored to any concept of what used to be his reality.

And then they came for him.

52

They took Eric's car. It was the lunch hour, which only partially explained the traffic.

"Are these people freaking crazy?" asked Eric as he slammed on his brakes to avoid a jaywalking octogenarian. So far he had been cut off by a pickup with tires off a 747, been tailgated by an SUV-driving trophy wife and had waited behind a Cadillac in a turn lane, the driver of which thought the green light was part of a conspiracy and damnit, he wasn't going to bite.

"I forgot to tell you something," he said once they were fully under way on Scottsdale Road, which carried more traffic than most self-respecting freeways, and faster, too.

"Why not, can't get any worse."

"Actually, it can."

"If you tell me Paul was married the whole time, I'll throw up in your car."

"Not that bad. Sort of worse, only in reverse."

"I can't wait."

"It's about Wesley. Something that doesn't fit."

"Right now I'll believe anything."

"Well, my buddy with connections at the FAA, he calls me back. Tells me he learned some things about the Oar Research jet . . . specifically, the flights to Dallas in the months prior to Peggy's death."

Bernie drew a deep breath. Hearing Peggy's name

took the sass out of her. She nodded, signaling that he should continue.

"The guy helping my buddy is connected at the airport, so he asks around. Turns out Wesley wasn't flying to Dallas on business. In fact, Wesley wasn't flying in at all."

"Right. Paul was. Using his name while he fucked up my sister's life."

"That, too. What I'm saying is, Wesley loans the plane out, gratis. Those trips to Dallas were to pick up a twelve-year-old kid and bring him and his mom back here to the Mayo Clinic for chemo sessions. Did it twice a month for four months. Plane would fly in the night before, leave with the kid the next morning. Bring him back again that night. That puts the pilot here two nights in a row, twice a month."

She tapped Eric on the shoulder and motioned he should take a right onto Lincoln.

"Guess it made the papers, sort of a big deal at the airport. Flight services would fuel it for free, local grocery chain filled it with food for the kid, stuff like that."

"Probably wasn't real hungry," said Bernie with a scowl.

"Ice cream," said Eric.

"Great PR."

"Listen to you. You're a cynic."

"No shit."

"I'm serious. When this is over, you need to take care of yourself, find that little girl again. Take her to the circus or something."

His voice was so sincere it brought tears to her eyes.

"Why weren't you my dad?" she said, turning away.

Eric grinned and reached to pat her hand. "Seems he does that all the time, loans the plane to medical transport patients, people who can't afford it. Belongs to some organization that matches patients and private jets with downtime."

Bernie stared at him.

"What, I'm supposed to feel sorry for the guy now?"

"No. It's just . . . nothing's simple, ya know? There's no black and white. That's all I'm saying."

They drove in silence to the turnoff into Paul's neighborhood.

Moments later a white Ford Escort turned off of Lincoln following them up the hill. They hadn't noticed, but the car had been tailing them since the moment they left The Fountains parking lot, where it had been parked for hours, waiting for them to leave.

The security gate was open. As Eric drove through, he leaned forward to look at the house looming above them, a squared-off architectural jewel blending seamlessly into the burnished hillside. He quietly mumbled, "Show me the money," as they drew closer. There were no cars in the area in front of the three-car garage, which was closed. The service door next to the garage doors was wide open in invitation.

They hadn't noticed a white van parked on the street outside the gate.

Eric was anything but naïve, but he was nothing if not a working stiff at heart. His father had worked in a cannery, and his mother was a hotel maid who spoke English not as a second language, but as a last resort. As he followed Bernie through the utility room, which was larger than some apartments he'd lived in, into the kitchen, which he was sure he'd seen in one of his wife's magazines, through the family room with its walk-in fireplace—as if anyone would want to walk *into* a fireplace—and then up the marble and iron staircase leading to the twenty-five-hundred-square-foot master suite, he was truly speechless.

But there was something else on Eric's mind besides interior decorating—regret that he'd left his gun in Dallas, because each and every strand of his inbred animal DNA was screaming *danger! danger!* at full volume. In lieu of the gun, he'd opened his glovebox and withdrawn the next best thing, which was now in his pocket. Bernie didn't know because she'd been in a hurry to get inside.

They entered the master suite, with its expansive glass wall and a panoramic view of the city and Camelback Mountain. The massive bed was on a pedestal, looking like a prop from *Gladiator*. On the wall above it was an oversized movie poster for a flick called *The Matador*, and there were three other equally huge movie posters on other walls.

Nadine was standing outside on the deck, gazing out at the view. She was wearing the same black pants suit she'd worn early that morning, only now with the cat burglar gloves and her hair tied back. Bernie thought she looked trimmer than she did in her business attire, ironic since *this* was really her business, after all, the profession of corporate espionage. Eric simply thought she looked like bad news.

Eric was the first to see bloodstains on the off-white carpet at the foot of the unmade bed. He tapped Bernie on the arm and pointed to it, but all she did was nod and continue toward the doors leading out to the deck.

"Thanks for coming," said Nadine, still facing away from them.

Drama queen, thought Eric, noticing how she stood with her gloved hands clasped behind her back, how she'd spoken without turning to give the effect of omnipotence.

"Where's Paul?" said Bernie, no small amount of impatience in her voice.

Nadine now turned. "He's dead," she said flatly. Then she walked back into the bedroom, passing Bernie without meeting her eyes. She walked to a cabinet built into the wall, with a smokey black glass door hiding a panel of controls for the house sound and audiovisual systems. She hit a button, and a panel opened in the ceiling about six feet from the foot of the bed, followed by the lowering of a forty-eight-inch flat-screen television.

"Sit, please," said Nadine, indicating the foot of the bed. "I want to show you something."

She hit another switch and the screen came on, a solid blue with the number O3 in the upper right corner. Ber-

nie and Eric exchanged skeptical glances, then sat beside
each other on the bed.

"What is this?" asked Bernie.

Nadine stepped forward and extended a gloved hand
to Eric. "You must be the Lone Ranger. I'm Nadine."

Eric shook the hand, noticing the glove, but said
nothing.

Nadine seemed smug about this as she returned to the
panel to hit another button, and again without looking
she said, "Think of it as a trial by a jury of peers."
Now she turned and added, "You *do* want to know,
don't you?"

Eric could tell Bernie was just barely holding it together. An hour ago she learned her supposed lover had
seduced and probably played a role in killing her sister,
and now she had just been told the man was dead, by a
woman who had been posing as her partner but most
likely had hijacked her e-mail and completely duped her
into stealing proprietary software on her behalf, for God
knows what purposes. All in all, thought Eric, she was
doing a pretty good job just staying coherent.

Bernie nodded. Of course she wanted to know. She'd
kill to know.

Nadine pushed a button, starting the tape. The screen
blinked into a magnified image of a dark Camelback
Mountain, which quickly zoomed to a close-up of the
top. It was barely dawn, and the silhouette of a man
standing alone on the top was the only movement in the
frame. After a moment another image appeared, entering the frame from the right, stooping as if to catch his
breath as he put his hands on his knees. The first man
was at the far left, right next to a severe drop-off.

Bernie's breathing was deep and forced. Her eyes
were bolted to the screen, and Eric had a feeling she
knew what was coming next.

Now the first man turned as the new one approached,
and they seemed to be having a pleasant conversation.
The image zoomed even closer, as if the camera were
less than a hundred feet from them. But from the initial

shot it was obvious where the camera had been—right here, on the deck of this house.

Suddenly all hell broke loose. The first man leveled the smaller newcomer with a series of blows and kicks, the moves of a highly trained martial artist. The injured guy tried to get up, but the attacker kept him down, placing a foot on his chest as he leaned over him, saying something. That lasted less than a minute before he suddenly sank to a knee and took the man's head in a choke hold, snapping his neck with a vicious twist.

Seconds later he hoisted the victim to his feet and tossed him over the cliff.

Eric didn't need to ask who was who. The attacker had been Paul, Bernie's lover. Had to be—he was handsome and fit and moved with the grace of a dancer, just her type. The victim, Eric guessed, was Jerry, the brilliant little nerd programmer—definitely not her type—who the world believed had died in a climbing accident.

One look at Bernie confirmed this analysis. She held a balled fist over her mouth, her eyes pools of scarlet sorrow, something that had never failed to move Eric for the past twenty-five years of his life. He felt it now, the urge to spring to her defense, make it all go away, bring back the schoolgirl, life-affirming smile. For all his anger and resentment at Shannon's jealousy of Bernie, he at least respected his wife's intuitive sensibilities. It was hard to make her wrong when it was truth that fueled her pain. He loved Shannon, but he would always have a place in his heart for Bernie. Somehow, they would both have to learn to live with truth.

The screen went to blue, then to black as it was swallowed up into the ceiling.

Nadine turned, holding something in her hand.

"Paul lived with a woman named Victoria Garlington, but he called her Diana for some reason. They were demonic lovers and their games involved other people who didn't have a clue they were nothing more than props in a sick little game. One of those games involved

Jerry . . . they had a thing going with him, and when
they found out what he was up to with the Serpent program, they got greedy. She talked Paul into killing him
so they could steal the code and sell it to the highest
bidder. Takes a lot of cash to meet the nut on a place
like this, and with the market these days they were hurting. Or at least that's what Paul thought. Turns out
Diana had yet another game going on the side, unbeknownst to poor naïve Paul—she had seduced our very
own Wesley Edwards, which was probably how she
found out about Jerry and the program in the first place.
At first she was just going to use the video to keep Paul
quiet while she took all the money herself, or maybe it
was all part of their game playing, who knows. But then,
you see, she changed her mind. Paul was dangerous and,
with Wesley in her life, suddenly very expendable. So
they killed him, right here, where you're sitting. Hung
him from that beam."

Bernie and Eric looked up to where Nadine was pointing, noticing a thick eyebolt affixed to the base of the
beam.

"You are so full of shit," said Bernie. "Wesley
wasn't here."

Nadine grinned. "Got to you, didn't he."

"No, he got to you. Why did you tell him I was in
his office?"

"Because I needed him to trust me, and with a guy
like Wesley, you earn that trust. When the time came, I
needed him to believe anything I said."

"Like his dead pilot calling in sick."

"Bright girl."

"Wesley didn't kill Paul. And he has no clue who this
Vicki-Diana woman is."

"Could be. Look around, kiddo. These people . . .
they were freaking monsters! See that?"

She pointed to the six-by-eight movie poster above
the bed, and both Bernie and Nadine had to strain their
necks to have a peek.

"*The Matador.* Story of two lonely people with a thing for death, they get off on it. Against all odds they find each other and pursue their mutual interest."

Nadine pivoted and pointed toward another movie poster to the left of the double doors leading into the master bath and closet area.

"*The Comfort of Strangers,* remember that one? Christopher Walken playing himself? Story of two lonely people with a thing for death, and against all odds they find each other and pursue their mutual interest."

She pointed to the poster flanking the doorway on the side.

"That one, *Natural Born Killers* . . . story of two lonely people with a thing for death . . . wake up and smell the embalming fluid, baby."

"You're still full of shit," Bernie interrupted.

Nadine was grinning. "Yeah, that's true. It's all illusion, isn't it. I mean, look at the ways it can play. Wesley and Vicki—I mean, Diana—dupe Paul into getting Jerry out of the picture, then they take him out. Or, how's this sound—Paul realizes he's about to be fucked over, so he kills both of them in a suicidal fit of jealous rage."

"Wesley looked pretty healthy to me this morning," said Bernie. "So did the woman."

Nadine's grin widened. "Ah, more illusion. You see, they were dead the minute they stepped onto the plane. A flight to nowhere, bye-bye birdie, crash and burn."

"So where's Paul in all this? Certainly not at the airport."

Nadine was having a delightful time of it, judging from her expression.

"Depending on who you ask," she said, "he was flying that airplane this morning. Flew it right into the Pacific Ocean, in fact."

"That's not what happened."

"Isn't it? They'll think so when they find his body with the others, if they find them at all. If they don't, they have his car in the hangar, his signature on the logs, his prints all over the place . . . he was Wesley's pilot, of course it was him. Who else could it be?"

"Paul's car wasn't in the hangar this morning."

"It is now," she said. Her smirk was deliberately infuriating. Eric considered putting his foot in her ass right then, but held himself back.

"Where's Paul?" asked Bernie again.

"I assure you, he was on that airplane."

"Already dead," offered Eric.

Nadine's smile widened as she walked to the dresser and opened the top drawer.

"We all have a secret little hiding place for our treasures, don't we," she said. She began withdrawing items, mostly sex toys, holding each one up for viewing before dropping them at her feet. Finally she pulled a gun from the drawer, a hefty thirty-eight caliber.

Nadine turned and pointed it at them.

"Now there's a surprise," mumbled Eric.

"Paul's gun," said Nadine. "Some sex toy, don't you think?"

"That explains the gloves," said Eric. "It's a hundred degrees out there, didn't think it was a fashion statement."

Nadine fished a pair of handcuffs from the drawer and tossed them to Bernie.

"Put them on him, hands behind his back," she said.

"Fuck off," was Bernie's reply.

Nadine was amused, but only for a moment. She fired the gun, the bullet entering the mattress right between Eric's legs, inches from home plate. Eric and Bernie both scrambled backward onto the bed.

"Yes?" she offered, her voice stern this time.

Eric rolled onto his stomach and put his hands behind him. Bernie clicked the handcuffs in place, then helped Eric roll onto his back.

Nadine found another pair of handcuffs in the drawer. "Now you," she said, motioning with the gun for Bernie to roll over. Nadine placed a heavy knee between Bernie's shoulder blades as she expertly snapped the handcuffs onto her wrists. Then she helped Bernie roll over so that she was lying next to Eric on the bed, both of them faceup.

"They'd have loved this," said Nadine, standing at the foot of the bed now, the gun held at her side. Bernie flashed on the night she was here, the dream no longer quite so opaque and confounding. She had been unwilling to consider the reality, but now she felt sick. It had been real. She'd been their toy for the evening.

"Of course," said Nadine, "if Paul really snapped, he'd go off on you, too. He was falling for you, but then he found out you were fucking your old friend the Lone Ranger here, that he'd come out to Scottsdale to see you, and it just killed him to know you'd betrayed him, too. First his lover Diana, then you. Too much all at once for a nice sensitive boy like Paul. So he gets you over here, no one will care how, and kills you both before he goes to the airport to take care of Diana and Wesley. I mean, you can read about it yourself on his computer, he left a suicide note explaining everything."

"How convenient," said Eric.

"I was on that plane," said Bernie.

"Hey, you make it up as you go along."

"But why? What's this about?"

Nadine's smile was distant and complex. She looked out the window for a moment, as if considering whether to answer this or not. Finally she said, "Do you have any idea how much the Serpent program is worth in the open market? No, you don't. Take your wildest guess and triple it."

"Thank God," said Bernie, "for a moment there I thought we had a government conspiracy on our hands. Good Feds gone bad."

"Same shit, different pension plan," said Nadine. "Actually, I work for a single buyer."

"The New York boys sold him out," offered Eric.

"Whatever," said Nadine. "Wesley was thinking small, it was all about his stock options. Big fish eat small fish, it's the natural law of business."

"Wesley wouldn't kill anybody," said Bernie.

"You're so cocksure of yourself, aren't you. Who do you think killed Jerry's programming partner before you got here? Guy wasn't playing ball, he disappears. Jerry gets a conscience, he falls off a cliff."

"You make it all so neat and tidy, so easy."

"I do, don't I. *You* were easy, Bernie, from the get-go. At first I thought you might walk away from all this, you get your pound of flesh from Wesley, be willing to just disappear, take your money and run. But you turned out to be Batgirl, calling in the troops . . . it could have been different."

Nadine dug into a pocket and withdrew a thin silver chain, on the end of which was what appeared to be a red jewel. She held it up, and the light shone through— a vial of crimson liquid.

"They wore each other's blood around their necks. Sick, isn't it? But in a sweet and twisted sort of way. This is Paul's. They'll find some of it under your fingernails and on his hands, as if you were fighting him off. It'll match DNA from hair samples in the bathroom. The blood on the carpet is Diana's, and they'll conclude she struggled, too, that he dragged her off to the airplane after having a little fun here first."

She held up another necklace with an identical vial.

"Diana's. They'll find traces of this in Paul's car, and on the pavement in front of the hangar. Those forensic people are good, they'll put it all together and get a citation from the attorney general's office. They'll find out Paul was a fifth-degree black belt, so of course the two of you didn't stand a chance against him. He beat you senseless before he got bored and shot you. Then he goes down and writes the suicide note—they'll find his blood, and yours, by the way, on the keyboard."

Nadine knelt on the bed, crawling up between them.

"I thought about making you get naked, as if Paul caught you together. Fun as that sounded, it didn't make sense, you wouldn't come over here and make love in his bed. Would you? Didn't think so."

"Not gonna fly, lady," said Eric. "It's *too* tidy. Doesn't work like that."

"Oh, I assure you it does. This shit happens all the time. Half the important software in the world has blood under the label."

Bernie tugged on her cuffs, hoping they might not have been secured correctly. If she could get one hand free, she could turn this around in two quick moves. One to her head, the other to her throat.

"Here's the tricky part," Nadine went on, settling into the mattress on her knees.

"Those forensic guys, they can tell what happens in what order. So if he shot you before he beat you to a pulp, which a man in his state of rage wouldn't do, it wouldn't fly. So we have to do a little rough stuff first."

Nadine still had the gun in her hand. She suddenly lashed out with it, the butt slamming into Eric's jaw with a sickening thud.

"I'm sorry, but that's in the script."

She put both hands on the gun now, raising them above her head before she brought it down with a hammerlike blow toward the bridge of his nose. As a reflex, Eric swung his legs up, trying to put a scissors hold around Nadine from which she would never escape. Bernie saw what was happening and swung her own legs up, trying to kick Nadine in the head or shoulders. The result was an alteration in the path of the blow, which glanced off his temple.

Nadine had been through some training of her own. She moved forward to the head of the bed, away from the pair of swinging legs. She grinned, but it was that of someone who had been angered rather than amused. Again she lashed out with the pistol, whipping it across Eric's face. Blood poured from a cut below his eye and from his nose.

Nadine was breathing hard, and the smile had evolved into something dark. "Don't think I'm enjoying this," she hissed. "Not for a minute."

Now she drew back to strike Bernie, but stopped, puzzled by what she saw.

Bernie was laughing. Her smile was ear to ear, completely out of context. "Good-bye, Nadine," she said.

Nadine grinned down at her. "Same to you. It's been fun."

As she again cocked the gun over her head, Bernie flicked her eyes toward the door in a *see-for-yourself* manner.

Nadine pivoted her head in time to see someone standing in the entrance to the master suite. It was a woman, holding a gun in both hands, posed in a wide military stance, ready to fire. The scene froze in time for an eternal moment, nobody on the bed believing their eyes.

Shannon fired. The bullet struck Nadine full in the chest, slamming her against the headboard.

Shannon took a step into the room and fired again. This shot cleanly penetrated Nadine's throat, the force of it propelling her body over Bernie's prone form and onto the floor.

She lowered the gun slowly. She appeared calm, her face a steely resolve that was neither angry nor afraid.

Nobody said anything for many seconds. Eric's face was swelling, and he wasn't likely to break the silence. When he saw his wife, his expression alternated between relief and utter confusion. It hurt too much to smile, so he said it with his eyes.

With a low voice, Bernie finally said, "Remind me never to piss *you* off."

To which Shannon replied, "Day's not over yet, sweetheart."

53

Shannon walked calmly to the bed, sitting on Eric's side. She cupped his head with her hand, raising it slightly. By now her eyes were moist, her mind giving way to the realization that her husband was injured and she had just blown away a woman she'd never met. She lowered her face to the nape of his neck and began to weep.

Eric shot a glance over at Bernie, still bound behind the back as she lay on the bed next to him. She shrugged back at him, thinking of nothing she could say.

"Let's hope there's a key in that drawer," Eric said, his voice shaky. Shannon either didn't hear or didn't care, because she didn't move. "Honey . . . a little help here, okay? See if there's a key in the drawer."

Finally she sat up, still holding Eric's gun, which she'd taken from his briefcase at home. She had no agenda for it initially, her only rationalization being that he might need it if things went south. But she knew this was bullshit because she didn't intend to interfere or even let him know she had come.

She had come to watch. To test his word.

Shannon went to the drawer and rooted around, returning with the key to the cuffs in her hand. Within seconds Eric was free, and he immediately took the gun and the key from her, using the latter to release Bernie. Eric and Bernie both sat upright on the bed, rubbing their wrists. Bernie snuck a look at the floor to her left, but glanced away quickly. It looked as if a wolf had torn Nadine's throat out, the blood still flowing into an expanding pool around her head, soaking into the thick off-white carpet.

"We're in some deep, deep shit here," said Bernie.

Eric had his arms around Shannon, who rested her head against his shoulder almost serenely. She was in a daze, only half present. Later she would explain how she came to be here, her suspicions getting the best of her after Eric left and after the phone call with Bernie, the insanity of not knowing . . . how she caught a red-eye to Denver and then an early flight into Phoenix, renting a car and driving straight to the address she'd memorized off the envelope Eric had brought home. She'd waited there for an hour before she saw them arrive in his car, sick to her stomach with guilt and the certainty that her suspicions had been valid. But there was something about the way they got out and rushed inside, it wasn't natural. Lovers walk arm in arm, they don't run to their bed. Something had happened. Within seconds a white van pulled up, as if it had been following Eric's car. Curiously, that driver, a woman wearing gloves, remained in the vehicle, her eyes glued to the door of Bernie's condo the entire time she was there, which was well over an hour. Intuition was Shannon's strong suit, and it was in full harmonious raging glory now—something was very strange about all of this. Bernie had indeed gotten herself into something, and Eric had driven straight into the middle of it. She considered joining them, but something told her to hang back, the same voice that whispered doubts, that suggested there was still a chance she would find what she'd come for. Strange, to desire that which you dread. So she waited, living the hell of the paranoid lover hiding behind her own deceit, the minutes ticking by in tiny lifetimes of wild imaginings, interrupted only by the need to vomit onto the pavement next to the car. The white van left

without explanation, further confusing her. Finally Eric
and Bernie emerged from the condo, once more in a
great hurry, getting into Eric's car.

Something *had* happened. So she'd followed them
here.

When she saw them pull through the gates of this little
estate, her weakness got the best of her. This was a
lovers' rendezvous after all, Bernie's place of seduction,
Eric's place of betrayal, belonging to a friend who
loaned this lovely home out for secure adultery with a
view. She would kill them all—Eric, Bernie, even the
friend, and depending on how she felt about it, perhaps
herself. But then Shannon saw the same white van that
had lurked at the condo, and the part of her that didn't
want to listen to the little voice once again hoisted a red
flag—this was trouble. With the gun in her purse, she'd
walked up the long driveway, entering the house through
the open door next to the garage. Moving slowly through
the various rooms, she heard the voices from upstairs,
so she'd made herself invisible as only the truly paranoid
can, creeping to the cusp of the doorway. Standing there,
listening, she was certain her pounding heart would give
her away.

It was then that Shannon heard the entire thing. From
the moment Nadine introduced the video, to the shot
she'd fired—this was when Shannon extracted her own
gun—to the beginning of the beating. Overcome with a
sudden rush of love for Eric, and even for Bernie, Shannon chanced a glance into the room. When she saw the
woman straddling her husband, beating him, she did
what any loving wife would have done. She saw Bernie
meet her eyes in the moment of commitment, saw her
sudden laughter, and she knew what she had to do.

And now, whatever doubts she'd harbored about
Eric's loyalties were about to be dashed forever. All
would be forgiven. But first, they had to get out of this
with their skins intact.

"Maybe not," said Eric, referencing Bernie's *we're-in-
deep-shit* observation.

"Eric, *think*!" said Bernie. "We have to call the police, now."

"Do we? *You* think. Better yet, you *listen* to me. My wife just shot a woman, and any way you cut it, it's murder. Self-defense, you say? Shannon wasn't the one under attack. How do we explain all this? We don't know what's true, all that crap about the airplane and Wesley and the woman. But what if it is? Why else would she say it, and why would she kill us if that wasn't what went down? What possible reason could there be for this little masterpiece theater if what she said happened wasn't the case?"

Bernie's eyes fogged as she listened. She trusted Eric, had always considered his judgment holy. She wasn't sure where he was going with this, but he had her attention.

"She has the program," said Bernie. "We were the only ones left who could stop her."

Eric was holding on to his wife as if she were on her deathbed.

Eric looked down at his gun, visibly processing a solution. Then he glanced at the headboard, where the bullet had gone through Nadine's chest and imbedded there in a grisly little photo-op for the *Enquirer*. A moment later his eyes scanned the glass wall, where a small hole was visible from the bullet that had torn through Nadine's neck. Spatters of blood dotted the glass, a few of them dripping toward the floor.

"Stand back," he said, and when she didn't move he said it louder. He guided Shannon toward the door leading into the bathroom, well away from the bed, indicating that Bernie should do the same. Then he knelt by Nadine's body and, pulling his handkerchief from his pocket, picked up the gun that belonged to Paul Lampkin from the floor next to her.

"Eric, don't," said Bernie, beginning to understand.

He moved to a position near the hallway door, where Shannon had emerged as if from a dream to shoot Nadine dead. He steadied himself as he raised the gun and

pointed it at the headboard. He emptied the clip from
Paul's gun, firing four bullets into the bed, hitting the
very hole Shannon's shot had created, saving the last
two to shatter the glass just beyond where Nadine lay.

Bernie now knew what this was about.

"Get her gloves," said Eric. Then he disappeared
downstairs for a few minutes. Later he would tell her
he'd gone to find Paul's computer, where Nadine had
indeed written a convincing suicide note that explained
how one lover had betrayed him and the other had manipulated him into killing for her. All he did was change
a few words, altering the context that implied that the
callous lover had been Bernie so that it now put Nadine
in that role. Nadine and Paul, a secret liaison, as unknown to the outside world as Bernie and Paul had
been.

With any luck it would work. With any luck the neighbors wouldn't have taken note of a new Avalon in the
driveway or a pair of white vehicles on the street. With
any luck no one heard the nine shots, the last six coming
in rapid succession several minutes after the previous
shots. With any luck they'd conclude the van was Nadine's, regardless of who it was registered to. With any
luck, the video and the note and the bullets from Paul's
own gun and the disappearance of the pilot and his ex-
lover and his ex-lover's new man . . . with any luck it
would all be enough.

If it wasn't, he always had the handheld tape recorder
he'd put into his pocket before coming into the house.
Everything Nadine had said to them was on tape. Al-
though he liked the current option better, it was nice to
have a net below the wire.

Eric returned to the bedroom, and after wiping it
down tossed the gun onto the bed. Bernie had removed
the gloves from Nadine's cold hands, creating a memory
that would never leave her. She'd also wiped down everything they might have touched since they arrived.

"Look at me," he said when everything was done. He
waited until Bernie's full attention was on his eyes in a

way that shut out the rest of the world, connected in a tunnel of understanding.

"We were never here," he said.

Bernie nodded. It wasn't right, but it wasn't wrong, either. It was simply the best choice at the moment.

Shannon still hadn't spoken a word. Later she would have much to say, but for now she just walked in the embrace of her husband, away from a crossroads in their lives that, for the moment, led in equally blind directions. Only one, however, the low road in this case, was lined with hope.

Bernie followed them through the elegant house, walking alone once again. Eric had finished here, had yet again stepped up and saved them all.

But Bernie had one more thing to do before the healing could begin.

54

Four Days Later

The press had been having a field day. Either story would have been career-making stuff—the private jet containing a Scottsdale computer executive, his girlfriend and his pilot disappears over the Pacific on a routine flight; the subsequent discovery of a body in the pilot's luxurious home who turns out to be the assistant to the missing executive, a home in which until recently the pilot shared with the woman reputed to be the executive's girlfriend. But it gets better from there—a suicide note was found in the house. In it the pilot confesses to the murder of a programmer who worked for the executive and had been seen in the company of the girlfriend. And as if to prove it, he left a videotape of that murder on top of Camelback Mountain, which had apparently been shot from his own balcony.

Leeza Gibbons and the *Extra* crew were in town for interviews and location footage, which was indeed spectacular in the well-heeled valley that lies between Mummy Mountain and Camelback. The *America's Most Wanted* team was right on their heels, investigating rumors that there had been conflicting evidence found at the crime scene. On the surface that evidence was overwhelming. The murdered woman had, in the past, been romantically linked to the missing computer executive. Blood traces suggested a struggle in the home involving the assistant, the former girlfriend and the pilot, includ-

ing samples taken from the pilot's car and the pavement
in front of the hangar from which the jet departed that
day. The police were saying nothing, but the newspaper
reported that one investigator, speaking on the condition
of anonymity, said it was a classic case of a love triangle
gone south, with one of the participants cracking wide
open.

Nothing was mentioned about any connection to the
Serpent worm, or to any other individuals. When inter-
viewed, the neighbors had nothing to contribute, nor did
their domestic help. It was just another day in paradise,
gunfire and all.

Nadine's body was discovered by the cleaning lady the
next day. She had left for the day before Nadine arrived,
and when she came to work the following day she
fainted dead away at the sight of Nadine lying on the
floor with half her neck gone, hitting her chin on the
footboard and requiring three stitches. She told police
about the earlier bloodstain she'd found, leading them
to conclude that the violence in the house had been
building to a breaking point for some time.

The forensic team did their usual bang-up job of
things. Four of the nine bullets were recovered, three of
them from the wall behind the headboard. They were
fragmented and distorted to the point of uselessness,
having passed through that two-inch-thick piece of ma-
hogany before embedding themselves behind the drywall
in two different pine studs. Spectral analysis confirmed
that one still had traces of blood on it, which was confirmed to be Nadine's. Other blood samples, including
those taken from the car in the hangar, were compared
to DNA samples taken from the bathroom, and were
confirmed to have come from Victoria Garlington and
Paul Lampkin, co-occupants of the house until recently.
Neighbors of Wesley Edwards confirmed seeing Ms.
Garlington's red Corvette parked at his house recently,
remaining overnight.

One of the members of the crime scene team, a rookie
with too much enthusiasm and, in the words of the senior detective assigned to the case, not enough experience, was making things tough on everybody. For
example, she was concerned that there didn't seem to
be fingerprints of the victim anywhere in the house, including the bedroom, or in the van found outside. She
also pointed out that she'd never known a woman who
drove a utility van. Time of death estimates conflicted
with the reported departure time of the missing airplane,
on which the prime suspect was supposed to have departed the city—but the two-to-five-hour gap was within
the standard deviation of accuracy, and therefore might
or might *not* mean anything. And lastly, the blood samples taken from the victim's fingernails and hands, shown
to be that of the pilot, were unlike anything she'd ever
seen in practice or studied in school, more like she'd
dipped her fingers into a puddle of blood rather than
dug them into the flesh of an attacker. There were no
skin remnants present, which usually accompanied blood
in such cases.

All in all, it wasn't perfect. But it was a busy time of
year here in the valley of sun, and with the press breathing down their necks it was good to be conclusive. Unless something new popped up, this would go down as
a domestic nightmare of the first order, end of story.

The air traffic controllers at the Tijuana Airport tried
unsuccessfully to raise the Cessna Citation that had requested approach clearance for an hour before notifying
San Diego control of the situation. For a while there
was a bit of a pissing match over whose jurisdiction this
was, and long after the plane had angled into a deserted
Baja beach some three hundred miles from the nearest
electrical outlet, the U.S. Coast Guard was notified that
a small aircraft may have ditched in the sea off the coast
of the U.S.-Mexico border. Anxious for a training exercise, a local base scrambled three C-130 aircraft for low-
altitude recon, but by nightfall there had been no sign

of debris or any other hint of a crash on the surface of
the water, so the planes were recalled. Another search
was mounted the next day, but by early afternoon they
had canvassed a computer-plotted matrix of all possible
ditch sites to no avail.

There was a sketchy report from the Mexican authorities of a sighting of a small jet flying at low altitude
approximately four hundred miles south of Tijuana. But
as luck would have it, the report could not be pinned
down and was not pursued.

There had, in fact, been a sighting, by a farmer and
his wife driving a 1959 Chevy pickup along a dirt road
not far from the beach where the plane went down.

On the evening of the murder, CNN reported that
eleven more companies had reported "denial of access"
attacks from hackers, supposedly linked to the recent
outbreak of what had become known as the Serpent
worm. In reality only eight of them were attributable to
an infected magnetic strip remotely accessing their systems, followed by the machinations of a very creative
and hostile cyber-vandal. The other three were the work
of a seventeen-year-old president of his school's computer club, who wanted in on all the action and believed
he could emulate what he'd read about the Serpent's
venomous symptoms. He was good, too, because his
work would never be separated from the actual Serpent
code, actually enhancing the legend of the worm because
of a few new twists he'd developed. Hacking, it seemed,
was a wide-open field for those with the stomach for it.

In La Jolla, California, three executives of a major
software protection firm had been caught with their
pants down. They had promised several clients that they
could, and would, deliver an anti-invasive firewall program within the day that would protect them from an
attack by the Serpent. But by day's end they had nothing
to deliver, and their clients were left sitting on what one
of them called a pile of Serpent shit. The three would
be terminated within a week, the internal memo an-

nouncing the departures stating they wished to pursue other opportunities while spending more time with their families.

Shannon and Eric drove back to Dallas that night. The three had spent the afternoon by the pool at Bernie's condo, reassuring themselves that they had done the right thing. The conversation waxed philosophical at times, and when it wasn't philosophical it was emotional. They repeatedly dissected the parameters of good and evil and the relationship of those standards to accepted definitions of right and wrong. Shannon came clean on her reasons for following Eric to Arizona, and by the end of the afternoon all had been forgiven, with Shannon possessing a new understanding of the bond of childhood friends. They practically begged Bernie to come home with them, but she declined, stating she had something important left to do here in Scottsdale. She promised to follow in short order, but she had begun to build a life for herself, and it would take some time to tie off an assortment of loose ends.

That wasn't exactly accurate, however. There were two loose ends to tend to, and only one that she truly cared about.

She didn't mention that she wanted to finish the Web site for the presentation of Jerry's Serpent white paper. In her mind it was a memorial to his genius, and a way to give back what he and Wesley had intended to take from the marketplace. She would not only publish his theory, which was intended to whet the appetites of infected companies who would pay anything to get their systems unlocked, but she would put the entire programming solution on the site, available to anyone with the knowledge to implement it.

Jerry and Wesley may have unleashed the Serpent, but she would give the world a collar for it. And in doing so, position Wesley Edwards as the Serpent slayer, an irony that was exclusively hers.

As they said their good-byes in the carport, Bernie

handed Eric a paper sack, saying it was a little something for Max. She made him promise not to look inside before they hit the Arizona state line, and while he thought this was cute he also gave his word that he wouldn't. She made him promise, on the soul of her dead sister, that he would say nothing about it to anyone, even her, that he would not try to give it back, and that he would see that Max got her gift in its entirety. They shook on it, and it was done.

With so much else to talk about, Eric and Shannon quickly forgot about the gift, remembering it was on the floor in the back when they stopped for gas a hundred miles into New Mexico. It was Shannon who opened it, and as she gasped she dropped it onto the pavement next to the car. She held her hands over her mouth, her eyes wide. Eric thought Shannon's response was exactly what she might do if a snake had been inside that bag.

He was close to correct, in a metaphoric sort of way. Because the Serpent was indeed responsible for the gift.

Eric dumped the contents of the sack on the hood of his car under the bright lights of the gas station. He gazed down at forty-nine thousand dollars in cash, one-hundred-dollar bills wrapped in bundles and secured with rubber bands. He would never know that there had originally been fifty thousand, or that Bernie had withdrawn a thousand to cover the cost of what remained for her to accomplish.

Next to the steps he'd taken to protect his wife, keeping his promise was perhaps the most difficult thing he'd ever done.

Max was going to college someday, thanks to his new godmother. The latter had been Shannon's idea, not so much because of the money, but in return for Bernie teaching her about the essence of forgiveness.

On the fourth day after the disappearance of the Oar Research airplane with its CEO and pilot on board, Bernie stepped into the morning sunshine wearing shorts, a sexy new halter top and sunglasses. It was ninety degrees at nine in the morning, but it didn't matter today, a day when the balance would be restored.

She had gone into the office and finished her Web site over the previous two days, posting it on the company server the previous night. Like a quietly published book or an unheralded movie, it would go unnoticed until someone of influence stumbled upon it, or more likely, heard about it from someone else. Word of mouth was the key to the Web, and she would seed that phenomenon with what she held in her hands this morning. The news of Wesley's disappearance had for all intents and purposes frozen the company, with many employees simply staying home. Men in suits had appeared out of nowhere, the whispers being they were board members looking for a clue as to how to proceed from here. One of them introduced himself to Bernie, asked what she did here and if she knew Wesley, and she answered both questions truthfully. He took down her name, but nothing came of it.

At least, not for a while.

She got into her Volvo, putting the grocery sack containing her work in the seat next to her. Inside the bag were over a hundred six-by-nine envelopes, all with adequate postage, each with two CD-ROM disks inside—one containing the code for the Serpent worm, the other delivering the full antidote program, complete with specifications and a context-creating user's manual, which announced the new Web site she'd just posted. She'd duplicated the disks at the office, with no challenges as to why she was hoarding the CD burner. But she'd purchased the envelopes and postage with the money Wesley had given her, not wanting to steal another penny from the company.

In matters of the universe and the balance of karma, even the little things counted.

The envelopes were addressed to the top IT executive at every major software and hardware company in the computer industry. There were also packages addressed to the *Wall Street Journal,* the major computer periodicals, the FBI, several universities with software protection and investigation departments, and the Federal Office of Computer Security, where an old acquaintance would become a bit of a hero. It took her a total of nine hours surfing the Internet to gather the proper names and addresses, and at fifty dollars an hour—a hefty little discount from her normal day rate—she paid herself four hundred fifty bucks out of the remaining stash.

No names or claims of responsibility were included with the package. She did, however, state that Oar Research believed in an open market environment, and that when one of us was under attack, all of us should rally to the cause.

The press loved that kind of shit. And indeed, they would pick it up and run with it in a way that had never entered Bernadette Kane's mind.

She just wanted to do the right thing. To be cleansed. And after all that she had been through, at peace.

On the day Bernie returned to Dallas, an article appeared on page five of the *Arizona Republic*. A body had been discovered in the desert twenty miles west of Chandler, believed to be that of a programmer named Jason Hillman, who was employed at Oar Research at the time of his death. DNA tests were expected to confirm the identity, using hair samples taken from the programmer's car, which had been abandoned in Peoria three months earlier. Investigators were looking into a potential connection between this death and the recent disappearance of Oar CEO Wesley Edwards and his pilot, as well as the murder of Edwards's assistant.

Eric would show Bernie the article while she was at the house for a pleasant evening barbeque. He'd been picking up a copy of the *Republic* on a daily basis, suddenly very interested in Phoenix politics and sports.

But they wouldn't talk about it. There was nothing to say, really, and there was so little time remaining.

Near the close of the evening Bernie announced that she had decided to stay in Scottsdale. Eric wondered if this was a wise move, making his case with fatherly concern. Bernie just smiled, exchanged a warm glance or two with Shannon, then made a comment about refusing to live in the shadow of fear, which was almost as toxic as the stench of revenge.

Besides, someone had made her an offer she couldn't refuse.

The next day Bernie visited Peggy's memorial gravestone. She'd come to say good-bye, and to ask forgiveness for a multitude of sins. Shannon had been wrong—Bernie didn't understand how it all worked, this life and death business and the supposed connection that remained, but she did indeed firmly believe that Peggy was in what we, with our simple human minds, like to think of as heaven, which meant Peggy was a lot closer to the Creator than her. She spent an hour, in no hurry to leave, as if her departure would signal a new chapter in her life.

As she reached her car, a gentle puff of wind kissed her neck. It was warm, and it seemed to linger for a moment in an unnatural way that made the skin on her arms prickle.

She smiled, wondering who it was that had just kissed her good-bye.

55

Three Months Later

It was the Web site that did the trick. Because the mass mailing of salvation of the Serpent program to the industry at large had credited Oar Research as the bene- factor, intense scrutiny was suddenly focused on the new Web site, which became a sort of Serpent central for companies with retail-based, remote-access servers in a position of risk. Within days there wasn't a firewall in the country that hadn't implemented some portion of Jerry's antidote code, revising their programs to prevent anything like the Serpent from reaching into their secret realm ever again.

But no one who knew would sleep too soundly for too long. There were other worms, other insidious software demons, and other minds like Jerry's with the capacity to circumvent the best intentions technology could realize.

The press needed a hero, and with Wesley and Jerry gone, and given the storm of controversy surrounding their disappearance, they landed in Bernie's lap on the day she was leaving town. An interview in the *Wall Street Journal* commenced her fifteen minutes in the spotlight, but it also got the attention of not only the investment group that had hired Wesley Edwards to turn their company around, but of the company who was itch- ing to buy them.

Wesley's old bosses had no interest in or experience with the particular niche in which Oar played. That's why they'd hired Wesley, and with him out of the picture, they were ready to swallow and move on. So with their hearty endorsement, Bernie was asked if she would come to Los Angeles and meet with the principal investors in a partnership that intended to acquire Oar Research in an all-cash deal. This new group would happily send their private jet for her—a Gulfstream V this time, no chopped-liver Cessna for these guys—but while she accepted their offer of the interview, she insisted on flying commercial.

Two weeks later she had a new job, paying two forty a year plus an obscene benefits package and a page full of performance clauses that would make her a rich woman. Bernadette Kane, an experienced project manager for a variety of major groundbreaking Internet assets, former VP of Technology for a company five times the size of her new one and therefore fully qualified for the job, was now the new president and CEO of Oar Research, suddenly the hottest ticket in the computer security business.

On a Monday in late August the temperature would hit one fourteen in the Phoenix area, hot enough to make a girl regret her million-dollar decision and hightail it back to Texas, where the high was a measly ninety-four. Bernie's strategy on days like these was to arrive early, stay late and have lunch brought in. She liked noon meetings, and her staff appreciated the tasteful catering she preferred, rather than the Subway and bento culture of her predecessor. Life was good—she'd purchased the condo she'd been renting, and she'd discovered that the traffic wasn't so bad if you adopted their kill-or-be-killed philosophy and joined the race. The city was a cultural treasure chest, and if you were bored it was your own fault, even if you were single and lonely and new in town. Hell, they had bars here where you had to show your single-and-lonely-and-new-in-town card just to get in.

It was after seven when Bernie knocked off for the day. The parking lot was pretty much deserted, and her car—still driving the Volvo; no sense in flashing the new credit rating quite this soon—was a chip shot from the door. She'd had Wesley's Reserved stall painted over—these days it was first-come-first-served at Oar Research, and the employees had labeled her a saint for it. Small move, big return. So much so that when she arrived first, which she did on many mornings, she deliberately parked in the middle of the lot. Snagging Wesley's old stall had become a sort of black-humor *thing* at Oar, and she didn't need to win that one to evoke his spirit. She was sitting in his office, and he was everywhere she turned.

As she walked to her car, carrying her laptop and a purse, she noticed a car on the other side of the landscaped meridian that divided the lot. Its door opened, and a man got out very slowly, reaching back in to retrieve something.

She was twenty yards from her car, and while she hadn't really registered a state of alarm, she had been brought up to keep an assessment of the battlefield always at the ready. The man began walking toward her car, and she could see now that he was using a walking cane, moving carefully. It was hard to tell how old he was because he had a beard. He was slight of build, but wore pants and a printed shirt from the Tommy Bahama store over in Kierland Commons, just across the street. He looked like Willy Nelson after a binge and a shopping spree.

He stopped a few yards from her car, directly in her path. He was watching her approach, leaning hard on the cane.

As Bernie got closer she stopped in her tracks. Her stomach detonated, an explosion of acid as vivid as if she'd swallowed a whole packing crate of Alka-Seltzer.

It was Wesley. Back from the dead. But just barely. He'd aged twenty years and lost forty pounds.

They stared at each other for half a minute. Bernie glanced back at the building to see if there was anyone around, hoping there was, knowing there wouldn't be.

He gently moved his hand up in a sign of greeting, or perhaps reassurance. A feeble smile emerged on his face.

She walked to him, seeing no alternatives. When she drew closer she could see that his face was badly burned, the skin still red and rough. He was also wearing a medical burn glove on one hand. She stopped ten feet away. Close enough for now.

"You're wondering if you should faint or kick me in the balls," he said. His voice confirmed what her eyes were having trouble accepting. Wesley was alive.

"Still telling people what they think," she said.

This made him laugh, and it melted her defenses enough to permit a smile.

"I'd say you look great, but frankly . . ."

He said, "Still telling people what *you* think, I see."

Where before she had nodded, now she was shaking her head. Wesley held up his hand, as if to stop her from saying anything. Which didn't stop her.

"I hope you don't want your old job back," she said.

"Heard my replacement has nice tits."

"You heard right."

The obligatory joust dispensed with, a moment of quiet now commenced. Wesley lowered his eyes, searching for a jumping-off point.

"I almost died," he said.

"Who else *almost* died?" There was a sudden toughness in her tone.

"No one. They bought the whole ticket."

"The world thinks Paul was flying that airplane."

"The world thinks a lot of things about Paul, I hear. If they ever find it, they'll find what's left of him, too."

"So who *was* flying that day?"

"I was hoping you could tell me."

"You don't know, then. That's interesting. The world thinks you do."

"Not a clue," he said. "I barely remember what happened, and when I do, I picture an airplane with no pilot and an open hatch."

Bernie nodded in understanding. "How did you make it out?"

"I didn't. I rode it all the way down. I woke up in a little shack that smelled like burned toast and bad cheese. An old couple fished me out of the fire, took me in, fed me burned tortillas and sour gouda. Didn't speak a word of English. God knows how long I was out or how I survived. Tequila, I think."

"Never underestimate tequila," she said.

"I was in and out for six weeks before they put me in the back of their truck and took me to a village with what they considered a hospital. Didn't want me to die in their place, I guess. Two cots and a pass-around syringe, actually. They didn't speak English, either. I found out later the people of that region don't trust the authorities, which means they don't talk to them, which means no one knew I was there until ten days ago. A guy passed through who spoke passable English and had a cell phone with him, and here I am."

"Bet the shit hit the fan then," offered Bernie.

"Not when your lawyer is the first person you call."

Bernie shuffled her feet, chancing another glance back at the building. Not because she was frightened, but because she was afraid to look at him and let him see her wince.

"You're nervous," he said.

"Wouldn't you be?"

"I suppose. I'm not here to cause trouble for you, Bernie. If anything, I'm here to thank you."

A wave of unexpected emotion descended on her, not unlike that warm breeze in the cemetery in Dallas a few months ago. As it had then, her skin prickled and a chill slid down her spine.

"Thank *me*? I don't understand," she said.

"For doing the right thing. Finishing the Web site.

Letting the Serpent run free so it could be captured and killed. For not stomping on my name. You deserve everything that's come your way."

"Don't be so sure," she said.

He looked around at the surrounding terrain, the McDowell Mountains with their evening shadows, the buildings of Kierland Commons and the bustle of Scottsdale Road, all of it once his kingdom. Kingdom come, kingdom gone.

"There was this nurse," he said, "in Tijuana."

"Sounds like a joke I remember."

He smiled, then went on. "I spent five days there, getting some real medicine, arranging things with my attorney. But it was that nurse I'll always remember. It was like she knew things, like she was there when the plane went down, when I woke up in that hovel, like she was in that truck with me while they drove me two hundred freaking miles. Try that with a fractured pelvis, five cracked ribs and a concussion."

"Wesley, I'm so sorry. . . ."

He held up his hand again, and this time she stopped.

"She made me see it for what it was," he said. His eyes were glazing, and she knew that he was not the man who'd once ruled this roost. He was broken. And perhaps, better for it.

She only nodded, encouraging him to go on.

"She talked to me about things."

"Sounds like an angel," said Bernie. "I believe in them, you know."

"That's the thing . . . I don't know if she was real or if I dreamed her. I was on a morphine drip, pretty whacked out, actually . . . but I remember her. She was gone when I got straight, nobody'd seen her. But I remember what she told me. I'll never forget it."

"What'd she tell you, Wesley?"

He looked up at the sky, which was laced with pinkish condensation trails from a dozen airplanes already gone over the horizon.

"To forgive myself," he said. "To start over, go forward, and if I can forgive myself then I can get my life back."

Bernie watched her own feet as she traced the line of one of the parking stalls.

He said, "You look death in the eye, you smell its breath . . . you see things for what they are. For what they *were*. And in my case, I didn't like what I saw."

"They think you killed that programmer."

"What do you think?"

"I think that pilot killed him. The one that flew you that day."

"That's what I think, too."

"What the world wants to know is, how were you connected to Jerry Grasvik's death? Your new girl-friend's ex-lover tosses him off a mountain . . . she shows up on your airplane the next day . . . doesn't look good for you."

"Only you know that, Bernie."

Wesley's eyes drifted, almost embarrassed. "I had nothing to do with Jerry's death. Vicki was a drug, irresistible, totally addictive. You'd have to be a man to understand her power. She tells me she's fucking my best programmer, says she heard all about me from him, that she had to meet me, sleep with me. Call me naïve, egotistical, whatever, but it worked. She was doing both of us when her boyfriend found out about him. I had no idea she was living with Paul Lampkin. None. Guy goes ballistic, tosses Jerry off the cliff. Could have been . . . Christ, it *should* have been me. But when all was said and done she had Jerry's computer, and that's all I cared about at the time."

Bernie nodded, knowing it was all true. No one that broken could fabricate a story that lame and tell it with a straight face.

"You know what else?" said Bernie. "They killed my sister in Dallas. I came here thinking it was you, did you know that? I was after your ass from day one."

He shook his head.

She chuckled sadly. "Maybe you just said it—you look

death in the eye, you smell its breath . . . you see things for what they are."

He processed this for a moment, his thoughts unreadable. Finally he said, "You want to hear something funny? My lawyer says I'm rich. I had a performance clause in my contract, a piece of the pie if they sold the company. And guess what? They sold the company. Money's in my estate, which resides in probate hell for now. It's a big freaking pie, Bernie, I swear to God."

"I'm happy for you."

"I owe you a German car and a hundred grand."

"Black. Keep the money."

"Deal."

His energy suddenly shifted, as if he'd been working up to this very moment.

"There's something else. I need your help."

She drew a deep breath. This was where he would try to draw her back into the Serpent's lair.

"I'm not sure I can do that," she said.

"You haven't heard me out."

She nodded, folding her arms in the body language of resistance.

"I need you to tell the police I wasn't with Vicki the night before the flight. They think I had something to do with Nadine's death, that I was involved with her."

"Why would I do that?"

Indeed, why would she? The police had barely registered her existence on the landscape of the investigation. He was inviting her straight into the deep end of the shit pool, and if they looked close enough they might find something that she and Eric hadn't been careful enough to hide.

But she knew. She'd seen Nadine die. Whatever Wesley had done, he wasn't guilty of *that* crime.

"Because it's the truth," he said. "I was with you that night. *All* night."

That he was. She was down on the second floor boning up on the customer demo she was scheduled to perform, and he was upstairs in his office, probably talking on his mobile headset to his stockbroker, visiting her every hour or so.

A breeze caressed her head, flipping her hair playfully.

"I'll think about it," she said.

He nodded, then turned and began the agonizing walk back to his car, a rented Taurus. As she watched, she realized the truth had caught up with them all.

She had already thought about it. Every night when she was alone, unable to change the past, accepting that she had created her own fate. To hide, to continue to chase and be chased by ghosts, was to deny truth. She had wasted months of her life pursuing a lie, and it had nearly killed her.

She waited until he reached his car, then she called to him.

"Wesley!"

He turned, eyebrows raised.

"I've thought about it." She added a wink, followed by a grin that she hoped would give him hope. He had paid his debt, and the angel had shown him the error of his ways.

And now, he needed another angel. One with merciful eyes. Her.

His face broke into a warm smile, and for a moment the scars were gone and the Wesley of old was back, charming his way toward a dream only he could visualize.

Bernie got into her car and started the engine. There was a song playing on the radio, one she hadn't heard in months, since Peggy's death, in fact. It had been one of her sister's favorites.

More than ever, Bernie no longer believed in coincidence.

. . . it's about forgiveness . . . even if, even if, you don't love me anymore . . .

Even if. A chill caressed her spine, licking like a lover she once knew.

ONYX

Danielle Girard

COLD SILENCE

"High speed, high stakes, high suspense."
—*New York Times* bestselling author Lee Child

When Cody O'Brien's son is kidnapped in broad daylight, her greatest fear is knowing the true motive behind it.

A former FBI agent with a new identity, Cody knows that old secrets—and vendettas—die hard. Now she's on the run again to save her son from an enemy who wants only one thing: cold-blooded revenge.

"Danielle Girard writes thrillers guaranteed to keep you up at night."
—*New York Times* bestselling author Lisa Gardner

0-451-41059-9

S607